HOUSE OF MOONS

But why was she here? Her heartbeat accelerated: was this the person responsible for trying to drown her? Could she really be so single-minded that she was prepared to see someone die, in order to get what she wanted? Looking at that fine-boned face, the question answered itself. The woman was clearly both ruthless and determined; not the sort to let anything stand in her way. Though she shrank at the thought, it seemed important to find out who she was yet there was no-one Tess could think of who might know. Yet it was out of the question to ask the woman herself: only someone very brave or very insensitive would have dared interrupt that intense sorrow.

As Tess watched, she raised her head and looked up at the sky. The long mouth quivered; although there were no tears, the dark eyes were full of such desperate grief that Tess felt her own tears rise again.

She turned away, not wishing to intrude, wiping her own eyes; when she looked back, the woman had disappeared.

Also by Susan Moody

PLAYING WITH FIRE
HUSH-A-BYE

About the Author

Susan Moody is author of *Hush-a-bye*, *Playing with Fire* and the highly acclaimed Penny Wanawake crime series. A former Chairman of the Crime Writers' Association, she also represents Britain in the International Association of Crime Writers.

House of Moons

Susan Moody

CORONET BOOKS
Hodder and Stoughton

Moody, Susan
House of Moons.
I. Title
823 [F]

ISBN 0 340 59028 9

Typeset by Hewer Text Composition Services, Edinburgh
Printed and bound in Great Britain by
Cox & Wyman, Reading, Berks.

Hodder and Stoughton Ltd
A division of Hodder Headline PLC
338 Euston Road
London NW1 3BH

For Victoria Trotman,
my god-daughter.

1

MERCEDES

For the rest of her life she would remember those scarlet evenings, the sun going down behind the roofs, the streets thick with crimson-edged shadows, the curve of the cobbles under her shoe-soles.

At the end of the afternoon, the gates were opened to let the women – mothers, usually, or wives – bring food and clean clothing for the prisoners, and at least Fernando was allowed visitors.

The older women of the house – Luisa and Rosita, Francisca and Isabella – would not go, not wanting to distress him with their tears. Besides, they said, she was a child, it would be safer for her than for them . . .

But she was not a child. Her breasts were full under the white blouses she wore to school, and each month there was blood; as she passed, men turned to look at her. Yet she was glad to pretend an innocence she did not have, if it meant she could spend the precious evenings with him, watch his fingers on the white paper, hear his beautiful voice.

Every evening, as the shadows began to lengthen on the high sierras and to glide slowly up the walls of the salt-white houses, she would take the basket from the chair in the hall. Carefully closing the door behind her so they would not know she had gone and thus start to count the minutes until her return, she would begin the climb up to the old convent which sat just outside the town. The *fascistas* had commandeered it, turned it into a prison; no-one knew what had become of the nuns, no-one dared enquire.

Rape, abduction, murder, these had become common-place since the war had begun. Questions were dangerous. Every day there were bodies dumped in the street, some-times outside the victims' own front doors for their families to discover: old men, children, women with babies at the breast. Once she had passed the corpse of her friend Concepción, lying half-naked by the gate to the cemetery: there was blood on her thighs, it had formed a pool between her legs.

The basket was often heavy. Luisa and Rosita, Francisca and Isabella would have spent the day filling it: with chocolate, wine, paella, a tube of paint or a new paint-brush, charcoal sticks, clean linen. Despite the fear which lurked in the doorways and round the corners in the tight late-afternoon heat, life in the little town appeared much as it always had. Supplies came in from the countryside or from the city; here, at least, no-one was short.

She was thirteen; her blood surged. She loved him more than life itself; she would have died for him. At the convent gates there were guards, wearing blue shirts, lazily hoisting guns across their shoulders. To pass them she had to give the clenched fist salute although it made her grind her teeth to do so. They laughed at her, they teased – "Such a little thing, such a big basket!" Sometimes they plunged thick brown fingers in among the contents, tasted the paella, sniffed the wine; sometimes they put a hand on her shoulder, or round her waist. She would stare at them, sometimes touching the mark on her face, and, superstitious, they would look away, wave her through. Her mother was a *vascongada*, a woman from the Basque country far to the north: in the little town, it was whispered that she had been a witch. Emilio Sanchez, the baker, cousin to Federico Cabrera Ramirez, the *alcalde* no less, swore that he had seen her one starry night astride a black goat whose horns were tipped with silver, riding across the bridge which spanned the narrow river to the west of the town; since it was well known that witches could not cross running water, no-one believed him.

Behind the guard-house, formerly the porteress's lodge, was the convent garden. Nuns once trod the paved walks between high box hedges, fingering their rosaries; under the orange trees they had said prayers or exchanged serene conversation. Now the walks were muddied with the tramp of soldiers' boots and the hedges were unkempt.

She hurried through the thick aggressive scent of the box avenues to the main front door. He would be waiting for her, sitting on the floor, face uplifted to the light from the window: it was too high for him to see out. The guard unlocked the door then relocked it behind her, the turning of the key always a reminder that he was a prisoner.

Sometimes she would want to cry out, to demand that he at least be left the dignity of an unlocked door. She wanted to say that he had not been tried, that the charges brought against him were not specific, were unproven, but in these uncertain, these erratic times, such an action could lead directly to the firing squad.

3

The possibility of his death was something she chose deliberately to ignore, yet at night her dreams were punctuated by bullets thudding not into his flesh, but her own. Sometimes, in those dreams, the face behind the trigger was his. Already they had kept him there nearly three weeks: having taken him, they dared not release him, yet they were too frightened to take further, more final action. She did not think they ever would: he was too important, too well known in the world beyond the country's borders, it would be shameful, dishonourable, if one of Spain's leading artists were to be shot for no more than a few injudicious remarks, a suspected sympathy with the wrong side. She saw him there in his conventual cell, waiting out the war, and because it kept him close to her, because it seemed somehow to reverse their roles so that she, for once, became the powerful one, she found it bearable.

She raged, sometimes, keeping her voice low so that the guards might not hear, unable to understand how he could remain so calm.

"They have no right," she protested fiercely, "no right," and he would smile gently, point at the canvases propped against the wall and his brushes beside it. "They let me paint," he would say. "What more could I want? Except you here with me, of course."

When he said that, she could feel her body tremble. *She* wanted more than that; *she* wanted – but she dared not speak. Her eyes would grow huge with longing, she could feel the pupils expanding, she would reach out and take his hand, crush it to her bosom, her mouth. Her love for him – if love it was – would swell inside her body until she could not speak, could scarcely move.

*　　*　　*

4

The basket was lighter than usual that night. Coming home from school, she picked it up from the table in the cool hall and slipped out again, before the aunts could detain her with conversation and tears. She ran quickly up the cobbled street to the convent. The guard on duty was a boy from the next village; when he winked at her, she tried to smile as she pushed past him. He called after her, told her to stop, but she took no notice. His name, she knew, was Ramón; in the past, she had seen his eyes on her breasts.

Out in the convent garden, the green leaves were dull, the orange blossoms very white, almost silvery in the dusk. Evening had come early to end a sullen day; she could hear the murmur of voices from the open windows and a woman sobbing. At the top of the main staircase, more guards lounged; there were empty wine bottles on the table at which they sat. One of them, a big man with scars down one side of his face, blocked her way as she walked by.

"Not so fast," he said. He tried to pull the basket from her arm, as Ramón came running up the steps behind her.

She forced herself to look innocent, to meet his eyes. "I'm already late," she said. "Fernando will be hungry." She raised her hand to touch the blemish on her face.

"Not tonight." The big man shook his head and grinned at the others. "Not any more. Isn't that right, *compadres*?"

The others shuffled their feet, nodded, looked away.

"What do you mean?" But even as she asked, his words struck her chest, each one a mallet blow. "What do you . . .?" *Not any more.* Her head felt heavy, hot, unbalanced on the stem of her neck; she thought she might fall over. "Is he . . .?"

"This morning," one of them said. She knew they had heard the rumours about her mother; they would not look at her. "The orders came . . ."

For a moment the passage was silent. She could see the whitewashed walls – she would see them always – stretching away, all the grilled doors shut except for his, which stood half-open, a crucifix high on the end wall. Somewhere a fire was burning; she could smell the smoke, and hear music too, from a distant guitar, melancholy.

"No," she said. "No." The pain she felt was unbearable; each separate rib seemed to contract about her heart. She put out her hand and held on to the table, her head swinging, breathing through her mouth, searching for words, for comfort, for help.

"Who?" she said finally. Her voice did not shake. "Who was it?" She stared at them, from one to the other, not bothering to hide her contempt, for after all it did not matter now.

They stared at her. "You don't – " one of them began.

"I have every right to know," she said, cutting him off before he could tell her she did not. "Tell me." Her voice was rising, rising, like the wind in the winter when it shrieked down from the hills and raged between the houses. She turned. "Ramón. You must tell me."

He shrugged, looked at his companions then down at the floor.

"A name, Ramón," she said. She grabbed his arm, squeezing, digging in her nails until he slapped her away. "Just a name." She stared deep into his eyes, willing him to do as she said, feeling her pupils grow huge, feeling power

6

sweep across her shoulders, from fingertip to fingertip. "Give it to me, Ramón."

So, turning away his head, furtively crossing himself, he gave her a name.

2

TESS

White petals fading, water
flowing, snow:
these are immutable, yet
they come and slowly go.
translated from the Japanese by Teresa Lovel

The night before her birthday, Tess dreamed again of the Casa de las Lunas, the house where she was born. In dream, she revisited the dark panelled rooms, the shuttered windows, the wood-coloured shadows; in dream climbed the wide staircase and felt once more the smoothness of the baluster rail under her palm.

At the top of the stairs, the narrow strip of coir matting stretched away from her, perspective elongated by the vagaries of sleep so that its two edges seemed to meet at some distant point of infinity. Its ridges were harsh beneath her bare feet. The house smelled, as always, of wood, of strong tobacco, of lemons and clean linen. She passed closed doors, shuttered windows, until, dreaming, she came to her mother's bedroom; through a half-open door, she saw her lying there on the carved four-poster hung with flower-sprigged cream satin – and saw herself, too, newly-born, lying in the crook of her mother's arm.

The dream had no sound track. Her own infant mouth opened but no cry emerged: her mother murmured but no words could be heard.

Behind her the house waited, hushed, crouched around its secrets. Even dreaming, she was aware of them, hidden like man-traps behind the doors of the Casa de las Lunas, the House of Moons, the house where she was born.

The wind got up during the night. The oceanic roar woke Tess around four o'clock and she lay listening to the surge of turbulent air in the street as it tore at roofs and trees and sent loose objects clattering noisily along the Cambridge pavements.

She thought: today is my birthday. It is the first day of the new year and I shall be twenty-nine years old.

And alone.

Tension gathered somewhere at the base of her brain. Whatever else she had achieved, whatever reputation she had established in her field, whatever feminist principles she upheld about independence, there was no gainsaying the fact that she lay alone in the big carved bed which had once been her mother's when she would rather have had someone else alongside her.

While the wind nagged at the window-panes, she grabbed the word. *Alone*. She held it tightly, shook it apart, broke it down into its separate resonances, analysed it until she was finally able to prove to herself its absolute irrelevancy as far as she was concerned, to show herself that being alone in bed on the morning of her twenty-ninth birthday made no difference whatsoever to her life. She had friends. She had Jonas and Henry. If she wanted, she had Dominic. *Alone* was inapplicable, irrelevant.

Besides, age was meaningless. This was a year in her life like any other, neither more nor less remarkable than the ones before it or those which would follow. None the less, it seemed a watershed: time had slipped away from her before she could seize it, and suddenly the years between now and forty, fifty, sixty, telescoped, crushed together, no more durable than a snowball.

She turned over, hunching the bedclothes around her shoulders. While she slept, cold had invaded the room. Yesterday, there had been ice on the river; in the park across the street, silver birches stood frosted, white against a grey sky. Today would be colder, snow would fall, pipes would burst.

The wind gnawed; the house shuddered in a new onslaught from the gale. She tried not to remember what other anniversary this birthday – every birthday – marked. Instead, she recalled other cold awakenings, other chilly birthdays, one in particular: a conference, a castle, central Europe. The castle, painted a dusky rose, stood like a fairy-tale on the shores of a frozen lake. There had been utter silence: no birds, no voice. Only the crunch of her feet in the snow and the hiss of her skates across the ice while below her, in another glassy world, long strands of weed streamed stiff as steel, silver fish hung suspended in an element grown suddenly rigid, bubbles were trapped like balls of mercury. Fur-hatted, long-coated, a Hans Andersen ice-maiden, she had flown above them, skimming through air as sharp as glass towards an illimitable horizon, free.

*   *   *

She awoke again to the sound of the doorbell. Dressing-gowned, she opened the front door to a delivery boy who thrust flowers into her hand, pale rosebuds tied with white ribbon, peach pink at the centre shading on their outer edges to a vanilla that was almost green. From Henry. Her friend. Her fiancé – until she broke the engagement off nearly a year ago. She smiled over his card: *For my always Dulcinea*. His disarming resemblance to Don Quixote, the tall angularity which gave the impression of being nothing but elbows and limbs, had been one of his attractions. It was a pity things had not worked out between them.

The wind was still gusting down the street which lay white now under a pewter sky, its edges softened by snow. Imprisoned in ice, plane trees tossed, their branches cracking against each other, sucked this way and that by the snapping gale. Looking out into the cold, Tess felt restless, overrooted. She thought: I have never travelled overland to Afghanistan, never lived with gorillas in an African rainforest, never hunted orchids nor married a Bedouin sheik, not even been to a rock concert.

The fact that none of these were things she had ever wanted to do was immaterial: opportunities were there, and she had ignored them.

She thought: I do not belong here, in this bleak East Anglian town. I need sunshine; I wish to bloom, to flower. Sun glittered inside her skull, black shadows, white walls. Spain took brief shape on the cold doorstep, a multilayering of impressions, of memories which were not all her own: the ancient Arabic wail of flamenco, bulls dying slowly in the afternoon, crowned skulls, castanets clicking like knuckle-bones, black shadows, red blood, a song drifting from a grilled window. Clichés. Clichés of a tourist's Spain, an idealised impossible Spain, yet hers, surely, if she only dared to look for it.

The postman appeared. Shivering, she took the mail from him and hurried back up to bed. There were cards from friends, from Henry, from her father, from a colleague in Tokyo, this one enclosing a letter. She read it slowly, recalling Japan, recalling the years before her mother's death, years which in retrospect had been as spare and fragile as a porcelain bowl. Her memories of that time were elusive; she could remember so little. If she closed her eyes and thought of them, she saw only white chrysanthemums, lacquered dragons, a bare branch framed against a window, three fragments of composite memory, each one framed in a darkness into which she did not dare to venture. And a once-loved, still-remembered voice, *If you touch the child I will –*

Quickly, she picked up the last envelope. Inside was an auctioneer's catalogue. The colour photograph on the cover showed Brantwell Manor, described as "a gentleman's residence, the small but exquisite 17th-century manor house which was formerly the home of the late British Consul in Madrid." House and contents were to be auctioned the following day.

She leafed through the thick list of contents: Venetian girandoles, gilt and crystal; French furniture; Chippendale chairs; a Sèvres dinner service for twenty-four; mahogany teapoys; crystal, silver, marquetry, ormolu; all the paraphernalia of a life both privileged and public. The Consul and his wife, she remembered, had both been killed in a helicopter crash early the previous year, on their way to a performance of *Orfeo* at Glyndebourne.

One section listed the late Consul's collections. Obviously a man of considerable private means, he had been eclectic in his tastes, pursuing everything from antique timepieces and firearms to modern paintings and ceramics. Turning a page, her eye was caught by an item half-way down which someone had outlined in red ink:

Lots No. 584–627:
Various paintings of the modern Spanish school, including works by Luis de León, Ramón O'Donnell, Sancho Guzmán, Ricardo Sanchez etc.
A separate catalogue is available on request.

She frowned. Where had it come from? Why had it been sent to her? Who had marked the item so that she could not miss it? There was no accompanying note, no explanation. The envelope had been posted in London the previous day; it gave nothing else away.

Beside her bed, the phone rang suddenly.

"Teresa?" The voice using the Spanish form of her name was hoarse and elderly.

"Don Pedro," she said, trying not to sound surprised. Two weeks ago her employer, Pedro de Torres y Morena, had caught a virulent strain of flu and had been confined to bed ever since.

He spoke the soft Castilian Spanish, tongue tripping over sibilants, thickening on the 'd's. "Please forgive my telephoning you at your private address," he said, in his usual formal way. "By now, you will have received my letter."

"Letter? I have no – "

"The catalogue." He cut across her, imperious as always.

14

He kept his voice low, as though afraid of being overheard; she wondered where he was, whether he spoke from his sick bed or had dragged himself, in defiance of authority, to some less public place, away from nurses or his domineering wife.

"It's in front of me. I didn't realise it was you who had sent it." Tess too spoke in Spanish.

"I who caused it to be sent, yes," he corrected. "Teresa: you must go to this sale."

It was not difficult to guess what he wanted: Don Pedro was an avid collector of contemporary Spanish art and had the means to indulge his taste.

"All right," she said. She was used to carrying out his instructions since that was what he paid her to do. "I suppose you want me to buy a painting for you."

"Naturally I would go myself, Teresa, if I were well . . . You saw the item I marked?"

"Yes."

"You will buy the separate catalogue when you arrive at the house. You will bid for Lot 602."

"Let me guess," she said in a hollow voice. "A Sanchez."

"How did you know?" He coughed; faintly came the sound of his laboured breathing and she guessed he had turned away from the telephone in the hope that she could not hear it.

"You know my views on Sanchez, Don Pedro. Let's hope none of my friends sees me bidding for it and thinks I'm buying it for myself."

She heard his dry chuckle. "I knew that, as always, I could rely on you, Teresa. As for the money, I have already made arrangements so that you will have access to as much as you need. The Consul was a great friend of

mine – I was with him when he bought this particular example of the artist's work and I have always coveted it."

"So money's no object?"

"Teresa," he said reproachfully. "When is it ever? What
does money matter?"

"Easy to say when you've got lots."

"But in this case, it is the picture which matters.
However high the bidding, you must bid higher. Do you
understand?"

"Of course, Don Pedro."

"Remember, whatever is bid, you will bid more."

"I hope this doesn't mean that when you get back to the
Banco you'll expect me to make your coffee or buy flowers
on your wife's birthday."

"No danger of that." Another cough. "I read in the
papers this morning that your guardian has been hon-
oured. You must be very proud."

"What do you mean?"

"The Honours List. He has been made CBE. As you
know, I have often expressed the wish to meet him but
now he has been elevated it is impossible, you will say it is
only old Don Pedro wanting to climb the social ladder."

"You?" Tess said. "Never!"

He laughed again. "It's good to talk to you once more.
When this stupidity with my chest is finished, we shall have
lunch together, yes?"

"You know how much I should enjoy that."

"And remember: tell no-one. For the moment, this
matter remains a secret between the two of us."

"Of course." She knew his blue-blooded American wife
looked with disfavour at the amount he spent on paintings.
In the silence, she added: "We miss you, Don Pedro."

"Someone's coming," he said and softly replaced the receiver.

For a moment she stared unseeing at the snow-laden branches of the trees in the park across the street. Over the years she had carried out many confidential transactions for Don Pedro. He was the London-based head of the Banco Morena, a small but prestigious family-owned merchant bank in the City; the Morena family originated from Burgos and after the war had been encouraged to expand by the Franco government, anxious to improve Spain's chances in the international monetary markets. It was not the sort of place where she had anticipated making a career.

After studying fine art at the Courtauld Institute, she was disconcerted to find that her diploma did not guarantee her a job. The kind of places into which it might have granted her an entry – museums, art galleries, auction houses – were in the grip of recession and laying people off rather than taking them on. Eventually, needing to earn a living, she had registered with a London translation agency.

Spanish and Japanese: it was an unusual combination of languages and one ideally suited to the needs of the Banco Morena; for the past few years, Don Pedro had been paying a generous retainer for the exclusive use of her skills. She had originally been sent to the bank as a replacement translator when the man who usually dealt with their requirements was off sick. The speed and efficiency with which she worked on the documents just faxed in from a Tokyo bank had impressed the Financial Management Officer with whom she had collaborated; next time he needed a translator, he asked for her by name. Shortly after that, she was called in to sit in as interpreter on a series of confidential meetings between the directors of the bank in Tokyo and those of the Banco Morena. She found, to her own surprise, that she was following the complicated financial discussions with both interest and excitement.

The internationalism of money intrigued her. Despite the different names given to any particular currency, money flowed across borders, crossed language barriers, meant as much to those who had it as it did to those who had not. She had grown to be fascinated by the way it rocked like a great golden sea, lapping at the shores of continents, now a giant tidal wave of yen, now a ripple of Deutschmarks, now a flood of dollars, a billow of sterling. It was the theory of the money supply, rather than the actual balance in her account, which beguiled her, which kept her involved despite the fact that the work was arduous and unpredictable and the hours lucratively long.

She began to read the financial pages of newspapers, to subscribe to specialist publications. Once, while the executive board of the Banco Morena discussed some complicated transaction involving the exchange of yen, she found herself contributing an opinion on the current state of the markets – and being listened to. Increasingly she found her role as interpreter being combined with that of commentator.

It was perhaps seven months after she had first acted as interpreter for him that Don Pedro approached her privately and offered her the chance to become a permanent member of his small but powerful team.

Flattered, she accepted immediately. Gradually, she

had begun to travel with Don Pedro to meetings; though he spoke excellent English, it sometimes suited him to behave as though he did not, and on such occasions she was able to act as a linguistic backstop, maintaining a discreet check on the highly sensitive negotiations with which he was often involved. Yet she still saw herself primarily as a person with a fine arts degree, so she was delighted that Don Pedro, discovering this, had begun to send her along to appraise works of art belonging to various clients, either for tax purposes or, on a couple of occasions, for the purposes of drawing up wills or paying out legacies. This was the first time he had asked her to undertake a commission on his own personal behalf rather than for the bank.

However high the bidding, you must bid higher . . .

She nodded to herself. That was what he wanted; that, then, was what she would do.

At six o'clock, she drove through a dark winter evening to Jonas Fedor's cottage outside Cambridge. As well as being one of the outstanding potters of his generation, up there with Bernard Leach, Lucie Rie, Hans Coper, Jonas was her friend, her unofficial guardian, the person she loved best. He was all the family she had: there were no grandparents, no cousins, no siblings. Without Jonas she would have felt herself truly orphaned. She swung into the gravelled courtyard and felt her spirits lift. Jonas's house was the place she considered home; in childhood she had spent most of her school holidays there, only returning to Japan in the summer, and not always then, since occasionally her mother flew over from Tokyo to spend the vacation weeks in England.

The back door opened, throwing light across the courtyard. Jonas's ample form stood, as so often in the past,
with arms outspread to welcome her.

"Happy birthday, my darlink," he called, his accent
untamed by the years of living in England. "Congratulations!"

"It's you who is to be congratulated. A CBE!" She
knuckled her forehead. "You're almost too grand to speak
to now. My boss was terribly impressed that I consort with
such famous people."

Jonas chuckled. "The phone has never stopped ringink
all day. The newspapers, the BBC, even that young man
who does a chat show on the television."

Tess hugged him, breathing in his familiar odour of
garlic and cigar smoke, wine and clay dust. "About time
too," she said. She thrust a sheaf of yellow roses into his
arms. "Here, these are for you."

"But Teresa," he said. "It is your birthday, not mine.
You are the one who should be receivink the presents."

In the cluttered sitting room, he poured wine for them
both. "This is a good one," he said, raising his glass. "I
am very pleased by this . . . Teresa, my darlink, this is for
you with all my love."

He handed her a parcel and then sat back, watching
her as she struggled with knotted string and thick layers
of tissue paper. Finally she uncovered a bowl, delicate yet
sturdy, the hallmark of Jonas's work. It was exquisite, the
wide brim standing on an elegant foot, the whole glazed
in a pale sea-green.

"Oh, Jonas," she said. Looking at his broad red face,
she felt tears prick the back of her throat. How long had
it taken him to make it, how much effort had it cost him

now that his fingers had grown stiff and breathing was an effort? "It's absolutely beautiful."

There was an accompanying note in Jonas's fine italic script:

> Happy Birthday, my darling Teresa: I saw a pot
> like this many years ago, in Spain, and seeing
> it, realised instantly what I was meant to do.
> I fear that it is the last pot I shall make . . .
> I wanted you, who has always loved me without
> question, to have it.
> With all my love.

He had signed it, as always, simply with a J, the long tail dipping towards the bottom of the page before curling upwards and down again in the suggestion of a heart.

She got up and hugged him again. The atmosphere was suddenly overcharged. She wondered if it was because of his apprehension about his forthcoming trip abroad. Although she had offered to go with him, he had insisted on travelling alone – 'unfinished business', he had called it, winking at her, implying that there was a woman involved, an old flame, or even a new one. She assumed his worries were logistical, involving the carrying of heavy bags, the demands of steep steps on old legs: she wished now she had insisted on accompanying him.

He chuckled. "What a lucky old man I am," he said. "A beautiful woman to embrace me; good wine, and now even the chat show hosts beggink me to appear on their programmes. I shall tell them about my book – it will be excellent publicity."

"I can't wait to read it. I hope you'll give me a signed copy."

"Of course. It will be a sensation, I guarantee. A bestseller." He rubbed his big potter's hands together.

"Is it finished?"

"Almost. This is why I go to Spain, to check up on one or two final details. Then it can be published and I shall become filthy rich at last."

Tess refilled their glasses. "I thought you didn't care about money."

"I don't, Teresa. You know I do not. But it would be wonderful to have some finally, before I die." He grinned at her. "I could build a Jacuzzi at last. I could give the money to deservink causes, and appease my sense of guilt."

"Guilt? For what?"

He was suddenly serious. "Things." He stared sombrely into the leaping flames of the fire which burned in the grate.

"What things?"

"You will have to read my book to find out," he said. Unexpectedly, he seemed uncertain of himself.

She smiled at him, hoping to joke him out of his downbeat mood. "You do realise that for a bestseller you need certain ingredients, don't you?"

"Such as?"

"Money. Sex. Violence. Corruption."

"But, my darlink, my book has all of these, pressed down and running over," he said. He laughed richly, his hand trembling slightly as he lit one of the five cigars he allowed himself each day. "Naturally I have made the women prettier, the dangers more desperate, and myself more heroic, like Superman."

"I hope you had a better dress sense than he does," Tess said.

Jonas sipped wine, his face thoughtful. "There are some people who will not be very pleased about my book."

"Why not?"

"Because they will not wish me to speak of the days in Spain during the Civil War. They would rather it remained secret, that I let sleepink dogs lie. But a long time has passed since then, and I would like it all to come out before I die."

"I wish you'd stop talking about dying," Tess said. "Especially on my birthday."

"Of course." Jonas checked his watch. "You must be late: you are havink dinner with Dominic tonight, yes?"

Tess was annoyed. "How do you know?"

"He told me."

She did not enjoy the idea of Jonas and Dominic discussing her when she was not there. "Do you two often get together?" she asked.

"Of course. He is writink a book on the Civil War; I actually took part in it." Jonas chuckled again. "For him, I am a piece of livink history." In the grate, a log collapsed onto itself, sending up a shower of sparks. He said: "I am pleased that you are to be with him on your birthday. Believe me, Teresa, he is exactly the right man for you."

"For someone, perhaps."

"Why not you?"

"For a start, he's loud and arrogant and opinionated."

"Like me."

"But without any of your charm."

"If he is so horrible, why do you go to his house tonight?"

"Because . . ." Tess stared into the red glow of the fire. *Because there is no-one else to spend my birthday with? Because although I am afraid, I am compelled by him?* "Because he invited me before anyone else," she said lamely, and knew that Jonas was far too acute to believe her.

Dominic Eliot had been courting her for some time, without a great deal of success. Part of that lack stemmed from the fact that Jonas not only approved of him but constantly – and obviously – tried to push the two of them together: she did not care to be manipulated. Yet, despite the fact that she found him overbearing, she had continued to see him at regular intervals in the six months since Jonas had introduced them: why?

Only to herself could she possibly have admitted the real reason. When she was with Dominic, she was aware of urgent possibilities, of lives unlived. When he touched her, however casually, her whole body leaped; when he kissed her, desire raced like fire. Yet the worlds he offered she dared not enter and terror forced her to keep him at arm's length. However strongly she longed to draw him in, she feared that if she ever relaxed her guard against him, he would, dragon-like, consume her in the heat of his flame and she would be devoured, annihilated, reduced to ash. It was easier to keep him at a distance, and much less frightening . . .

There were eight of them round the table. Tess found herself sitting between Dominic and the corpulent young

Something-in-the-City in an expensive suit and gold-rimmed glasses with whom, over Dominic's excellent preprandial sherry, she had already established a mutual fascination with the abstract notion of money. Conversation ranged, as always on such occasions: the latest shocking novel from the States which led on to a discussion of a writer's obligations to his readers, the political situation, the awfulness of the current government, the correct way to make a vinaigrette. Someone mentioned a TV programme which had shown the behind-the-scenes activity prior to a major sale at Sotheby's, and they got on to art and the ethics of creation.

"Life and art have nothing to do with each other," Tess said. "The creation should stand alone."

Jerome, the Something-in-the-City, said: "Unfortunately, though, it seldom does."

"Why should a painting be worth millions with a signature, and almost nothing without it?" someone asked.

"Part of the intrinsic worth surely must lie in the fact that a particular person painted it," Dominic said. He ran a hand through his rough dark hair and down over the back of his head, a frequent gesture of his. He smiled at Tess, leaning towards her until their shoulders touched. "After all, you're paying partly because the signature guarantees that this particular painting, these very brush-strokes, were the work of a man who subsequently went mad and chopped off his own ear." Beneath the sleeve of his jacket she was acutely conscious of blood and nerve and muscle.

"Or died of the demon drink," said Jerome.

"Or slept with his own daughter," said Dominic.

Eric Gill, Tess thought. Augustus John. Blood pounded

in her ears. "You're right, of course, in a ghoulish sort of way," she said, moving away from Dominic. "Naturally, it's much more fun to know that X or Y painted the picture hanging in front of you while he was recovering from the suicide of his mistress or was high on drugs. But it shouldn't be. The thing should offer its own aesthetic, without needing a signature."

Jerome said: "Because of the value of those signatures, my bank has just decided it can't afford *not* to go into the art consultancy business." He looked solemnly round at them. "These days banks have their own arts programmes, staffed by experts who can not only advise clients on how much to spend and where to spend it, but are also able to invest in art for the bank itself." The thought seemed to depress him. He stared morosely into the bottom of his wine glass.

On Tess's other side, Dominic laughed ironically. "The acceptable face of capitalism: I suppose it makes sense. Art provides moral statements about those who own it, after all."

"It certainly helps to make a corporation less faceless," Jerome said stiffly. He was not quite sure whether he was being laughed at or not. He turned to Tess again. "Ever thought of going in for that sort of thing yourself?"

"Not really. I've done some appraising for the Banco Morena from time to time. As a matter of fact, I'm off to Texas shortly for precisely that purpose. One of our bigger clients has just died and turns out to be something of a collector."

He narrowed his eyes. "Interesting. Would that be the Cramir collection, by any chance?"

"It might be."

26

"Lucky you."

"I'm looking forward to it," said Tess. "But advising the bank on what to buy for its own purposes? I don't know that I'd dare."

"Perhaps you should have more faith in yourself. You obviously know a lot about the subject, and you seem to have a sound financial brain. I think you'd do rather well at it."

"Something to consider in the future," Tess said lightly.

Dominic tapped on the table with a fork and raised his glass, his eyes warm and slurred. "Let's drink to the birthday girl," he said. "Here's to lovely Tess." He turned to her and said in a lower voice, meant only for her: "Happy birthday, my darling."

Tess smiled back at him, nodded at the others, drank his fine claret. She put her face close to his and said quietly: "Darling? Since when?"

"Come on, Tess. Just because I use a term of endearment doesn't mean I'm asking you to marry me." He looked at her large dark eyes, the generosity of her mouth. When would she realise what she was missing? He remembered his mother brushing his sister's hair when they were children and quoted softly: "*Oft do I think of this wild thing wedded; much more love should I have, and far less care.*"

He put a hand on her thigh. Her face flushed as she removed it and he said mockingly, "You know, you've really raised self-control to an art-form."

The words, as much as the tone in which he spoke, stung. Did he know of the passions which sometimes raged in her? Could he see behind her cool exterior to the real naked Tess?

As Dominic produced careful cheeses, a delicate dessert, liqueurs, the phrase continued to nag her. As a linguist, a translator, constantly moving back and forth between one language and another, balancing meaning against accuracy, needing to match the spirit of a statement with its intention, words were the daily currency of her job: they were three-dimensional, alive. Dominic had been speaking in coded messages, she knew, but perhaps he was right. Perhaps she was over-controlled. If so, it was because she was terrified of what would emerge if she let go. Perhaps she hid herself behind words because they were pin-downable, skewerable, like butterflies. Certainly she could not deny that there was something contained about herself, something enclosed, as though she feared her personality might dissipate if she was too prodigal with its essence. Was that the same as controlled? And anyway, was being controlled such a negative thing to be?

Next birthday, I shall be thirty, she thought, catching Dominic's eye, only ten years off forty. The years she had already lived crowded behind her; she saw them as somehow thin, attenuated, the lean kine as opposed to the fat ones which could be the next thirty. If she allowed them to be.

Later, leaving, she refused Dominic's offer to escort her home, but kissed him with more warmth than usual so that his arms gathered strongly about her and she felt him harden against her body. She wanted desperately to give in to her own impulses, wanted to feel his lips warming the cold places of her heart, but dared not, knowing she sought only temporary comfort. Drawing back, she saw the sadness in his face and wondered if it was only for himself or for her as well.

Walking home, slipping on the frozen pavement, she shivered in the bitter cold. The temperature was dropping. There had been stars earlier, pure and piercing in a dark-blue sky; now snow was falling again, thick flakes settling on the sleeves of her coat and glistening like tears in the light of street lamps. Snow clung to the branches of evergreens and dusted the tops of garden walls; her breath led the way, cloudy in the cold. She spoke aloud Ramirez' lament for a lost love: "*White roses, whiter snow, roses and snow, and between them my bloodied heart.*"

For a moment she half expected the words to materialise and hang suspended there, snow and roses, like ice carvings or decorations on a birthday cake, pendant in the frozen air.

Unexpectedly, there were tears in her eyes; she could not have said whether they were caused by the cold or by the bleakness which seemed to have settled in her marrow. She had a sense of flying time, of winged wheels, of tumbrils rattling across cobblestones into darkness. Roads not taken mocked her; sharply, her heart ached.

In bed, alone, depression weighed on her. She was not the first to find that despite its realities, life was no more than an illusion, ungraspable. Like the house she had dreamed of, the Casa de las Lunas, the house where she was born.

Friends, Henry, Dominic: she had used them earlier as a defence against loneliness. Yet, Henry was no longer hers and she did not have the courage to accept Dominic. As for her family . . .

In reality, Jonas was all she had.

She thought about what he had said earlier that evening, concerning his autobiography. For a moment, prescience, foreknowledge, apprehension, squeezed her brain in an ugly grip, and events not yet known to her glimmered briefly and were gone.

Leaning against her pillows, she stared at the painting which hung beside her bed. *The Tears She Shed* had been a present from Jonas on her twenty-first birthday; it was her most treasured possession. The girl in the painting on the wall watched her with melancholy eyes; she felt a rush of guilt which she tried to tell herself was irrational. Were it not an absurd emotion to connect with Jonas, she would have said he had sounded almost afraid: was the trip to Spain something more significant than she had believed? After all, she *had* suggested accompanying Jonas, albeit in a voice which invited a negative response; Jonas had duly refused her offer. Her only fault lay in not making it again, though she knew (and suspected he did too), that only her own fears held her back.

The picture was about two feet by three, painted in oils. It showed a dark-haired girl, no more than thirteen or fourteen, seated on a rumpled bed. She wore a rudimentary shift which suggested the outline of young breasts. The colours, violent swirls of pigment laid on thickly with a knife, were muted: ochres, chestnut, a cinnamon shade which she knew was a hallmark of the artist's palette. The only bright colour came from a bowl of lemons on the high window-ledge. The wall behind was of rough, cream-painted plaster; the effect was that of a nun's cell, or a prison. The bed-linen was very white, almost glowing; the girl's face was sad. Slung over one end of the brass bedpost was a meticulously painted necklace of glass beads. The outline of a shoulder occupied the lower left-hand corner of the little canvas.

Tess looked at it for a long time. As always, questions hung in the air: had the girl just risen from sleep, or from a rude forcing? Why did she wait with such fear and yet such resignation? Did she know it was useless to struggle? Was the person whose gaze she met her aggressor or her comforter?

There had never been any need to speculate on who the artist was. As soon as she had unwrapped it, that first time, even before she had found the tiny signature inscribed along the rim of the bowl, she knew his name.

Fernando Vicente, dead for more than fifty years, imprisoned during the Spanish Civil War and then shot. According to the legend which had sprung up about him, he had been released at dawn from the cell where he had spent his last night, led out into a cold Andalusian morning and set against a cemetery wall. She had often wondered what he thought as he looked beyond the gravestones and the soldiers to the slopes where the olives blew. Had small birds sung as he saw for the last time the blue light on the mountains? Had his artist's eye put together a painting, a final possible canvas, there in the cold morning with the black line of the hills against the gold of a not-yet-risen sun? Did he think of his parents, his sister, the high-breasted aunts, or had he been beyond thought by then?

It was known that he had not been a brave man; small things terrified him: spiders, rough voices, children, knives. She had always hoped he died with dignity, lifting his chin to the sky, perhaps even smiling briefly, before they raised the barrels of their guns and he slowly crumpled beneath a rain of bullets, his blood smearing the wall behind him, one hand lifting briefly towards the sky.

There was no stone to mark his grave; what was left of Fernando Vicente lay somewhere in the hills of southern Spain, his dust mingled with their bitter soil. She had always promised herself that one day she would go there, stand under the sun with flowers in her hand, red flowers, the kind he had loved. She should have done so long ago; that she had not was due in part to fear, but also to a conviction that the right time had not yet come.

Looking at the painting, at the frail arms of the girl, at the almost scented lemons, she wondered if perhaps it had at last arrived.

3

TESS

Hannya is the female demon traditional to Noh drama, the equivalent of the western witch. The emphatic horns on this mask show that she is angry, as does the ferociously twisted mouth. The mask portrays her with sternly parted black hair, sharp gilded teeth and lips the colour of blood.

Catalogue: *Wood Sculpture of the Edo Period* edited and translated by Teresa Lovel

"So it wasn't until after the war that you realised in which direction your artistic talents lay?" the man in the linen jacket said earnestly.

"Oh, I realised," Jonas said. He settled back comfortably in the TV studio chair. "But I wasn't able to do anythink about it until the hostilities were over."

"What led to your realisation?"

Jonas smiled lazily. A dimple showed in one of his broad red cheeks. "It was durink a rainstorm. I was with a . . . friend, in Granada. It began to pour with rain, and we ducked into a little museum of local artefacts." He leaned forward, staring at the presenter. "And there it was. A

Roman pot, standink on a single leg, glazed in green. A most beautiful piece."

"The single leg has become a trademark of your work, hasn't it?"

"I would not like to think that I had a . . . *trademark* . . ."

"A recognisably Fedor characteristic, shall we say?"

"Possibly." Jonas smiled again, this time to camera.

"You know Spain well, I believe," the presenter said, referring to his cue-cards. "In fact, you fought against Franco in the Spanish Civil War, didn't you?"

"Indeed I did." Jonas's bulk moved towards the front of his seat. The dimple disappeared. "And terrible days they were."

"You ran a resistance cell, isn't that right?"

"Yes. For some time I was based down in the south of Spain. There were twelve of us . . . they called us the Apostles. I was named Águila."

"Águila?" The presenter turned to camera and the unseen audience. "That means Eagle, doesn't it?"

"Yes."

"And you were given this nickname because you used to swoop down from the mountains after your prey?"

"Perhaps. Or perhaps because eagles have talons, and beaks which can tear apart the flesh of a lamb – or a man."

The presenter looked startled, then laughed. "The Apostles? Águila? To modern ears, it all sounds a bit like an adventure story from a – "

"Believe me, my friend, it was no story. It was blood and guts and death and pain," Jonas said forcefully, cutting across the other man. "We had nicknames in those days because it was sometimes the only way to survive. If your identity became known, not only you but your entire family could be killed."

"I see. So you – "

"We were not fightink this war for fun," Jonas growled angrily, "but for freedom, for justice. And it was a vicious war, an evil war, from which neither side emerged with much glory."

The presenter said: "Perhaps you heard some of the discussion with my previous guest on the nature of good and evil . . ."

"I did. And I disagree with what the Bishop said. I believe very strongly that truly evil men can and do exist."

The presenter cleared his throat. "Have you ever met any such men?" He looked down at the notes on his clipboard.

"Twice," Jonas said, and he frowned, his face dark. "It was durink the Civil War. One of them betrayed everything that makes civilised men stand out from the animals: his family, his friends, his honour. Above all, his art."

"What happened to him?"

"He died the death he deserved," Jonas said baldly.

There was a pause. "And the other?" prompted the interviewer.

"The other?" Jonas seemed to come back from somewhere far away. His face set in stern lines. "The other was the man I fought against during those terrible times. We knew him as El Malo – "

"Which means the Evil One?"

"– and he more than lived up to his name. A man without a single redeemink quality, a man who – "

"Have you ever identified him since?" The interruption, designed to put a stopper on Jonas's rising emotion, was smooth.

"No. But as you know, I have almost finished writink a book about those years. I am goink next week to Spain, to check a few facts." Jonas shifted in his seat, stared straight at the camera.

"And when you return, you'll know who he is?"

Jonas gave a grim smile. "I think so."

"He's still alive then?"

"As far as I know."

"And you intend to tell the world?"

Jonas grinned. "Not the world. Only those who buy my book."

The telephone rang early. Sleepily Tess picked it up and heard Don Pedro's voice. "You haven't forgotten about the auction, Teresa?"

"Of course I haven't."

"I just wanted to check with you . . ."

"I'm to buy the Ramón O'Donnell, right? And however high the bidding – "

"*Not* the O'Donnell," Don Pedro exploded. "The *Sanchez*!"

Tess laughed. "I was only kidding."

"Don't kid at the auction, Teresa."

"I won't."

"I saw your guardian on the television the night before last."

"So did I."

"I was impressed."

"Me too."

"He is not a bit like I had imagined him. I suppose you are very close to him."

"Very close indeed."

"Like me and my daughter." His voice grew husky with emotion as it always did when he spoke of the beloved only child his wife had belatedly produced some twenty years ago. "Total trust, no secrets from each other."

"More or less," Tess said, knowing there were secrets she would not wish to share even with Jonas.

"And this book of his, have you read it?"

"Not all of it, but most. It should cause a stir when he finishes it."

"I can imagine." He coughed. "Er – perhaps he might be persuaded to sign a copy for me when it is published."

"I'm certain he would."

"You sound . . . distant, Teresa."

"I'm not. Just sleepy."

"But you have an auction to go to, a painting to buy."

"If you can call Sanchez' work 'painting'," Tess said.

"Now you are teasing me again."

Brantwell Manor was nearly three hours by car from the house she rented in Cambridge. She had often thought about moving into London – it would be much more convenient and she could certainly afford it – but preferred the space between work and home, the limbo provided by the train ride in which she could shed Tess Lovel for a while and become anonymous.

Beyond Buckingham, the river began to flatten out between the water-meadows, its course gauged by the lines of pollarded willows along its banks. After a while, rain began to fall. A dank grey sky nuzzled the crouched fields where sheep plodded.

Last August, she had driven this way with Dominic. It was shortly after Jonas had introduced them; she knew almost nothing about him except that he was an historian researching the Spanish Civil War and she had not yet realised his power to terrify her. It had been high summer then, the pastures tall with grass; the air blowing in at the open window had been rich with the scent of hay. Dominic was going to interview someone who had fought alongside Franco during the Civil War and suggested she came with him, made a day of it.

They had picnicked beside a calm reach of reed-fringed water, lunching off the chicken salad which Tess had prepared, drinking chilled white wine provided by Dominic. They had talked desultorily.

"You don't sound entirely English," she said, at one point.

"Odd, because I am." He had been lounging on one elbow. Now he leaned forward and brushed the tip of a grass stem slowly along the side of her jaw, smiling lazily when she flushed. "But not brought up here, for the most part. My father was a consultant for one of the big oil companies – we moved around a lot."

"To where?"

He had shrugged. "Australia, Hong Kong, Spain, South Africa. Places where they needed his particular petrochemical expertise."

"So you speak Spanish?"

"I do. And Afrikaans." His mouth was suddenly grim. "For what that's worth. French, too. And some German."

When he looked up at her, something chill and hard stirred behind his smile.

"Did you go to university?"

"Of course. A year in New Zealand, two years at the university of Michigan, a post-graduate year in Spain. That's where I first got interested in contemporary Spanish history."

He reached over and put his hand on hers; one of his fingers trailed along the thin cotton which covered her thigh. Goose pimples rose on her arms and she shivered suddenly. "And after that?" she asked quickly.

"Lots of things, mostly bumming around. My father wanted me to get a proper job; I wanted exactly the opposite."

"Bumming around."

"India, China, South America – proper Boy's Own stuff," he said lightly. He jumped up and pulled her to her feet. "Come on. Let's walk for a while, and you can tell me about you – much more interesting than I am."

Unlikely. None the less, she told him something of her earlier years in Japan – the sanitised, acceptable version, and wondered, when he looked at her, how much he perceived of what she chose not to tell . . .

Reaching the open gates of Brantwell Manor, she turned in to follow a line of cars towards the house and a makeshift parking lot. She had already checked that the picture sale was due to start after lunch, which gave her plenty of time. She bought an itemised catalogue from an overalled woman seated behind a table at the front entrance. The house was old, the hall panelled in linen-fold, a huge fireplace burning logs which straddled a pair of wrought-iron dogs. Above it, a portrait of a disdainful youth in a tight green coat looked down on mellow parquet flooring and diamond-paned windows.

Somewhere, in the recesses of the house, Tess could hear the voice of the auctioneer – "What am I bid, ladies and gentlemen?" – and a bustle of footsteps and under-the-breath conversations. There was something distasteful about this laying bare of two people's lives. They had lived here, the British Consul and his Spanish wife; they had entertained friends, read books, listened to music, walked their dogs, made love. And now strangers fingered the intricate patterns of the existence they had woven together. She found the room where the paintings were displayed. A guard stood at the door; he watched sternly as Tess took in the fact that few of the canvases hung round the walls were by internationally known names. She opened her catalogue, and read:

Lot No. 602: Ricardo Sanchez (1865–1928)
Boy on a Horse, oil on canvas, 104.5 × 84 cm.
acquired from the artist in 1921.

There followed a brief description of the artist and his life which she did not trouble to read. Don Pedro already owned a number of works by Sanchez: Tess did not care for them. Over the years, she and he had engaged in a number of enjoyable arguments about them, the most recent only days before his attack of flu as they had dinner together in Paris after a hard day of discussions with a group of French businessmen. Tess maintained that Sanchez' style was too facile and his subjects hackneyed.

"Hackneyed!" Don Pedro said, outraged. "What on earth do you think Murillo was?"

"Wash your mouth out!" cried Tess.

"Or early Velasquez . . ."

"How can you speak of Sanchez in the same breath as Velasquez? Even *early* Velasquez."

Don Pedro had pounded the table with mock-rage; Tess had continued to eat, imperturbable. Smiling at the recollection, she wandered round the room.

And then she saw it.

A woman stood partially blocking the view but even so, Tess could see most of the picture and the sticker attached to a corner of the frame which announced that this was Lot 617. It drew her across the room as though she had been caught by some invisible hook. The colours, the sunshine, the magical tree . . . although there was no need of the printed word to tell her who the artist was, she none the less looked down at her catalogue.

And looked again.

There was some mistake, surely. The title was as she expected it to be but the painter . . .

She read the page again.

Lot No. 617: signed A. R., Granada Group, (1947–)
Casa de las Lunas, oil on canvas, 72 × 60 cm.
purchased from the artist in 1966.

The canvas was dream made actual. She would have recognised it anywhere, the Casa de las Lunas, the house where she was born, the house from which her mother had been so disastrously married. It sat in creamy sunshine, four-square to the road which ran below it past the gates. There was a tangle of indeterminate leaves in the foreground – bougainvillaea, plumbago, oleander – and, above them, the house itself, softly glowing, melon-coloured, green-shuttered beneath a roof of umber tiles. A balustrade set with pots of geranium and fuchsia dripped purple and crimson and flame down over the front of the house; to one side a fruit tree, round as a child's, was hung with gold and silver fruit.

"*The golden apples of the sun, the silver apples of the moon,*" Tess said under her breath. Or was that improbable tree inspired by something older, by a present from a King of Spain's daughter, by the romance of a silver nutmeg, a golden pear?

Large in the foreground of the painting were the gate-posts, blocked in with thick layers of ochre and grey. Each bore the outline of a stylised moon, one waxing, the other waning, the moons from which the house took its name. Tess knew the shapes were made of beaten copper. Her mother had drawn them for her many times, the two solid gateposts, the sweep up the short drive to the house, the iron gates spread wide.

Tess was not given to materialism, to possessions. But now she thought: *I want it. I must have it*. She remembered herself skating on the lake below the pink castle, an ice-maiden with a band around her heart; she felt a literal loosening, as though upswept hair had tumbled, as though dammed water had been given freedom. For the first time she understood the grip of desire.

A Vicente – no question of that, whatever it said in the catalogue. She bent closer to search for the familiar hidden signature but could not find it. Centimetre by centimetre she went over the little canvas but all she could see were the initials A. R. painted in midnight blue in the lower left-hand corner, over the creamy-grey at the foot of one of the gateposts.

She shook her head. Whoever had compiled the catalogue had got it wrong. The style, the technique, the mixture of reality and fantasy in which the artist often indulged, the palette, were all unmistakably those of Vicente. She was prepared to stake almost anything on it.

Besides: "I didn't even know there was such a thing as the Granada Group," she said, only realising that she had spoken aloud when the woman beside her said tersely: "There isn't."

Tess turned her head. The woman wore a white silk shirt, a black jacket and jeans, handmade brogues; the casualness of her attire was more than offset by the top quality of the material and its beautiful cut. Her dark-streaked grey hair was pulled into an elegant chignon around a face as arrogant and beautiful as an Aztec carving. She had the carriage of a ballet-dancer; her expression was disdainful. Black eyes flicked across Tess's face without interest then suddenly her eyes widened, the pupils appearing to enlarge until her gaze seemed one black stare. Meeting it, Tess could not move. Her mind filled with sudden images: dragons stirred in the depths of caves, a sword flashed, a silver-horned goat streamed across a starry sky.

Was it for infinity that the two stared at each other, or only for seconds? Certainly, when the woman turned back to the painting, Tess felt as though she had been swept up by some giant force and then allowed to fall. She shook her head, as though to clear it, and wandered over to look out of the window while she considered what to do.

She had a hard decision to make. Don Pedro had authorised her to spend money on the Sanchez but she knew that if he was aware there was a Vicente on sale he would most certainly wish her to buy it too. However, she did not have authorisation. It would not be possible to telephone him: his fearsome wife fielded all calls. But to let a Vicente, even a doubtful one – though in her own mind she was convinced that the painting was genuine – go: she was sure he would never forgive her. She would have to stick her neck out, take the decision on her own. Or could she afford to buy it for herself? That would depend on how much it went for, of course, but she doubted it – even if she counted on Jonas being willing to chip in a loan.

Dammit. What ought she to do?

The doubtful attribution explained why it was here at a country sale when it should have been whisked off to Sotheby's, given the big sales hype. The puzzle was why someone should wish to pass a genuine Vicente off as being by someone unknown – which, as far as she was aware, this AR certainly was. It was obvious that he must have substituted his own initials for Vicente's signature – but what possible reason could he have?

She decided to go for it, to use Don Pedro's line of credit and deal with the consequences later. Perhaps technically she would be guilty of some financial misdemeanour – embezzlement, perhaps even theft – but she was certain she was right and it would be money well spent. She walked back to the painting and studied it again: there was definitely something odd about the signature. When she straightened up, the woman in jeans was watching her.

In films, auctions are always conducted in an orderly

fashion. The punters sit on small gold chairs and decorously nod their bids; the auctioneer, gentlemanly in old school tie and good suit, is orotund and seemly. Here, there were no chairs; the auctioneer wore a cracked Barbour over a tweed jacket and carried a small wooden stool which he moved round the room from picture to picture as the sale proceeded, while the prospective buyers milled and surged about him, as amorphous as a flock of sheep.

Tess had no problem with the Sanchez: it seemed that she was not the only one to dislike his work. The painting was knocked down to her at less than she expected and she knew Don Pedro would be pleased. She waited in a muted frenzy of excitement and trepidation for Lot No. 617. By the time it came up, she found herself at the back of the room, wedged against a wall. It was like travelling on the Tube during rush hour; she wondered whether she would be able to catch the auctioneer's eye over the heads of the crowd. Behind him, a man slung about with straps and bulging at the hip stood with folded arms, his eyes wary under a peaked cap.

Looking about her, Tess became aware of someone standing outlined against the long leaded windows, his features unclear because of the haloing daylight behind him. A man. A small man, in his middle thirties, perhaps. She could tell he was staring directly at her, his expression somehow both perplexed and mournful, as though she reminded him of things he would rather forget. At the front of the crowd a small commotion began: someone felt faint. Faces turned, the auctioneer called for a chair, the guard at the door found one and it was passed over the heads of the crowd.

"Ladies and gentlemen," the auctioneer began. "Lot No. 617: a prime example of the work of this talented school of artists, whose reputation has grown enormously over the years." He looked around at them, playing them like a fisherman. "A fine investment for the future. Shall we start at, say, three thousand pounds?"

There was a murmur. He looked around, and smiled indulgently. "Come along then, ladies and gentlemen: two thousand. Just two thousand pounds."

The audience, mostly middle-class county women in quilted jackets and sensible skirts, with a sprinkling of dealers and yuppies, shuffled again. He said benignly: "Very well then. I'll say fifteen hundred. Who'll start us off at fifteen hundred pounds?"

Someone did. The bidding rose jerkily to two thousand pounds, three, four. At four thousand five hundred, the auctioneer took a deeper breath and, looking at his audience, began to increase the pace. Tess guessed that the estimated price had been reached and overtaken. She had not yet bid; there had been no need. The man by the window was bidding; a couple of other people had come in for a round or two and then dropped out.

Feeling sick, she unobtrusively raised her hand.

"Ah, a new bidder," the auctioneer said: "six thousand pounds."

The bidding continued, gradually reaching nine and a half thousand pounds. She nodded again at the auctioneer.

"Ten thousand pounds," he said. He looked around, casting for further bids, found one, said: "Eleven thousand pounds, ladies and gentlemen. Any advance on eleven thousand pounds."

Tess swallowed and nodded again.

"Twelve thousand pounds," said the auctioneer. From her experience of men and money, Tess could tell he was astonished. So was she; someone else in the room must have realised the painting's true worth.

There was a small sound at the front of the room; a hiss like that of a snake. "Thirteen thousand," the auctioneer said.

The man at the window raised his hand.

"Fourteen thousand," said the auctioneer. This was far more than he had expected to get for Lot 617; already he must be wondering what had gone wrong with the pre-sale estimations. Sweat had appeared on his upper lip; he looked behind him at the guard, as though checking that he was adequately protected.

The thrill of the chase took hold of Tess. Someone badly wanted something which she was not going to let them have. She bid again; the bidding moved to fifteen, sixteen, eighteen.

She nodded again. "Nineteen thousand pounds," said the auctioneer.

People were turning, trying to see who was bidding so recklessly. Exhilaration seized her, made her weightless as though she breathed a rarefied air. There were only two of them in it now, herself and someone at the front whom she could not see. "Twenty thousand," said the auctioneer. "I'm bid twenty thousand pounds."

The man by the window dropped out and began pushing through the crowd to the door, passing her with a stir of cashmere, a faint odour of cologne, a sideways glance from large mild eyes; he was not an Englishman, Tess judged. Close to, she could see that he was older than she had thought, in his middle fifties at the earliest. The boyish figure belied his drawn features, refined down to the bone; his hair, cut close to the scalp, was grey. Other people came in, waiting for the following lots, or drawn by the sudden tension which had developed. Behind the windows, the sun seemed about to break through the clouds.

Tess dipped her head once more.

"Twenty-one thousand pounds." The auctioneer's expression was disbelieving as he cleared his throat.

Again Tess heard the hiss at the front of the crowd. She found herself smiling. The outcome was inevitable. *However high the bidding, you must bid higher*. Don Pedro had said that about the Sanchez: she applied it to the Vicente, despite the false signature, despite the fact that she did not have the funds behind her to pay him back were he to refuse to take it. It did not matter. She no longer cared. She felt as though she had entered some mythological landscape where nymphs became trees, lovely boys changed into flowers and everything she touched would turn to gold.

She wondered who the unseen bidder at the front was. The auctioneer glanced from one to the other, picking up their nods; the two of them were bidding against each other in silence, gladiatorial.

At twenty-two thousand, she realised, with a sense of exultation, that her opponent was weakening. There was a distinct pause before the next bid was announced. At twenty-four thousand, the auctioneer dropped his gavel onto the clipboard he carried. She knew she had won.

"Sold to . . .?" At his enquiring eyebrows, she mimed writing on her catalogue; she was reluctant to release her name into the charged air. Luckily he remembered her name from Lot 602. One of the guards approached and she followed him to the office set up in what must once have been a cloakroom.

A man in dark suit and heavy-framed glasses completed the details of the transaction. Earlier she had checked with him that Don Pedro's arrangements for payment were satisfactory; she dealt with temporary insurance, papers of provenance, proof of ownership; she signed something and saw that her hand was not quite steady.

Outside the room, she leaned against the closed door and smiled. For the moment, until she passed it over to Don Pedro, the Vicente was hers. She was overcome with the desire to snatch it from the wall and drive off at full speed. Yesterday, apart from *The Tears She Shed*, she had only seen Vicente's work on the walls of museums; now, suddenly, she owned, if only temporarily, two pieces of his work.

Coming back into the wide hallway, she hesitated at the sight of the man she had noticed earlier. He stood gazing up at the portrait above the fireplace; he was clearly waiting for someone. She was about to duck into one of the other rooms when the woman who had been viewing the Vicente earlier appeared. There was something familiar about her though Tess could not immediately pin down what it was.

"I lost it," the woman said furiously, her voice as deep and harsh as a man's. "I cannot believe this. Did you see who bid against me?"

"No," said the man. The two of them spoke Spanish, she much more fluently than he.

"Are you sure? You were at the back of the room."

"I p-paid no attention."

Tess wondered why the man should lie; he had been watching her for most of the proceedings, he must have known that she was the one bidding against the elderly film-star – if that was indeed what she was. Perhaps he was the woman's agent.

"I curse her," said the woman slowly, and Tess was suddenly struck by chill, as though an icy wind had just blown through the hall.

"How do you know it was a 'her' and not a 'him'?"

"I feel it." The woman pressed one elegant hand against her chest. "Here, I feel it. I saw her earlier, before the auction began: she knew that picture was a Vicente, she was . . . *fighting* me for it. And this time she has won."

"F-fighting?" The man broke into English. His accent was faintly American. "Not everyone is as aggressive as you, you know." His gaze moved around the wide hall and Tess stepped back further into the shadow of the doorway. He stared at it, as though he knew she was there.

The woman tapped her catalogue. "I don't think much of your friend's little trick, by the way. Painting over a Vicente signature. A strange idea of fun."

"Very strange."

The woman changed tack. "That girl," she said venomously. "There must be a way to find out who she is."

"You are only angry because she wanted the painting as m-much as you did. Or even m-more."

"But it is the *Casa de las Lunas*. I needed it. And now she has ruined my plans, the work of years."

"Ruined your p-plans? Even if you had this so-called Vicente there are many others s-still unaccounted for." The man turned his mild gaze on the diminutive figure

50

beside him. Tess wondered if the woman knew that he himself had been bidding for the picture.

"Whoever she is, I curse her," the woman said again.

"Why didn't you go higher?"

"Because I knew – halfway through, I became certain that whatever I bid, my opponent would bid more, that there would be no end to it."

Would I have gone on and on? Tess wondered. Surely I have more sense than that. The notion that perhaps she did not was both unexpected and pleasing.

The woman standing by the fireplace said fiercely: "I shall simply have to find some other way. I don't care how it happens, but that painting must be mine."

She spat into the fire, causing the logs to hiss, and the flames, momentarily, to writhe.

Like an addict, Tess could hardly wait to unwrap the newly-acquired painting. Despite the fact that the early morning rain had given way to intense cold, that frost now sparkled on the roads, she drove dangerously fast through the quiet country lanes, her mind preoccupied with the woman's strange curse. Was she serious? Did she really intend to try and gain possession of the *Casa de las Lunas*? As she neared Cambridge, she saw the turn-off towards Jonas's cottage and hesitated, her foot on the brake, then swung left. Maybe it would be best to leave the Vicente with him for the moment, until she had worked out what course of action she should take.

Jonas was not at home, but Kate welcomed her in. While the housekeeper prepared a pot of tea, Tess unwrapped the Vicente and propped it up on Jonas's untidy desk. She gazed at it for a long time, feeling herself fall into it, feeling the mellow sunshine, the sweep of the drive, the intoxicating profusion of flowers. This was the house where her mother had lived as a child; it provided a link with a past which her mother's death had rendered impenetrable. The old ache of loss suddenly overwhelmed her; she swallowed, forcing it back. Looking at the two symbols, new moon and old, on the gateposts, she thought: I have roots but they are not planted deeply enough, nor can they be until I see for myself where I began.

She found Jonas's flashlight and played it over the left-hand corner of the painting. Scrutinised closely, it was obvious that the AR signature was of a more recent vintage than the rest of the canvas. Searching diligently, inch by inch, she found a place, running up the trunk of the nutmeg tree, where it was possible that Vicente's own tiny repressed signature might have been painted out.

She puzzled over the reason behind it all the way back to Cambridge. It was late; she had lingered over Kate's beef casserole, hoping that Jonas would return before she left, but he had not done so and eventually she had decided to leave the paintings at the cottage and drive on home.

The house waited for her. As always, when coming back to it, she wondered whether she could ever share it, or, indeed, her life, with anyone else. Other people produced pressures and complications she was not sure she wished to take on; other people wanted things she was not prepared to give . . .

As soon as she opened the front door, she sensed that something was not as it should be. The hall was too chilly to linger in, yet she stood staring into the blackness at the end of the hall. What was it? Had she heard a sound as she came in? Had there been some slight adjustment to the oriental runner which covered the Victorian tiles, some rearrangement of the garments hanging from the bentwood hat-stand?

No. It was more subtle than that: a sense of disturbed air, an almost imperceptible odour of unfamiliarity. And as she thought that, she realised that not only was the door into her sitting room slightly ajar but that a small feather lay curled against the skirting board. Yet she had a very clear recollection of turning as she left the house that morning, and looking back, sweeping the terrain as conscientiously as a security camera. She was sure that the door then had been shut, the hall floor immaculate, unfeathered.

Shutting herself in with a possible intruder did not make much sense. She opened the front door again, letting in a surge of wintry cold; the feather lifted, drifted, settled again. She walked towards the sitting room and pushed the door wider, reached in to flick down the switch on the wall so that when she stepped inside, the room was brightly lit. There was no sign of disturbance, no indication of an alien presence. The room looked as it always did, calm and peaceful. The same was true of the rest of the ground floor, and of the bedrooms when she went upstairs. She frowned. Perhaps she had merely imagined it. Perhaps the novelty of being cursed by a stranger with the cold eyes of a statue had unnerved her.

She tried to laugh at herself but it was not easy. If someone had broken in, might he not still be in the house, waiting to pounce on her? A cold draught of air reminded her that the front door still stood open, providing another possibility: suppose someone was lurking outside and, seeing the open door, seized the opportunity to come after her?

The frosty doorstep glittered in the light from the hallway; out in the street, branches creaked. Running towards the front door, she slammed it to, then went back upstairs, leaving all the downstairs lights on.

It was bitterly cold; the central heating had been off for hours. She rechecked the two bedrooms, looking under the beds again and into the wardrobes to assure herself that there was nobody in either of them.

Then she went into the big bathroom and turned on the taps to run a bath. The room was warm, heated by a hot-water radiator independent of the heating system. She poured lemon-scented bath oil into the bath and watched it form citrus pools on the surface of the water.

Undressing, she stepped into the bath and lay there, freeing herself of sensation, of apprehension; somewhere at the back of her mind lay the *Casa de las Lunas*, waiting for her like a childhood treat, something to be savoured, pleasurably anticipated. She was tired. As the warmth of the water permeated her body, her eyes closed, her mind drifted. Copper moons, the hanging trees, flowers tumbling over golden stucco brilliant in the noonday sun, the smell of –

The light snapped off.

At the same time, she was pushed violently beneath the surface of the water. The shock was so sudden that for a moment she lay passive, then she was frantically flailing, gasping, choking as water filled her throat, her nostrils, her lungs. Something weighed her down so she could not rise. Her lungs heaved; her mouth was solid with unbreathable water. As she twisted and splashed, panic-stricken, the realisation trickled slowly into her terrified brain: someone was trying to drown her. She flexed herself against the edge of the bath, pushing with her forearms, but the oiled water gave her no purchase and the pressure keeping her underwater was too strong. Her feet scrabbled at the end of the slippery porcelain. She felt the knobby chain of the bath plug. In what was more a reflex action than a conscious thought, she curled it between her toes and tugged. Her chest felt as if it was on fire; the blood roared in her ears; already fingers of blackness were seeping from the edges of her brain towards the centre. When they met, she would be dead.

The water began draining away. If she could last, if only she could last another few seconds, she might be able to survive. Yet at the same time she knew it was impossible, that she was dying, her lungs were collapsing and she with them. Through a dim haze, she felt her face emerge, and then she was coughing, spluttering, feeling sick, drawing in great heaving breaths of air. At the same time, she slid forward and up, away from the iron grip on her skull, slithering sideways over the edge of the bath, her body fluid as a seal's, finding herself on hands and knees on the tiled floor. The only light came from the hall, and silhouetted against it she could see a man's figure, thickset, the features indistinguishable in the dark. Afterwards, she would realise that he must have been wearing some kind of scarf around his face; at the time the featureless outline made the whole encounter doubly terrifying.

She drew in a breath to scream. At the same time he threw himself at her. With horror, she saw the faint gleam of a blade and twisted sideways, rolling up against the wall, feeling the roughness of the towels which hung from the rail. She tried to stand but her body was slick with oil; she could not get sufficient grip on the floor to stand up. Equally, her assailant could not hold her still long enough to drive his blade into her vulnerable heart as she floundered and threshed beneath him on the floor.

Her mind was still working sluggishly, as though each thought had to push through a thick black curtain, but she none the less understood that her only chance of staying alive lay in immobilising him long enough for her to get downstairs to the front door. But she had no weapon. The bathroom contained nothing useful, no heavy objects, nothing sharp or dangerous. As he kicked viciously at her head, she slithered again across the tiles and fetched up once more against the hanging towels. Big towels, bath sheets . . .

She yanked at one and threw it at him like a net, over his head, over the upraised arm with the knife, as he lunged once more towards her. Frantically she jack-knifed away from him, but not before the blade had dragged down her side. Even through the covering towel, it produced a red-hot line of agony. The pain brought tears to her eyes and anger to her brain.

It was the anger which saved her. How dare he? How *dare* he? Once again she twisted away from him, the tiles bruising under her shoulder-blades, painful against her elbows, but this time she drew her knees up as he came at her again and kicked out with all the furious strength she could find, knowing that this was her only chance.

He lost his footing. As his feet fought for a hold on the wet tiles, he grabbed at air, teetering, off-balance. Tess dragged herself towards the door and found a foothold on the fitted carpet. On her feet, she raced for the top of the stairs and the lighted hall.

At the same time, the front door opened and Dominic

appeared. He stood for a moment gazing up at her, a grin appearing. "We-ell!" he began.

Then the expression on his face changed. "Tess!" he said urgently, running towards her, taking the stairs two at a time, reaching for her. "What the hell's going on?"

She fell against him, clutching at the banister, feeling the belated screams rise in her throat. Before she could answer, the man who had tried to kill her came down the stairs like a fired torpedo, the knife vicious in his hand. Dominic, one arm round Tess, grabbed at him, but was pushed violently back as he ran for the front door and was through, out into the frosty dark.

Dominic turned as if to follow, but Tess pulled him back. "Don't leave me!" she said, hearing her own hysteria. "Let him go . . . stay with me!"

Her knees suddenly gave way and she sank down until she was sitting on the stairs. Burying her face in her hands, she began to weep, huge sobs shaking her.

"Tess," Dominic said tenderly. "Sweetheart." He tried to pull her up but she resisted.

"You're hurt," he said. "You're bleeding. He must have . . ."

Tess pulled her hands away from her face. A thin line of blood wavered through the oil on her skin. There was a gash running from the side of her breast to just above the hip bone; a line of blood continued from the severed flesh down one leg, dripping steadily. For the first time, she was aware of her own nakedness, the soft lines of breast and belly, the dark pubic tangle. She looked away, shock and pain not able to diminish her embarrassment and, at the same time, her sudden inappropriate desire. If Dominic were to make the slightest sexual movement towards her she knew that she would be unable to resist him, that if he threw her down on the carpet, the bathroom floor, anywhere, she would open herself to him. Horrified by her body's reaction, she squeezed her eyes shut. If he kissed me, I would be lost, she thought.

"Come on, my sweet," Dominic said softly, as though talking to a child. He took his coat off and put it round her shoulders. "Let's get you cleaned up. Then I'm going to call the police. And a doctor."

"No," she said, rousing herself from the cold torpor which had overtaken her. "No."

"Why not?" He seemed astonished at her vehemence.

"I can't face it," she said, tears coming to her eyes again and falling heavily down her face. "Besides, what good will it do? They'll never find her."

"*Her*? That wasn't a *her*."

"No, but she was behind it, I just know it."

"Who was?"

"Some Spanish woman." Tess's eyes were suddenly lead-heavy. "I bought a picture she wanted."

"And she tried to kill you because of it?" She could hear Dominic's scepticism.

"She cursed me," Tess said, and remembered the silver-horned goat racing across a star-scattered midnight sky.

"This sounds totally bizarre," Dominic said. "I'm going to get you into bed."

Deliberately he turned his gaze from her. Taking both her hands in his, he led her back to the bathroom, sponged her expertly down, taped gauze over the knife cut. Exhausted, she let him take charge, glad he had not further mentioned a doctor; the wound bled a lot but seemed superficial enough and she could not have managed to talk to anyone about the hideous experience she had just undergone.

"He tried to *kill* me," she whispered against Dominic's shoulder, as he half-carried her into her bedroom.

He ignored her. He turned down the covers of her bed. "In you get," he said. "And take this." From the inner pocket of his jacket, he pulled out a small plastic packet and extracted a round tablet. He handed her a glass of water.

"What is it?"

"Something to make you sleep."

When she had swallowed it, he said: "Don't worry. I'll stay here with you."

"With me?" She opened her eyes and stared apprehensively at him. Hot images filled her mind. She wanted to reach for him, pull his head towards her breasts, sink into the safety of his mouth on hers. But to do so would be to lose control. "You mean . . .?"

He sighed. "Same old Tess," he said. His sister Valentine had told him she was worth waiting for; he knew she was right, yet at the same time he wondered how much flesh and blood could stand, how long the wait would be, whether, indeed, it would ever be over. The indeterminate darkness of her eyes compelled him, the siren shape of her mouth beckoned. That there was some trauma tucked away behind her self-containment, he was aware. What he wanted was the key so that he could help her unlock it, open it to the fresh air, watch it blow away like morning mist. But so far she had withheld it.

He shook his head and smiled. "I'll be next door if you want me," he said. Leaning over her, he kissed her forehead. "Don't worry, you're safe with me."

Through half-closed eyes, she watched him cross the room to the door. *You're safe with me*, but she knew she was not, that dragon-like, he waited to sear her with his breath.

Waking in a sweaty panic from a claustrophobic dream, of lying in a grave, drowning in her own blood, hands shoving at the unyielding coffin lid, knowing that even if it gave, she would not be able to break through the depth of soil which pinned her down, she wondered for the first time at Dominic's opportune arrival. How had he got in? He had told her the front door was open when he arrived, that her assailant must have left it open for a quick getaway. But she distinctly remembered closing it, and by then the man must already have been hidden in the house. He said he had been passing, that seeing a light on, he had wondered if they could share a nightcap.

Thinking about it now, his words rang falsely. *A nightcap*? It was not their habit. She blinked in the darkness, feeling her heart begin to beat more rapidly. Switching on the bedside light, she sat up. The room looked familiar yet unknown, the objects still recognisable but different, tainted with the knowledge that someone had tried to kill her. On the back of the upright chair near the bed, Dominic had hung his jacket. She suddenly reached forward and pulled it towards her, feeling the weight of his wallet, hearing the faint rattle of his keys. As though a sponge had wiped away her normal feelings of shame or embarrassment, she quickly opened the bulky leather wallet and whipped through it.

Credit cards, a photograph of a woman she knew to be his sister, business cards from all over the world, bills, money, receipts from shops, garages, old bus tickets, train tickets, plane tickets – carefully she scrutinised them one by one and then put them back, not even caring if it was obvious she had looked through it. In the outside breast pocket was the small cellophane bag from which he had taken the sleeping pill he had given her earlier. There were half a dozen like it left, as well as some long blue capsules and a handful of big white ones. She wondered whether she dared extract one but decided he would notice so replaced them. She hung the jacket back over the chair and lay back against her pillows. What kind of a man carried strong sedatives in his pocket? What kind of a man would yield so easily to her pleas not to send for the police?

For a moment, she saw Dominic clearly. Then sleep claimed her again, and by the morning, she had temporarily forgotten her doubts.

4

MERCEDES

She stalked him.

Subtle as cobwebs, she set her traps; hung them across his paths. With the sly skill of the fisherman, the poacher, she dropped her bait and watched him sniff, then take.

Nature helped, of course. The task she had set herself might not have been so easily accomplished if she had been ill-favoured. Nor, indeed, if he had been baser born, less educated and therefore superstitious. It was as if some Providence not only approved of her plans but was determined to further them. By the time she was sixteen, she was accounted a beauty. The sorrowing aunts, Isabella and Francisca, Rosita and Luisa, walked with her through the sad and bloodied streets, they waited for her outside the school, they sat with her, slowly fanning themselves, through the long airless afternoons. None the less, there were opportunities for her to display herself, to make sure he noticed: she could occasionally walk alone in the hills, or ride with Pepe around their land, visit the workers, cross his path. It suited her, however, that the aunts should guard her; she welcomed her lack of freedom since it gave her time to prepare her campaign. From the first, she had no doubt that she would be victorious; when the moment came, she intended to be merciless.

The aunts exulted as the years passed. "Such hair . . ." "Such eyes . . ." "That waist . . ." She would listen patiently, smile at them, seeing the grey shadows lying like sickness beneath their own eyes, watching the tremor of Isabella's hand, listening as Rosita wept in the night. Listening, watching, she could feel herself, under the soft covering of flesh, grow harder than any rock.

Did they, the four of them, have any notion that she was less than complete, that where there had once been a heart there was now only a black and bleeding wound? Could they not feel her pain, as she felt theirs? They told her she was beautiful; staring at her reflection in the chestnut-framed mirror she saw only the force of her desire for vengeance. Although conscious of beauty, she viewed herself with dispassion, with the eye of a hunter: her hair was no more than the noose from which he would dangle, her dark eyes only the decoys which masked her true intention, her breasts and tiny waist merely the hooks with which she would snare him.

Fernando's paintings had been removed from the walls at the time of his arrest in case they became a target for abuse. When it was over, when all the dead had been counted and order was restored, the pictures remained where they were. "Tomorrow," Francisca, the oldest of the aunts, would say. "Tomorrow I shall go up with Pepe in the cart and fetch them down. Or maybe the day after . . ."

The paintings, wrapped in sheets, had been removed, when the *fascistas* came, to one of the deserted *cortijos* now used for drying almonds, up in the hills. Sometimes, at dusk, while Francisca and Isabella prepared the evening meal, she would walk with Luisa or Rosita up the street to the edge of the little town and watch the shadows come down across the lines of hills, changing against the evening sky, silvery pink, lavender, mist mauve. Up there, somewhere up there, buried in straw, under the piles of soft green-grey husks, lay all that was left of Fernando.

One day, without telling them, she walked through the narrow alleys to the house of Pepe's son and told him to tell his father that tomorrow she would be waiting by the gates of the old convent. He had not wished to; there was hay to harvest, a sick goat . . . she touched the witch's mark beside her nose and watched him turn away, nodding surlily.

She chose the place deliberately, as a scourge, as a lash; waiting for Pepe, she remembered her younger self, the weight of the basket on her arm, the high pearled light of those early evenings. It seemed to her that her whole life was condensed into those three weeks, that never again would anything fill her with such intensity, never again would she love. Circumstance had forced her to grow up too fast. Then, her life had seemed infinitely wide, a multiplicity of possibilities; now, shattered by events, it had narrowed, refined into a single determination.

Bumping in the cart up the precipitous track between vine-covered terraces and groves of olive, she thought about the pictures. It was best that they remain, for the most part, hidden. Sooner or later, buyers would come, from Madrid, from Paris, from New York. Although they had seen no newspapers, she could guess that the world must know of Fernando's death, that the news would have been greeted with shock and disbelief. Eventually the paintings would have to go; they were his legacy to them, all he could do to see that they were able to maintain their comfortable life, keep up the substantial town house, the trips to Paris, to the apartment in Madrid, now that he was dead. Besides, the aunts would wish Fernando's genius to be shared with the world. She knew that she herself could be no more than their temporary caretaker, but while she could, she would indulge herself. She had decided to pick four of them; for days she had been debating which to choose, wandering in imagination among the subtle colours, remembering his hands, the smell of oil paint and turpentine, the look of concentration on his face, the way his hair crinkled back from his brow.

The village fell away behind them: sharp-angled orange roofs, white walls, acacia trees, the stone front of the church, the belvedere at the southern end of the main street overlooking the sweep of the valley. Cicadas trilled; above their heads were swallows and a pair of hawks, motionless against the blue sky. From up here, she could look down on the Ramirez estate stretching towards the steep massif of the sierra, its sloping fields planted with vine and olive and almond. Hidden among the trees were the roofs of the *finca* and behind them, the ruined tower built centuries earlier by their Moorish ancestor, in the time before Islam was finally expelled from Spain.

The *cortijo* was one of many which dotted the hillside, a two-roomed building once painted white and surrounded by prickly pear and oleander. It stood close to the edge of a plunging ravine, space held back by the remnants of a retaining wall. Once there had been a small garden scratched out of the soil by a previous owner; now only an overgrown hibiscus and a group of rusted cans remained to show where there had once been fertility.

She climbed down from the cart, telling Pepe to stay. He nodded; the mules waited, quiescent in the solid heat; silence descended. She walked round the side of the little building and looked over the retaining wall into the plummeting depths.

Once, when she had first heard the news of Fernando's murder, she had come here, climbing up through the dry terraces left by the Arabs, limbs torn and scratched by the spiky shrubs, mind screaming with loss, and contemplated throwing herself over. She had imagined then how it would be, that long descent into oblivion, her body dropping through the cool air past the wild thyme and the clinging scrub and the cries of birds; she had even climbed onto the flat stones of the wall, ready to launch herself towards the dried river-bed below.

Bells had saved her. Not church bells, drifting up from the valley, a message from the God she felt had abandoned her, a reminder of mortal sin, but goat bells, knocking, mocking, pulling her back from the edge of Eternity. Fernando, writing once from Madrid, had said it was the sound he missed most; long afterwards, she would interpret their sudden appearance that day as a sign from the Devil. At the time, as the goats flowed past the walls of the *cortijo*, grey, brown, white and black – the colours of the landscape, the colours Fernando loved – as she faced the collective glare of their yellow eyes, saw the wicked thrust of horns, she had seen them in a way as a message from beyond the grave, a message telling her death was something to be postponed, that there was work to be done.

She had followed them downhill through the crushing heat of mid-afternoon, feeling the hatred flow and burn, solid inside her as lava, until the goats had suddenly wheeled away and lost themselves among the rocks; by then, she knew she had to live, to avenge.

After the bright sun, the bigger of the *cortijo*'s rooms was dim. She could smell the almonds, the scent like the essence of summer meadows; they lay like heaped dust, spilling into the centre of the floor. The pictures were hidden on either side of the square hole cut into the wall to let in a minimum of light. She plunged her arms into one of the piles of furry grey husks and felt for the wrapped canvases. Finding an edged corner, she pulled; the almonds scattered, rolling softly across the earthen floor like the soft bodies of moths. She did the same with the other heap.

The paintings had come to no harm for their long incarceration. She unwrapped the sheets as though they were shrouds, kneeling in the light cast through the open door, and saw his images come alive again: a house, a tree, a girl lonely on a bed, a young woman laughing, the *corrida*, a man looking down from a balcony. With the pictures came recollections of the man who painted them. She clenched her fists until the nails bit into the palms of her hands; she doubled over, agony squeezing her chest. Oh God, Fernando . . .

For a moment she lifted her head and gazed out into the open air, seeing the hills back away from her, the clear sky above them, the whole tremendous view he had loved, and nearer at hand, dry soil, a clump of yellowing grass, a line of ants.

She swallowed. Four, she had allowed herself. She selected the canvases she wanted, rewrapped the rest, working them in among the velvety almond husks until they were covered up again, scooping almonds from the floor with both hands and flinging them back onto the piles from which they had slid.

Pepe had not even raised his head as she lifted them into the back of the cart. As she took her seat beside him, he turned the mules towards the town far below; neither of them spoke. It was best that way. In the confused days of the war, it had not always been easy to know who was friend and who was not. For centuries the little town had survived on the mutuality of shared interests, but trust had been destroyed. Who wished to sit in the café and play dominoes with a man who might have betrayed your son or your father? Who wished to wash the linen of a woman who had sold secrets, or buy oil from someone who might have murdered his neighbour?

She had chosen that day deliberately; it was the third anniversary of Fernando's death and the aunts had gone to Mass to pray for his soul. She unloaded her canvases and carried them two by two into the dark, cool hall of the house. The mules clopped away, the sound of their hoofs dying away along the cobbles as she took Fernando's paintings up to her room and ranged them round the walls. Later, she would decide where to hang them; for the moment it was enough that she had them. The faint aroma of oil paints still rose from their surface, mingled with the smell of the almonds which had been their protection. Looking at the sad-eyed girl on the edge of a bed, at the sombre self-portrait, at the soft colours of the Ramirez house on the edge of town, at the still life – lemons on a linen cloth, a knife, butter in an earthenware bowl, a wine-glass – she was filled with exultation. She *knew* that embroidered cloth, that dish, that glass, she had shared them with him, nothing could take that away.

The tears came later.

And the nights, the oil-lamped nights when she lay naked on her bed, watching the glimmering colours on her walls, touching herself, wishing, wanting, seeing again his smile, his hands on her shoulders, his mouth, feeling the blood surge from the furthest edges of her body to concentrate in a single lifting moment at the centre, teeth clamped on the sheets so that she would not cry out.

She planned her strategy, seeing Ramirez there as though at the wrong end of a telescope, tiny. Hers to destroy.

5

MERCEDES

They were reluctant to let her go but she was firm.

"Fernando would have wished it," she told them and they nodded at each other, Luisa and Rosita, Francisca and Isabella, each unsure that it was really what Fernando would have advised, yet giving in because each thought that her sisters would say, if asked: "But of course, yes, this is what Fernando would have wanted for the little one."

She supposed she loved them; they were her family and she had watched with rage as grief and passing years greyed their hair and dimmed their once-fine complexions. Of the four of them, only Luisa had had a *novio*, the mayor's son, and even he had gone to America in 1938 and never returned.

As the years went by, she had grown adept at interpreting Fernando's wishes. "You remember," she would cry as they sat in the jalousied drawing-room in the heat of the day, Luisa reading, Francisca writing a letter, the other two sleepy on a sofa. "You remember what he said, that time we were in Madrid . . ." Or it might be: "that time in Paris . . .", "when we were at the *corrida* . . .", "driving to Granada . . ."

And the aunts, languorous with heat, stout with lunch-eon, would nod, almost sure that they did remember, and she would get her own way. This last suggestion, however, was proving more difficult.

"A young girl alone in Madrid," they said. "No. It cannot be allowed."

"But I have to go," she said. "When the war in Europe is over, the dealers will come. We must be ready for them, and I am the only one who can acquire the necessary knowledge."

"No," Francisca said, her fan vigorous. "You are just a girl, it would not be safe, it would not do."

"What would Fernando say if you sold his pictures for too little?" she retorted. Sunlight pierced the slats of the blind to spear the dim air of the room with brightness. The aunts nodded and murmured.

"What would he feel if you let his work go for less than its true worth?" she demanded, remembering as they did not that for Fernando the real worth of his painting had only ever existed in the joy of its execution and never in whatever monetary value others placed upon it.

Again the aunts nodded.

"But without training, without knowledge, we shall never know what we should be asking," she told them, "after the war in Europe is over, when the dealers come."

When the dealers come . . . It had grown into a kind of mantra for them all, as emotive for these four sisters as the thought of Moscow was for Chekhov's theatric three. Although the Civil War in Spain had come to a bitter and bloody end, Europe itself had erupted into an even grimmer struggle, and although Spain remained neutral, life was harder for them now than it had been during the years of civil war.

In the end, worn down by her insistence, they agreed that she should go to Madrid to study art for a year, but only if Luisa went along as companion and chaperone.

She did not tell them her real reason for wishing to go. She did not say that he too was in Madrid, a lawyer now, one of the more brilliant of the new generation of post-Civil War advocates.

In Madrid, Luisa bloomed. At home, she was seen in the town as a woman disappointed, abandoned by the man of her choice, left to wither. In Madrid, established in the family's high-ceilinged apartment near the Puerta del Sol, Society knew nothing of her, she could be anonymous, just another handsome young woman, not albatrossed by circumstance. She made friends, acquired a circle. She bought new dresses, had her hair done every other day, attracted the attention of older men who wore formal suits of pale cloth and stiff white collars.

This was ideal. When Luisa suggested they give a buffet supper, she was enthusiastic. She wondered shyly whether she might ask some of her student friends; she mentioned in passing that Ramirez was here, that it might be a friendly thing to include him, for old acquaintance's sake.

It was the first time she baited the trap.

She wore a dress of white eyelet cotton, her small waist emphasised by a wide belt of blue suede. She had watched him for weeks, learning him. She followed him from the roomy apartment he maintained behind the Prado, observed the women he took out, the men with whom he conversed. She had calculated that his appetite was jaded, that the freshness and innocence she offered, her apparent lack of sophistication, would tempt and captivate.

The calculation was based on close observance. She knew the women he was most often seen with. She had sat in the corners of the cafés and restaurants he frequented and seen the lines of boredom on his face, seen him frown as his female companions chattered, crossed their silk-stockinged legs, lit cigarettes, lipsticked their mouths.

On the evening of the supper party, she deliberately kept away from him. Every now and then she looked across the room at him, and then, when she had caught his eye, turned away as though in confusion. She engaged herself in conversation with one of her tutors in drawing and design, a dark, devilish-looking man who lived with his wife and five children in a cramped apartment to the north of the city. Anyone watching them might have wondered whether so young a girl was safe in the company of an obviously older and more experienced man, a man, moreover, whose black eyes were sunk in decadent shadow and whose cheek was rakishly scarred from eyebrow to jawline.

The two of them spoke of Degas and Cézanne; they discussed Picasso and the Cubists. She lowered her eyes demurely, knowing that from a distance it would look as though the conversation had taken a *risqué* turn. She mentioned El Greco, one of her tutor's greatest enthusiasms, and waited for him, as he always did when passionate about a painter, to lay his hand upon her arm.

The bait was taken.

Ramirez sauntered over. She looked up at him as though

in surprise. He was tall and well set; even through the cloud of her nurtured hatred, she acknowledged his physical attraction.

"Don Carlos," she said, moving away in order not to have to introduce her tutor and so reveal his harmlessness; the manoeuvre might have looked like that of a person released from a siege.

"It is some time since I last set eyes on you," he said, bowing. The warmth in his look was everything she had hoped and worked for.

"When was that?" she said, wrinkling her brow in perplexity. "I don't recall . . ."

"I was out riding," he said, eyebrows pulling together as though he were annoyed that she should forget an incident he obviously had not. "You were sitting under a tree – surely you remember – your ankle . . ."

"Ah yes. Of course." As if she could forget so carefully staged an accident, or the smell of the olive leaves silver against a pale hot sky as she waited for him to complete his daily circuit of the Ramirez estate, the hawks circling lazily above her, the silence absolute, the baking brightness of the soil beyond the shadow of the tree. "You were kind enough to take me back to my aunts."

"Yes." But the way his eyes held hers, she knew he remembered more than that: remembered, as he was intended to, the feel of her waist as he set her into the saddle, the brush of his hand against her breast, the smell of her hair as she leaned into his arms when he lifted her down outside the door of her house.

She smiled at him uncertainly. He cleared his throat. "I didn't know you were in Madrid," he said. "I would have called sooner . . . Are you here for long?"

"I'm enrolled at the university," she said.

"Aren't you a little young to be a student?"

"I'm sixteen, almost seventeen."

"Indeed? What are you studying?"

"Art and design. Art history." She gestured vaguely. "I also take classes in painting, both in water-colour and in oils."

"Of course. After all, Fernando Vicente was your . . ." He stopped.

Hatred, grief, swelled her heart so that for a moment she thought it would burst from her lips. *Fernando, Fernando* . . . That this man, of all men, should use his name . . . "Yes."

"So it runs in the family," he said, as though he spoke of blue eyes or a way with words.

"Hardly," she said, ferocious. "Vicente was a genius."

"Are you interested in the work of contemporary artists?"

"Yes. Very much so." She held her breath, anticipating the approach of a goal she had waited for.

He said: "So am I. I've been given tickets to a private view. Ramón O'Donnell and Luis de León are good friends of mine. Would you care to come with me?"

It was what she wanted above all. She had seen him with the two artists; it was not difficult to assume that they would ask him to the first night of their latest exhibition.

"If my aunt permits, I should very much enjoy it," she said primly, though adrenalin surged through her body and she wanted to shout aloud. She looked up at him and felt her pupils expand; she saw him react, tense, step back.

The trap was sprung.

*   *   *

It was the first of many such outings. Although she felt she had achieved the object she had set herself in coming to Madrid, she none the less continued to study hard. It was important that she learn all she could; her growing acquaintance, through Ramirez, with the modern generation of painters would eventually stand her in good stead. In front of the O'Donnell canvases, she listened attentively as Luis de León – small, dapper, mustachioed – explained his friend's work to her, the symbolism behind the abstract sweeps of colour; she did the same when big blond O'Donnell waxed enthusiastic about de León's miniature paintings.

The fact that she was Fernando Vicente's sister made her an icon among them. Some of Ramirez' artist friends – Castán, Sanchez – had known him, had studied with him or even shared a studio. They had admired his work; as a martyr they had begun to clothe him in myth.

Seated beside Ramirez in cafés, in restaurants, in dingy studios and shared apartments, she saw ahead of her the paths she would take. For years she had merely had a fixed goal to aim for; now she saw beyond that point to a world where she wielded power not just over one man but over many; she saw herself manipulating markets, establishing trends.

Taking one of the dozen or so Vicentes she had brought with her from the south, she found a reputable dealer and sold it to him. The amount he first offered she rejected, wrapping the picture up again and walking to the door. The revised offer he made as she tugged at the door handle was slightly more than she had calculated on getting.

She began to buy, discreetly, cheaply. New names, using her own judgement on those which would become famous when peace came at last to Europe. She learned to have confidence in her own choices for this was not a matter she wanted to discuss with anyone else.

She bought several of de León's tiny jewelled canvases; although she did not care for O'Donnell's work, she recognised his importance and bought those too, using a false name each time. She did not wish either of them to know who was buying their paintings since it would alter the image she was so carefully building. She never looked at her acquisitions. They lay stacked under her bed, her investment for the future.

After a while, confident, she bought in order to sell immediately, always making a profit, always ploughing it back into the business. The dealers and gallery owners began to recognise her; they learned what she went for and kept paintings back until she had seen them first. She saw how the artists she favoured began to command higher prices than those she did not; young though she still was, she knew she was on the way to where she wished to be.

Luisa, caught up in a social whirl of her own, courted by no fewer than three eligible men, was happy enough to allow her more freedom. Ramirez, after all, was known to her, a local man, the son of the largest landowner within miles of Montalbán. She knew from the expression on his face when he called to collect Mercedes that though he loved the girl, he none the less saw her as nothing more than a child; no harm could come to Mercedes in his company. It did not occur to her for a moment that it was Ramirez himself who was in danger.

One evening they were joined in their favourite restaurant by a young man Ramirez knew: Jonas Fedor. He was a refugee from Austria who had gone to England at the start of the Nazi persecutions and then come to Spain to fight against Franco as a member of the International Brigade. He fascinated her; she could sense the man inside, pulsing, chafing, quite different from the snub-nosed, dark-curled boy who listened to their talk and said little. She was drawn to him.

He spoke vaguely of studying at the university and occasionally she saw him in the hallways or the student cafés, talking fiercely, seriously, watched by a group of rapt faces. She never joined them; she sensed that the Fedor who harangued and encouraged was a different being from the Fedor who often joined Ramirez and his friends after that first evening. He found her beautiful, she knew; his eyes were always upon her yet he kept barriers between them. She saw him eyeing the mark alongside her nose and wondered if he knew what it was supposed to signify.

One evening, they gathered in O'Donnell's studio to celebrate the big painter's thirty-fifth birthday. They had crusty rolls, a basket of peaches from Ramirez' estates in the south, a brandy-soaked cake baked by Luisa. Bottles of *vino tinto* passed from hand to hand; someone had brought in a platter of hot sausages cooked for them by the butcher in the street below.

O'Donnell lurched about the room, lubber-like, his big face red. "I never thought I'd make it this far," he said. "They had me once, you know. They had me, the bastards."

His friends groaned; they had heard the story before. "No," he said, "listen," and she saw how his hands shook at the memory. "They had me, they came for me in the middle of the night, knocked my mother about, marched me off saying they knew I'd been involved in the attempt to assassinate Jiménez de Asúa. They showed me corpses, people I knew, people some of *you* knew. It was dreadful. Innocent people." He looked round the room but she knew he did not see them, only the bodies of men he had once known. "We talked," O'Donnell said. "Of course we talked, who didn't in those days? We were political, we wanted reform, like everyone else. But they were shooting people for the wrong reasons, because they had cheated their wives over the price of a loaf, or stolen an egg or two from them or refused to sign their identity papers. They forgot nothing, those people, nothing, every slight, every insult . . . they were taking revenge for things which had happened years before. There were children lying there, too, dead children, and women. The guard lifted the skirts of one as he led me to the cells, showed me her petticoats, her stockings . . ."

She knew that by telling it, O'Donnell hoped to forget. She wondered if he realised that it was the remembering that fuelled his paintings. She picked up a guitar leaning against the wall and began to pluck at the strings. Fernando had taught her to play; heavy in her heart lay the memory of his voice as he hugged the instrument against him holding it as he might hold a woman, his dark eyes insisting that though he played to the aunts as well, he sang for her alone.

Almost unaware, she began to sing '*Adios mariquita linda*' in her small husky voice, and saw Fedor turn away, tears falling down his cheeks. He told her later that his sister used to sing the same song; he explained why he had not seen his sister for years, nor ever expected to again.

It was her first close acquaintance with the horrors of the European War; until then, she had concentrated on her own horror.

She would have tried to say something about Fernando, how the lightness had gone from her life too, how she needed him, but Fedor touched her then, for the first time.

"I'm sorry," she said. "I'm sorry that you should weep."

He smiled at her and his smile filled her soul. He said: "Don't be. Tears water the heart. They keep it supple."

She could not remember when she had last wept and wondered how supple her own heart was. She was moved by him; she thought, surprised: I could love this man.

6

TESS

A dried leaf, a feather
blown on the wind:
What else is a man?
translated from the Japanese by Teresa Lovel

"*Dios*!" At the other end of the line, Don Pedro drew in
a sharp breath. "Are you really all right, Teresa?"

"Yes, really. I – "

"But *really* all right? Are you sure you still want to go
to Texas?"

"Of course."

"But Teresa, why should someone want to kill you?
This means something more than an ordinary theft, does
it not?"

"It looks that way," Tess said reluctantly. It was
something she had not wanted to face up to. "But the
woman behind it – "

"You *know* who is responsible?"

"I – I think so."

"Then you must go immediately to the police, Teresa."

"I don't know her name," Tess said lamely. "She was at

the auction. She was extraordinary, like a witch – I don't suspect of her of trying to kill me with her own hands, but I'm sure she paid someone to do it."

"Someone must know who she is. The auctioneers, perhaps."

"I don't think so."

"But to kill you for a picture? Why not just steal it?"

"If you'd met her, you'd understand."

There was a pause, then Don Pedro said in a troubled voice: "If I had dreamed for one moment that my request to you would result in this terrible attack, I would never have asked you to go to that auction."

"It's not your fault there are weirdos about."

"I begin to appreciate what your guardian said the other day on the TV – that true evil really does exist."

"Please . . ." But Tess could not speak for the tears which since the attack had seemed only just below the surface.

She had a week in which to recover before she was due to fly to Texas. The wound to her flesh healed quickly but her mind was less adaptable. Endlessly she wondered what led a man to kill, especially on behalf of someone else. How could anyone enter the home of a stranger and deprive him or her of their lives, merely for money? The idea of murder grew more monstrous to her as she relived those moments of horror: the sudden darkness, the water covering her face, the pressure in her chest as though her lungs were about to burst through skin and bone, the choking terror.

Dominic stayed with her, visibly subduing his normal exuberance in order not to jar. She appreciated his thoughtfulness, glad to have him near; she knew this was not the real Dominic and even found something healingly comic in the way he wrestled with his own energetic temperament for what he perceived as her sake. At the same time, she found herself treating him with caution, even with suspicion, though she could not exactly recall why.

Until Don Pedro offered her the Texas assignment, Phil Cramir had been no more than a name filed away at the back of Tess's mind. Since then, she had taken time to familiarise herself with the man. The Banco Morena was one of the trustees of his considerable estate; Tess's role would be to assess for insurance purposes the few paintings in his collection which had not already been designated as bequests to museums and galleries in both Europe and the States. Cramir had elected to break his collection up, sharing its contents out among the kind of small provincial gallery for whom a Rembrandt cartoon or a Picasso drawing would have been out of financial reach. In a handwritten letter to Don Pedro, written shortly before his death, he stated that it was better that a hundred museums should each own a single Velasquez or Goya or de León than that one museum should have a hundred.

She wondered if he had had any inkling of the headaches his gifts were causing among administrators as they looked at the increased costs of insurance and the need for better security. Already one small gallery in Montana had declined to accept its legacy, on the grounds that it would be impossible to meet the security expenses; there would doubtless be others.

She was astonished at how little personal detail Cramir's

file contained. His money came from textiles: he had made millions when synthetics first came onto the market, and millions more when ecological awareness took off and there was a customer swing away from man-made fibres, by drawing up contracts for up-market natural fabrics with some of the top fashion houses. No rainforests destroyed; no destruction of the ozone layer, just pure silks, linens, hundred per cent cottons from Egypt and China. A shrewd operator, obviously, but one who kept his private life to himself. The files did not even state what his origins had been.

One item of information had particularly interested Tess. Some five or six years earlier, Cramir had made headlines around the world when he sold off his collection of Impressionist paintings and gave the multi-million dollar proceeds to various 'green' organisations. The Banco Morena had been involved not only because Cramir was one of its clients but because, coincidentally, the principal beneficiary of his generosity, the Madrid-based charity Save the Earth, also held an investment account with them.

Tess recalled all this as she and Martin García, Don Pedro's Harvard-trained assistant, took off from Heathrow on the long flight to Houston. They worked well together; like herself, Martin was the product of an Anglo-Spanish marriage and fluent in the languages of both parents.

During the flight, Tess returned to the files. In his later years, Cramir had rarely given interviews, and purchased additions to his art collection in conditions of great secrecy. The trustees of the estate were already experiencing some difficulty in drawing up a definitive catalogue of the works he owned since it appeared he had often used a go-between and sometimes even a false name when making new purchases.

She read with some interest the transcript of an interview he had given over the telephone three years ago to the Arts Correspondent of the *New York Times*. Asked why he had moved from Impressionists to relatively unknown painters whose monetary value could not be guaranteed, he had replied: "In buying the works of these artists I'm relying on my own artistic judgement and not that of others. That's what makes it fun."

As if unable to believe there was not some other, deeper significance for the switch, the interviewer had persisted. "Is that the only reason, Mr Cramir?", to which he had answered: "Perhaps it's also a matter of conscience." When the interviewer wondered exactly what he meant by that, Cramir had moved on to talk of something else.

They came out through the automatic doors of Houston's Intercontinental Airport into cool sunshine. A hire car waited; Martin drove, pulling out onto Interstate 45 to head south towards the city before taking the West Loop Freeway towards Cramir's estate. On the horizon, skyscrapers shimmered against a pearly sky; sun glittered blindingly on the cars which moved slowly along traffic-clogged freeways.

Cramir's estate lay in acres of rolling countryside west of Houston, and was surrounded by a double row of electrified storm fencing which could be floodlit at night. At the entrance gate, a guard with a gun on his hip let them through after checking with the main house that they were expected.

The house itself – a sprawling ranch-style building of white adobe with curved tile roof and heavily shuttered windows set among pines and shade trees – might have come straight from southern Spain. Cramir's daughter waited to greet them at the top of a shallow flight of pillared steps; she was a handsome middle-aged woman, with dark hair drawn into a knot on the nape of her neck. She introduced herself as Leónie Cramir Westlake. Tess murmured something suitable about her recent bereavement; Mrs Westlake was brisk.

"Dad was seventy-four and had been ailing for some years. I don't want to sound callous but it was better for him not to linger – he'd been active all his life and found it unbearably frustrating to be an invalid." She looked from one of them to the other. "Which of you is the picture expert?"

"I am." Tess smiled encouragingly, thinking that expert was somewhat overstating the case. "I've been reading about your father's collection on the plane. It sounds quite something."

"I think it is, though I had no real idea just how famous some of the pictures were, not until he died and the dealers started calling up."

"So you aren't really familiar with the collection?" Tess said.

"I don't even have the keys to the gallery. We'll have to wait until the manager of his bank in Houston gets here: he's the only one with access." Mrs Westlake was clearly embarrassed at not being entrusted with the keys herself.

"Most of the paintings have already been assigned to various museums and galleries, I believe," Tess said.

"That's right. You're here to assess what's left. It was one of the stipulations of Dad's Will that someone from the Banco Morena come over."

"We're a Spanish bank – was he Spanish?"

"Well . . ." The woman hesitated. "I'm not really sure *where* he was from. He always refused to talk about the past, he said the present was more interesting and the future more important. I often wondered if perhaps he was an illegal immigrant. I've heard him speak fluent Spanish on the telephone. But he also spoke French and German."

"Is that him?" Tess nodded at the painting which hung over a huge open fireplace in the living room. The room was enormous, a sixty-foot expanse of shining slate tiles broken up by various arrangements of furniture. Picture windows on three sides provided extensive views of flat green land stretching away into the far distance. Anyone approaching, whether by car or on foot, would be visible for miles between the pines.

"Yes. It's very like him. He must have been in his late forties when that was done. I can remember him quite clearly, sitting in that chair in his study, with exactly that expression on his . . . Oh dear." Mrs Westlake began to sniff. "Excuse me, will you? I'll – I'll go see if the man from the bank is here yet." She hurried out of the room, dabbing at her eyes with a tissue.

Tess walked over and studied the portrait more closely. Phil Cramir had been a good-looking man. Dark hair, well-marked eyebrows, a humorous mouth, an air of confidence despite the melancholy expression in the eyes. "What kind of a name is Cramir?" she said to Martin.

89

"Could be anything." Martin shrugged. "French, German, Scandinavian: who knows? Don Pedro told me once that he was always very cagey about his origins. Maybe some criminal connection in his youth which he preferred to keep to himself. Maybe a pay-off which enabled him to get his first business venture off the ground, something like that." Martin's forehead creased as he looked uneasily at Tess. "Nothing we should bring into the general conversation, don't you agree?"

Tess laughed. "Don't worry. I'll be discreet."

The Cramir collection was housed in a series of interconnected underground chambers built out under the huge living room and reached by a circular staircase which led down from a doorway beside the hearth. Air-conditioning hummed almost inaudibly; the atmosphere was cool and dry, unscented.

The long rooms were vaulted like wine cellars, the stucco walls painted white. Despite the bright lighting, the low ceilings made Tess uneasy. Since the attack on her the week before, her incipient claustrophobia had become more pronounced. She felt the need for wide-open windows, long vistas; she liked to know where the nearest exit was. On a recent trip to the Banco, she had been seized on the Underground with an almost tangible panic which left her sweating and breathless, forced to continue the journey by taxi.

Now she looked around, the back of her neck prickling. "Is there only the one exit out of here?" she said. "Suppose there was a fire or something at the door, how would you get out?"

"The possibility of a fire is remote," the banker said

frigidly. He was tall and thin, inclined to be stand-offish with his British colleagues. "In any case, the very latest technology has been installed to deal with such an eventuality."

"Yes, but suppose the door jammed," Tess persisted, aware that Martin was looking at her oddly, of the hysterical note in her voice.

"There is a second subsidiary exit, in case of emergencies," the banker said, "but as far as I know, it hasn't been used for years. If you're really worried, I'll show you where it is."

Tess felt suddenly foolish. "No. I just wanted to know."

In each room, a pair of chairs was set back to back. They were uncomfortable chairs, upright, wooden, with rush-bottoms and no arms; they reminded Tess of peasant homes she had glimpsed in Greece, where entire families would settle round the kitchen table after supper, talking softly, watching television, seemingly unmindful of the discomfort of chairs just like these. She could easily imagine the reclusive Cramir sitting here, straight-backed, staring at the visual treasures he had accumulated, losing himself in them, drawing something from them, some essence which would necessarily have been diffused if they had been shared with others. Feeling an unexpected rapport with the dead man, she thought: that kind of selfishness doesn't really matter since he always intended to share them eventually.

There were some wonderful paintings. A Murillo self-portrait. A Valdés Leal street scene, crowded with energy. A pair of small portraits, husband and wife, by Velasquez.

An El Greco. A Ribero. Still lifes by Fernandez and Arellano, a sombre Zurbarán.

"He obviously liked Spanish painting," she said to the banker. The man had barely glanced at the walls as he led them from room to room.

"It was his particular interest."

"It shows." She stopped in front of a print of a prison scene by Goya. "Are all these paintings authenticated?"

"I believe so."

"And you have the documents to prove it?"

"Of course, where they are available."

Something about the Goya etching worried her. Her specialisation during her time at the Courtauld had been Spanish painting; she had concentrated on Francisco de Goya, in particular on his scenes of sorcery and witchcraft. She moved on, remembering how disturbed she had grown after weeks of poring over the frightening images on the paper in front of her.

Cramir had been eclectic in his tastes, ranging over centuries and nationalities. In the final couple of rooms, however, he had concentrated on an ever-growing collection of modern painters.

In the first of the two, Tess drew in a sharp breath.

There were three or four paintings by Sanchez on the walls, some of the little miniatures which were the hallmark of the tragic artist de León, various exuberant canvases by O'Donnell, representative works by Castán, Picasso, Miró, Dalí. There were other canvases by names she did not know: Antonio, Andreo, Judeo. And then, to her amazement, among a handful of charcoal drawings, portraits by Fernando Vicente, she found herself face to face with Jonas.

She stepped back. The face was younger than the one she knew, the curls black instead of grey, the cheeks gaunt, but it was indubitably Jonas.

But if Vicente had drawn Fedor, the two must at least have been acquainted. So why had Jonas never told her that they had known each other? Although he seldom spoke about those days, she knew he had been in Spain before World War Two, that he had fought in some capacity during the Civil War; she had in fact learned more from Jonas's appearance on television than he had told in the whole of the time they had spent together. But not to speak of a familiarity with the painter seemed mysterious, bizarre – even, in some way, alarming.

Why, for instance, had he not mentioned it when he gave her *The Tears She Shed*? Wouldn't it have been natural to do so? And how extraordinary, how *surreal*, it was to find Jonas here, in an underground art gallery in Texas, with the air-conditioning murmuring in the background and one of the spotlights blinking defectively, on, off, on, off.

She took her camera from her bag and focused it on the drawing. Before she could ask permission, the banker stepped in front of her, holding up his hand.

"No photographs," he said. "Sorry, but it's one of Mr Cramir's own conditions."

"'Fraid so," Martin said, when she turned to him for confirmation. He raised his eyebrows and shrugged.

She looked again at the other Vicente portraits. Although they were unsigned they were as unmistakably his work as *The Tears She Shed*, or the *Casa de las Lunas*. Young men, for the most part, hollow-eyed, their faces marked with suffering. They caught at her heart. Who were they? What secrets lay behind those poignant gazes? The drawings disturbed her, as though she were seeing something that was not for public viewing; she turned and walked quickly into the last room.

Although it was longer than some of the others, it held only half a dozen paintings, as though Cramir had left space to add more. And once again, she stopped dead. They were all by Fernando Vicente – she saw a landscape, a curious Madonna, a still life.

And, unbelievably, *The Tears She Shed*. She glanced quickly at the others, half-expecting them to be as taken aback as she herself was. The banker was consulting a piece of paper resting in a folder which he held open between his hands. Martin was staring at the still life, his eyes narrowed and one of his eyebrows raised enquiringly.

"Weird stuff," he said.

"Isn't it, though?"

"Seems perfectly ordinary until you really look. Then you see it's something quite different."

"Exactly. Illusion was one of Vicente's specialities, making the extraordinary look ordinary. And vice versa."

Tess bent closer to *The Tears She Shed*. It seemed perfect in almost every detail, almost exactly the same as her own. Yet it couldn't be. From the biography of Vicente, she knew that, unlike some artists, he never painted more than one version of a canvas. She was prepared to swear that the one in her possession was the authentic version; Jonas had always assured her that it was and there was no reason why he should be wrong, particularly in the light of her discovery that he knew the artist personally. In that case, it must follow that the version in front of her now had to be a fake.

She bent to look at the signature, then straightened up. Logic insisted that if there was one fake, then there could be others. If so, had Cramir known? Was that why he had not allowed other people to view his paintings, not allowed photographs? Or had it been easy for the dealers selling to him to pass off fakes as the real thing precisely because they knew that once the paintings passed into his possession, they would not be seen again?

The Houston banker cleared his throat. "These pictures are to be destroyed," he said.

"*What*?" Tess did not trouble to hide her scandalised disbelief.

"We have specific orders that all the paintings in this room were to be destroyed when Mr Cramir died."

"Did he say why?"

"No."

"But that's . . . vandalism," Tess said. "He's not allowed to do that, surely."

"He owned them. As far as the law is concerned he can do as he pleases," said the banker, expressionless.

"But – "

"All of them," the banker said, looking down at his file and extracting a long document, "except *The Tears She Shed* – "

"Oh?" Tess looked again at the painting on the wall. Something about it was different from her own version, some small detail which she could not quite put her finger on. Was it the number of glass beads, the exact pattern round the rim of the Delft bowl, the lemons in the bowl, or –

" – which is bequeathed to 'the Aragon Gallery from whom I bought it'," the banker read out impassively.

"What about the Vicente drawings in the previous room? Are they to be destroyed too?" asked Tess.

The banker looked at the document again. "Those are bequeathed to the Vicente Museum in the artist's home town," he said.

Tess turned away. The Vicentes to be destroyed? Cramir must have had a reason: what could it have been?

"I'd like to look at all the documentation on the various paintings which haven't already been allocated elsewhere," she said briskly to the banker. "I believe that's most of the modern stuff, isn't it?"

"Mostly," agreed the banker. "I've got it all in my briefcase upstairs."

"And I shall need to have access to the gallery, if that's possible. I may have to come down here several times."

"I don't think that will be poss – "

"It's going to be extremely inconvenient if I have to wait for you to drive out from town each time I want to look at something," Tess said sharply. "I should have thought that my colleague and I could vouch for each other's honesty. Besides, since we are acting for the Trustees of the estate, I can't see any reason why we shouldn't have access. I don't need to remind you that the late Mr Cramir left specific instructions in his will concerning the role of personnel from the Banco Morena."

"I'm aware of that, but – "

"I can sign any kind of guarantee you wish. And countersign a disclaimer from you, if you think it's necessary."

He frowned. "I most certainly do."

"Good. Perhaps you could draw up a document immediately. The sooner my colleague and I can get on with the job in hand, the sooner the estate can be wound up." Tess kept her voice deliberately crisp, realising that with a play-by-the-ruler like the Houston banker, an air of authority was everything.

She looked at Martin. "You've brought a copy of the Will, haven't you? I'd like to go over it again."

"Right."

Faced with her discovery, Tess was too impatient to feel hungry, but Martin insisted that they drive in to the city to eat. She found the place alien, uncomfortably rich, improbably glitzy. Somewhere, she knew, ordinary people lived ordinary lives, but ordinariness was in short supply at the restaurant Mrs Westlake had recommended. She ate quickly, too preoccupied to be aware of the expensive food she was eating or the taste of the wine in her throat.

It was the first time that she and Martin had worked together on Banco business without more senior bank officials accompanying them. At first their talk was of Banco affairs. Then, ordering a second bottle of wine, Martin began to talk about himself and his family: the grandfather who had fought against Franco, the father who had been traumatised by his own father's death at the hands of the Republicans, his own early years.

"My father was obsessed with the death of his father," he said. "It ruined my childhood."

Tess had been thinking about Cramir's paintings. She forced herself to concentrate on her companion. "Why exactly?" She was guiltily aware that she had not been paying attention.

"They tortured the old man," Martin said. "Not that he was old, of course. My father was born after he died. I spent my entire life compensating for my grandfather's loss." He waved a glass around; his fair hair glinted in the light from the scented candle in the middle of the table. "I'll tell you something, Tess. I grew to hate my grandfather almost as much as I hated the people who killed him."

"I never knew either of my grandfathers," Tess said.

"I never wanted to know mine," said Martin. "On the other hand, I'd do anything to avenge him, if only to get him off my back." The whites of his eyes were red, as though with weeping; she realised he was slightly drunk.

Tess was glad to be driving back up the drive to Cramir's house with warm, faintly salt-tinged air flowing in through the car windows, and darkness all around.

"I'm going to look at the paintings again," she said, as soon as Martin had brought the car to a halt.

He groaned. "I suppose I'll have to come with you. Otherwise you'll get blamed if something goes missing. And no photographs, remember?"

"Bring a book," Tess said, ignoring him. "I might be there a while."

Without the banker in attendance, she felt free to leave the door open, and felt much less imprisoned than on the first visit to the collection. Belatedly, she remembered that she had not been shown the second exit.

It took her nearly four hours to draw up a list of paintings whose authentication she felt was at least doubtful.

There would be other experts who could pronounce more definitively than she; there might also be paintings she had missed. The Goya etching she was certain was not genuine; there was a Dutch interior she wanted checked out. And there were the moderns. In addition to *The Tears She Shed*, at least one other of the Vicentes was wrong; two or three of the de Leóns struck her as very suspect, and there was a Sanchez she knew categorically must be a fake – unless the almost identical painting hanging on Don Pedro's walls was.

She checked provenances where she could. Cramir had purchased mainly from galleries, though occasionally, through an intermediary, at the bigger auction houses. The New Age Gallery, Galeria 2000, Legrand's in Paris, Leónardo's of Rome. Of the galleries, the one from whom he had purchased *Tears* was the one which most interested her, especially as it had also sold him the other Vicentes: the Aragon Gallery, in New York.

Before waking Martin, who was dozing uncomfortably in one of the hard chairs, she took a last look at the Vicente sketches. They had a kind of doomed power about them: she wondered who the subjects were, if any of them were still alive, where they were now.

She told Martin some of what she suspected. Some, but not all, because to do so would mean explaining about *The Tears She Shed* and Jonas had always been insistent that she tell no-one about the painting he had given her.

"Fakes?" Martin was apprehensive. "Are you sure?"

"Pretty well."

"This could make headlines. Bad ones." He smoothed down his rumpled hair and yawned.

"It could. But I'd like the chance to look into it a bit further before we go public."

"Do you think old Cramir knew?"

"It seems unlikely. Not at the prices he paid. On the other hand, perhaps he knew and didn't care."

The two of them were staying in one of the guest suites situated behind the main house. They walked across to it, the cool pre-dawn air blowing against their faces. The sky above them was black, pierced with stars. To the east, the golden glow of Houston warmed the horizon.

"I'm going to ring up the Aragon Gallery in New York where Cramir bought some of these suspect paintings and make an appointment to see the owner," she said.

"But that'd mean flying back to England via New York," objected Martin.

"So let's change our tickets."

"I don't know if the bank would authorise such a – "

"Of course it would." Tess touched his arm. "Look, Martin. I know for sure that *one* of those paintings is a fake; I believe some of the others are too. It would make my case stronger if I'd had a chance to confront at least one of the gallery owners involved."

The Aragon Gallery seemed a good place to start making enquiries: she was sure of her ground in stating that Cramir's version of the *Tears* could not be genuine. Although confident she was right, she none the less found herself hesitant to challenge other galleries on her list of those who had supplied Cramir with fakes. She looked at Martin, who shrugged.

"OK by me," he said.

"I'm sorry," the assistant said breathily into the receiver.

He spoke with a lisp. "The gallery owner's away right now, in San Francisco, and won't be back until next week."

"Oh." Tess was surprised at the strength of her disappointment. "There's a couple of urgent matters I'd like to discuss as soon as possible. Could you take down my number and make certain the owner telephones me as soon as possible?"

"OK. The Banco Morena, you said. Can I know what exactly you want to discuss?"

"It's too complicated to explain. But it concerns some paintings you sold to – to one of our clients." About to mention Cramir's name, Tess decided it would be wiser not to.

"Right. We'll be in touch."

She dropped her bags in the hall. As always now, she stood and listened, snuffing the air in atavistic reflex. Instinct told her that the house was empty, was safe: she had to trust it, or live the rest of her life in fear.

She went to look at her Vicente, *The Tears She Shed*. Was it ridiculous to say that she knew it was genuine because it *felt* genuine? Because it gave off the sense of work done, because she knew that Vicente himself had drawn that bowl of lemons, painted each bead in that glass necklace? It sounded perilously close to a hunch, and Tess mistrusted hunches, impulses.

She looked again at the lemons. There were seven of them, sharply yellow, one for each day of the week. But there had only been six in the Houston version, she was positive of that. It only added further proof to her suspicions.

She was on her way to bed when the telephone shrilled.

She wondered who could be calling so late. Lifting the receiver, she half expected to hear again Don Pedro's fastidious Castilian accent asking about the trip to the States and the details of Cramir's collection.

But the caller was not Don Pedro. The voice was inarticulate with tears and sorrow; it took her a while to realise that it belonged to Kate, Jonas's housekeeper, and even longer to take in the full horror of what she was saying.

Jonas . . .

Jonas was dead.

7

TESS

Wine lay on your lips like blood;
Your shadowed kisses
Your widowed kisses
Trapped my soul in a shroud.
      from Amador Ramirez' *Elegías españolas*,
                    translated by Teresa Lovel

The pain of losing him was huge. As she wept, she remembered how he used to say that tears water the heart and keep it supple. They had not had nearly enough time together. The thought of spending the rest of her life without him seemed almost unbearable. All she had were the bare facts: Jonas dead of a heart attack, found at the bottom of the ravine into which he had fallen when taken ill.

As she read the obituaries in the soberer newspapers, the appreciations, Tess's view of him began to alter subtly, to be overlaid with a communal veneer, like bread and butter spread with honey; the man she had known most of her life became something else, the public image and the private merging into a different whole . . .

*   *   *

She had met him first when she was eight. Despite Lovel's resistance, her mother had insisted that she was to go to school in England. She and her mother flew to London from Tokyo; Jonas met them at the airport.

"Conchita," he said. That was all. He smiled, holding out his arms to Tess's mother. It would be years before Tess came to understand how a single word can contain an entire universe. At the time he simply seemed old to her, and unusual, nothing like the European businessmen who came to the house in Tokyo for dinner parties, nor the neat Japanese in silk suits and whiter-than-white shirts.

Jonas wore crumpled corduroys, a baggy sweater, espadrilles. His hands were very far from clean; she could not help wondering what would happen if Jonas tried to sit down at a meal with them in Japan with nails like that.

Her mother smiled back at him in silence, then let go of her hand. "This is Teresa," she said, and Jonas swept Tess up in a bear hug. She did not remember having met him before yet he seemed at once familiar. He crushed her against him, so that for the first time she smelled the odour – good wine, cheap tobacco, garlic, clay – she would always afterwards associate with safety, with warmth, with love.

England was wet and cold. Jonas led them through driving rain to his car, a veteran soft-topped Citroën. "I borrowed it from one of my students," he said. "He drove me here. Can you manage it, Conchita?"

"Of course." Her mother smiled at him, getting into the driver's seat.

Tess sat in the back, sniffing the leather, running her finger round the dark whorls of the walnut veneer. "Why is my mother driving?" she asked, frowning.

Jonas turned round in the passenger seat. "Ah, Tess. We

have known each other only a little time, and already you have found me out. Unerringly you have put your finger on my weakness."

"What do you mean?"

Jonas shrugged his big shoulders. "I cannot drive, Teresa. Many times I have tried to learn, but each time the instructors scream at me, they beat me, they jump from the vehicle before I can understand what it is I must do."

"They *beat* you? What with?" She bit her lip, not wanting to think of this man feeling pain, hearing the thud of fists into wincing flesh.

"With their hands, their feet." Jonas groaned theatrically. "Or sometimes with their books of instruction. So it is best, I think, if your beautiful mother drives us, don't you agree?"

"Yes."

Once on the road, Jonas cursed good-naturedly at other vehicles, confused left with right, offered directions then changed them at the very last moment, so that Conchita was forced to apply the brakes, causing Tess to lurch forward. She enjoyed the drama of it, the complete dissimilarity to the more conventional way of driving to which she was accustomed. Her mother put a hand on Jonas's corduroyed leg; Tess hoped she was not afraid. They travelled dangerously away from the airport through suburban streets, past unfamiliar shops and houses, out into a countryside rich with early autumn, all umbers and oranges, entirely unlike anything Tess had seen before.

After a while, Jonas began to sing, a song with which Tess was familiar but Jonas obviously was not.

"You're singing that all wrong," she said severely. It was

not a criticism she would have ever dared to make back home, but instinctively she felt that this odd man would not mind.

"I'm sorry," Jonas said. "Please sing it right for me."

She leaned forward and sang breathily into his ear, Jonas humming a rumbling accompaniment. When she had finished, he said humbly: "Thank you, Teresa. From now on, always I shall sing it right."

In the driver's seat, Conchita laughed. "Of course you will," she said. "He's tone deaf," she said over her shoulder. Tess did not wonder how she knew.

Later, Jonas ordered Conchita to pull to the side of the road. "I cannot breathe," he exclaimed, clutching at his throat. "I must have air. We must put the roof down."

"But it's raining," objected Tess. "We'll get wet."

"Have you ever driven in the rain?" demanded Jonas.

"No." Tess wondered why her mother kept silent, why she did not appear to disapprove.

"Then you must do so. Never turn down a new experience, Teresa." Jonas leaped out of the car and began tugging at the wet canvas roof until it lay in untidy folds behind the back seat. They drove off again, rain streaming past them, filling their hair, prickling their faces.

"Does this not please you?" Jonas shouted over his shoulder. "Is this not exhilarating?" and Tess nodded, for indeed it did please and exhilarate her.

"You must always embrace life, Teresa," he said and holding onto the back of his seat, she screamed: "Yes!" seeing life as some kind of amorphous shining bundle and herself struggling to get her arms around it, to hold it to her narrow body.

Looking back at this incident as an adult, she realised

that they could not have been more than half a mile from Jonas's house. At the time, it seemed as though they drove for hours through the falling rain; it was an experience she would never forget.

That first time, she and Conchita followed Jonas down the narrow passage from the back door past a long row of old-fashioned brass hooks hung with a thesaurus of outdoor wear: tweed coats, Barbour jackets, quilted jerkins, waterproofs. Enwreathed in these were scarves, caps, hats and sou'westers. Beneath was haphazard footwear: walking boots, brogues, wellingtons thickly encrusted with mud. A tall cylinder of Japanese porcelain decorated with dragons held walking sticks of various kinds and several black umbrellas. Much of the mud from the boots had detached itself from between the ridges of their soles and lay in dried or powdered form upon the floor. From the ceiling swung a gilt cherub on a thin chain, chubby hands clasped in prayer, innocent eyes uplifted, the spiritual tone lowered by the fact that whatever his outward appearance his thoughts were clearly on matters carnal, as attested by his rampancy.

Used as she was to Japanese spareness, the kitchen at first seemed to Tess to be unbelievably untidy. A pine dresser took up all of one wall, its shelves crowded with odd bits of pottery and china. A red-enamelled Aga, covered in pots and pans, sat in the alcove where formerly there would have been an open fire. Every surface was covered in a salmagundi of bottles, baskets, candlesticks, newspapers, stones, sketchbooks, jars full of pebbles, paintbrushes, dried grasses. There were bowls, too, hand-made and beautiful, Jonas's own work. They held lemons, avocados, letters, glass marbles, nuts, pot-pourri. Despite the clutter, the effect was warm, comforting. Without needing to express it, Tess was immediately aware of eternals here, of solidity, of life swelling, of good things continuing.

The house had been thatched once, Jonas told her, taking her on a tour of the place while her mother rested. That was why the roof was so steep-pitched.

"It's a bit small, isn't it?" Tess said, critical. "You're too big for it, really."

"I know." He looked at her glumly. "Perhaps I should slim, perhaps I should live on bread and water until I am like a shadow. What do you think, Teresa?"

She surveyed him. Lovel was thin; she decided she preferred men like Jonas. "No. You're all right that way," she said.

"Look at this," Jonas said, flinging open the doors of various outbuildings. "I bought the house because of these."

"But they're all full of cobwebs."

"Now, yes. But once they were full of horses – can you not see their ghosts, Teresa? Those big round haunches? Those mangers full of hay?"

Now he mentioned it, she almost thought she could, could hear the jingle of harness, the scrape of iron shoes on the uneven floor.

"And think of what I could do with these places one day," he went on.

"Like what?" said Tess, dubious.

"I could have a theatre here. Or a zoo. Or a mushroom farm." His face glowed. "Think of the mushrooms growing there in the dark, bald and white, hundreds of them, thousands. Close your eyes, Teresa, and imagine it."

She did. Mushrooms grunted quietly in her mind, pushing up through rich black soil, gleaming like miniature skulls in the dark.

"Or I could have a tea-shop," Jonas said. "Or a . . . um . . . a Jacuzzi." He sighed gustily. "Oh, so much potential . . ."

He beamed and although the word 'potential' had no meaning for her then, it took on a particular beauty of its own so that ever after when she heard it, she would see Jonas standing there and behind him, the outbuildings. None of them was ever turned into anything; they decayed gently through the years, roofs falling in, bricks loosening, hinges rusting, yet for Jonas, and for Tess, too, they remained always full of possible magic.

She did a special drawing for him, using her new crayons. When he saw it, he said: "What is this, Teresa."

"It's the driving instructors beating you up," she said. "The one with big feet is the one who kicked you, and this one here's banging you on the head with his book."

He said nothing at first. Then he asked: "Who is this beautiful princess with black hair?"

"That's me," she said. "Coming to rescue you."

"And what are you holding?"

"A *gun*. Can't you tell? Look: I've already killed one of the driving instructors."

"This is a very violent picture," he said slowly.

"Is it?"

"Little girls should not know of such things as guns."

"I got that off the telly," she said. She bent over the

109

paper, carefully drawing in drops of blood; there was a pool of it already on the floor. She did not add that little girls should not know about beatings, either, but they sometimes do.

"Oh, my Teresa," Jonas said. His voice sounded funny; when she looked up at him his eyes seemed to be full of tears.

"What's wrong?" she said.

"Nothing. I am very touched that you should draw me a special picture. And because it is very precious to me, I shall put it in the secret place where I keep all my most valuable possessions." He took her hand. "Come."

He led her to his big untidy desk and pulled down the lid. He looked round the room as though afraid of being overheard, and lowered his voice. "There is a secret drawer in this desk which only a few people know about – a few *special* people."

"Does my mother know?"

He shook his head. "Even Conchita does not know."

If even her mother did not know, it must be a really exceptional secret; she was proud to be entrusted with it.

Jonas pulled out one of the drawers and felt around at the rear of the space it had occupied. There was a click, and another drawer moved forward. She saw a dried flower, a lace handkerchief, a heart made of solid silver, some photographs.

"My mother used to have a heart just like that," Tess said, reaching forward for it. "Just exactly the same."

"Did she indeed? And does she no longer have it?"

"Not since – " Tess stopped suddenly, aware that she had said too much, that she had violated the unspoken agreement between her mother and herself, the one which allowed them to shut the door on the demons and the dragons and never hear the sound of claws on wood, the puff of poisonous steam – until they broke loose again.

"Since what?"

"Um – since she lost it."

"And how did she do that?"

Tess shrugged. She waved her hands about. "Honestly, my dear, I really don't remember," she said airily, mimicking, pretending it didn't matter.

Jonas frowned. Then he looked down at her picture. "I'm going to fold this up very carefully and put it away in here," he said slowly. "And then you must swear never to tell *any*one about this drawer, not *ever*. And you must never *ever* look in there without asking my permission first. Do you swear?"

"Yes," she said, impressed by his solemn tones.

"I'm not sure I believe you."

"But I really promise. Cross my heart and hope to die."

"I think you'd better swear an oath," he said.

"All right."

"A solemn and binding oath, Teresa." He put his head on one side and stared at her. "Will you do that?"

She nodded, eyes round.

"Then repeat after me – but first you must cross your arms on your chest and close your eyes."

She did so.

"Now, say after me . . ." and, with Tess stumbling after, he chanted:

"May manticores munch me,
Vultures eviscerate me,
Salamanders swallow me,

Dragons – " Tess hesitated here. "Dragons devour me, if I ever divulge the secret of Jonas's desk

To anyone, living or dead, in the entire universe."

Later that night, after she had gone to bed, she heard them through the floorboards. Jonas's voice was thick with rage; as always, her mother made excuses.

"The man is obviously a sadist."

"He is my husband."

"You must leave him, Conchita."

"I cannot. I made vows before God."

"For the sake of the little one."

"It would not be right, Jonas."

There was a pause then Jonas said: "Look at this drawing she gave me this afternoon." Tess heard her mother gasp.

Jonas went on: "If this continues, the child will grow up seriously disturbed."

"I try, Jonas. Believe me, I – "

He interrupted, his voice harsh. "What did he do when he found the silver heart I gave you?"

"How did you know?"

"Something Teresa said."

There was another pause. Jonas spoke again. "Leave him. Come to me."

"It would be a mortal sin."

"But you know who and what he is. Do you really think God would give a damn?"

"If I did not think so, then my whole life has been pointless," her mother said. Her voice was almost too low for Tess to hear.

"And the child's life?"

"Don't, Jonas. Please."

Perhaps it was then Tess truly understood that Jonas was the only rock she had to cling to.

One summer, instead of Tess flying to Tokyo, her mother came to England. The two of them travelled up to London to see a Picasso exhibition on the South Bank. Crossing Hungerford Bridge, they leaned elbow to elbow and watched the brown river slide beneath them while behind them, the trains sauntered southwards out of Charing Cross.

Big Ben chimed the half-hour. "Teresa, you must promise me," her mother said. Her voice was urgent.

"Promise what."

"That one day you will go back."

"Back where?"

"To Spain. To the Casa de las Lunas. You will get back the house, restore it, make it happy again, for my sake, you must do this, Teresa, and for your own. I want so much for you to see how it all was once."

Below them, a barge came slowly under the bridge and drifted up-river with the tide. A boy was up on deck, sitting on a piece of rusty machinery, stroking the head of a black-and-white collie. He looked up at them and laughed, throwing back his head, waving at them; Tess laughed too, caught by that moment of ease, waving back. "All right," she said. The barge left no wake as it moved away from them. The dog laid its head on the boy's knee.

"You must truly promise me, Teresa."

Tess turned, alarmed by the passion in her mother's voice. She had no inkling of disaster, of time about to cease. "OK," she said, thirteen years old, wondering at the oddities of adults. The idea of buying a house seemed remote, yet the notion had a drama about it, as though she were a fairy-tale princess making a death-bed promise to fulfil a dying wish.

"OK? This is not enough." Her mother's voice rose.

"Yes. All right. I promise." Embarrassed, Tess looked up and down the narrow length of the footpath. Luckily it was almost empty; there was only a man a few yards down, also watching the river on his way to the exhibition. Turning back, she said: "Anyway, I thought the idea was that we'd go together some day. That's what you've always said."

"Yes. But this may not be possible now."

"I wish you wouldn't talk like that," Tess said uneasily. "You sound as if you're going to die or something." For the first time she noticed how thin her mother had become; that there was grey in her dark hair.

"We are all going to die."

"Yes, I know, but – "

"It is only a question of whether it is sooner, or later."

Tess clutched her mother's arm. "You haven't got anything wrong with you, have you? I mean, that's not why you came over this summer, is it, to see a specialist or something?" She was stricken with the intimation of another's mortality; with the selfishness of the young she saw a stark glimpse of her own loneliness if anything were to happen to her mother.

"Of course not."

But she felt for the first time that her mother lied. A bird rose suddenly from under the bridge, almost at her mother's feet, and Concepción shrank back in fear, a hand rising to her throat as Big Ben struck the quarter-hour.

114

It was three nights later that Tess heard the cry in the night. That evening her mother had cooked a paella, the kind of dish she was not allowed to make in Tokyo: yellow rice, red strips of pimiento, the tight curled bodies of prawns, the green of parsley.

"It is like a Van Gogh!" Jonas cried. "Such yellows, such reds." He poured wine, made them read the label. "I am very pleased by this . . ." he said, savouring, noisily swallowing. They laughed. Tess, relaxed in a way she never was in Japan, watched the two of them across candles, the graceful droop of her mother's head, Jonas's hand on her mother's sleeve moving slowly down to stroke her fingers, his thick thumb running back and forth across the curve of the wedding ring she wore, the dimples in his red cheeks, the glances between them. They were happy together; she sensed that. She wished the three of them could always be together like this, in a firelit room smelling of wine and saffron, linked by an indefinable urgency.

They spoke in Spanish, the soft unstaccato chatter alien under Tudor beams and plaster.

"Some things were meant to be," Jonas said suddenly.

"Yes." Her mother's eyes were languid. "I know."

"Don't fight, my beloved." He pulled her close to him. "Oh, Concepción, Concepción: how much I love you .."; with a kind of groan, he kissed her mouth. Tess, watching, knew a moment of fleeting comprehension of things incomprehensible; before it passed away, she was shaken by something lovely and not hers.

For a moment her mother yielded to Jonas's embrace, her face uplifted towards his. Then, breaking away, she smiled. "What about Tess?" she asked.

Jonas turned swiftly, swiftly gathered Tess to his side and kissed her too.

"Her I love even more than you," he declared. Then looking down at Tess, added: "My little sleeping beauty. One day you too will waken and make some man happy."

Lifting the wine bottle, he waved it over Tess's glass. "She may have more, may she not, Conchita?"

And though her mother protested, she laughed too, and Jonas poured more wine. They toasted, glasses clinking about the candle flames: to youth, to beauty, to love and creation. Tess thought: this is what it is like to be grown up.

Her mother sent her up to bed when the longcase clock began to strike midnight. Holding hands, the three of them watched its face, saw the metal discs of sun and moon slide together and part again, saw the painted stars dip. Then she went up the steep wooden stairs, hidden behind a door, to her bedroom. Later, she heard Jonas say goodnight, his deep voice loud through the floorboards; her mother's step sounded lightly along the passage and the latch of her bedroom door, across from Tess's, lifted.

Through her open window, Tess heard footsteps on the gravelled path below. She slipped out of bed; the air was honeysuckled, fragrant with the tobacco plants which Jonas had planted to remind him of his boyhood home in Vienna. She saw him standing by the little gate which led out to the back lane. He had a cigar in his hand; smoke clouded the outlines of his head. She wanted to call out to him but did not do so. His shoulders seemed somehow so unbearably sad that she found tears rising in her throat.

She went back to bed and fell asleep. The cry woke her.

She sat up abruptly against the pillows. Outside, owls were calling among the trees; she wondered if it had been them. Vividly the memory of her mother's face on Hungerford Bridge returned: thin and somehow desperate. She was old enough to know about cancer; she jumped out of bed and ran to lift the catch of her bedroom door.

"Mama! Mama?" she called, suddenly terrified.

Across the narrow passage, she heard the jangle of bedsprings, a cough. "It's all right, darling. Go back to sleep."

"But somebody shouted," Tess said. "I heard them."

Her mother's bedclothes rustled, floorboards creaked as she crossed the room and opened the door. "Sweetheart, probably it was a bird."

"But suppose someone's out there in the woods," Tess said. "Needing our help . . ."

"I don't think they are. And how should we find such a person in the dark?" Her mother's hair hung loosely about her face; Tess was embarrassedly aware that under her Japanese robe, Conchita was naked.

"I hope I'm never walking in the woods in the middle of the night and some mad rapist jumps on me and when I scream for help nobody comes," she said sulkily, conscious that she was being silly, that a hooting owl had woken her, nothing more sinister than that.

"So, my darling, do I," her mother said. She touched her daughter's cheek; her hand smelled of perfume and something sharper, more pungent. "Go back to bed now."

Behind her in the darkened bedroom, bedsprings twanged. In the dim light of the passage, her eyes were huge and shadowed in the whiteness of her face.

*　　*　　*

117

Once, prepubescent and troubled, Tess tried to tell Jonas. "I don't want to go back to Japan," she said.

"Why not?"

"I'd much rather stay here with you."

"You know, darlink, that nothink would give me more pleasure than to have you with me always. But there are others with . . . with stronger claims to your company."

"Jonas," she said slowly. "Is it wicked to hate your own family?"

He gave a sharp intake of breath. "Not necessarily. You can't choose your family, and sometimes the one you get given isn't the one you'd like. Why do you ask?"

But she could not utter the blasphemous words: "I hate my father." Everything she had ever been taught, everything she had read, suggested that only the most unnatural of children could ever think such a thing, let alone voice it . . . She imagined the flames of Hell engulfing her, the little scarlet devils darting at her with their red-hot toasting forks.

"I just wondered," she said.

Jonas looked at her. "Teresa. What is wrong?"

It was too late. By then her own defences were difficult to breach. And once, later, when she ventured further, stammering and hesitating, into the emotional territory where she herself feared to walk, he grew so alarmingly angry that she immediately pulled back.

"Are you tellink me," he said, his face reddening with rage, a thick vein springing up under the skin at his temple, "are you seriously tellink me that the man – "

"No, no." Hastily Tess sought to repair the damage, stick her thumb back into the crack and keep it there as she had done for so many years, holding back the waters which might otherwise engulf her.

"Then what? What are you sayink to me, Teresa?"

"It's just that . . . Well, you know . . ." She tried to hide behind vagueness but he would not have it.

"No," he said, more sharply than he usually spoke. "I do not know. But I wish to. You say that he – "

"It wasn't him, it was my mother."

"Concepción? You mean that Con*chita* has . . ." He gulped air. "This I cannot believe."

"You know how she feels about her stepmother," Tess said, seeing the ground firmer beneath her feet again. "How she hates her. I mean, she makes her out to be some kind of monster." Which was exactly how she herself saw Mercedes, flame-eyed, smoke-breathed, with claws that could rip out your heart if you weren't careful and a hide as scaly and impenetrable as a dragon's.

He let out a long breath. "For a moment there, I thought you were tellink me something quite different," he said. He allowed himself to be sidetracked. "Yes, Mercedes was – is still, I am sure – a monster. Self-created, self-constructed, as artistic a piece of work as any of my pots. Yes." He nodded, pursuing the image, eyes vague. "Fired in a kiln of vengeance, and glazed with hatred. Finely decorated, of course. Beautiful, at first sight. But fundamentally flawed." As his eyes refocused, he added: "Conchita was right to warn you against her. I myself have felt the heat of her obsessions."

When she was fourteen, Jonas said: "You're big enough now to use the wheel. You must throw a pot. Who knows: one day you may even become a famous potter yourself."

He dug into a plastic bin covered with a piece of damp sacking and fished out a couple of handfuls of dark clay. With his foot he started the wheel turning and then, when it had reached a certain speed, he slammed the clay down onto its surface, keeping his hand on top of it.

"You must show the clay who is the master here," he said. "You must not let the clay conquer you." He demonstrated the way to work the wheel with the foot. "Go on, Teresa. Take over. Just knead it as hard as you can. We call it 'wedging' – it's more or less the same as kneading dough."

Tess had often played with clay before, had built a few coiled pots; this was the first time he had shown her how to use the wheel. Under her hand the clay fought her, displaying its strength. She leaned onto it, turning it over on itself, feeling its brute force.

"There are those," Jonas said, "who maintain that the whole art of potting lies in the wedging. Some of the Japanese masters will make their pupils wedge clay for months on end before they're allowed to even think about throwing a pot."

"It's jolly hard work," Tess said breathlessly.

"Of course. So is anything that's worth doing." He watched her critically for a moment. "These days you can get machines which do the wedging for you but the medium you end up with is very different from hand-worked clay. Not nearly as plastic, for one thing. And without the same spirit."

His hands, huge, thick-fingered, enclosed hers. She smelled the deep strong smell of garlic which habitually hung about him; he ate it often, enthusiastically, by the clove.

"Lean! Lean!" he commanded. He showed her the way to use her thumbs to open up the clay, how to control the spinning lump. She made pots, misshapen, awkward. Together they glazed them; he promised to fire them for her in his kiln. At lunchtime, Kate, his housekeeper, gave them a *Sauerbraten*, the gingery sauce heavy with dumplings. Jonas drank long glasses of beer.

Sighing, he said: "This reminds me of Vienna, when I was a boy. Often my mother would make a *Sauerbraten* . . ." His voice trailed away.

"Tell me about your family," Tess said, and he talked his childhood for her, the comfortable bourgeois father with his waistcoats and watch-chain, the plump mother, the pretty sister, picnics in the mountains, coffee in the garden under the chestnut trees, Putzi, the little dog.

"Then it ended," he said harshly. "As childhood always must."

"Yes," Tess said. Her own stretched before and behind her, endless, a brew of memories and hopes.

"We were Jews. You understand?"

Tess nodded. Suddenly she was afraid to ask about the sister, about Jonas's parents; they had just finished studying the Second World War in her history class.

"We grew up fast in those days, we became men overnight, bewildered men, even cruel men, when we were still boys in our hearts. So I came here, to England, in the hope of leaving persecution behind. And then I went to Spain, to fight against the *fascistas*." He shook his head. "More repression, more cruelty in the name of freedom. Sometimes I hope that we can all live in peace some day, but mostly I think it will never end, that our most powerful urge is to kill."

Then, seeing her face, he laughed and raised his glass. "Or is it to love, Teresa? Is love what motivates us more strongly than any other passion?"

"Have you ever been in love, Jonas?" she asked.

"Only once. Maybe twice."

"Why didn't you get married?"

"It was not possible," he said. He put his glass down on the table and lifted a dumpling to his mouth, as though to stopper up words which might otherwise flow.

"But why not?" Tess had just read *Jane Eyre*, *Wuthering Heights*; love seemed worth dying for.

"We were . . . prevented."

"And all these years you've secretly yearned for her?" asked Tess eagerly, seeing Mr Rochester, seeing Heathcliff and the long, lonely moors.

"That is right. Secretly . . . and perhaps not so secretly."

"Have you got a picture of her? Can I see?"

"You must leave me my secrets, Teresa," he said.

Kate came in with an apple pie, a jug of yellow cream. Tess jumped up to help her clear away the plates, while Jonas leaned back in his chair and gazed thoughtfully up at the ceiling.

After lunch they sat for a while in the untidy sitting room. Jonas gave her a book of pictures, reproductions of art treasures from around the world, while he, as he put it, would commune for a while with his Maker.

"Have a snooze, you mean," Tess said. "I hope you don't start snoring."

"How brutal you are, darlink." Laughter rumbled behind the thick loops of Jonas's coarse grey sweater. "Anyway, I do not snore. I am too much of a gentleman."

things romantic. It became a book she went back to again and again over the years.

Reading the descriptions of Vicente's paintings, she could visualise them almost as clearly as if they hung in front of her; reading of his death by firing squad, one early morning during the Civil War, she wept. But the book determined her on her own career.

She went to the Courtauld to study fine art and found herself sharing a flat with a couple of students reading history at the university. One day, with nothing much else to do, she went with them to hear a lecture on Europe in the fourteenth century. The lecture room was too hot, the lecturer himself, Professor Henry Adams, unprepossessing. But as his voice rolled across the heads of note-taking students, the European continent took form for her, ceased to be a flat map and grew hills, forests, was armied with horses, cannon, supply-waggons, soldiers, each one individually wrapped in the centuries of history which had gone before him. Pikes, muskets, gun-carriages slowly advanced, bodies lay trampled into mud, women wept for lost husbands and sons. He brought alive what had until then been no more than words on a page, a pygmalionic miracle.

Afterwards, she went up and introduced herself, saying how much she had admired his lecture; he asked her to join him for a drink and they discovered, over lukewarm beer, that they shared a passion for Velasquez, for rugger, for asparagus and the works of Jane Austen.

She was twenty-one. Jonas threw a party for her to celebrate. Before the guests arrived, he drew her into his studio. Something wrapped in sacking leaned against a table; he had stuck on a made-up bow of green tinsel. "I should have wrapped it better," he said. "But what matters is inside."

She unwrapped the sacking and saw *The Tears She Shed* for the first time.

"Oh, Jonas," she said, stunned.

"I bought it many years ago," he told her. "I always thought that if I ever had a daughter, I would give it to her. Now, I give it to you."

"How come I've never seen it before?"

"I have kept it hidden. And I'm afraid you must do the same – not from yourself, of course. But don't tell people you own it – and do not lend it to exhibitions, or sell it, however tempting an offer you are made."

"Why not?"

"It would be better. Otherwise you might come home one day and find – pouf! – that it was gone."

"You mean because it's valuable?"

"Something like that."

"What's the mystery about?" she demanded.

Instead of answering, he said: "I had intended to leave it to you on my death, but recent events have persuaded me that the sooner it is in your hands, the better."

"I wish you'd stop being so enigmatic," she said crossly.

Again he sidestepped the unspoken question. "She never told me who was the model," he said vaguely, "but how like her is that face, those eyes."

She kissed him. There were tears in her eyes. "I love you, Jonas," she said softly.

"And I you." There was a kind of fierceness in his embrace.

*   *   *

Jonas was furious when she and Henry got engaged. "He is dull," he shouted. "He is too old for you."

"He's what I want," she said.

"He is dreary and – and thin, like a grasshopper. He will not make you laugh."

"He makes me feel safe," she said.

"Goddammit!" He slammed both hands down on the table, making her jump. "Teresa, you are still asleep. You need a prince who will kiss you awake, not a watchdog to keep you safe."

"Also," she said coldly. "I love him."

"But he is old," Jonas said again. "Two hundred years old."

"He is twenty years older than I am, that's all. We share a lot of things, we have the same tastes, the same aims. We respect each other."

"Respect," groaned Jonas. "Respect? You should be burning, Teresa, you silly child. You should be on fire."

He began peeling cloves of garlic and cramming them into his mouth.

"I wish you wouldn't do that," Tess said disapprovingly. "It makes you smell terrible."

"I have to," he said. "I need to keep away colds. And witches."

"Witches," scoffed Tess.

"Indeed. Do you not believe in witches?"

"Of course I don't."

He gazed soberly at her. "Perhaps you should."

She and Henry went to Spain for a fortnight. She quite enjoyed making love with him; occasionally she wondered what all the fuss was about, and why she had dreaded it so. Together they looked at cathedrals and art galleries, castles and museums, drank warm red wine, went to the *corrida*. Henry suggested that while they were in Granada, they drive into the hills to Montalbán to see the house where she was born; she refused.

She realised she could not share with him the terror which rose in her at the thought of deliberately entering such alien territory. As a child, her mother's refusal to discuss Mercedes Ramirez had built the woman up in her own mind as a monster, and the place she occupied as too dangerous to approach. As an adult, her rational mind told her this was nonsense. None the less, the shreds of fear still hung about the very mention of the word Montalbán, her doubts and uncertainties not helped by the contradictory fact that the Casa de las Lunas was the place where her mother had been happiest. Her mother . . . increasingly she found that the thought of her mother brought sudden tears. For years she had cauterised the raw wound of her loss by detaching herself from it; dimly she had begun to see that this was the wrong way to mourn, that beneath her surfaces, grief writhed.

On their last night, driving back to catch the ferry at Santandér, they found a hotel in a small village about to hold its annual *feria*. They sat on long benches in the street, hemmed in on all sides; lamps were slung between leafy trees round the village square and behind them lay the thickness of a Spanish night. There were tables set with wine bottles and huge blackened pans of paella, there was the smell of hot oil, bursts of sudden music, a voice wailing an ancient alien song.

Some time during the evening, Henry turned to her. He

stared as though he had never seen her before. "What's the matter?" she said.

"You look . . . as you ought to look," he said.

"How is that?"

"Your hair all round your face. Wine on your chin." He wiped it away with a finger. "Excited."

Yes: she had been excited, transported. The dark stares of the village youths heated her. Dancing with one after another, thigh pressed tightly to thigh, wine-stained breath hot against her throat, abandonment gripped her; under her skirt the tops of her thighs grew damp. Returning to their hotel, she had urged Henry into her body as the rising sun had crimsoned the sheets of their bed. Yet, when it was over, she was miserably aware that whatever it was she yearned for, she had been unable to find.

Afterwards, she stood naked on the wrought-iron balcony while Henry slept. She beat her fists against the apricot stucco of the walls while on the slope below the olive-trees stirred silver in a pre-dawn breeze. Weeping, she squeezed her breasts together, ran her hands down the curves of her body; she thought of her dead mother and wondered what kind of woman she had been; whether such longings had once stirred her, whether she too had been pierced by such desires. Back in England, she told Henry she could not, after all, marry him.

Jonas gave a party to welcome her home. She drove to his house through a summer evening, the sun still high, the fields heavy with heat. Harvesting had not yet begun; there was a sense of breath-held lushness, of expectation. Soon the year would turn, the fields would be shorn and leaves begin to fall, but for the moment everything waited, at its peak. The bold ripeness all around mocked her.

Jonas came out to greet her as she parked her car. "Darlink, you are late. Already several hundred people are here." Then, seeing her face, his ebullience had shifted rapidly to delight. "You seem very cast down," he said eagerly.

"I am, actually, though why you should be so pleased about – "

"Is it all over? I have spent many hours hoping it would end soon, soon."

"What *are* you talking about, Jonas?" Already Tess felt better.

"This so-impossible engagement of yours."

How could he have known? "I'm not sure what you mean," she said.

He took her arm and led her into the house. "Yes. I can tell. You have finished it, broken it in two, smashed it like a badly-made pot."

"Yes, as a matter of fact, I – "

"Thank the dear Lord!" Jonas cried. He ran across to the harmonium which stood in the wide hall, and pressing keys haphazardly, began a wild hymn of thanksgiving, while Tess stood with a hand on his shoulder, shaking with laughter.

Later, during a quiet moment, he found her in the garden. "Teresa," he said gently. "Please do not think I am making jokes about your broken heart."

"That's just it," she said. "That's exactly the trouble. My heart *isn't* broken."

"And you feel it should be?"

"Of course it should. That's what love's all about."

Turning, she saw him catch his breath.

"What is it, Jonas?" she said quickly, concerned. "Are you all right?"

"Perfectly. But with the sun on your face, and that cream dress – for a moment you looked so like – " He shook his head. "I almost thought . . ."

"Who, Jonas?"

"Someone I . . . loved."

"My mother?"

"Someone else. She was – is – a most beautiful woman. But – " Again he snapped the sentence off.

"But what?"

He hesitated. "An evil one."

"Evil. That's a strong word," Tess said.

"It's the best word."

"And beautiful?"

"Yes."

"Jonas," she said suddenly. "Am I like my mother?"

He sighed. "Too much so. She was such a timid creature. So afraid. So much in need of protection. That's what I loved about her."

"Timid? Afraid? I'm not a bit like that."

"Aren't you, Teresa?"

"Definitely not."

"Sometimes I think you are just as frightened as she was, but you hide it better. With Conchita it was all on the outside; with you, it is hidden very deep."

Her face was hot. Apropos, it seemed, of nothing, she said: "I've never seen any pictures of Mercedes Ramirez, you know."

"I have some. Many. Kate shall put them in your car." He pulled her towards him and kissed her forehead.

"Come, darlink, let us go and dance. Kate's granddaughter has been teaching me the latest steps, and I wish to practise them and make you proud." And he pulled her with him back into the house.

Later, opening the albums, she saw them all, reduced now to squares of cardboard: Jonas, younger, darker, in grey V-necked sweater and baggy flannels; her own mother, shading her eyes from sunshine, dressed in white lace with roses in her hands; narrow streets bisected by shadow with unidentifiable strangers smiling; men lounging on grass, beside rivers, in punts; women picnicking, laughing, in the seats of cars, turning to gaze at the camera from under the brims of hats, made mysterious, made beautiful by the passage of time.

She saw too, rows of men in strange uniforms, squinting sternly into the sun, and a face she took to be that of Vicente, the artist who had been her stepgrandmother's brother. But when she asked Jonas, he shook his head. "No," he said. "I did not know this man."

Visiting, Jonas identified some of the people for her: "That's your mother, that's Mercedes, this is a good friend, here's my own mother, this must be my uncle, these are men I fought with in the Civil War . . ." breaking off frequently to reminisce, to clothe the two-dimensional with flesh.

"I remember how your uncle Amador cried because Mercedes refused to give him another drink," or "This is me with my sister – I loved her very much; she was wearink a new dress that day, so proud, so pleased she was."

And seeing the sad little boy in shorts, the fierce gaze of Mercedes under a broad hat of straw, Tess's own throat had grown parched with thirst; looking at the two solemn children holding hands in some long-ago Viennese drawing-room, she felt brief terror, recalling where the sister had later died.

"Here is my sister with Hansl," Jonas said, on another occasion, picking up a studio portrait of a young woman in a black dress, holding a shawled baby. "They had taken away her husband by then; poor Hansl never knew his father."

One day, as she walked round the side of his house into the garden, she found him talking to a stranger. "I want you to meet Dominic Eliot," he said.

She shook hands. Eliot was tall and spare, bony, wearing a black polo-neck sweater under a denim jacket. There was something rakish about him, something swashbuckling, as though in an earlier age he might have swept from his head a plumed hat and bowed low instead of simply taking her hand.

"Dominic is an historian," Jonas said. "He is writink a book about the Spanish Civil War – "

"And naturally I came straight to Jonas," said Dominic. His manner glittered with energy; the words came out with the kind of enthusiasm she had only ever seen before in Jonas himself. For a moment, looking at the two men, Tess had the curious notion that they might have been father and son.

"He wishes to include a chapter on your hero," explained Jonas, eyes bright.

"Which hero is that?" Tess said coldly. She hated it when Jonas patronised her.

"Fernando Vicente."

"There's only been one biography since the war," Eliot said, "and that was written by his sister."

"I've read it," said Tess.

"The thing is, it's nothing more than a hagiography," Dominic said vigorously. "No-one in their right mind could take it seriously."

"*I've* always found it very illuminating," Tess said.

"Come *on*. It says almost nothing of any importance about the man," Dominic said, waving his hands about. "It makes him out to be some kind of saint in artist's clothing – which we all know he wasn't."

"Do we?"

"Of course we do." He laughed, throwing back his head, savouring the day, the sunshine, the conversation, the wine he and Jonas had been sharing.

"Who's publishing your book?"

"Ah." He grinned at her. "No specific promises, unfortunately. Although I think the world is ready for something new on the subject and I'm willing to supply it, I haven't yet managed to persuade anyone in the publishing world that they are too." He laughed again.

"I have read some of the chapters," Jonas said, "and they please me. I have recommended him to my own publishers."

"I see." Tess was ashamed to realise that her chief emotion was a childish jealousy at the way this man had so obviously won Jonas's affection.

"I have told Dominic you own a Vicente," said Jonas. "You must invite him round to your house some time."

"I'd very much like to see it," Eliot said eagerly. "Would that be all right?"

"I'm awfully busy right now," Tess said.

"What about an evening, if you're out during the day?"

"Of course," Jonas said. "She will give you a drink, and you perhaps will take her out for dinner. What could be more pleasink?"

A great many things, Tess thought sourly. She knew why Jonas was pushing this Dominic Eliot at her; ever since the split with Henry he had been urging her to marry.

"Before it is too late, darlink," he would say.

"Too late for what? Me, or you?"

"Me, of course. I wish to see tiny Teresas in my garden. I wish to give them sweets and cream buns and thinks their mother would never allow them. I wish to feel their sticky little fingers on my face. I even wish to change a nappy or two: it is one of those experiences which life has so far denied me."

Tess had looked away from the sadness in his red face. Remembering it, now, she said grudgingly to Eliot: "Next Thursday would be all right, if you can make it."

"Perfect." Eliot grinned at her, showing good teeth. She could have sworn she saw him wink at Jonas.

And now, unbearably, unbelievably, Jonas was dead.

8

MERCEDES

He was on fire. She could feel the heat of him through his clothes; even across a room she could hear the thump of his heart.

In her white dresses she flitted through the evenings with him, virginal, moth-like. Yet she knew that she was the candle, and he the blundering fragile insect. He was desperate for her; he burned. She did not have to enter his mind to know that behind his civilised veneer lurked a creature of primitive lusts, that while he talked to her of painters and politics, he was visualising her naked, helpless, at his mercy. Somewhere deep inside herself, the thought of his thoughts excited her.

Deliberately, she tantalised him. She taught herself to stand so that her small breasts stretched at the thin fabrics which covered them; she developed a habit of innocent carelessness about the way in which she sat when he was near, so that he caught sudden glimpses of ankle or thigh. Yet whenever he inadvertently touched her, she drew away, biting her lip. If he should venture to compliment her, she would raise her eyes to him, full of wonder and surprise. He dared not go too fast, for fear of frightening her, of losing her. Having made her opening moves, she now played the middle game and found it exhilarating, the more so because he never suspected for a moment that he was merely a pawn, that she was the Queen.

Coming lightly up the stairs to O'Donnell's studio one afternoon, she heard his friends discussing the matter. "Carlos needs a woman," she heard O'Donnell say.

"Needs, yes," said little de León. "But *wants* only Mercedes."

"He's not going to get her, though. Not this side of a wedding ring."

De León said soberly: "Would that be a good idea? Carlos is easily led, she seems too strong, too . . . *determined*."

"But she's only a child."

"Why else do you think he's held back all this time. Unlike you and me, poor Carlos is a man of honour. We must arrange something, get him drunk, get him a girl."

"We'll invite Juanita and Pilar, borrow some of those new American records," O'Donnell said eagerly. He dah-di-dahed to the tune of 'Everybody loves my baby', clicking his fingers. "They're good girls. They'll know what to do."

"They'd better. Carlos looks as though he's about to explode."

"When's a good day? Saturday?"

"Why not. But we'll have to get him on his own."

"Tell you what. Why don't we ask one of the foreigners to invite her out? I've seen her looking at the Austrian, the Jew. If she agrees, we'll have a chance to cure Carlos of his fever."

"The fever he's got is the kind which keeps coming back."

"Or do you mean coming up?"

The two of them laughed boisterously as she tiptoed back down the stairs. She had not looked beyond marriage, though children figured in her plan. Now she saw, in Juanita and Pilar, women she did not know but whose way of life she could guess, a possible weapon for the future.

When Jonas suggested that she go with him to the theatre, she blushed, looking down at her hands. When she glanced back at him, ready to accept, his eyes were fixed on hers in a manner which disconcerted her. For a moment, she thought he was seeing inside her brain, could read her plans. When she accepted his invitation, his mouth moved, almost as though he were trying not to laugh.

Seated at his side as the house lights went down, she was acutely aware of him, of his arm on the seat, of his flesh through his sleeve. His face was gaunt and beautiful, his hands ugly. Yet throughout the play, she could think of nothing except those hands on her body. What would he be like in bed? she wondered. She imagined his mouth on her, his full red lips tasting her nipples; she felt herself loosen, grow moist. Her limbs quivered. She thought: If he kissed me, I would be lost, and for a brief moment, saw herself gladly abandoning all that she had worked for over the past few years.

Afterwards, as they sat in a café, she found herself unable to talk to him. She breathed through her mouth, lightly, fighting for self-control, aware that with the slightest encouragement she would throw herself at him. She, who gladly watched Carlos burn, was on fire herself.

He told her that he did not know what he wished to do with his life. He said: "I will settle in England." He spoke to her of trout-streams and the smell of burning leaves on November afternoons, of water-meadows and small churches crouched between yew-trees. "I have friends there," he said. "It's a good place to find peace."

Peace. Briefly, she closed her eyes and saw his England, a country of green fields and gentle hills, a place without passion. Perhaps she too might one day go to England and be quiet, the turmoil of grief and loss which swirled inside her stilled at last. But not yet. Not yet. There were still battles to fight and wars to win.

She opened her eyes again. Resolution returned. "Peace?" she said scornfully. "I'm too young for that."

"So am I," he said. He took her hand in his. "And you are right, Mercedes. We are both too young to give up yet."

She did not wish to ask him what he meant. What should a man like that have to give up? She pulled her hand away from his and stared fully at him, feeling her pupils expand. He did not react. He stared back at her steadily, and she could not read his expression.

"You are very beautiful," he said softly.

Oh God, and so are you, she wanted to cry. Instead, not caring whether he believed her or not, she worried her lower lip with her teeth, a young girl confused by the advances of a crude man. "I think perhaps we should . . ." she said, starting to rise.

"Go? Oh, surely not, Mercedes," he said, and this time there was no mistaking the mockery in his voice.

"What do you mean?"

"Surely you can handle the situation," he said. "I can't be the first man who has told you that you are beautiful."

"No, you are not."

"Have you ever acted as a model for your friends?"

"No."

"Would you, for me?"

Danger glittered in front of her, potent as a drug. She wallowed in the thought of it, saw herself naked, spread, open to his gaze, knowing that she would do whatever he asked. But if Ramirez should ever find out, it would mean the destruction of the edifice she had spent so much time in building. She dared not risk that.

She shook her head. "I think not," she said, and this time the blush was real. They both knew what she really wished to say.

It was the start of a relationship as ritualised as the movements of the *corrida*. But which was bull and which was baiter? She was never sure. Sometimes one of them held the hidden sword, sometimes the other. She found it excruciating.

She spoke to him occasionally of her aunts, of Vicente. She told him about Montalbán, about beautiful Granada, and saw his eyes change. "I would like very much to go to Montalbán," he said thoughtfully. "I did not realise you came from there."

Later, as they all sat in a café, she turned to Ramirez. "I must go south and see my aunts," she said.

"And my parents write that they wish to see me. Why

don't we travel together," Ramirez said. He turned to his English friend, Maitland, who had just joined them. "You too, Julian. My parents would be so glad to see you again."

"Well . . ." Maitland hesitated, looking at Jonas.

"Fedor, too, of course," said Ramirez. "And anyone else who should wish to come. You can stay with me: the Casa de las Lunas is big, there is room for all of you, isn't that right?" he said, turning to her.

"Very big," she said.

"So what do you think, Jonas?"

They turned to Jonas, all of them. She wondered if they realised that in some strange way, this stranger, exiled, had become the focus of their activity, that it was his tentative suggestions which they eventually adopted, rather than the more robust plans put forward by themselves. Also, she began to suspect that Jonas was playing a game as deep as her own. There was nothing she could put a finger on, could pinpoint and say "Aha, I have him now." Yet, in her wanderings around the city, she saw him in odd places, coming out of doorways where afterwards, she thought she would not have expected to see him. He said he was a student, but what did he study? If she asked him, he looked at her with hard eyes, laughed, said things about pretty women being enough in themselves, about pretty heads not being bothered, and because she was playing a role, she had no choice but to pretend, to pout and push his arm and say how silly he was, while Carlos watched, enraptured.

"I think this is an excellent idea," Jonas said. Very deliberately he turned his head and stared deep into her eyes. A pulse beat against his jaw. Knowing she could not have him, not if she were to succeed, she looked away, hating him for his knowledge of her, wanting to rip, to tear, to be torn.

In the end, eight of them took the train and travelled down through Spain. Ramirez was proprietorial; she was demure. She half-suspected that he would visit Francisca during their visit, that he would offer for her. If he did, she had already decided on her response. Sleepy in the dusty railway carriage, she watched Fedor from under her lashes as the train plunged southward, as the country grew dryer and more elemental.

Softly she placed her hand on Ramirez' sleeve then drew it away again as though she had not intended to be so bold. "We must take Jonas to Granada," she said. "I think he would enjoy that."

"Of course. What a good idea." He spoke as to a child. She stared down at her hands, tightening her lips: one day he should see how little of a child she was, how little of childhood he had left her. Forcing herself to smile, she looked up to meet Jonas's unsmiling gaze.

The expedition to Granada took place the following week. They went in two cars – the Ramirez family had no difficulty in getting hold of gasolene. They called for her at the big house in Montalbán: three young men in straw hats and white jackets, Maitland, Fedor and Ramirez, three handsome young men, and though Carlos, with his strong black hair swept back from his brow, with his blue Celtic eyes, was the most handsome, Jonas was the one she wanted – and could not have. In the hall the aunts fluttered like butterflies, exchanging significant nods over her head, twitching and plucking at her skirt, her middy blouse, the ribbon in her hair.

They were less pleased to see that she was to travel alone in the car with them without a chaperone, but she whispered at them not to be so silly, two of them were foreigners and did not count and surely they did not for a moment imagine that Carlos Ramirez would try take advantage of her.

Had they imagined such a thing? The aunts, three now, with Luisa still in Madrid, caught each other's eye and looked away, ashamed of such unworthy thoughts, reminding themselves that this was 1942, not the eighteenth century. Yet watching the delicate dark-eyed figure of their niece – their child – as she was helped into the back of the car, they could not suppress a collective pang at her fragility, her innocence. It did not occur to any of them that Mercedes was not the one in danger.

"She should marry," Francisca said firmly, as the car took off down the street. "We must do something about it very soon."

"A nice man," pleaded Rosita, as they climbed the staircase to the *sala* on the first floor. "Someone she likes." She dared not use the word 'love', knowing Francisca would be brisk, even scornful.

"Someone to take care of her," Isabella said.

"I shall talk to the advocate; I shall consult Don José," said Francisca.

"Jonas has made himself at home," Ramirez said, lighting a cigarette with one hand as they drove down the steep mountain road to the plains below.

"Has he?" She could feel Jonas's hand on the seat

behind her head; if she leaned back his fingers would touch the back of her neck.

"By now he knows everyone in the village," Ramirez said. "In a few days he has made more friends in Montalbán than I have all my life."

She said nothing, thinking: That is because he is not a murderer.

It rained suddenly, in Granada. She and Jonas, waiting in a palm-shaded square while the others searched for stamps or cigarettes, found themselves getting wet.

"Come on," he said. "There's a good place over here." They ran across the street to find shelter, clinging together, laughing. His arm was around her shoulders. The doorway they chose led to a small folk museum.

"Let's go in," he said, trawling for pesetas in his pocket. "Shall we?" He took her hand.

"Ah, no," she sighed, feeling nothing at all but the sensation of their fingers entwined, of her flesh and his.

"What? Don't you want to?" He gave her his direct stare and smiled.

"The others," she said faintly, not giving a damn about the others. Did he really not know that the smell of him, his nearness, his touch, intoxicated her?

"They'll find us," he said firmly.

The museum contained local artefacts: spearheads, Moorish tiles, swords, pottery. He said: "I'll be only a moment . . ." and she looked away, embarrassed.

There were only two rooms; she was bored with shards and had seen all she wanted. She wandered towards the door and heard Jonas's voice; it seemed odd that he should be talking to someone in German. She backed away and pretended an interest in some crudely fashioned amphorae.

Minutes later, Jonas rejoined her. He took her arm and moved her around the exhibits. In front of a bowl glazed a soft green-blue which reminded her of the sea, Jonas stopped. "Look at that," he said. "Look."

"It's lovely", she said.

"But not deliberately so. Whoever made that was more concerned to make a bowl than to make something beautiful." His hands curled at his sides, his thumbs kneading imaginary clay. "Do you understand what I am saying?"

"Yes," she said. "Of course," though at the time she did not.

Afterwards, when he was famous, when his work was prized and sought after, she was often to think: I was there when he saw for the first time what he was meant to do. *I* am the one who was there; he was with *me*.

9

TESS

Time is a series of parallels, of lives played out in front
of mirrors; you recognise the reflections even when they
aren't your own.

> *The Looking-glass Corpse* by I. C. Sanyoshi,
> translated by Teresa Lovel

Later, when the body had been cleared for shipment
back to England, a nephew appeared. Pleasant enough,
impersonal, a small man, fiftyish, overwhelmed by the
dark overcoat he wore. He was the son of Jonas's sister
who had died long ago in Dachau; he took over the
funeral arrangements, asked her advice about solicitors,
undertakers, the right person to give an address.

"I don't know," Tess said, scarcely able to think
straight, still shattered by the absence of Jonas. "One
of his colleagues, perhaps."

"Most of them are dead," said the nephew. "I could
look through his address book." He cleared his throat.
"You knew him better than I did. Wasn't there . . . uh
. . . someone he . . . uh . . . I seem to remember he had
a friend, a woman? Shouldn't she be notified?"

Tess shook her head. "There was someone years ago; I don't know who."

"He told me once his heart had been broken when he was a young man and never mended."

"Whoever she was, I think she must have died," said Tess. "Or perhaps married someone else." Her eyes were full of tears; she wiped them slowly away with the back of her hand.

"It is sad," the nephew said, trying to be brisk with Jonas's clothes, his soiled tobacco pouch, the collection of stem-bitten pipes on the mantelpiece, the back copies of newspapers he had always intended to clip cuttings from.

"Cuttinks," he called them. "My cuttinks." Remembering, more tears welled up in Tess's eyes.

"Is any of this . . ." The nephew waved a hand at the paintings which crowded the walls of the untidy sitting room, and upwards to indicate the rest of the house, the studio outside ". . . worth something?"

"A lot," Tess said. "I don't know what kind of a will he made, though I believe most of the pictures have been left to the Fitzwilliam, in Cambridge, though there have also been a number of letters from dealers asking to buy specific items they knew he had. He was friends with so many artists; he knew everybody."

"What about his pots?"

"Most of them are in private collections or museums. He hasn't made any recently – except one – because it was difficult for him to work with clay any more."

Again Tess's eyes filled. "*A man who can earn his livink doink what he loves is a happy man,*" Jonas used to say. Yet the arthritis in his hands and the incipient emphysema, the result of years spent breathing in clay dust, had prevented him from potting; latterly, frustration had drawn sorrowful lines down his face. It must have been a tremendous effort for him to throw the pot for her birthday.

The two of them walked across the yard to the converted barn which had been Jonas's studio. The heavy iron key stuck as it always had; the door squeaked as usual on the hinge which Jonas had kept forgetting to oil.

"It's not that I want anything for myself. I have all I need." There was the same teutonic shading to the nephew's voice as Jonas had had; it brought the man back more vividly than his possessions. He said carefully: "I believe he has left me many things: if there was anything which could be sold, I would want to give it to Amnesty International, or something similar. He suffered enough; I always wish I had seen more of him . . ." He stared at Tess with eyes full of worlds she had never known: refugees, grey roads, wrists tattooed with blue numbers, prejudice.

"We'll go round the house together later," she said. "Perhaps after . . . after . . ."

The nephew patted her arm. "Of course. There's no hurry. And you – I know he loved you as though you were his own child. I don't know exactly what is in his Will . . ." He gestured helplessly.

"He gave me so many things already," Tess said. *The Tears She Shed* sat warily in her mind, enigmatic, and made more so by the existence of the fake in Cramir's collection.

She walked across the dusty floor and stood looking down at the chair where Jonas had sat so often. A picture burned her brain: a bare hillside, sharp shadows, blood spilling from a body torn and battered by the stones at the bottom of the ravine into which it had fallen.

"What happened to him?" she said urgently. "Does anyone know for certain?"

"No. As his last surviving relative, it was me the Spanish authorities contacted. They didn't seem too sure themselves. They said . . ." Momentarily at a loss for words, he shrugged, the big coat lifting from his shoulders. "They said he must have been taken ill, that he must have stopped for a rest and perhaps suffered a spasm of the heart which caused him to lose his balance and fall over the retaining wall into the ravine beyond."

Tess's throat felt hot. She hoped passionately that Jonas had not had time to be frightened at death's sudden snatching. When she said something to that effect, the nephew looked at her oddly.

"I think Jonas learned a long time ago not to be afraid of death," he said. "Either his own or that of others."

"What do you mean?"

The nephew shrugged. "It was all a long time ago," he said softly.

But it was the present which occupied Tess. "It doesn't make sense," she said. "What was he doing up there in the first place? Does anyone know?"

The nephew shook his head. "The police in Spain said he had been walking a lot during his holiday. There are witnesses who have stated they saw him several times up in the hills."

"But that's impossible," Tess said. "He couldn't have walked. He had arthritis in his knees, and his breathing was bad."

"I don't know. Really I do not."

"Where was he staying? And why was he there in that particular place?"

"These are questions I cannot answer." The nephew looked at her sadly. "Does it really matter? Isn't it enough that he is dead?"

"No!" Tess's voice cracked. "Not for me." Heat, rage, clutched at her. But seeing the nephew's expression, seeing pain he did not want to confront and realising that in his lifetime he had already faced more than a man's fair share, she tamped it down and said nothing more, for belatedly she had realised that this diffident little man in his too-big coat was the same Hansl she had seen as a baby in photographs of Jonas's family.

All Jonas had told her before he left was that he had some unfinished business to attend to. She assumed it was something to do with his work: an exhibition, a book, a *catalogue raisonné*, the sort of thing which these days took up much of his time, presuming that he had spoken for dramatic effect rather than truth during his television interview.

"Someone ought to go out to Spain, just to make sure," she said quietly.

"I agree. But who? I cannot take the time . . . my work . . ." Again the big coat moved, almost independently of its wearer and the sad eyes blinked. "I have a family . . ."

"I understand," she said. "But perhaps I could go . . ."

She looked round. Thinking of the dead man whose absence was only made more palpable by this dust, these walls, those tins of glaze, that vase full of peacock feathers, the crude horse of painted china whose face he had liked, she could feel grief rise in her like yeast. Words chased themselves through her mind: farewells, eulogies, endings, a scrap of a letter by Cicero, a couple of lines of Dylan Thomas. She shook her head. Death is too powerful, too immense to be parcelled up in phrases and secured with ribbons of sentences. It occurred to her that as a means of emotional communication, words are almost meaningless.

"Oh God," she said painfully. "I'm going to miss him so much. He was all the family I had."

Awkwardly the nephew patted her arm. "If you would come and visit us one day, we should be so pleased," he said. "My wife was so fond of Jonas – it might help you if there was someone you could talk to about him." He cleared his throat. "In the past, I have found that it helps to talk to someone who has shared the same experiences."

Enviously, Tess pictured it: the bustling wife, the constant coming and going of friends and family, a smell of fresh-baked *strudel* and coffee; the house would be warm, over-stuffed, full of dark *fin de siècle* furniture brought over from Austria and heavy lace curtains; there would be old ladies with rich middle-European accents sitting with their skirts pulled up over their knees; an air of kinship and sharing. "Thank you," she said. "I would really like that."

He tried to be brisk again. "Now, the housekeeper – Mrs Holden – has offered to stay on for a while. But there will be very much – uh – clearing up to be done . . ." His eyes, strangely large in so small a man, peered vaguely about, asked for her help.

"Later," Tess said. "I can deal with it later."

His face brightened. "I would be most obliged . . ."

Letters of condolence came from all over the world. Answering them, and the numerous telephone calls, at least gave her something to do. One letter, addressed to Jonas's publishers and forwarded by them to her, was written on thin blue paper and headed with a name already familiar to her. She read it with growing anger, her eyes smarting with furious tears. There was no word of sympathy, just the stark words:

TO WHOM IT MAY CONCERN

Jonas Fedor always promised that when he died, I should receive a picture which he owned. It was painted by Fernando Vicente, and is called *The Tears She Shed*. I should therefore be grateful if arrangements could be made for this to be dispatched to me at the above address.

The letter, signed M. Aragon, came from the Aragon Gallery in New York. Dully, she registered that she had already had contact with the place, but for the moment there were more important things to attend to.

She wrote a courteous reply, saying that there was no question of M. Aragon receiving the picture as Mr Fedor had given it to the undersigned Teresa Lovel years before, and she had no intention of parting with it.

Searching the newspapers for further information about Jonas's death, she came across a newspaper report which was mildly interesting:

CASTLES IN SPAIN?

Is it now time for a major reappraisal of the work of the Spanish moderns? *writes our Salesroom Correspondent.* A de León was recently sold at Sotheby's for a price well above the estimate. A Vicente was bought by a Spanish museum for almost double the previous price paid for a work by this artist. And recently, in a dramatic duel between two anonymous collectors, an oil painting, *Casa de las Lunas*, by an unknown member of the Granada Group, of which Vicente was perhaps the most notable representative, sold for the sum of £24,000 at a country house auction when frenzied bidding sent the price rocketing to three times the expected figure of £6,000–£8,000.

There was speculation today that one or other might have been fronting for some major commercial interest, such as the Getty Museum, or one of the large Japanese electronic groups. If so, it surely heralds a new look at the work of the artists working in the difficult years immediately prior to the Spanish Civil War and during it.

Due to his tragically early death in front of a firing squad during the Spanish Civil War, Vicente's output is relatively small. This belated focus on the work of the Group he founded could force prices up all over the world, and generate a revival of interest in the work of his contemporaries, a development which would be a cause of celebration to the current Government in Madrid.

'Frenzied' was perhaps putting it a little strongly, Tess considered. She wondered who had passed the information on to the newspaper since it was unlikely that a reporter had been sent to cover a country house sale, and again wondered about the identity of the other 'collector', the woman who had been so furious at losing the *Casa de las Lunas*. Shivering with remembered terror, yet again she speculated fruitlessly on the identity of the person who had broken into her house and tried to drown her. But her immediate concern was all for Jonas and she gave it little further thought beyond reminding herself that she must get both the Sanchez and the AR-signed Vicente to Don Pedro as soon as she could.

"Julian Maitland," the nephew said.

"What?" Although it was three o'clock in the afternoon, his telephone call had wakened Tess from sleep; since Jonas's death, she had felt herself enormously exhausted, unable to find hours long enough for the rest she seemed to need.

"Maitland worked with my uncle after the War," said the nephew, on the other end of the telephone. "I found his number in the address book. He is devastated by what has happened."

"So are we all." The horror she was trying to avoid by sleeping time away began to engulf her again. "I still don't understand it."

"Why did he go to Spain in the first place?"

"He wanted to check some details for his memoirs, and he also mentioned some unfinished business." Tess pulled herself tiredly up against her pillows; bare tree branches swayed outside her window, grey against the grey sky above the park. Her bedroom seemed unnaturally cold. "I didn't realise Julian Maitland was still around."

"Oh yes. He was some years younger than my uncle. They became associates for a while . . . perhaps you did not know."

"The Kelmscott Pottery," Tess said. "Jonas told me about it and, of course, I've read about their work there."

"Maitland said that my uncle visited him just before the . . . the tragedy and seemed in fine spirits. He will be in England shortly and he has agreed to give an appreciation of my uncle's life and work at the memorial service. I am very pleased about this."

How long would it be before the corners of grief grew blunted? In just the same way had Jonas so often exclaimed, beaming: "*I am very pleased about this* . . ." whether it was a fresh-thrown pot, or a fine day, or a new wine he had just discovered. Oh Jonas, she thought, how I will miss you, how very much I wish you had not died and left me.

"Yes. That's good," she said and was struck afresh by the constrictions of the language of mourning; how unsuitable 'good' was to describe something which concerned a death. Yet, indubitably, it was good. She knew to what extent Jonas used to value Maitland as both colleague and friend.

There was a pause. She realised he did not know how to ask whether she was free then, or whether she would help him.

"Obviously I'll help you all I can," she said, "Just let me know what you'd like me to do."

Putting down the receiver, she got out of bed. From her closet shelves she reached down a large cardboard box and spread its contents over the floor. Albums, a dozen of them, padded, gold-engraved, hung with tassels, tied with faded tape; photographs jumbled into envelopes, plastic bags, or simply loose: Jonas's life caught between marbled covers.

Her life, too. Or part of it.

The night before Jonas's funeral she slept in his house and again wandered in dream the wood-lined rooms of the Casa de las Lunas. Objects caught her attention: a pile of starched linen, a bowl of acid-yellow lemons, a wine glass with a twisted stem. Each room led into the next; each room was dominated by a blown-up photograph of Fernando Vicente's sombre beautiful face.

In dream she reached a room with a tripod-legged table. On it stood a silver platter, on the platter, a head, trepanned. As though it were some kind of ornate pot, it held a long-stemmed golden spoon. She moved towards it on silent dreaming feet, pulled by the hollow eyes and anguished mouth. Beside the the table, a black-clad figure wearing a horned mask took the spoon and, curving it gently round an eyeball, coaxed it from its socket and lifted it towards her. She felt her mouth open and her lungs strain but no sound emerged; in front of her, the devil-faced figure swayed, its blood-red lips twisted with menace, its golden teeth ready to devour.

She awoke with the taste of bile at the back of her throat and, on the edge of her mind, the words: *If you touch the child I will* . . . In the past, she had often dreamed of the house – her mother's obsession for the place transferring itself to her – but this was the first time there had been any sense of threat. Though she could not have said whether the masked figure was male or female, other details remained clear in her mind: sharp yellows, white sheets, blue sky behind a window and, on the walls, the famous photograph of Fernando Vicente, taken only days before his death.

A clock blinked on the table beside her bed, marking the passage of electronic seconds. 4:18. She had known it would be; it was impossible not to shiver at the fortuitous synchronicity which had led her to wake at that particular moment. She pushed back the covers and walked across thick carpeting to the window, not needing lamplight since the room had been dear and familiar from childhood; long ago Jonas had allocated it to her.

Outside, frost glittered in moonlight. The cottage windows looked out on a narrow river, imprisoned now, glassed in by ice; like piles of snow, swans lay asleep beside it. Beyond lay a rise of wooded hill and somewhere among the trees was the small church where in the morning Jonas would be buried. He had not been a religious man, not even a Christian one, but in leaving Austria behind he had embraced England and the things he saw as epitomising its culture: village churches, thatched roofs, pubs, royalty. His Will had specified most of the details of his funeral service; having dealt with the problems of having his body brought back from Spain, Tess and the nephew had been glad to have this small burden, at least, lifted from their shoulders.

When she turned back from the window, the green blink read 4:21. The moment should have passed, but had not. She wished not to remember; the proximity of Jonas's body, somewhere close by, waiting for the cold earth, made it impossible for her to forget.

*　　*　　*

She buttoned her navy coat, tied a bright silk scarf around her neck. From a cupboard, she took a hat, new and dramatically, aggressively, red.

"Wear red at my funeral," Jonas had often said. "It does not please me to see women in black."

He had said it again only a few weeks earlier, as they tramped through the woods behind his studio. "No black, Teresa, no tears."

Now, she was fulfilling the first part of his wish, though she doubted she would be as true to the second. The hat, as well as being red, was jaunty. Jonas would have loved it.

She had refused Dominic's offer to drive her to the funeral service; since Jonas's death she had been brusque with him, as though by wanting him, she was somehow being disloyal to Jonas. Instead, she and Kate would go together.

The housekeeper, still shaken and disorientated, waited for her in the kitchen. For the moment she would be staying on in the house; later she would move to Eastbourne where she planned to share a flat along the seafront with an old friend from her days as a Land Girl.

Tess drove her to the church, which was already packed with mourners. She found a parking place and helped Kate out of the car; Hansl, the nephew, had saved them a pew at the front of the church. Two rows behind, she saw Dominic's dark head, shoulders bony under a navy-blue top coat she had not known he possessed. A cold light fell through the stained glass of the east window; above their heads angels hung from beam-ends, their spread wings tipped with gold. As Jonas had directed, the church was filled with roses, hothouse and unscented but none the less beautiful, set off by thin sprays of winter jasmine and forsythia.

Tess picked up the Order of Service sheet lying in front of her: Jonas had chosen four hymns – and reading the titles she felt the tears begin to gather. She could remember so many Sundays with Jonas, sitting in some village church, kneeling for the prayers, light falling through an east window, and the sound of an organ, Jonas's tuneless voice uplifted, cheeks shining with pleasure as he bawled away: 'Guide me O Thou Great Redeemer'; 'Abide With Me'; 'For All the Saints'.

The sound of the vicar's voice intoning the Opening Sentences and Preface called her back to the present. The service continued. As Jonas had directed, Hansl read from the *Rubáiyát of Omar Khayyám*: *There was a door to which I had no key*, his faint accent adding a piquancy to the Englishness of the scene which Jonas had doubtless relished fully in advance. The organ swelled from the loft; the congregation stood, sat, knelt; beside Tess, Kate wept.

The address: from across the aisle a tall, white-haired man rose from his seat and strode to the front of the church. Julian Maitland; Tess recognised his face from television arts programmes. His bronzed face was dominated by a nose of considerable aquilinity, his eyes were strongly blue. He reached into the inner pocket of his dark jacket and brought out some folded sheets of paper. And then, without reference to them, leaning on the brass lectern, he talked gently of Jonas and the art of a master potter, linking his life and his work in an extended metaphor.

"Like Jonas," he began, "I dislike the modern attempt

to turn pottery into a form of sculpture. Like Jonas, everything I make is a container. Containing is an integral part of a pot and in the same way, containing was intrinsic to Jonas's life. What he filled the vessel of himself with was love, for his fellows, for his art, for the huge rumbustiousness of life as he saw it . . ."

That did it for Tess. She began to weep, remembering Jonas over the years, all the years, it seemed, of her own life. Dimly she heard Maitland's voice " . . . discipline of the wheel . . . fusing of the cultural and the functional . . . profound influence . . . compassion and concern for others . . . a European, never part of the British tradition . . . strength . . . love . . ." while slowly the images reeled through her mind: picnics, laughter, candles, wine, Jonas's red face, his big safe hands, her mother's secret smile.

Perhaps the tears were as much for that lost smile as for Jonas himself: with Jonas gone, so was nearly the last link with her mother. And thinking that, she recognised she too had much unfinished business still to deal with, that she would never satisfactorily lay either of them completely to rest until she had faced up to it. If she was to continue without them, there really was no choice.

The congregation was rising for one final triumphant hymn: 'Glorious Things of Thee are Spoken', sung to the tune called Austria. Jonas's wave at the end of his life to its beginning, Tess thought. She sang loudly, lifting up her voice for him, sure that somewhere he heard her.

Afterwards she shook hands numbly with celebrated faces, humble faces, colleagues who had worked with Jonas in the past, young artists who had benefited from his encouragement. Dominic embraced her; she stood numbly in his arms. Don Pedro was also there. He too had folded his arms about her, murmured that he knew what Jonas had meant to her, how much she would miss him, hoped she would not mind him coming. To everyone, she could only nod, and try to smile.

Later, finding herself beside Julian Maitland, she said: "That was a wonderful address."

Maitland looked down at her. "I'm glad you thought so," he said. "Jonas and I were good friends."

"I know."

"And you are . . .?"

"Teresa Lovel."

"Ah yes. Teresa," he said warmly, as though the name was somehow familiar to him. It seemed to be a practised response. When he smiled, deep lines umbrellaed out around his eyes.

She put a hand to her hat as a vicious wind frenzied the yew-trees and set the lych-gate banging back and forth. "I was wondering if there was something of Jonas's you would like, a keepsake, a memento. Perhaps you'd like to come back to the house and choose something."

He looked regretful. "My dear, what a splendid idea. I'd have loved to, but I can't see how it can be squeezed in."

"Come down some other time. Spend the night – there's plenty of room, and I know Jonas would have – "

"I'm afraid I leave tonight. God knows when I'll get back again." He winced at another attack by the freezing wind. "These days I'm increasingly reluctant to leave my own hearth."

"I know you live in Spain, but where exactly is your hearth?"

He looked down at her. "In the south. Near a little place called Montalbán."

Montalbán . . . it was only a word, yet those nine letters contained for her a whole sphere of experiences still unexplored, held echoes which until now had resonated silently, unheard. It was also the place where Jonas had met his death.

She stared at Maitland. "I believe Jonas came to see you just before he died," she said. She tightened the scarf round her throat; it was bitterly cold, the sky promising more snow, freezing rain already spitting down.

"He did, yes." His blue eyes strayed beyond her to the two women hovering behind her, clutching at their hats. "I'm sorry, my dear, but the Press is here. That's the girl from *The Times'* Arts Page, if I'm not mistaken, and someone from Sotheby's. I must talk to them. Even at my advanced age, I still have a living to earn."

"If I came over to Spain, could I visit you?" she said quickly, aware that his attention was straying. "I'd love to hear about Jonas in his younger days, how the two of you set up the Kelmscott Pottery and so on."

For a moment he looked at her thoughtfully. Then he said: "If you're prepared to travel, I'm more than prepared to talk about it – though God knows I don't really have any more information than you do. But what could be more seductive to a man of my advanced years than an excuse to drink red wine and chat about an old friend with a beautiful woman?"

She ignored that. "You're sure it wouldn't be inconvenient?"

He put a hand on her arm. "Just let me know when you're arriving."

"I haven't made any concrete plans," she said. Indeed, the idea had only come to her in the past few moments, triggered by a need to hang on to anything connected with Jonas. "Presumably there's a hotel near by – what about the one where Jonas was booked in?"

He looked vague. "Do I even know which one it was?" he said. "I'm sure it's not one I could recommend. Either way, we have plenty of room, even if there are other visitors – there always seem to be. Stay with me if you like."

"That's very kind of you, but – "

"I am almost never kind," he said. "I've found that I get far more pleasure out of being selfish. Talking to you would be an act of simple self-indulgence." He fished in his wallet and handed her a card. "Let me know when you're arriving. All right?"

"Perfect."

Turning away, as the women behind came up to talk to him, Tess was astonished to see the woman she had encountered at the Brantwell Manor auction. She stood beside a cold slab of granite, her expression blank, stunned. She was elegant in a coat of dove-coloured wool cut like a riding jacket, with matching trousers tucked into knee-high leather boots polished to a high shine. Again, Tess felt that there was something familiar about the wide imperious mouth and the way the tawny skin stretched tight across the high cheekbones. It was the mark beside her nose, Tess decided, which gave the woman her unusual beauty: by its very nature an imperfection, it emphasised the perfection of the rest.

But why was she here? Her heartbeat accelerated: was this the person responsible for trying to drown her? Could she really be so single-minded that she was prepared to see someone die, in order to get what she wanted? Looking at that fine-boned face, the question answered itself. The woman was clearly both ruthless and determined; not the sort to let anything stand in her way. Though she shrank at the thought, it seemed important to find out who she was yet there was no-one Tess could think of who might know. Yet it was out of the question to ask the woman herself: only someone very brave or very insensitive would have dared interrupt that intense sorrow.

As Tess watched, she raised her head and looked up at the sky. The long mouth quivered; although there were no tears, the dark eyes were full of such desperate grief that Tess felt her own tears rise again.

She turned away, not wishing to intrude, wiping her own eyes; when she looked back, the woman had disappeared.

10

MERCEDES

She had thought she was winning; suddenly the game began to go against her . . .

He took her out to dinner, just the two of them. It was a warm evening; they ate outside, under a vine-covered pergola. She wore white, her hair loose and caught back in a red scarf. His blue un-Spanish eyes lingered on her, as always. From a nearby park came the sound of music, the sharp hand-claps of a flamenco singer and a hoarse voice singing of love gone sour.

"I'm going to New York," he said. "I've been offered a chance to work in a law firm there. Now that America has gone into the European War there are fewer young men around . . ." He tapped his leg. "And I am available."

"This is a splendid opportunity for you," she said, hiding her shock, realising how easy it had been until now. She thought: What I can do? I could lose him, lose the game. The mere possibility made her realise just how vital it was to her that she should not.

"I agree." While he spoke of the advantages of working in New York, her brain whirred as she calculated and planned and always came up with the same conclusion: she would have to stay here until she came of age in another fourteen months. Unless, of course, she was prepared to defy the aunts.

They would never allow her to go alone to New York. And after the years she had spent perfecting her role it would be impossible for her to change it now, impossible to start throwing herself at him, bind him to her with sexual favours.

His mouth was soft; she wondered what it would feel like to kiss him, whether it would be bearable. For years she had schooled herself to accept the fact that eventually she would have to make love with him. Clinically, as a mental exercise, she had gone over the way it would be, forced herself not to shudder as his hands touched her breasts, her belly, opened her thighs, as he put himself between her legs, entered, violated her. As if to confirm her suspicion that she had overplayed her hand, had made herself out to be such an innocent that he could not see her as a wife, he leaned towards her, the heat from the candles between them blurring the lines of his face.

"You are so young," he sighed. "So innocent . . ."

Not that innocent, she wanted to say. In fact, of the two of us, you are the innocent, despite your guilt. She touched his hand timidly. "I shall miss you."

"And I you," he said. He was a big man, and handsome; the effort he made not to pull her into his arms was almost palpable. "You must stay here and finish your studies."

"Of course." She spoke as though there were no alternative, while she decided that if necessary, she would pay her own way, cross the Atlantic without permission from the aunts. She had cash, she had assets in the paintings she had collected. And in New York lay the future of which she intended to be a part, as well as – soon – the man she intended to destroy.

His departure was a setback, but not an insurmountable one. During the days before he left, she set herself to further enmesh him, while she laid other plans.

As she had expected, the aunts were adamant at the suggestion that she go to New York to complete her studies. She tried to use Fernando as a lever but this time it did not work. Having not expected to win it, she retired temporarily from the battle. She bided her time.

Carlos wrote, saying he was living with distant cousins while he looked around for an apartment. New York was bigger than they could imagine, much more cosmopolitan than Madrid or Barcelona, or even Paris. There was something exhilarating about the place, a sense of opportunity which did not exist in Spain, where everyone had their future determined more or less at birth.

He spoke of his employer, Blevitsky, a man whose father had been an immigrant from Russia, a man who had pulled himself up by hard work and determination, until he was now a respected lawyer. He said that he was almost ashamed to be Spanish, since in Spain it was taken for granted that those who worked the hardest – the peasants – should be rewarded the least.

In other letters he spoke of the art scene, mentioning the names of those who had taken refuge in New York. The list excited her: Marcel Duchamp, Tanguy, André Breton, Chagall, Piet Mondrian . . . He had met them all, through his cousin who was a patron of the Museum of Modern Art. He told her how difficult it was for indigenous American artists to get a showing, especially since so many of the gallery owners were refugees who considered that the only art worthy of the name came from Europe.

Once he wrote to say that he was trying to promote some of the Spanish artists they both knew: O'Donnell and de León and, of course, Fernando Vicente . . .

Fury filled her at the thought that he, of all people, should be promoting the works of Fernando. Imagining the scene, the people, the parties, the pictures, she seethed with impatience. She longed to get to New York with the same intensity with which she had once prepared her trap for Ramirez. Now the one obsession was subsumed in the other. She began to prepare her escape from the prison she now perceived Spain to be; it drove her mad to feel that so much was going on, in the world she had decided to make her own, while she was exiled here.

Increasingly he wrote of the social conditions in New York, the work he did among the Jewish immigrants, the horrors they endured on being uprooted from their own homes and finding themselves in a country they did not understand and whose language they did not speak.

Mercedes grew bored by his letters. She did not want to hear about immigrants and deprivation, she wanted information about the artistic world, she wanted scandal, gossip, names, something to keep her in touch with the centre of things. Carlos seemed to be growing more and more serious. He wrote:

I work alongside my employer and his daughter, Marguerite. She is a very gifted young woman, not only possessed of a fine legal brain, but also an artist of some merit and with an abundance of compassion for the poor sufferers we are endeavouring to help. You would love her, Mercedes. She is like you, very gentle and kind.

My little friend, I wish you could be here with us. I think your tender heart would be as much moved by the plight of these poor refugees as ours are.

When she showed this letter to Jonas, he smiled, his mouth quirking upwards.

"Dear me," he commented drily. "It sounds to me as though you had better get over to New York as soon as you can."

There was no point in pretending that she did not understand what he meant. Part of his attraction for her lay in the fact that he seemed to see straight through her into the very depths of her brain, as though she were transparent, made of glass, or ice.

"I mean," pursued Jonas, cruelly, "does one really call a girl one is madly in love with 'my little friend'? Or is that what one calls a girl when one has already met another girl with whom one has or is beginning to fall in love?"

It was so exactly what she had supposed herself, that she said nothing.

Madrid was hit by a heat-wave. In the parks, the trees drooped, the pathways turned to dust; the streets collected heat and threw it back so that walking became a penance, an ordeal by fire. Luisa, engaged to be married to a widower who worked in the Mayor's office, was kept busy meeting an elaborate tangle of his parents, his brothers, his cousins and former in-laws.

171

Mercedes spent long hours alone, lying in the shaded rooms of the empty apartment. It was too hot to move without discomfort so that each action required a mental effort before it could be accomplished. Her body ached intolerably; when she touched herself her hand burned. She thought of Jonas, of Fernando and yearned for them both. Over and over she repeated scenes inside her head, Jonas and her, their bodies entwined, his ugly hands, his eyes swallowing her.

One afternoon, the doorbell chimed. She was alone in the flat; as so often these days, Luisa was away, and the two maids were visiting their families. She went slowly to the door, barefooted, wearing only her wrapper, a gauzy thing of ivory lace and silk. The high polish of the parquet flooring reflected her movements as though she walked on water, treading on the soles of a drowning woman beneath. Jonas stood outside. Seeing him, she stepped back and opened the door wide.

"Are you alone?" he said.

She nodded, closing the door behind him, locking it.

She followed him into the drawing-room, watched him turn to look at her, saw the need in his face and, aware that it matched her own, knew already what would happen. He opened his mouth; she said: "Don't speak." She undid the belt of her wrapper and let it fall.

He stood staring at her. He took his time, eyes lingering like hands on her shoulders, her breasts, her slim hips, the dark patch at the base of her stomach. She began to breathe fast through her mouth, she could feel the blood running through her body, flushing her nipples, caressing the root of each hair. She was wet; she moved towards him as though through water but he held up a hand. "Wait," he said. "I haven't had enough."

"Jonas, I – "

"Ssh."

His gaze was like electricity; she flinched when his eyes touched her. At last, he drew in a deep breath. "You are even better than I had imagined," he said.

She could not let him see how elated she was to know that he thought of her when they were not together. It was part of the duel they fought.

Slowly, he began to undo the buttons of his shirt.

When he was naked, he took a step towards her and she shivered. It was the first time she had seen a totally naked man. She watched as he swelled and hardened; she held out her arms to him but he did not move.

"I am going to take your breasts in my mouth," he said. "I want to feel your nipples harden under my tongue. I am going to kiss your shoulders first, I am going to hold you, to touch that soft skin, I am going to hold your waist between my hands, I want to touch your soft places, to taste you, smell you, put my hands into your body first and then put . . . *this*."

"Oh, Jonas . . ."

"I want to hear you call for me," he said.

"I'm calling."

"I want to feel your desire for me, I want to smell it on you, Mercedes, I want to taste it."

Longing overwhelmed her. Her legs trembled; she could no longer stand.

"Jonas, please . . ." she said, sinking to the floor, ready to explode, wanting nothing except his body inside hers. He continued to watch her, eyes half-closed, and she put a hand on her own body, thrust her own fingers inside herself since he would not come to her, moaned. She lay in front of him, legs spread, lost in sensation and felt no shame that he should see her with such totality, should see her need, hear her gasps of longing.

"Do you want me?" he said.

"Yes," she gasped. "Oh . . . please . . ."

He dropped to one knee beside her. "The first time will not be the best," he said. He took her shoulders between his hands and pulled her up against him so that her nipples brushed the dark hair of his chest. "Feel my heart beating," he said softly.

She thought she was swooning; reality was gone, she had lost the ability to think, giving herself up to the feel of him, semi-conscious with pleasure.

She took his hand and thrust it hard between her legs. "Feel *mine*," she said.

"I do, Mercedes," he said. Fiercely he kissed her mouth; his lips opened and closed on her body, hungry and possessive; his tongue explored her. He kissed her, all of her; he guided himself around her, using her moans of pleasure as signposts, her movements in his arms.

She could no longer wait. She thrust herself onto him, impaled herself, dragged his hips forward to meet hers, moved him frenziedly inside her, until he took over the rhythm she had set up and she came in a series of languid shocks like the ripples round a stone dropped into oil, and felt him too pulse rhythmically inside her, heard him groan into her hair.

When she could speak again, she said: "Do you love me?"

"Love?" He drew back to look down at her. He drew

a finger down the side of her face and she smelled herself on him. "No, Mercedes. Not love. I could never love a woman like you, so white and black, so . . . obsessed."

"Never?"

He shook his head. "But want? I want you all right. I don't think I could ever get enough of you, ever. You have what the French call *la beauté du Diable*, the Devil's beauty. Ever since the first time we met you've beckoned me onwards, like a siren, like a will o' the wisp. You have enslaved me, Mercedes."

She smiled as she heard the extravagant words, then realised that he was deathly serious.

He came to the apartment many times after that. The heat continued, draining her of energy except when they were together in the hot afternoons, and then she pranced about his naked body, delicate as a unicorn, the sheets beneath them tiger-striped in the light which fell between the blinds. He took her on the floor, on the sofas, over the tables, they lay together on the brocade chaise-longue, the bed, once even in the huge old-fashioned bath, while the taps of the basin dripped a slow accompaniment to their crescendos.

All the time she was aware of danger, knife-edged. What she did now could so easily jeopardise the future. Not only her soul was imperilled but her life's purpose also, yet throughout the long summer, it ceased to be of importance.

The apartment reeked of sex. Luisa, returning from yet another party, another shopping expedition, would raise her head and sniff, saying "What's that funny smell," staring suspiciously about her but Mercedes, realising that since she did not recognise the animal scent, she must be a virgin still, simply raised her eyes from the book she appeared to be studying and say: "I smell nothing."

When he was not with her, she dreamed about him, about Fernando, the two merging into a composite whole of eyes and hair and scent while she brought herself to climax. He occupied her completely; he took everything of her that he could, he told her he was bewitched, his kisses burned on her body like crosses.

One afternoon, as they lay sweating, hearts still racing from the strenuous love they had made, she said: "Do you know anyone with money, Jonas?"

She felt him tense beside her. "I can get hold of money myself, if the need arises. Why do you ask?"

"I may need some. A lot."

"I can give you – "

She put her finger across his lips. "Ssh. I don't want your gifts. But I have some things I could sell."

"What things?"

She got off the bed and walked across the room. Naked, she always felt at her most powerful, as though she knew that her body was her strongest means of binding him to her. She carried a chair from its place between the tall windows and set it beside the wardrobe. She looked at him. "I always keep my valuables up here: the maids never clean anything higher than their own noses."

He seemed amused. "Really? I'm sure my mother's did."

"Only if she ordered them to. And Luisa is too wrapped up with her fiancé to think about such things," she said scornfully.

"So would you be, if you were in love," he said.

Her heart pounded. She wanted to scream at him, to demand whether he was blind that he could not see she was in love, sodden with it, soaked through and through, unable to eat or think or sleep for love. Instead, she climbed up on the chair and carefully brought down from the wardrobe a pile of the canvases she stored there.

"What are those?" He leaned on one elbow.

"You must never tell anyone that I have these," she said. She spread them out on the floor in front of him like a horizontal picture gallery. In the shaded room the Sanchezes and the de Leóns, the O'Donnells and Castáns, glowed on the polished planks of the floor like a spilled sackful of precious stones.

She heard him gasp. "Where on earth did you get them?"

"Here and there."

"Did you steal them, Mercedes?"

She laughed. "They're all mine. I've got the papers to prove it. I bought them, bit by bit. I got some of them cheap – and O'Donnell gave me this as a present." She held up a big splashy abstract. "I don't like it, but he's going to be an important painter one day."

"And you want to sell one?"

She nodded, her eyes greedy on his body. Although they had both climaxed only minutes before, desire clawed at her again; she wanted to take him in her mouth, taste herself on him, she wanted to feel the ruthless slam of his body forcing its way into hers. She took a deep breath and let it slip out through her clenched teeth.

"Why are you asking me?" Jonas said. "You're obviously quite used to buying and selling on your own behalf."

Why was she involving him? She did not really know – unless it was to show him that she was more than a body, more than a partner in their sexual lingerings. She wanted him to love her, and feared he did not. She lowered her eyes. "I need money at the moment, and I thought you might be interested. If you're not – " She knelt with the intention of picking the paintings up.

"Have you any others?" he said.

She hesitated.

"Any Vicentes?"

She could see her kneeling reflection in the long looking-glass of the wardrobe door: the girlish breasts, the slight curve of her belly and the thicket of black hair beneath. The mark beside her nose seemed bigger than usual, swollen, disproportionately large. She touched it, fancying that it throbbed under her finger. Then she rose to her feet. "Yes. But they aren't for sale."

"Let me see them," he said.

She spread them in front of him, fingers reluctant. She did not want the man she loved now to see, judge, maybe to criticise the work of the man she had loved once and would always love.

"This is interesting," he said, leaning over what seemed at first to be an idiosyncratic Madonna and Child, though looking closer it was clear that the mother was no more than a child herself and the bloated baby was far too big for her slight lap. The child-mother sat in a garden which was enclosed by a tight hedge of thorn like the mediaeval virgins in their rose-gardens;

in one corner a unicorn pawed the ground under a tree of gold and silver fruit. "What did Vicente call it?"

"*A Monstrous Love*," she said, holding a corner of the canvas between her finger and thumb. She did not want him to have the painting.

"Why?"

"Look at it. It looks like a standard Virgin and Child, but everything's wrong, everything's perverted. The flowers in the garden are really weeds; the unicorn's horn is black and its face is debauched. The Virgin couldn't possibly have produced that hideous child."

"It's intriguing. I'll buy it."

"What about this one?" she said, pointing at one of the still lifes.

He contemplated the skull, the plate, the peeled lemon. "It's good . . ." He reached for another. "What's this? Does this have a name?"

"It's called *The Tears She Shed*. Look: you can see the title painted along the brass bedstead."

He pointed to the necklace which hung over one end of the bed. "Are these the tears she shed?"

"Symbolically, I suppose they are."

"I'll take all three, including this one."

"It's not for sale."

"But it's the only one I really want."

"You can't have it."

"Name your price for them, Mercedes."

Of all the paintings, *The Tears She Shed* was the only one she did not want to sell. On the other hand, if she was to get to New York, she was going to need money. Besides, somewhere in the corner of her brain she calculated that if they should part, the picture might be an excuse for them to meet again some day.

He pulled her towards him on the bed, pushed her underneath him, kneed her thighs apart and came roughly into her. "How much?" he said, his body penetrating the furthest reaches of hers. "How much? How much?"

She could feel herself wet and slippery around him; each thundering movement he made seemed like a long streak of ecstasy. She was coming again, shuddering, fainting under him.

"How much?" His teeth were gritted. Familiar with him now, she knew that he too was on the verge, on the very brink of his climax.

Melting into orgasm, she told him her price.

"Done," he gasped, as he exploded inside her like a firework.

One afternoon, draped across her like a drowned man, he said: "I am going away."

"When?" she said.

"Tomorrow."

She did not wish nor try to argue. Afraid of his answer, she did not ask why he had not told her before.

"It's over, then?"

"For the moment."

Was there a promise in those words? From the beginning she had recognised that for him this was an affair of the body, not the heart. None the less, at the thought of his absence, she felt the start of an intolerable anguish. "How am I to survive?" she said.

He shook her. "You will be busy, Mercedes. You will go to New York, do what you have waited so long to do."

Did he, could he know the purpose which filled her? "And you?" she asked.

"I shall learn my trade. The war is ending, I too must do what I have to do."

"Shall I ever see you again?"

"Who can tell where our paths will lead?"

"Tell me you love me," she said.

"But I don't."

"Tell me anyway."

He smiled; slowly he shook his head. She did not think she would ever be happy again, unless he said he loved her. She did not think he ever would.

Her aunts travelled up to Madrid for Luisa's wedding. When it was over, the three of them sank into the sofas in the apartment, sleepy-eyed and complacent. "Beautiful," they murmured. "He is a kind man. Luisa will be happy. She has forgotten Felipe: I thought she never would."

Rosita looked at her niece. "And you, child. The summer is almost over, soon you will be back home with us, yes?"

"No."

"What?"

"I am going to New York."

"New York?" Isabella fanned herself; there was sweat on her upper lip. "But – none of us can go with you." She was the youngest of the three sisters, she knew she would be the one to go, but she was nearly fifty, she was too old. She felt faint at the thought of New York, the streets, the skyscrapers blocking out the view, the dirt. She longed to be back in Montalbán where she was known and respected. In New York, she would be just another of the teeming millions, she would be jostled on the pavements and stared at by the hungry eyes of men.

Aware of her thoughts, Mercedes said: "I can go alone. I don't need a chaperone."

"But – "

"We know people over there. We know Carlos Ramirez. I have friends who are living there now. Or I can go to a hotel."

Francisca roused herself. "I cannot allow it."

A cold rage settled in Mercedes. She had to prevent herself from leaping at Francisca and putting her hands around that fat self-satisfied neck. "You can't stop me."

"You are not yet of age, I believe." Francisca said haughtily, her face appalled. It was the first time in her life that Mercedes had defied any of them.

"That makes no difference," Mercedes said.

Rosita trembled. The child sounded so cold. She had known no good would come of allowing her to go to Madrid. She looked at her niece and saw something hard and steely there; she was afraid.

"Don't expect us to give you money for this madness," Francisca said. She was used to commanding. She had held the family together for years, ever since the deaths of her parents and later, of her brother and his wife. Although a virgin, not a mother, she had raised the two children left behind, Mercedes and Luisa, aunt and niece though the years between them were few. She had organised her sisters, run the house and the small estate. She was unaccustomed to insubordination. "You will come home with us and we shall – "

"I have money of my own," Mercedes said. "I don't need yours."

"You may not go." Francisca snapped her mouth shut. The syllables clanged like bells in the hot wine-fumed drawing-room. "The entire world is turned upside down. Japan has entered the war, they are fighting in Africa, Europe is in turmoil. How can a young girl like you expect to – "

Mercedes stood up. In her white dress she seemed as frail as a flower. "But I have to go. I must."

"Why?" Isabella trembled. She knew she was the one they would send as chaperone. "Why must you?"

"Because . . ." Mercedes paused, looking round at them all.

Rosita closed her eyes. The child – except she could see all too clearly that she was no longer a child – was about to say something unforgivable, she was about to destroy, simply for the pleasure of it. She thought: I have never really looked at her before today – she is quite different from what we have always assumed her to be, she is . . . She remembered the strange woman her brother had married, the one they said was a witch, and looked at the mark beside her niece's nose as the girl opened her mouth. She was afraid that when she had said what she was about to tell them, they might never see her again.

". . . because I'm pregnant."

Their hearts surged with horror and indignation as they stared at her, their fragile innocent child now fatally besmirched.

"What?"

"Who?"

"Where . . .?"

Hideous images affronted them, pictures they dared not allow into the privacies of their minds: bodies, mouths, innocence defiled, a child on a bed, a man taking what was not his.

"I shall have to have an abortion," Mercedes said.

The horror multiplied: not just one sin, but two.

"An ab – " Francisca could not bring herself to utter the word. She straightened her back. "Who is the man?"

"No-one you know."

"My poor child . . ."

"I can't get an abortion here. That's why I must go abroad, to New York."

"But Mercedes – " began Isabella. It was Rosita, usually so indecisive and anxious, who cut her off. "There is no point in arguing with her," she said. "Even if it is true – and I think perhaps it is not, it was just said to hurt us – she will still go to New York. So let her go."

For so long had she been obsessed with her own plans that it had never occurred to her that others might also have been planning.

By the time she got to New York, it was too late.

11

MERCEDES

The journey had been arduous and tiring: a long train ride from Madrid to Lisbon, weeks of waiting for a passage, the constant fear of arbitrary arrest, the struggle merely to exist among the thousands of refugees who had descended on Lisbon. Before leaving Madrid, she had assumed it would be merely a matter of buying a ticket and taking off for New York. Instead, along with all the other hopefuls she was put onto a waiting list and told to check in every few days to see when a flight might be available.

Lisbon proved impossibly tedious, filled as it was with refugees and hysteria, the hotels crowded with people wanting to escape, the cafés doing better business than they ever had in peacetime as the anxious and the desperate whiled away the long hours of idleness. Every day there were queues at the shipping office, heads shaking, bribes passed, tears. She often had cause to reflect that at least she was not trying to escape persecution, she was not mourning the loss of a husband, a wife, children, she was not in fear of her life; she looked with an indifferent eye on those who were. The streets were full of contrast. Thin sad women with pale faces and tired hair waited alongside those in furs and silk stockings; shabby-suited men shared tables with cigars and handmade shoes. She often felt, watching them, that nobody was exactly what they seemed, that all of them, including herself, played a role, putting up a façade to hide a reality too awful to contemplate.

In a queue one morning, she saw a face which made her catch her breath. Surely that white-blond hair, those cool aristocratic features belonged to, yes, indeed, to Max Ernst, one of the most famous of all the painters of the Surrealist school. She could hardly believe they were standing together in the same wretched line for a ticket to New York, but it proved to be so.

He told her he and his companions had recently moved to Monte Estoril, a seaside resort not far from the city. "Join us, my dear," he said, his round blue eyes lighting up. He seemed perpetually on the verge of laughing for pure joy. "Join us: at least we can sunbathe and swim and make love while we wait."

Did he mean with her? She was not sure; it did not matter. She moved her bags out to a cheap hotel at the resort. It seemed as though every nationality was represented; the beach was polyglot, the tea-rooms and esplanades cosmopolitan. She spent much of her time lying on the beach in a state of limbo, free and anonymous, just one of the crowd. Sometimes the police came round, ever vigilant against indecent bathing suits; sometimes she walked with others in the evenings, or danced, legs cramping with anxiety as she wondered how long this non-life must continue.

Every few days she put on a dress and took a train in to Lisbon to see how far up the waiting list her name had travelled; it never seemed far enough. Once she took a half-hour trolley-bus from the centre of the capital out to the ugly brick American Consulate in order to get her exit visa, to be prepared when her flight finally came through.

Once she saw Ernst again, in the middle of a crowd of women and children; for some reason his beautiful white hair was turquoise blue. She saw in that crest of flamboyant hair a signal, an indication that soon she would be living a quite different life from the one she had always known. She learned that the unattractive woman with the big nose who gazed moonstruck at Ernst and laughed whenever he spoke was called Peggy Guggenheim, a well-known patron of the arts, a collector and gallery owner. On the beach, she struck up an acquaintance with Señora Guggenheim, on impulse, introducing herself as Mercedes Aragon. She talked of Vicente, of Sanchez, spoke knowledgeably about art, making sure that she would be remembered if – *when* – they met again.

At last she was told there was a seat for her on one of the clumsy Pan American Clippers. She sent a cable to New York. The journey took thirty-six hours; the vibration from the propeller engines, the air turbulence, the lack of facilities, children whining, babies screaming, the delicate-stomached vomiting into paper bags, combined to turn the hours into a nightmare. She refused to let it get her down; in the leather bag on her knee was her – as she saw it – seed corn, the carefully rolled canvases which would make her fortune. She had several O'Donnells and de Leóns, a few paintings by Sanchez and Castán, and the precious Vicentes, their number supplemented by a visit, just before she left, to the *cortijo* on the hillside above Montalbán where the protective almond husks still lay piled.

He was waiting for her on the quayside, together with a plain woman in round spectacles, some years older than he, whom she took for a maidservant. In his time away, he had broadened and strengthened; his body stood more solidly on the earth, it seemed to her, and there was an added sheen to his hair. As he embraced her, planting a fraternal kiss on either side of her mouth, she knew she had grossly miscalculated. These were not the new manners he had learned in a more relaxed society than their own, but an indication that she was no longer too precious for him to touch.

"You look well," he said, though, pale and frazzled after her hideous journey, she knew she could not.

Again Carlos touched her, putting an arm round her shoulders and turning her to face the woman standing a little apart from him. "You are prettier than ever, Mercedes."

The woman smiled, holding out a hand. "Hello, Mercedes. I'm Marguerite." Her voice was very low, almost a baritone and Mercedes, heart sinking, saw how these two factors – the voice, the smile – bestowed a kind of subterranean beauty which was far more aesthetically pleasing than mere prettiness.

Her heart raged; she took the woman's hand and falling easily back into the role she had perfected, smiled shyly, dropping her eyes, while above her head, the woman whispered, "Enchanting!"

The blow came suddenly. Carlos said: "Mercedes, you are the first, the very first to know that last night

Marguerite consented to become my wife. We have not even told her parents yet."

She clasped his arm with both her hands. "I'm so happy for you both," she said, looking up at him through her eyelashes, noting with scorn the fatuous smile on his face, thinking: the game is not over yet, my friend.

Hatred ran with the slow heaviness of mercury through her veins. How dare he be happy, how *dare* he, when the man whose every chance of happiness he had snatched away lay rotting somewhere unknown in the dry hills above Montalbán. And I cannot go there, I cannot lay flowers, red flowers, on his grave, I cannot even mourn, she thought, even that he has taken from me.

But it was still not too late. Engagements could be broken; fiancées did not always become wives.

Ramirez had arranged for her to lodge with the same distant cousin who had put him up during his first days in New York. He himself now owned an apartment on the upper East Side. "Once Marguerite and I are married, you must come and live with us," he told her. "I've already discussed it with her and she thinks it would a wonderful plan." He smiled. "She's always wanted a younger sister."

The cousin had connections which Mercedes used to find herself a job. Holding letters of introduction and commendation, she went from gallery to gallery until one of the owners agreed to take her on as an assistant, though at a salary which paid little more than the cost of her travel in each day. Ramirez was delighted with the news; she did not tell him that to get the job she had made promises with her eyes which she had no intention of keeping. The pay did not matter. She had money, she could make more if necessary. Meanwhile, she had a foot in the door of the art world which she intended to conquer.

The New Age gallery had an eye to the future: New York was full of European artists in exile and Simon Rabat, the owner, cherished them as though they were his own children – at the expense of indigenous American artists. Occasionally, helping some thin young artist – they were all thin, whether male or female, with the same poverty-haunted expressions on their faces – to set up his canvases for Rabat to assess, Mercedes saw pieces of work which she was certain would one day become icons of America's artistic movement. Although herself reared in the European traditions of what constituted 'Art', she was able to see a fresh and innovative vein of creativity running through the work which was brought to Rabat and which he consistently rejected.

He was wrong. She knew instinctively he was wrong. Once she ran after one of the dejected artists who had packed up his canvases and was walking away down the street.

"Meet me over there this evening," she said quickly, pointing at the café on the corner. "This evening, at six o'clock."

When she ran back into the gallery, Rabat was waiting for her. "What were you doing?" he asked curiously.

"I just wanted to tell him I didn't dislike his work as much as you did," she said. One of the great pleasures of her new life was the chance to be her real self, away from the smothering aunts, away from the need to entangle Ramirez. New York suited her temperament.

Here, she could be what she really was: abrasive, bold, knowledgeable, untrammelled by convention.

"I see," Rabat raised his eyebrows. "No doubt that comforted him considerably."

"I think it may have cheered him up a little," she said. In her mind, she had already chosen the canvas she intended to buy from the young man . . .

"I see." He laughed scornfully. "And you, of course, know so much about it, I suppose."

"I know enough to see that the person who starts taking American art seriously, instead of only looking towards Europe, could not only make themselves very rich, but would also become one of the most influential people in the art world," she said.

"So you think I should give that young man – Pollett, was it? – "

"Pollock."

"You think I should give him a show?"

"Yes. Before someone else does." She gestured angrily. "If I had the money, I'd subsidise him myself, without your help."

"What did he call his stuff?"

"Action Paintings."

"It was rubbish, Mercedes. Daubs. A mockery of everything art stands for."

'Daubs' was Rabat's highest insult, one he used indiscriminately for anything which did not accord with his narrow Europeanised vision. She had nothing but contempt for his blindness.

"Can't you see the violence, the momentum, the *power* of his work?" she demanded.

"No. I just see a mess."

"But he has a truly authentic original voice," she said. She was aware that she was shouting. "Oh, you're so short-sighted! If you handled things right, you could turn New York into the art capital of the world."

He put an arm around her shoulders. "My dear, you have a pretty face and a good eye, not to mention a lot of energy. But until you develop a sound commercial sense as well, I suggest you leave the artistic side of things to me, hmm?"

She shrugged away from the weight of his arm. "If you don't do it, someone else will," she said.

He patted her buttocks. "Make me some coffee, my dear, will you?"

His patronising tone made her furious. Rabat did not yet take her seriously, but the time would come when he did. She recognised that she was in the very eye of the artistic hurricane which would sweep the world when the war was over.

Meanwhile, she was prepared to suffer. But only for a while. Ramirez' cousin, a widow, was old and boring; despite her wealth, she expected Mercedes to help the elderly servants in the kitchen, to perform menial tasks about the house, to take meals with her. Mercedes was already sickened beyond measure by the woman's ill-fitting false teeth which scraped against each other in a most disagreeable manner each time she chewed. She hated the fusty smell of the big house, the old woman's clothes which, each time she passed, left a drift behind her of sweat and the sickly-sweet perfume of pressed powder. She disliked the ugly surroundings in which she lived, the long rows of red brick houses, each one identical, she hated the lack of space, of long views and open spaces.

There were compensations. The cousin was a patron of the arts, even something of a collector. There were wonderful pictures on the walls; the house was crammed with bronzes, silver, porcelain. Mercedes forced herself to be patient, to ask questions, to learn.

In spite of the excitement of the world she was moving in, she did not lose sight of her long-term goal. "I wish I could move in with you now," she said wistfully to Ramirez.

"But Mercedes, you must see that this is not possible. I am a man, and you are a beautiful child; it would be most unsuitable."

"I don't see why. We aren't in Spain now. Who would care?"

"I would," he said firmly. "Your reputation would be ruined. How would you marry?"

She thought of Jonas. If she had ever had a reputation, there could be little of it left now.

"I don't care," she murmured. She moved closer to him. "I know I would be perfectly safe with you, Carlos. You would never touch me, would you?" She stared up at him and saw, with satisfaction, how he bit his lip and would not meet her eyes. Although Marguerite occupied him now, his desire for herself had not abated. Men love to destroy, she told herself. He wants to defile me.

"Besides," she said, "I am worried by the journey each day. There are servicemen home on leave who whisper at me, men rubbing themselves up against me. Carlos, it is so shaming for me to endure this. And my aunts would be horrified if they heard about such things . . ."

"Then you must not tell them," he said. "I will see what I can do. The wedding is only five months away now, and after that . . ." He took her hand and raised it to his lips.

She wanted to snatch it away but instead she looked trustingly into his eyes, timid as a gazelle. "I know you will always look after me, Carlos," she said. "I know I am safe with you." She watched him react, a slow blush reddening his face as he released her hand and moved away from her.

"Of course you are," he said, and she knew he saw her at his mercy, readied, a sacrifice.

She met Marguerite's parents. Although they had lived in New York for more than twenty-five years, neither of them had lost the thick accents of Russia, the country from which they had fled. They were hospitable people, and kind: the house was always full of bewildered young refugees from Europe, dispossessed old ladies, the smell of apple cakes and coffee.

"We have been lucky," Mrs Blevitsky told Mercedes. "America has been good to us and it is our duty, our *pleasure*, to pass some of our good fortune on to others." She smiled universally at the old women forced to spend their last years in a country whose language they would never speak: she passed cake to wild-eyed men whose minds could not yet grasp that the horror of pogrom and persecution was far behind them. She provided a sanctuary.

There would be beer on the table, tall fluted glasses full of golden light, there would be wine and roast meat, huge dishes of potatoes, beetroot salad, bowls of soured cream, chopped egg, raw onion rings and soused herrings. On the sideboard behind stood cascades of fruit: grapes, pears, apples, melons; pies leaking blueberries or apricots, damp cakes full of crystallised cherries and marzipan, custards, cheeses.

The family accepted Mercedes as though she were Ramirez' sister, or one of the frightened escapees from tortured Europe. Mercedes disliked that. She was here in New York of her own volition, unwounded; she had no need for patronage or pity. Sometimes, she had to remind herself why she was here, that she had a plan, that this was a necessary phase she must go through, and looking at Ramirez, tried not to show her distaste at being included in this group of plain fat ugly people. How could Ramirez have so far forgotten his origins, his class, as to get engaged to one of them?

Blanche, the older daughter, did not live with her parents though they often urged her to give up her house and move back in with them. She had been married the year before America entered the war; her husband was serving overseas. It was his absence which had provided Ramirez with his chance to join the Blevitsky law firm.

Blanche often watched Mercedes. At first Mercedes had assumed it was curiosity, perhaps even envy, which prompted her stare. But she began to realise that Blanche saw through her, just as Jonas had done, that Blanche recognised the overpowering obsession below the surface of the artless exterior, even if she did not understand its focus.

Mercedes thought: I have let my guard slip. I must be more careful, even my mind must pretend.

She moved into the the second phase of her two-pronged plan: she sold one of the canvases she had brought with her from Spain. The operation required a certain amount of planning, of cunning, but the times were right. New York, though on the periphery of the European war, was none the less in an unaccustomed state of cheerful chaos: there were too many artistic refugees, too many famous names seeking asylum, for the old habits of caution and rigidity to apply.

Without telling Rabat, she made an appointment to see the owner of a rival gallery. For the interview, she wore a dramatic black dress and a large hat with a swathed veil which partially concealed her face. Her make-up was heavy, designed to make her look older; to complete what was effectively a semi-disguise she borrowed – without permission – a silver-fox fur coat from the wardrobe of Ramirez' cousin, and a spectacular diamond ring.

She had chosen this particular gallery with care. The owner was younger than some of his colleagues, and although American, known to be sympathetic towards refugees; she had recently read an article by him in the art magazine *View*, extolling the virtues of new artists currently working in the United States and new movements which were starting up in Europe but not yet known over here. She was encouraged by the fact that of the names he mentioned, she had barely heard of more than three.

In addition, he had conducted an acrimonious correspondence with Rabat, accusing him of sharp practice in obtaining an important canvas by one of the exiled Surrealists. He had assumed a deal had been made; before he could clinch it, Rabat had offered more money and the artist sold to him instead.

He stared at her with interest as she came into his

gallery, leading her to his office without question. With the door closed behind them, she took from her bag the canvas she had brought and put it in front of him.

"A Vicente," he said.

"You recognise his work?"

"Of course. I've seen examples here and there. I heard what happened during the war in Spain. Tragic. A great loss."

"What do you think?" she asked.

"It's not his best."

The remark impressed her. "I know." Both of them stared in silence at the tortured image in front of them, the skull-faced young man staring horrified out of the canvas, hands tightly clasped in front of him as though to hide or protect his sexuality, while behind him a series of blood-red doors opened endlessly on to each other, receding into the distance. What did they represent? Doors he had not yet gone through, opportunities as yet unexplored? Or were those sinister beckoning thresholds symbolic of a hidden world he dared not enter, on which he had turned his back?

"None the less," the gallery owner said, "It's interesting. Where did you get it?"

Her story was prepared. "My sister," she said. "She was a good friend of Vicente. He lodged with her when he lived in Barcelona. He gave her many canvases over the years, sometimes he could not afford the rent." She judged that he would not know nor could prove, that she was lying.

"You have proof of ownership?"

"Here." She patted her bag. She had spent several weeks perfecting letters in Vicente's handwriting. "Not

all of them have such proof, but you can check in Spain –
or with Vicente's own family – if you doubt my word."

"He would have made a name for himself, had he
lived," the dealer said.

"I thought he already had done so." Mercedes was
haughty.

The dealer laughed. "Is that what he told your sister?
In Spain, perhaps. Not yet outside it." He bent down to
peer further at the canvas. "This isn't bad."

Not bad? Mercedes stared at him, feeling her eyes
grown huge, her pupils darken. *Not bad?*

Oblivious, the dealer said: "How big was his output, I
wonder?"

"His family still has a number of canvases, I believe."
Mercedes had difficulty remaining civil. "And my sister
has others. After he was murdered, the *fascistas* came to
her house, they threatened her, she decided it would be
better for us to leave Spain. She does not wish to sell,
but now we have no money and she has no choice."

"No money?" His glance fell on the diamond ring
she wore.

"It was my mother's. All I have left of her." Mercedes
managed to make her upper lip quiver.

The dealer ran a considering hand over his face. "And
how much does your sister want for this?"

She named a sum somewhat lower than she thought the
canvas was worth and saw him working out the kind of
profit he might expect to make on it. "And you say there
are other canvases available?"

She nodded. "If I can persuade my sister that it is better
to sell than to starve."

"What's your sister's name?"

"She made me promise not to tell. She is frightened, even here in New York. And one day she would like to return to Spain." He seemed to accept what she said. The volatility of European politics was taken for granted in the States, and the brutal repressions of the Franco regime were much talked about among the artists-in-exile.

"And your name? Or can't you tell me that, either?"

She shook her head. "I will leave this with you, señor. Tomorrow I shall come back and you can tell me whether you wish to buy."

"I wish to buy." Unexpectedly he smiled. "But not just yet. Some preparation is needed if I'm to make any kind of a profit out of a virtual unknown."

Mercedes raged. A virtual unknown? Fernando Vicente? She remembered how often she had taken comfort from the thought of the dealers who would flock to buy his work. In the end, she had taken Vicente to the dealers – and found him rejected.

"So you won't take the canvas?" she said.

"Bring it back in a year or so," he said carelessly. "I might do a deal then." He leaned forward to stroke the sleeve of her fur coat. "I do hope you and your sister will survive in the meantime."

"That is one thing you can be sure of," she said. Silently she rewrapped the canvas.

He asked: "Where can I get in touch?" but she did not reply.

At the street door, she turned. "I think you will regret your decision," she said.

From his expression, she saw that he agreed with her.

After that, she waited. Eventually, as she had expected, an article appeared on the Arts pages of the *New York*

Times. 'Death of an artist', over the by-line of the gallery owner, retold the story of Fernando Vicente's imprisonment and death. She thought she recognised it as the first stage in his purchase of the Vicente canvas she had shown him.

A little later, the same contributor, this time writing for *View*, wondered whether it was time to redefine the Spanish contribution to twentieth-century art. She herself submitted a short article to *Focus* magazine. She used the name of Schleeman, the gallery owner; she figured that by the time they discovered that he had not written it, it would be already in print. Besides, he did not know how to find her. In the article, she gave a judicious overview of Vicente's work, exaggerated his reputation in his own country, ended with a moving account of his final days, claiming to have spoken with members of Vicente's own family.

Casually she asked Rabat if he had read it.

He shrugged. "Typical of Schleeman," he said. "Always some new enthusiasm. Knowledgeable, admittedly . . ."

"And extremely successful," Mercedes said sharply. "I think he's right about Vicente: in Spain he is very highly regarded. Once the war is over in Europe, he will become an international figure, I'm sure."

"Mercedes, why don't you confine yourself to selling my pictures, and leave the art criticism to me?" he said unpleasantly.

"I have some canvases I brought with me from Spain," she said. "You should look at them."

He groaned. "Daubs by your grandmother, I suppose. Or maybe something your sister produced at her art classes."

"I have no sister," she said quietly. "But I had a brother."

Unwilling sympathy softened his face. He knew from the few personal details she had let drop that her family had suffered personal tragedy during the Civil War. "A brother, hmm?" he said, nodding.

"He was an artist."

Again he groaned.

"His name was Fernando Vicente."

She saw his mind travel from one point to another until it refocused on the article he assumed had been written by his rival.

"What?" He came closer until she could smell the raw onion on his breath. "Don't tell me. I never realised . . . *that* Vicente?" He gasped. "Are you really his . . .?"

"Do you want me to bring in my *daubs* or not?" she said coldly.

"Please." He looked at his watch. "Where are they?"

"Somewhere safe," she said.

"Go and pick them up now, if you want. Take a taxi back – I'll pay."

She took a taxi both ways. He did not quibble, helping her carry the canvases into the back of the gallery with hands that were not quite steady. As well as a Vicente – not one of her own favourites – she had brought a couple of the O'Donnells, a de León, a Sanchez.

Rabat's lips were wet as he looked at them. "My God, Mercedes. Have you got more of these? They're wonderful." He could see a new reputation for himself, as a promoter of a particular school of art.

"I can get hold of more," she said. She thought with impatience of the dangerous submarine-haunted sea which

lay between her and Spain. It had been hard enough
to organise the shipment of the few canvases she had
managed to bring with her; she had been forced to
leave others stored in Madrid. More frustrating than
that, however, was the fact that there were paintings
she did not yet own being produced at this very moment.
O'Donnell, Sanchez, Castán, others whose work she had
been buying for some years were still over there, still
painting, no doubt selling their work to people who did
not appreciate them, for the price of a week's food, a
month's tobacco or drink or women.

"What are they," Rabat asked, "all contemporaries?"

"More or less."

"We'd better give them a name – the Madrid School?
The Junta?"

"The Granada Group," she said. O'Donnell was from the
north of Spain, de León came from Madrid, but Sanchez
was born in a village between Seville and Granada: the
name would do for the present.

Rabat rushed into his office and started to telephone his
regular clients. She listened to the conversations, similar in
every case: ". . . something you ought to see . . . Vicente.
Schleeman's article in the current *Focus* . . . Yes, *that*
Vicente . . . others . . . Spain, the Granada Group . . .
no, neither had I but I have it on the best authority . . .
yes, someone *very* intimately connected . . . my dear,
these will be among the names of the future . . . if
you want to call your collection definitive, I'd advise
you get down here right away . . . *lots* of interest . . .
see you . . ."

When he finally emerged, beaming with satisfaction,
he found her on her knees, repacking the canvases. He

spread his hands. "But Mercedes, what are you doing?"

Feigning surprise, she looked up at him. "I can't leave these here," she said.

"But . . ." he said helplessly. "I have clients coming, I've told everyone, I thought you . . ."

"I only asked if you wanted to see them," said Mercedes. "I didn't say they were for sale."

His face hardened. For a moment he looked at her in silence. Then he said: "All right, Mercedes. What exactly do you want?"

"Two things."

"What are they?"

"Anonymity. I don't want anyone to know where you got these canvases. I don't want anyone to know who I am, or that I am here in New York."

"Anonymity, right. What else?"

"Half the gallery."

"Half the – " He blinked, frowned, half-laughing as though she had made a joke. "Are you crazy?"

"Not at all."

"What on earth makes you think I would – "

"I'll give you these canvases," she said. "Including the Vicente. In return, I want half the gallery legally made over to me. You don't have to tell anyone, I'm not looking for prestige – not yet, at least. But I want an equal say in what we show and who we buy. And I want to start a programme of – of patronage, if that is the right word."

"Patronage?" Rabat was thinking furiously.

"I want to put certain artists under annual contract to us, pay them a monthly retainer in return for their output, plus a percentage of any sales once they've earned out the advance we'd give them."

"And who would be responsible for choosing these artists, these *pensioners*? You, I suppose."

"Of course."

"You're mad," Rabat said faintly. "We'd go broke in a week if we started to underwrite painters people had never heard of."

"Of course we won't. Don't you see? Once you're guaranteed the supply of paintings, you start to promote it, you get the collectors interested, you create a demand. And when you've done that, when you've built up the reputation, you put the works on the market bit by bit."

"I'm in the business of selling art, Mercedes, not cookies."

She ignored him. "And above all, we should be giving more encouragement to the painters on this side of the Atlantic."

"Mercedes, my dear." Awkwardly he squatted beside her. "I think you have some good ideas, even some exciting ones, though they're a little too radical for my taste. But you simply don't understand the commercial cross-currents of the world of art. You can't seriously expect me to say: 'Here, here is my gallery, take half of it, do what you like with it, bring in every ragged Tom, Dick and Harry who shows up with a couple of daubs under his arm, turn the place into a flop-house for failed painters.'"

"That's childish." She continued to pack the half-dozen canvases carefully away, watching him struggle with himself. Indecision, caution, greed, a desire to score over Schleeman, warred with such artistic integrity as he still possessed. At the same time, he was too astute a businessman not to recognise that though her idea was a gamble, it was one which, if it worked, could lead to rich pickings.

Eventually, getting with difficulty to his feet again, he said: "Look, let's compromise on this, Mercedes. Leave your canvases here for the moment, let a few buyers see them, let me gauge the reaction of the public. And after that, we'll talk again, hmm?"

"All right."

She tried not to let him see the smile she could not conceal. She had got exactly what she wanted. The name of Fernando Vicente would rank as high as Picasso.

And Ramirez would tremble.

12

MERCEDES

In her younger days, she had wanted her revenge to be immediate, she had wanted to seize, to punish and then to destroy. As she grew older, however, she began to see that there were more subtle, long-drawn-out ways to achieve her objective. Originally she had intended, perhaps, to break his heart and crush his spirit, then move onwards into the rest of her injured life; anticipatory, she began to see that what had once seemed a single project of revenge might be infinitely expanded.

As a wedding present, Mr Blevitsky gave Ramirez and Marguerite the lease on a large apartment on the ninth floor of a new block of flats in Brooklyn. He made an occasion of it, calling the family together, opening the rich sweet wine he favoured, giving a speech, presenting the two of them with the deeds, scrolled and tied with red ribbon. Mercedes took part in the rejoicing; watching handsome Ramirez with his arm around Blevitsky's shoulders, she felt her hatred refuelled: he had no right to happiness.

At the wedding, Blanche and Mercedes acted as brides-maids; Blanche's husband, home on leave, was the best man. Because of the war-time conditions, the groom's relatives were unable to travel from Spain to attend, yet the list of wedding guests was long. It seemed as if half of New York had come to wish the daughter of the Blevitskys well.

As Ramirez circulated among the guests with his new bride, Mercedes thought: Two years ago I would literally rather have died than attend his wedding. She did not consider that she had failed either Fernando or herself. It no longer mattered, for such a multiplicity of possibilities presented itself to her that she knew she simply could not fail. Watching him, she could see that in New York he had found a place and a *métier* which suited him and despite her aversion, she had to admit he looked everything she knew him not to be: honourable, decent, kind. Seeing how warmly the wedding guests reacted to him, she thought, with anger: You may have fooled them, but you cannot fool me. I know who you really are.

He saw her staring in his direction and came over. He took both her hands in his and smiled down at her. "When we return from our honeymoon," he said, "we both hope very much you will make your home with us."

She raised her eyes to him. "It wouldn't be fair," she said softly. "As newly-weds, you need your privacy."

"The apartment is large enough for us all," Ramirez said.

She shook her head. "It would be wrong. Besides, your cousin has been ill recently, as you know, and I wouldn't like to leave until she has completely recovered. She relies on me more, I think, than she realises."

He hugged her. "You are always so considerate," he said. "But Doña Carlota has servants who can care for her. There is no need for you to sacrifice yourself." He flashed a smile across the room at Marguerite. How plain she is, Mercedes thought with distaste. How ugly. She wondered why Carlos would want to spend his life with such a woman but though she had looked for signs in him of venality or ambition which might explain the match, she had not so far been able to find either. Yet it was not possible that he was what he appeared to be; even if the rest of the world thought so, she did not.

"It's no sacrifice," she said bravely. "Why don't we consider the question of me living with you and Marguerite when you've had some time together."

"You must think of me as your big brother," he said. His eyes were warm. "You are such an unselfish child." And, hating him, wanting to strike him dead right there for the blasphemy he had uttered, she wondered savagely: How can you be so blind?

The truth was that although she had previously considered being under the same roof as Ramirez a requisite for the furtherance of her plans, she had begun to realise that it would be far too restrictive. Having constituted himself some kind of guardian to her, he would keep a constant eye on her movements and at this stage in her life, she needed freedom to come and go as she pleased. In fact the elderly cousin's house suited her perfectly. Doña Carlota, grossly overweight, suffered from a variety of complaints which occupied her to the exclusion of almost everything else. She kept few tabs on Mercedes, accepting what she had been told, which was that Mercedes had a time-consuming job in Manhattan which took up most of her waking hours. Doña Carlota had never shown much interest in the work itself; she knew vaguely that it involved the art world and beyond that was happy to confine her interests to a daily enquiry as to the state of Mercedes' bowels.

Mercedes tolerated the impertinence of these questions, along with her other dissatisfactions, for the sake of the independence which accompanied them. Her discussions with Rabat had reached a most satisfactory conclusion: she had allowed him to keep one of the Vicentes, the O'Donnells, two of the de León miniatures and the Sanchez, in return for a one-third stake in the gallery and the right to handle personally the gallery's protégés. Rabat thought he had the best of the bargain; she knew he did not.

Reluctantly he had agreed to her suggestion of placing young unknowns under exclusive contract; of those who had called at the gallery in the past year she selected three who, in her opinion, would one day make their name on the art scene. At first they had been inclined to disbelief when she turned up at their studios, then suspicious. She had convinced them. She pointed to Mrs Guggenheim, who operated a similar scheme with more famous artists; she told them they had been cho-sen above others because of their potential talent. She proposed a guaranteed fee every month, in return for the right to sell their work as and when it appeared. The offer was too good for a struggling young artist to turn down.

"But I can't paint with someone pushing at me to get on with it," one of them objected.

"No-one will bother you," she said. "The idea is to free

you from worry, to encourage you to concentrate on your work."

"I work slowly – suppose I don't produce as much as you hope."

"What you paint will be enough," Mercedes said calmly, though she felt a moment's qualm. Rate of work was one of the things she should have checked. She did not wish to put herself in the position of underwriting a non-productive unit. When she drew up the final contracts, she must remember to make provision for such an eventuality . . .

All three of her protégés wanted to paint her, either clothed or naked – or both. Foreseeing a time when she would be old and notorious, imagining a drawing-room which doubled as a gallery, its walls hung with paintings of herself by artists she personally had made famous, she agreed, paying out of her own pocket. Over Rabat's objections, she hung the portraits at the back of the gallery, making sure he understood these belonged only to her.

"My reputation," Rabat groaned, looking at them. "Pornographic daubs, nothing more."

"They're good publicity," she insisted.

"Who for? Yourself?" He fixed her with a shrewd eye. "Don't get too ambitious, Mercedes."

"They will act as hors-d'oeuvres to whet the appetite of the picture buyers," she said. "Who can resist looking at a nude? The women will be shocked; the men will drool. And after that they will marvel at the technique, at the painterly qualities, and want to see more by the same artist." She resolved in that moment to make certain Carlos never penetrated far enough into the gallery to catch sight of them.

"I hope you're right."

She did not tell him that roused by her lean, heavy-breasted body, all three of her artists had tried at different times to sleep with her. It was a development she had not anticipated but she did not find it difficult to handle, since only one of them was physically tempting. Yet, when after an afternoon of modelling, Richard Klein, the handsomest and most artistically promising, had put down his paintbrushes and gathered her breasts in his thin eager fingers, she remembered Jonas and shuddered.

"I can't," she said, turning her head away. Her hair drooped across her naked shoulders.

"Why not?" Klein's voice was thick with desire; his mouth was wet. He pushed his hand between her thighs and felt the dampness there. "You want to, as much as I do."

"Yes," she said. "But I can't."

"What about my artistic development?" he said. "I can't concentrate on anything but you, my painting's gone to pot, it's your duty not to deprive me of what I need."

"Deprivation produces inspiration," she said coolly, reaching for her clothes. Yet she was aware of inner despair. Would it be like that for the rest of her life? Would the shadow of Jonas, of an earlier love, fall across her bed each time she was physically drawn to another man? She wondered where he was, if he thought of her. Since their parting, she had pushed his image to the back of her mind; now she allowed herself to think of him, to wonder whether she would ever see him again. She realised that if she truly believed she would not, her life would be meaningless. She began to see that her desire for vengeance could only ever be part of it; there had to be construction as well as destruction.

It was 1945.

The war was over. And Marguerite was pregnant. Her thin face rounded, her angular body grew curves. Mercedes considered her an unlikely candidate for motherhood but hid contempt beneath apparent interest: the newly-weds behaved as though it was the first time in the history of the world that anyone had ever had a baby. She watched with repulsion as Marguerite's stomach distended the front of her dresses; she noted the softness in Ramirez' eye and thought: I have lost sight of my objective. He is too happy, it is not right. Yet, taking a longer view, she could see that happiness found would only emphasise the pain when happiness was subsequently lost. The coming of a baby provided a better way to achieve her aim. With a child, Ramirez was doubly, trebly vulnerable; as a father, he would be more easily hit and mortally wounded.

It was necessary for the maintenance of her cover to spend occasional evenings or Sundays with the Blevitskys. While they talked endlessly of birthing and babies, her mind roamed. Soon, she would persuade Rabat to hold an exhibition of the New Art, but first she must nurture her trio of painters, she must write articles, drop their names, interest her clients. She knew she needed more power: the problem was how to attain it. If she sold a second Vicente, would she have enough money to buy a bigger stake in the gallery? She had already proposed this to Rabat and been turned down: perhaps there was a way of making him change his mind. Or perhaps she should consider opening negotiations with someone else –

perhaps she should even consider the possibility of starting up her very own gallery.

The idea grew roots which burrowed deeper and deeper into her mind. A gallery where she could promote the works of Spaniards; a showcase which would foster the reputation of Fernando Vicente. One day, perhaps, a gallery devoted entirely to his work, where people could come and marvel at his skill. Schemes whirled in her brain, plans were made, analysed, discarded, replaced. Around her the women talked softly of confinement and labour, their hands busy with baby-clothes knitted from unravelled sweaters since wool was still scarce, or with quilting covers for the new child's cradle. She was with them but not of them, her mind ranging under a brighter, more star-studded sky than the one which hung above their heads.

Marguerite's pregnancy was difficult and exhausting; her labour, when it finally arrived, lasted nearly thirty-six hours. The baby was a boy: they called him Amador. Since Blanche was still childless, he was the first Blevitsky grandchild, the epitome of family hope, the one for whom two generations had suffered, emigrated, striven. Looking down at the creased red face in its cradle, at the slitted eyes and the squashed-flat nose, Mercedes saw only another Ramirez to hate.

She was increasingly glad that she had not moved in with Carlos and Marguerite when they first married: now, with the baby, she had a further excuse to stay where she was. She had toyed with the idea of getting her own place but the amount she paid Ramirez' cousin for her board was minimal and gave her the opportunity to save a little each month. In addition, the cousin owned jewellery and furs which Mercedes had learned to admire aloud: inevitably the offer to lend them followed. In her younger days, the cousin had been something of a fashion-plate; although she herself could no longer wear the clothes designed for her years ago in Paris, it amused her to see Mercedes parade in a day dress by Chanel or Molyneux, a hat by Lanvin, Dior's evening gowns. She sat chuckling on her sofas while Mercedes modelled coats of sealskin and fox, or strutted about the fusty drawing room with borrowed jewels in her hair and on her thin wrists. She had grown careless and forgetful; occasionally, discreetly, Mercedes was able to steal.

The first exhibition featuring the work of her protégés was not a success. Despite her best efforts, she had not been able to persuade the New York patrons that indigenous art was worth buying. Doña Carlota, driven for the occasion in her limousine, bought a canvas; so, surprisingly, did Mrs Blevitsky, over her husband's objections. Ramirez appeared, without Marguerite, and insisted that she advise him on what to buy.

"Something that will remind me of home, perhaps," he said, his eyes vainly searching the gallery walls.

"I'm afraid that's not the sort of thing we go in for," she said, trying to hide her contempt.

"Pity. But obviously we want to support you in your new enterprise. It doesn't matter what the price is: the firm is doing well. So what shall I take home with me as a present for my son Amador?"

Sourly she talked up two or three of the canvases and watched him make his choice. He seemed to be flourishing. In the past months he had filled out, grown glossier; she wondered how often women flung themselves at him, and whether he resisted their advances.

He put his arm round her shoulders as he left. "I am concerned about your happiness, Mercedes. Being so happy myself, I want the whole world to share my contentment."

She smiled. Inside she felt sick: Ramirez should not be happy, nor would be, if she could do anything to prevent it.

David Schleeman, the owner of the gallery to which she had sold the Vicente painting nearly eighteen months before, was buying one of the Richard Kleins. While Rabat dealt with the purchase, she watched Schleeman survey the thinly-attended opening, obviously searching for someone. Her? She approached him.

"Ah," he said. "Miss Anonymous." His eyes narrowed. "Or should I call you Miss David Schleeman? It seems to be the name you adopt for articles in the art magazines.

"You knew I'd written it?"

"Who else could it have been?"

"I only did what was necessary," she said coolly. She nodded at the Klein, with the sticker indicating that it was sold. "I see you bought something."

"Indeed. I had no idea that old Rabat was prepared to play such dangerous games. This is not the art of today, I think, but the art of tomorrow."

"Even old Rabats can learn new tricks," she said.

"But only if someone has the patience to teach them." His glance took in both the Dior dress she was wearing and the jewels at her ears, then returned to her face. "How is your starving sister?"

"My what?"

216

"Clearly doing better than when we first met if she can afford to dress you in Dior and diamonds." He reached out and touched her earrings. "Or were these also your mother's?"

"Uh . . ." She had forgotten the story she had told him. "Of course."

"Really?" He sounded unconvinced. "Does your sister wish to sell more of her Vicentes?"

"She spoke of it only recently."

"If she decides to do so, I hope you will come to me first."

"I'll make sure of it."

At the back of the gallery, the nude portraits of herself were labelled Not For Sale. None the less, he walked over to them and she followed. Waving a hand at them, he asked: "Do I recognise the model?"

"Possibly."

"She has a beautiful body, whoever she is. She looks as if she might be worth getting to know."

Mercedes stared fully at him then dropped her eyes, her brain busy. Opportunity beckoned. "Then perhaps you should make an effort to do so," she said.

Rabat did not attempt to conceal his satisfaction at being proved right. "Now we can boot out these bums," he said.

"No," she said. "We have an agreement."

"But nobody wants such stuff."

"They have contracts with us."

"You are bankrupting me, Mercedes, with your new ideas and your works of charity."

"It's not charity. It's a sound investment."

"For them, perhaps. For the three layabouts whose hideous daubs are disfiguring my walls. But not for me."

"For *us*," she said firmly.

A few days later, while Rabat was out having his morning shave, Schleeman came into the gallery. It was too late for her to move from behind the big desk placed near the back of the room.

He smiled. "So you work for Rabat? I wasn't sure."

"Yes."

"And your name?"

"Mercedes Aragon." It was not quite a lie – Aragon was her grandmother's name. And since her time in Lisbon, she had seen the advantages of not being too closely connected with Vicente.

"I see. Miss Aragon: I would be delighted if you would attend a small party I'm holding in my apartment next week."

The invitation was more or less what she had hoped for – or, at least, expected. She visualised the evening. By 'small', he meant just the two of them; at some stage he would start to make love to her, she could either respond or not. He was many years older than she was but good-looking, well-maintained. She thought she was prepared to go through with it, but only once – unless he paid the price she intended to ask.

"I'd be delighted," she said.

She was the youngest in the room by twenty years. She wore a glittering black dress of silk chiffon sewn with shiny bugle beading; there was a beaded orchid at waist and shoulder; the handkerchief hem dipped unevenly about the calf, showing off the slimness of her ankles.

The cousin of Ramirez sighed, seeing her before she set off. "Worth," she said. "I was wearing that dress the evening I met my husband."

"It's beautiful," said Mercedes.

"And so, my dear, are you." The old lady groaned, pressing a hand to her ribs. "Ring the bell before you go, Mercedes, I feel most unwell."

By New York standards the party was indeed small, though larger than she had anticipated. There were no more than thirty people present; she recognised most of the faces and all of the names. These were the people who moved and shook the New York art world. Here was the money, the taste and the power.

The room appeared to be a converted loft, long and arched, its walls painted white under black-stained exposed beams. Canvases hung at intervals, illuminated by carefully placed overhead lighting; the only furniture was a series of long sofas covered in bright Aztec-patterned shawls, and a few side-tables holding pieces of modern sculpture or pottery. Prominently displayed was the Richard Klein purchased from her exhibition. She did not fail to notice that throughout the evening Schleeman ensured that each of his guests was made aware of it. Watching, noting, she thought: this is how reputations are created.

Peggy Guggenheim, with Max Ernst at her side, crossed the room to exchange kisses with her and reminisce about the anxious days in Portugal, when they all waited endlessly for passage back to the United States. Mercedes saw Schleeman's astonishment at her apparent friendship with one of New York's most powerful art patrons.

"We should have seen something of you," Mrs Guggenheim said. "We've been so busy."

"Are you here with someone, child?" asked Ernst.

"No."

"You came alone?"

"Yes."

"We must invite Miss Aragon to our next gathering," Ernst said. His blue eyes under the thatch of white hair glistened at her. He gave his famous smile.

His wife, waving at someone else, said, with indifference: "Why not? Good idea."

Ernst nodded and winked. "See you soon," he whispered, as Mrs Guggenheim led him away.

Schleeman saw to it that she was introduced to everyone in the room. To each one he added some small remark of interest about her; she wondered how he had found out so much, and hoped that Rabat had done as she requested and maintained her anonymity. She wondered too when he would make his move.

When he asked her to stay behind, she resigned herself. With the last guest gone, he poured brandy for them both and sat down beside her on one of the long sofas.

"I recognise you," he said, without preamble.

She did not speak, waiting for what was to follow.

"I recognise you because you're exactly as I was, thirty years ago."

"What was that?"

"Tough. Ambitious. Manipulative. Completely ruthless."

She tried to laugh. "Thank you."

"Did I say dishonest?"

"Not yet."

"More importantly than all those, you have an eye.

When I saw those paintings hanging on Rabat's strait-laced walls, I nearly laughed aloud. I don't know what hold you have over him, but never in a million years did he choose to exhibit those artists himself; as soon as I realised that you worked for him, I knew you must have been the one to pick them out."

"What did you think of my choice?"

"One of them won't do as well as you expect. But the other two will. Particularly Klein . . ." Both of them turned their heads to look at the vicious colours of the canvas on the wall. ". . . he will be a star."

"Especially after this evening. You worked hard on his behalf."

"Just protecting my investment."

"When do you expect a dividend?"

"Give it a few months." Schleeman put his brandy snifter down on the table in front of him and took Mercedes' hands in his. "First, however, we have more work to do."

"We?" she said faintly. There was a surge of blood in her ears. She thought: it's happening. If I choose to play his game, I'm on my way.

"You tried hard to make your exhibition a success, I know," Schleeman said. "For a first effort it wasn't bad. I read the article you wrote in *View*, and several people have told me they've heard good things about Klein, as well as the other two. The word was definitely out on the street. You have the right ideas, but you don't yet have the necessary contacts."

"And you do."

"Of course. So will you, eventually. If I help you."

"Is there any reason why you should?" She shivered

suddenly, with a compound of fear and excitement. As never before, she felt that she held in her hands, in that moment, the whole of her future, hers to use as she wished.

He smiled. "None, really. By helping you, I could be signing my own professional death warrant. But I have to have faith in something: it might as well be you."

"I imagine there is a price to be paid," she said coolly.

"Isn't there always?"

"How much? And in what currency?"

"I think you can guess part of it, Mercedes," he said. Getting up, he knelt in front of her. He ran his tongue over his lips, his eyes flicking over her body; he put his hands on her thighs.

"What do you want me to do?"

He smiled. "What are you prepared to do?"

Calculations clicked in Mercedes' head. She had been prepared to sleep with him if it would further her own plans: she had guessed that he might want her to move in with him, become his mistress, maybe even his wife. If she agreed, she knew her career was set fair. But such a decision would mean that Ramirez would move out of her reach. The image she had spent so many years perfecting would, at one stroke, be shattered. She had to decide which was more important: her vengeance or her vocation. Or was it possible to have both? How manipulable was the situation?

Yet, she knew she had answered the question long before it had been shaped. She rose to her feet and stood in front of him. "Ask me," she said.

He slid one hand up her thigh beneath her skirt. She felt his hand stroke the silk of her panties, slide beneath the material, linger for a moment on the warm softness beneath. With a kind of gasp, he said: "I think it might be a good idea first to remove that beautiful dress you are wearing. What is it: Lanvin?"

"Worth."

She stood silently while Schleeman stood to lift the dress carefully over her head. Apart from her silk pants, she was naked underneath; his eyes lit up at the sight of her heavy breasts. "Your protégés – what an excellent idea of yours, by the way – "

"I borrowed it from Peggy Guggenheim," she murmured, implying by her tone that the two women had actually discussed it.

" – they did a good job, an excellent job, of painting you," he said judiciously, as though offering artistic comment. "But those canvases on the wall of Rabat's gallery – did he not recognise you, incidentally? – don't do you anything like justice."

She stared him in the eye, saying nothing.

He put a cold hand under her right breast and held it loosely. Slowly his thumb stroked her nipple. "Are you a virgin?" he said.

"No."

"Good. Then I don't have to be so careful." He pulled down the braces of his evening trousers and began to undo the buttons of his flies.

His words both frightened and at the same time, thrilled her. Once, she thought. I only have to do this once. After that, we talk on my terms, not his. She realised she needed more time to consider her options. Although she had anticipated this, she was less prepared for it than she had realised.

He put both hands on her shoulders and thrust her to her knees. "I wanted to do this slowly," he said. "but you're far more than I expected." He stood above her, tumescent and empurpled, glistening. He was enormous, bigger than anything she could have imagined.

She would not take him in her mouth, even if it meant the end of her hopes. Even as she thought this, she wondered how she could reject Richard Klein's advances for the sake of her lost love, and yet contemplate sleeping with this stranger. Was it because in the first case, she was attracted, in the second, she saw only the furtherance of her ambitions? And if so, what did that make her: a whore?

The idea excited her. When he pushed her backwards, she fell with grace, legs enticingly splayed. "What do you wish me to do?" she asked faintly. Her hand stroked the curve of her breast.

"Tonight – nothing. Just . . . *be*, Mercedes."

He knelt beside her. His fingers slid to the entrance of her body and she was surprised to find herself responding. The fibres of the carpet pricked her skin as he pushed at her. At the same time he took one of her nipples in his mouth and caressed it softly with his tongue. She closed her eyes, concentrating on the sensations he was arousing. His hands opened her, stretching her apart, wider and wider until she feared she might be torn. Suddenly he shoved his fingers inside her; smoothly he punched his hand back and forth, while she writhed, impaled. Sex should not be this way, she thought, divorced from love. None the less, the bubble of lust she felt began to expand; as he continued it became a ball, a balloon, growing bigger and bigger until finally it burst and she exploded over his hand.

"Good." He spoke calmly, though his face was red. "Now it's my turn."

He was huge. He crammed her, each movement he made tearing at the sides of her vagina, hurting her. Her own juices dried. Tears formed in her eyes.

"Are you in pain?" he asked, panting. One of his hands gathered her wrists together and held them tightly above her head.

"Yes."

He increased the speed of his movement in and out of her. The pain was unbelievable; she tried to get away from under him – nothing was worth this – but his weight pinned her down. She was determined not to scream; she told herself it could not go on much longer, that if she could just hold out . . . she had a sudden vision of Concepción, her friend, all those years before, the naked body tossed outside the door, blood on the white thighs. Would there be blood on *her* thighs when this man, this monster, had finished with her? And would he make it worth her while? She thought: He will have to.

He was built in such a way that few women could have taken him inside themselves. She guessed that by being able to, she already held an ace in her hand.

"I don't want to hurt you," he grunted, each word punctuated by a thrust of his body.

"But you are."

"You see how I am placed."

His eyes were squeezed shut; he bit his lower lip. "I'm – I'm coming," he gasped. She felt the pressure rise inside him, a final huge lunge of his body, and the enormous pumping of his release. She screamed loudly, threshing about beneath him. Jonas, she thought sadly; there was an ache in her mind. Where are you, Jonas? I want you. She thought of how it had been with him, and tears spilled over her face and down her neck. That had been love. This was . . . this was lechery. Self-disgust stirred.

For a moment Schleeman lay winded on her, then he pulled himself out. Even detumescent he was big; his departure from her body was exquisitely painful; she screamed again, holding her hands to her head.

"God. What have I done?" he said. She looked up at him. His face was appalled; he was streaked with her blood. His eyes met hers. "You said you were not a vir – "

"I'm not," she said.

"It wasn't rape, was it?"

She thought: I could say yes, and be believed, I could blackmail him. But I have more to gain if I – "No, no," she said. "I took part. I didn't have to."

He seemed relieved.

"Help me up," she said.

"Are you all right?"

She shook her head. "I don't think so. But I can take a cab back. I don't know what my – my guardian will say."

"Your guardian?"

"Doña Carlota Ramirez."

His eyes widened; he recognised the name and was awed by it. "Do you want to stay the night here?" he asked.

"Don't be silly. Do you want everyone to know what you have done to me?" she said. She had him where she wanted him.

"I'm sorry. It's difficult for me. Most women run a mile when they – when they see me."

"I could have run too. But I didn't."

"Usually I visit the – the houses," he mumbled. "The . . . brothels. But I want girls like you, pretty, *young*, the very ones who can't – can't accommodate my – my size." He sounded very different from the confident man of fifteen minutes before.

She thought: I can handle this. I can make him do anything I want.

One lunchtime, she met Ramirez by chance. He seemed older, dispirited, though his face brightened at the sight of her. He took her into his arms; by twisting her head, she ensured that his kiss touched her lips. She pulled away slowly, gazing up at him with the full force of her big eyes, and felt his grip tighten momentarily on her arms before he let her go.

"Have you time . . .?" He looked at his watch. "Let me buy you lunch."

"All right." Trustingly, she put her hand through his arm.

"It has been too long since we saw you," he said, when they were both seated in a small Italian restaurant.

"I know."

"Marguerite would love to see you. She is not well at the moment, I'm sure she would welcome a visit."

"But Carlos, I must not intrude on your happiness," she said earnestly.

"You know you would not do that," he said. He reached across the table and took both of her hands in his.

"Also . . ." She looked away, biting her lip.

"What, Mercedes?"

". . . I should not say this, but I do not come because – because . . ."

"Because what?" His fingers tightened around hers.

"It's hard for me to explain."

"Please try."

"When I came to the States," she said, not meeting his glance. "It was a – a shock to discover that you were engaged to be married. I had thought that perhaps you and I . . ."

He was silent.

"Oh dear," she said. Under the brim of her hat, she flushed. "Now I have embarrassed you. And myself. Let's change the subject."

"Mercedes," he said.

She began to talk brightly of a forthcoming exhibition, of a charity function at the Museum of Modern Art. After a while she pulled her hands from his. Under the table, she felt his knee gently touch hers and stay there for the rest of the meal.

Marguerite did not seem happy to see her. Mercedes, coming into the crowded house with its pervading smell of souring milk, could not help contrasting her own cool elegance with the tousled appearance that was becoming habitual to Ramirez' wife. On her shoulder Marguerite carried a fretful Amador; her eyes, behind the glasses, were red with lack of sleep and her hair did not seem to have been dressed that morning.

"How is the baby?" Mercedes extended a finger in Amador's direction and was glad to find it ignored as the baby slobbered on its mother's shoulder.

"According to the doctor, he has a digestive upset, maybe an allergy to my milk," Marguerite said. Her voice was depressed.

Mercedes laid her long leather gloves carefully across her knee and tried not to think of the baby's hungry little mouth fastened to Marguerite's inadequate breasts, drawing sustenance from them. Her own were still sore from Schleeman's manhandling of her two nights earlier, as were the tops of her thighs where his brutal hands had pulled her wider, wider, before he forced his way inside her. Although he begged for more, she limited her visits to no more than once a week. She made sure he realised how uncomfortable his huge size made her; she did not tell him that the feeling of being filled to overflowing had become unbearably exciting, that she could induce an orgasm in herself merely by remembering the slow inexorability of the way he entered her, the ruthless push up her vagina, the invasion of her womb which left no room for any other feeling than that of being totally occupied . . . The actuality, however, left her cold; it was something she merely endured.

"Nothing serious, I hope," she said. Soon, she would make her move; Schleeman was hooked. Already he had begun to keep his side of their bargain; the names of her three protégés had begun to appear in the magazines and art columns with increasing frequency. Without telling Rabat, she had taken on another, paying him herself from money which Schleeman gave her each time he slept with her.

"I don't think so," Marguerite said helplessly.

"*You* don't look terribly well."

"It's lack of sleep. I'm perfectly all right, otherwise."

But Marguerite did not seem healthy. Her face was pale, her posture defeated.

Blanche came in. Seeing the Spanish girl, she stopped short in the doorway, before coming forward to put an arm protectively around her sister's shoulders.

"Have you come for anything particular?" she asked rudely.

"I came to see Marguerite," Mercedes said, emphasising the name.

"And now you've seen her?"

"I should very much like a cup of coffee, if such a thing is available, and a chance to find how she is."

"Your eyes will tell you," Blanche said, her tone belligerent.

Mercedes smoothed her gloves and smiled secretively.

"Blanche, please . . ." Distressed, Marguerite glanced from one to the other. "Mercedes is our guest. Could you ask them in the kitchen to send up coffee for us all?" She looked uncertainly at the smart grey two-piece Mercedes was wearing and then down at her own house-dress. "And perhaps Nanny could come and take Amador for a while."

"I'll take him." Blanche almost snatched the baby from her sister and went to the door. "Sit down and rest."

When she had gone, Marguerite smiled nervously. "I'm probably a little over-tired at the moment. Did Carlos tell you we're expecting again?"

"My God. You didn't waste any time, did you?" She thought: No wonder he seems defeated, coming home each night to a wife who looks like this.

"You know how men are," said Marguerite, though,

230

thought Mercedes scornfully, she herself could not possibly know.

"He should take better care of you," she said. "The baby's what – six months old?"

"Five."

"It's too much. It's like some primitive tribe of savages. Surely he could have waited a little before putting you through another pregnancy."

"I wanted it too," Marguerite said. "I'm – I'm very happy."

"You don't look it."

"Amador is teething – it makes him a little fretful."

"Why don't you let Nanny deal with him?"

"I couldn't do that. Carlos and I feel very strongly that children need their parents' attention."

"Easy for Carlos to say. I don't suppose he's the one getting up at night to feed the baby."

"He's very – "

"Nor the one who gets pregnant."

Mercedes sat back as Blanche returned. There were spots of colour in Marguerite's pale cheeks.

Blanche looked from one to the other. "What've you been saying?" she demanded of Mercedes.

"Nothing at all. Merely expressing a certain amount of surprise that Carlos should have allowed Marguerite to start another baby when she so clearly hasn't fully recovered from the last one."

"What on earth does it have to do with you?"

"I speak merely as an old friend of the family."

"Not of our family."

"Quite right. But Carlos and I have known each other

231

all our lives. There was even a time when he – " Deliberately Mercedes broke off the sentence and lowered her eyelashes.

"He married Marguerite," Blanche said harshly.

"And I'm sure he's extremely happy with his choice."

Marguerite made a small distressed sound and Blanche immediately jumped up and joined her sister, putting both arms around her. "Can't you see what she's doing?" she demanded. "Can't you see how each time she comes here she tries to undermine your position with Carlos?" She stared through her glasses at Mercedes, her face flushed, her curly hair indignant, then shook her sister. "Carlos loves you, Marguerite. You know he does."

Quietly Marguerite began to cry. "How can he?" she whispered. "I'm so hopeless, so inadequate. I can't seem to cope with anything at the moment . . ."

"That's perfectly natural," said Blanche. "He knows that. He understands."

"And I look so terrible, so unattractive . . ."

"You do not." Over her sister's bowed shoulders Blanche glared at Mercedes. "You're a little exhausted at the moment, that's all."

"Carlos wants – wants – and I can't . . . I'm not able . . ."

"We'll talk about it another time," Blanche said hastily.

As coffee arrived, Mercedes thought cruelly: he wants sex. He wants to do things to her she shrinks from. It's me, he wants, you foolish woman. He wants *me*.

13

TESS

Terror is as compulsive as any drug. Confronting it,
wallowing in it, relishing the way the stomach churns,
the palms sweat, the balls shrivel – then kicking it in the
teeth. That's the sweetest high of them all.

> *Fear is the Spur*, by I. C. Sanyoshi,
> translated by Teresa Lovel

A solicitor's letter arrived, containing a copy of Jonas's
Will. He had not been a poor man: the bulk of his estate
– money, stocks, investments – went to Hansl. There
were bequests to various institutions with which he had
been connected; comfortable provision had been made
for Kate.

A substantial lump sum, together with the house and
its contents, except for a few named pieces of family
furniture from Vienna, were left to Tess. Once probate
had been granted and any outstanding fees had been paid,
she was free to dispose of them as she wished. Reading
the dry legalese, she found herself weeping. She missed
Jonas dreadfully; for years he had been the only parent
she had known. In addition, he had provided the last link

with her mother, a conduit through which she might one day be able to resolve her as-yet-unexpressed grief for that stupendous loss.

What could she do with a house so redolent of his ebullient persona? How could she bear to live there herself without him? Yet, equally, how could she possibly sell what was in effect all of him that was left? And why did she feel so strongly that there was still some task left uncompleted, that as he always had, he was presenting her with a choice and leaving her to decide for herself which way to go?

Frowning, she dialled the number of the direct line to Don Pedro's desk. Martin García picked it up, his voice warming when he realised who it was.

"Tess," he said. "How's it going? Ever get any further on those suspect paintings?"

Since hearing of Jonas's death, she had not given a thought to the Cramir collection or the possible fakes it contained. She said now: "I need some help."

"Anything at all that I can do . . ."

"Did you read about the death of the potter, Jonas Fedor?"

"Vaguely. In Andalusia, wasn't it?"

"Martin, Jonas Fedor was my – my guardian."

He stopped short. "Tess. I'm so sorry. I hadn't realised."

"And there's something a little off about it. He's supposed to have suffered a heart attack and fallen down a cliff into a ravine. I wouldn't have questioned it except that, as far as I can make out, it took place somewhere he would have had difficulty getting to unless he walked there." She swallowed. "And Jonas couldn't walk very

234

far: his health wasn't good enough any more."

"What do you want me to do?"

"I've telephoned the Embassy three times and each time they say they have no further details. The Banco must have local connections: I wondered if you knew anyone who could find out more about it."

"Leave it with me," he said. "I'll see what I can do and get back to you."

"Thanks."

She returned to the solicitor's letter: it requested that she call in person at the firm's offices at her earliest convenience, in order to clear up matters still outstanding.

They would have to wait. The wound of Jonas's loss was still too raw; she needed time for it to heal. Thinking of him again, as she did almost obsessively, of his kindnesses, his gifts, her thoughts led eventually to the Vicente picture she had bought at the auction and then on to the still unacknowledged debt she owed Don Pedro.

Uncomfortably reminded of it, she tried to call Martin back but the line was busy. She had already attempted to call Don Pedro himself but there was never any reply from his home.

There was another of the frail blue envelopes from M. Aragon in New York. Opening it, she read:

I am more than willing to pay whatever you think is reasonable for *The Tears She Shed*. Since it is one of Vicente's masterpieces, I appreciate that you will not wish to let it go for less than the market value. Would £200,000 seem a fair price? I need not remind you that since I once owned it, and only sold it to Jonas Fedor on the strict understanding that I should have first refusal if he wished to resell, I do have some moral claim to it.

M. Aragon.

£200,000? It was a huge sum, far more than the picture could possibly be worth. And who was this person who would not take no for an answer? For years Tess had carried around inside her, like a flat lake, an emotion which she was only just beginning to realise was anger; she had schooled herself to keep it under control but she felt it rising now, impossible to hold in check. Jonas's death had acted on it like a gale, whipping up the calm surface of her inheld rage; the arrogance of the New York dealer threatened to turn it into a tidal wave.

About to dash off a letter of refusal, she noted the numbers at the top of the page and instead dispatched a furious fax, making it clear that nothing M. Aragon could offer would induce her to part with the painting. Particularly, she added, in view of the fact that the Aragon Gallery had sold an identical painting to Phil Cramir, which by the terms of his Will had been returned to them.

She could not resist smiling at the dig.

There were other letters. One, from Jonas's publisher, said what a deep personal loss his death had been and added that though they understood how difficult things must be for her at the moment, they would much appreciate receiving the manuscript of Jonas's memoirs as soon as possible, especially since not only had he been paid a large advance but there was also considerable interest being shown in New York.

Which reminded her . . .

She dialled another number, and asked for Emma Lybrand. She and Emma had met at the Courtauld; the attraction between them was one of opposites. In complete contrast to Tess's cool composure and efficiency, Emma was scatter-brained, untidy, impulsive, one of a large network of exuberant relations. She shared a flat near Battersea Park with her brother, and for some years had been involved in an on-again-off-again relationship with Josh, an architect with a passion for tidiness, minimalism and hang-gliding. Every now and then, Emma's slapdash habits would exasperate him beyond bearing and they would split up, only to come tempestuously together again shortly afterwards.

"Em," she said, when the phone was breathlessly answered.

"Tess." A pause. "I heard about Jonas. I'm so terribly sorry. I meant to write but – "

"I'm not ringing about that. I wondered if you knew anything about a New York dealer – the Aragon Gallery."

"It rings vague bells. What do you want to know?"

"What sort of an operation it is, whether there's anything dodgy about it, what sort of stuff it specialises in, anything, really, you can find out."

"I'll see what I can do. And – I'm really heartbroken about Jonas, love."

"Thanks, Em."

Jonas's death preoccupied her.

There was something odd about it, she was sure. And there was the strangely valedictory tone of his birthday note. Had he had some kind of warning? Or did he suspect that he might be in danger if he went to Montalbán? What

237

was the 'unfinished business' he had spoken of? She tried to visualise his last moments: the heat, the low wall and the deep gulley beyond, the first intimations of pain. Would someone about to suffer a heart attack or a stroke really tumble backwards, or would they double over, clutching at their chest? Was the cliff absolutely sheer beyond this wall, or were there some inches of ground before the rocks fell away into space?

She drove out to his house, parking in front of the whitewashed spider-crammed outbuildings, doomed now never to become mushroom farm or Jacuzzi but to sink slowly back into the earth upon which they had been built. Unless, of course, she herself did something with them – but it was too soon to think about such things.

Kate was in the kitchen, staring out of the window at the woods, her hands resting on the table. It was the first time Tess had ever seen the older woman idle. She put her arms around her and for a moment the two stood together, weeping, not speaking. Then Kate, drawing back, wiped her eyes.

"Some people don't leave a hole at all when they go," she said, moving things around unnecessarily on the dresser, stacking up the correspondence which Tess would take home and deal with later. "But he's left a space I doubt'll ever be filled. Not for me, at any rate."

"Nor for me," Tess said, seeing that with Jonas's death, Kate's occupation had gone. She looked round the familiar kitchen and blew her nose. "I'd really love a cup of tea."

The housekeeper brightened. "What am I thinking about?" she said, and began to bustle, while Tess pulled out a chair and sat down.

"Kate," she said. "Did Jonas say anything to you about . . ." – it sounded ridiculous – ". . . about some danger threatening him? Did anything unusual happen just before he died?"

"What sort of thing?" Kate measured tea leaves from a Fedor lidded pot glazed with cobalt and grey and decorated with a single leaf in the oriental style.

"That's just it: I don't know." Tess made a helpless gesture. "Did he get mysterious phone calls or anonymous letters? Did he . . . um . . . keep having odd accidents? Was there anyone hanging about outside?"

Kate had been shaking her head. Now she looked up. "As a matter of fact, there was something," she said. "A couple of things."

"Like what?"

"There was this car one evening. Grey, it was, almost invisible. Jonas was away and I was just turning on the outside lights – it was starting to get dark – when I saw it parked out there in the back lane." She looked doubtful. "Doesn't sound very dangerous, does it?"

"Was there anyone in it?"

"I couldn't see. And it could have been somebody stopping to look at a map or have a pee or something, couldn't it?"

"Was that all?"

"Well . . ." Kate folded her arms across her chest. "I wouldn't even have remembered it if I hadn't seen what looked like the same car a few days later, driving slowly past the front of the house."

"Did you see the driver?"

"Only that it was a man, youngish, fairish hair. And that there was someone in the back. I couldn't see who

239

that was at all. I didn't say anything to Jonas; there didn't seem much point."

"Did you notice the licence plate?"

"No."

"Did you mention it to Jonas?"

"No."

Drinking her tea, Tess thought about it. "Anything else?"

"There were a couple of letters just before he died," Kate said slowly.

"What kind of letters?"

"Airmail. With foreign stamps."

"Where from?"

"One was from New York, that I do remember, since my niece lives there."

"Was the other one from Spain?"

"Could have been. I had a kind of impression of somewhere sunny and abroad."

"Were they from the same person?"

"Sorry, Tess. I just don't remember. That foreign handwriting all looks the same to me. But Jonas certainly wasn't best pleased by them. You know how he was when something made him angry; banging about and shouting and throwing things."

Involuntarily both women smiled. Jonas had never been one to hide his emotions.

"He didn't say anything about what was in them?" asked Tess.

"Nothing. But after the second one came, he went up to London." Kate pursed her mouth. "I knew he was up to something."

"How do you mean?"

"You knew him as well as I did, Tess. He had that kind of look in his eye, when he wasn't telling the truth. Or not telling *all* the truth."

"I see."

"And it was right after that he decided to go to Spain." Kate's eyes filled with tears again.

"Have the solicitors been in touch with you?"

Kate began to weep. "Yes. He was so good to me, always so good, so kind. I don't know how I'm going to go on without him, really I don't." Her shoulders shook. "Never have to worry . . . always said he'd see I was all right . . . all that money . . . I never expected . . ."

"Then you know," Tess said gently, "that he left the house to me."

"Yes, and who better?" sniffled Kate. "Like a daughter to him . . . loved you like his own . . . best thing he could do, considering . . ."

"It'll take months before everything's settled. I'm hoping you'll stay on for the time being. Obviously we'd – the estate would continue to pay your wages," Tess said, knowing that Kate would refuse to accept money if she thought Tess herself would be footing the bill. "Meanwhile, would you mind if I stayed here tonight? Someone's going to have to make a start on his papers and things."

"Course I wouldn't. And it's your place to do with as you want." Kate wiped her eyes vigorously. "I'll make something nice for your supper." She moved into domestic murmurings, obviously cheered by having someone to look after.

That evening, Tess sat down at Jonas's desk. The faded velvet curtains were drawn across the windows and the doors leading out into the little garden; the cosy firelit room was full of memories. Forcing herself to concentrate, not to think about the irrecoverable past, she pulled down the desk-lid.

Then stared in surprise. And some unease.

Instead of the clutter she had expected, she found nothing in the pigeon holes, nothing in the three little drawers.

She frowned. In the past she had so often seen Jonas pull the lid of the desk half open and toss in the latest batch of unwanted mail, then struggle to close it against the crush of letters already in there. What had happened to them all? She turned round.

Kate, knitting in an armchair by the fire, was looking at her over her spectacles. "He cleared it out himself, a couple of days before he went off," she said. "Burned it all."

"But why?" Tess tried to imagine Jonas going through the mass of discarded paper and found it impossible. "It's just not the sort of thing he would have done."

"I don't know. I asked him but he almost snapped my head off."

"You don't think he could have burned his autobiography too, do you?"

"Heavens, no. Ever so pleased with it, he was. Said it was going to be a bestseller. Why would he burn it?"

"I had a letter from the publisher, asking where it was. And so far I haven't come across it. And you'd have mentioned it if you had."

Kate put down her knitting. "That's odd. The publisher hasn't got it?"

"That's what she said."

"But that day he went up to London, he had it with him, I know he did. In a plastic carrier; I remember distinctly. He said he was going to take it in himself, said it was just about finished and there were only a couple of things he'd have to add when he got back from Spain. Wherever could it have got to?"

"I'll check with the publishers again. Perhaps they've made a mistake."

"That's probably it, pet," Kate said comfortably.

Tess sat thinking. Quite apart from the manuscript, if Jonas had tidied his desk, there had to be a reason. What was it? What had he known, or seen, or suspected, that could have caused him to behave in so uncharacteristic a manner? And where were the foreign letters which Kate had mentioned?

She pulled out the two big drawers below the desk-lid. The top one was entirely empty; the second held only a file of charcoal sketches and an envelope containing a folded piece of writing paper.

She spread the sketches in front of her on the green and gilded leather of the writing surface. As she took them in, her sense of some pattern outside her comprehension deepened. Surely these were the work of Fernando Vicente; although she was not a professional expert, as with the painting of the *Casa de las Lunas*, she knew enough about his style, his technique, the way he shaded a cheekbone or suggested the fullness beneath an eyebrow. Some of them were even familiar: she recognised what must be a rough version of Vicente's famous self-portrait, and a girl who could have been a preliminary study for *The Tears She Shed*. Remembering the sketch of Jonas which had hung – still did, for that matter – in

Phil Cramir's underground gallery, she wondered where and how Jonas had obtained these sketches. And why, knowing her own passion for the Spanish painter, he had never mentioned them.

She picked up the airmail letter. The postmark on the envelope indicated that it had been mailed three weeks ago in New York. She turned to Kate.

"Is this one of the letters you mentioned?" she asked.

Kate squinted at it then nodded. "I think it was." She nibbled at the inside of her lip. "I'm beginning to think the other letter was definitely from Spain, from Madrid, though I could just be persuading myself, with hindsight . . ."

Tess opened the folded paper. It was a note only a few lines long, typed in English, which said simply:

Against all advice, the Montalbán scheme is going ahead – we must finally move. After so many years, I'd hoped it wouldn't come to this.

I can guarantee the Vicentes. There's a Castán, too, and a de León, all from the same source. It's a pity about Felipe – but we'll have to go on without him. Time has run out.

But take care, my friend. You know how dangerous the enemy is, and how determined.

Vaya con dios.

It was signed with the initials A. R.

Tess stared at it; questions hummed like bees. Was this the same A. R. who had signed the wrongly attributed *Casa de las Lunas*? If so – and it seemed too much of a coincidence to think that it was not – how did he know

244

Jonas? What did the note mean? And who was Felipe? The name was Spanish – was that why Jonas had gone to Spain? Why did the note refer to a Castán, and a de León, two of the painters in the Cramir collection she herself had identified as fakes, while at the same time guaranteeing the Vicentes? *Which* Vicentes? If it meant the ones in the Cramir collection, did that mean that her own picture of *The Tears She Shed* was not, after all, genuine? And what did any of it have to do with Jonas?

She looked over at Kate; she seemed absorbed in her knitting. Slowly, guiltily (*May salamanders swallow me, Dragons devour me . . .*) she pulled out one of the drawers and pressed the hidden switch she knew lay at the back. The secret drawer slid open.

The silver heart was no longer there; the faded flower had gone. Only a few pieces of paper remained. She took them out; the top one was the picture she had drawn for Jonas years ago. The wounds inflicted on him by the driving instructors were still fresh; the pool of blood still red. Why had he kept it? Tears filled her eyes; she wanted to weep for the child she had been but dared not, for if she started she might lose control and never stop.

Beneath the picture were two more pieces of cartridge paper; the top one was another Vicente, this time a sketch of a young man, dark-eyed and handsome, vaguely familiar. She turned it over with careful fingers—and found herself staring at another face, a face she knew only too well.

Nausea flared in her belly. Her hands trembled; in the depths of her brain, her dragons strained at their golden leashes; the white chrysanthemum petals hissed like serpents. Repugnance, disgust, loathing threatened to overwhelm her. For a moment she closed her eyes, emptying her mind, breathing deeply. Instinctively she knew that the two sketches meant something significant – but what? Before she could further examine any of these new facts, information needed digesting, interpreting; courage would have to be mustered.

Unable to bear looking at the sketch again, she turned it over and was about to thrust it and its companion back into the secret drawer when she saw something else, pushed right to the back. It gleamed dully; even before it lay cold and heavy in her palm, she realised it was a gun.

As she opened her front door, the telephone rang. As always, a microsecond of memory flickered as she relived what had been, for her, the definitive telephone call: a winter wind flashed across her mind, wet mud, Jonas padding across a kitchen . . . She picked it up.

Martin's voice. "Hi. Glad I got you."

"Any news?"

"Not much. They're really being cagey on this one, for some reason. But I gather Fedor showed up in Montalbán about five days before he was found, and that's really all the police know – or so they say. He would go out each morning and not return until late at night, so it wasn't until a couple of days had gone by without anyone laying eyes on him that they thought to wonder where he might have got to. And even then, it was only pure chance that one of the local farmers happened to be searching for a lost goat or something and actually looked over the wall of this abandoned *cortijo* and saw his rucksack lying on a ledge half-way down. He called the police and they eventually found his body at the bottom of the ravine there."

"I see." Don't even ask what several days lying in the heat might have done to him, or what damage had been inflicted by predators while, in the soft air above, the goat bells knocked . . .

"Otherwise he might have been there for weeks." Martin's voice changed slightly. "The odd thing, Teresa – "

"Yes?"

" – I think you're right, there *is* something funny about it." He waited a heartbeat or two. "What did your guardian do?"

"I told you: he was a potter, a well-known potter."

"I don't mean now, I mean back then, years ago, when he was in Spain."

"I've no idea. He never said. Why?" Tess dragged a hand across her face as though she could wipe the images of death away.

"A couple of things. For one thing, they seem to know who he is – "

"I told you, he's a – "

" – and I don't mean because he's famous as a potter. I mentioned my grandfather and got through to someone very high up in the military. He actually consulted a file on him, dating back to before the war. He seemed to think that was what I was enquiring about. He shut up like a clam when he realised it wasn't. I only got on to him because I couldn't get any satisfaction from the Montalbán people though we'd expect full co-operation on something like this from the local police. They say that as far as they're concerned, they're satisfied as to what happened and the case is officially closed."

Tess realised that she was holding the receiver so tightly that her hand was hurting. She gritted her teeth. "Well, isn't that just too bad. Because I'm going to open it up again. I want to know how Jonas got up to this wall he's supposed to have fallen over, whether he saw anyone while he was out there, what he was doing. He certainly wasn't there for a walking holiday, whatever they say."

"You don't mean you're going to go out to Spain yourself?" Martin said.

"You bet I am." She remembered the impulsive suggestion she had made to Julian Maitland about coming to visit him. She was not going to let Jonas go without seeing that justice had been done. Someone should find out what had really happened to him and why. She owed him that much – she owed him infinitely more than that.

"Are you sure you know what you're doing?" asked Martin uneasily.

"No." She swallowed, taking a decision, setting her feet on a path which led for her only into a haunted darkness. "But that's not going to stop me."

She found she was shaking. Her palms were wet with sweat and there was more of it on her forehead. Montalbán. It crouched at the centre of her brain, unseen and unknown, yet all too terrifyingly real.

She knew she was not going only on behalf of Jonas. Montalbán was inextricably linked with her own past, the years she had not yet properly faced. And there was also the memory of a white face on a bridge, an urgent voice, a cold wind blowing. *You will make the house happy again,* her mother had said . . . But could she? Did she have the strength? Did she have the will?

"You still there, Tess?" Martin sounded alarmed. "Tess?"

"Jonas – my guardian – was a good man," she said fiercely. "And if someone – " The words choked her. She breathed in through her nose. "Listen, Martin. I'm going formally to request a leave of absence from the Banco Morena. Don Pedro won't mind."

There was a silence. Then Martin said quietly: "Good luck, Teresa."

Putting down the receiver, she wiped the sweat from her forehead. Her world had always been built on quicksand, except when Jonas was near. Now, she felt it shift beneath her feet; around her ears, chill winds howled.

She had been staring at *The Tears She Shed* for hours. Because of the adrenaline still pumping through her system, she saw it tonight with an altered perception. This evening the dark-eyed gaze of the girl on the edge of the bed was full of terror, the shadowed figure advancing from the left was clearly not her rescuer but her ravisher. The glass beads took on a new significance, not a rosary but a necklace of tears strung on a silver rope. Who was she? Who had she been? Could she, as Tess had half decided, have grown into the woman Jonas was supposed to have once loved? She'd asked him about her only days before he left for Spain, but he had refused to talk about it. They had been tramping across the fields behind his house and were making their way back along the sodden bank of the river to where Kate waited with hot tea and anchovy toast.

"Some things are better left alone," he had said, his

face unaccustomedly stern in the red light of a setting winter sun.

"But it happened so long ago that it can't matter now," said Tess.

He turned to look at her. "Teresa, Teresa," he said, shaking his head. "How can you possibly know that?"

"But surely – "

"Besides, by now you should have learned this: that sometimes the things which happened in the past matter more as time goes by, not less." He had raised his gloved finger and stroked her cheek. "Is it not so?"

How much did he know? She had looked away, over the cold plough towards unleafed woods. "Perhaps," she had said, knowing that he spoke only the truth.

He stopped beside the swirling river, full now with the winter rains, and poked with his stick at a tangle of reed and twig and mouldering leaf caught in the roots of a willow. "It is human nature to absorb the good things but to allow the wrongs done to fester and grow monstrous. Even when they have been forgiven, they are never forgotten."

"So there was a wrong done?" she said quickly. "Was it the woman you loved?"

He had chuckled. "You will not catch me out this way, Teresa. I shall say no more." Nor had he. They had continued their walk in silence.

Tess thought again of the picture of the Casa de las Lunas and the gateposts with their beaten copper symbols. If she went to Montalbán, she would be able to see them for herself, could actually push open the gates and walk up the steep slope of the drive to hammer at the front door.

What would happen then? What would it be like to look into the eyes of the woman whom Conchita – her stepdaughter – had hated so much that, twenty-nine years before, she had left the house with a new-born baby in her arms, and never returned?

14

TESS

If the plan is approved by our investors, it would involve over two hundred million pounds of long-term investment, and up to two and a half thousand jobs in an area of chronic unemployment.

Proposal Document, the Hayashima Corporation, translated from the Japanese by Teresa Lovel

"What do you think?" Tess said.

"It certainly looks like a Vicente," Dominic said cautiously. He bent his long frame for another examination of the painting of the Casa de las Lunas, lying flat on a table in front of him.

"You can be more specific than that, can't you?"

"I've never set myself up as an expert on the man."

"But you're writing a book about him."

"A chapter. No more than that."

"So you must know a bit more than the average person."

He turned an unsmiling face to her. "About Vicente? Yes. I think you could definitely say that."

She frowned. "What do you mean?"

"Oof!" Dominic straightened up, pressing both fists into the small of his back. "I'm getting old," he said. "It's high time I got married and started a family. Don't you agree, Tess?"

"Don't try and put me off, Dominic. Why did you say you knew more than the average person about Vicente?"

"Because it's true," he protested.

"No." She looked at him consideringly. "You meant more than that."

"Did I?"

Perhaps he had, perhaps not. Either way, he was not going to explain himself. She turned back to the painting. "Is it or is it not a Vicente?"

"In my opinion . . ." Dominic said. He paused. "If you'll go to bed with me, I'll swear on the Bible it is."

"Dominic . . ."

"Seriously, I don't think there's any doubt. As you saw yourself, what looks like the proper signature's been carefully painted over. And the style is really unmistakable. Yeah: I'll stake my rep – whatever that's worth – on it being by the man himself."

"That's wonderful!"

He bit his lip. He thought: If she only knew how I feel about her. When she looked at him like that he wanted to crush her in his arms, kiss her until she melted against him. He knew what her response would be if he tried. Why he should have fallen in love with this feisty, wounded, self-contained woman was a complete mystery to him. His sister, Valentine, called it the desire of the star for the moth. Tess was no moth, however, but a butterfly, a gorgeous hummingbird, still waiting to spread her wings and fly.

"Since I've authenticated your picture for you, you owe me one," he said. "So have dinner with me before you go."

"Well . . ." Tess tried not to sound as reluctant as she felt. Dominic had grown suddenly enigmatic; secrets drifted behind his eyes. She could not help recalling her doubts about his presence in her house the night she was attacked. But for the moment, the focus of her life had shifted from Cambridge to southern Spain; she did not want distractions. Least of all distractions like Dominic, who pulled her towards him like a whirlpool in which she could very easily drown.

"Come on, Tess," he said. "After all, this may be the last time I ever see you, if it's as dangerous as you make out."

"All right then. Tomorrow?"

"Fine." There was a pause. She looked so vulnerable that he wanted to wrap his arms round her like a shield. Despite the cool composure with which she faced the world he was sometimes shockingly aware of the turbulence she tried so hard to hide. He remembered her above him, naked on the staircase, magnificent, and swallowed. "And I promise not to call you 'darling'," he added lightly.

Her dark eyes were grave. "Good."

She grasped the leather handle of her briefcase a fraction tighter as she followed Don Pedro's assistant into his office. The Banco's porter came behind to lean the two paintings she had brought with her against the wall.

The room was familiar to her from other meetings. Though his assistant's office was crammed with fax machines, computers, personal modems and a bank of telephones, there was no sign in here of the modern technology which Don Pedro needed to conduct the day-to-day business of the bank. Outside the windows, metal and glass reared upward from the London pavements, symbols of the greedy Eighties when money ruled and most moral values had sunk out of sight. Inside, she might have been in the audience chamber of some mediaeval Spanish castle. Dark wooden panelling rose almost to ceiling height; a stone fireplace, its vast space filled with an elaborate arrangement of dried flowers, occupied one end of the room. Above it, a portrait of a man in black velvet and a white lace ruff dominated while other less imposing portraits hung here and there.

A desk was set diagonally on a faded Aubusson rug; leather chairs stood at intervals about the room; two massive candelabra of branching wrought iron loomed on either side of the fireplace. On a small Sheraton-style table stood a number of photographs in silver frames. Otherwise, the large room was empty. Behind the desk, a window gave onto one of those small prized courtyards which exist secretly at the heart of the City. Behind rippled glass, a plane tree spread generous branches; they were bare now, but in summer would be leafy, casting a green glow into the room.

Don Pedro rose quickly from his desk and came forward to greet her. Although he was no longer a young man, he was still conventionally handsome, dressed in a double-breasted suit of navy-blue and a very white shirt. Only his expensive silk tie, hand-blocked in swirling shades of peach and melon and raspberry, hinted at a different persona behind the official formality.

"My poor Teresa," he said. "Are you all right? After

such a devastating shock as you have suffered, it would not be surprising if you were not." He waved at the high-backed chair in front of his desk. "Please . . ."

Tess sat down. "And you, Don Pedro? Are you fully recovered?"

"Thank you, yes. And I have good news, too, which has speeded my recovery." Failing to keep the pride from his face, he picked up one of the silver-framed photographs and held it out to her. "My daughter has just announced her engagement."

"Congratulations, Don Pedro. What's he like?"

"From a most distinguished family. He's something high-ranking in the diplomatic corps and now that they are engaged, we hardly dare breathe in case we do something which will jeopardise Juan's chances of becoming an Ambassador!"

"I'm delighted for you."

He said gently: "What did you wish to speak to me about?"

She began to open her briefcase. "First of all, I've had no response so far to the report I submitted concerning the Phil Cramir collection."

Don Pedro held up his hand. "Teresa, please. I would much rather you did not feel you had to bother with working matters at such a time."

"That's all right," Tess said. "There are other things, too. With regard to the Cramir collection, I wasn't able to speak to anyone at the Aragon Gallery in New York. But someone else – other than me, I mean – should take a look at those paintings for which the Banco is responsible: I don't want the doubts about their validity to rest entirely on my judgement."

"Why not?"

"Well . . ." Tess gave a nervous little laugh. "Suppose I'm wrong. Someone must go over there soon, and give a second assessment before we make any kind of accusation."

"I have to admit I haven't yet read this report of yours."

She smiled at him. "There's also the Sanchez you asked me to buy."

"Good heavens." He registered surprise. "I'd completely forgotten about it."

"Forgotten?" she said, exaggerating her astonishment. "Your Sanchez?"

"There've been other more important things to deal with. And I've been off sick for so long. Then the Hayashima plans have taken up a huge amount of time. And of course . . ." He glanced a little sheepishly at the silver-framed photographs. "This is the season for charity balls."

"You really are a terrible snob," Tess said indulgently. She found Don Pedro's unabashed liking for the company of the rich and famous childishly endearing and tended to tease him about the photographs, which she called his Celebrity Collection.

"I know, Teresa." Don Pedro spread his hands and looked abject. "You must forgive an old man his weaknesses."

"I can forgive the way you lick the boots of the aristocracy," Tess said. "It's your admiration for Sanchez I just can't stomach."

Don Pedro laughed. "Show me my picture," he commanded.

She did, and told him how much she had paid. He gazed at it in silence, nodding with satisfaction. Then he said: "And the other?"

"Ah, yes. The other." Quickly she unwrapped the Vicente – the supposed Vicente. Seeing it again, she was seized with sudden doubt, despite Dominic's assurance that it was genuine and the overheard conversation at the auction which seemed to confirm his opinion. Had she made a terrible mistake? She held the painting up so that Morena could see it. "Look."

He did so. He picked up the gold fountain pen lying beside the papers on his desk and turned it around in his fingers. For some moments he stared at the painted sunshine, the fantastical tree, the flowing colours, tapping his teeth slowly with the pen. That it was beautiful, he could not deny. More than beautiful. The way the shadows moved behind those solid gateposts emphasised precisely their lack of solidity; the brilliance of leaf and flower merely reminded the viewer of how soon leaf would fall, colour would fade. Was it only a view of a house, or did it say something deeper about the malaise of Spain itself at the time it was painted?

"What do you think?" Tess said.

His reaction surprised her. "Why have you brought it to me?" he said. "Why should you imagine I would want it?"

"Well . . ." She sensed that he was both angered and, for some reason, apprehensive.

He peered at the painted signature. "What is it? Who painted it? Why did you bring it here?"

Tess had the impression that for some reason, although he recognised the artist perfectly well, he was playing for time. There was silence for a moment. The gold pen rotated, catching the light from the window. Behind the wavy glass was the cold grey sky of London, leafless branches, the upper storeys of mirrored citadels to wealth. On the other side of the door a telephone shrilled and was abruptly cut off.

Suddenly hesitant, realising she had grossly misjudged Don Pedro's reaction, Tess said: "While I was at the auction I saw this. I – uh – I was sure you'd have wanted me to buy it too, had you known it was there."

"Why should I? Who is this AR? I don't recognise the signature."

"That's just it," said Tess. "It's not by AR, whoever he is. I'm absolutely convinced it's a Fernando Vicente. I thought you would be furious if I let it go so I bid for it."

"How much did you pay?"

"Twenty-four thousand."

"And *how* did you pay?"

"I – uh – I used the line of credit you'd arranged in order to obtain the Sanchez."

He looked puzzled. "Let me get this absolutely right, Teresa. Are you saying that you paid twenty-four thousand pounds of my money for a painting by an unknown artist because you thought – without any justification at all – that it was really by Fernando Vicente?"

"Yes."

"But didn't you just tell me you were uncertain whether you were correct in judging some of the Cramir collection to be fakes?"

"That's different." Tess could feel her face redden. Don Pedro was hardly ever severe. "I know Vicente's work. I know this is one of his."

"Then why is it signed . . ." He peered again at the signature. ". . . with someone else's initials?"

"I'm not the only one who thinks there was something odd about it," Tess said, eager to justify what she could now see had been an act of foolish madness. "There was another woman there – she was bidding against me, actually. I heard her afterwards, saying it was a Vicente."

"But she was not prepared to put her money where her mouth was." Don Pedro smiled thinly. "Do you know who she was? A dealer? An agent? Someone whose opinion you could trust?"

"I don't." Tess was aware that she was not doing herself justice. "But she looked like . . . like somebody, if you know what I mean."

"I don't."

Tess hurried on. "I also had it looked at by a – by one of the leading experts in the field, who specialises in Vicente paintings."

"And he is?"

"An historian called Dominic Eliot. He's a specialist on the Spanish Civil War."

"I see." Don Pedro's face was glacial.

"But he's also writing a – a book about Vicente." Tess told herself it was almost true.

"I've never heard of him." Don Pedro said dismissively. He picked up the Vicente again. "In any case, I don't want this picture. It represents a period in my country's history which I prefer to forget. The cruelty, the treachery, the spilled blood . . ."

"But – "

"I do not wish to own this picture. You must find the money for it yourself."

"But I can't afford to – "

He held up a hand to stop her. "Then resell it. I don't need to remind you how serious this matter is. At best, a betrayal of trust. At worst, a breach of confidence if not actual fraud."

He stood and came around his desk again. There was a crescent-shaped scar beside his mouth, another down one side of his face. Parenthetically, she noted that he – or perhaps his barber – had missed a small patch under his ear when shaving that morning. Outside the window, sparrows dipped and chirped in the branches of the plane tree.

He said abruptly: "Why are you so keen on it?"

"As it happens, I was born in this very house," Tess said.

She did not add that the man who had painted the canvas was her link with a past about which she knew almost nothing but which she soon expected to plunge into.

"Vicente was active during the difficult times for my country," Don Pedro said.

"And before them. His first important canvas is dated 1929," said Tess.

"You've obviously done some research." He tried to smile at her, to blot out the severity he had shown earlier, but she was not looking at him.

"It's three or four hundred years since civil war last split this country in two," he continued. "It is barely fifty years since Spain was torn apart by one of the bloodiest wars in history. Certain things happened then . . ." He shook his head. How to explain to her, clever as he knew her to be, sharing some of the same blood as he, just how things had been in Spain? "I was not there, Teresa – my family was already settled in the States by then – but I heard

262

enough about it. The cruelties. The daily atrocities. The butchery . . ."

"If you're talking about the fact that Fernando Vicente was murdered for his political persuasions – " Tess began, her voice sharpening, but he cut across her.

"Fernando Vicente was a coward, a traitor and a pervert."

Tess gasped. "Don Pedro! Surely you can't believe that."

"Most certainly I can." He flipped open the folder on his desk and closed it again.

"But you know as well as I do that it was the usual practice, when they felt particularly guilty about killing someone, to denounce them first as a spy for the other side, and then as sexually undesirable. Exactly the same thing happened to Federico García Lorca, the poet."

"My dear Teresa, are you suggesting that García Lorca was *not* homosexual?"

"No, though I think it's entirely irrelevant. But they tried to suggest he was other things as well, just as you're saying about Vicente."

"Some skeletons are best left undisturbed."

"I think the bones of that particular skeleton have been kicked about too often by too many people to be swept back into their grave," Tess said. "Besides, it's all so long ago, now."

"Perhaps. But in my – *our* – country, it's still very much alive." He patted her hand. "Particularly in the remoter areas. People haven't forgiven or forgotten who was on which side in the Civil War or who betrayed whom." Holding the *Casa de las Lunas* upright, he went on: "Spain is now part of the wider European Community.

We're trying hard to emerge from under the shadow which Franco cast on our country. If we're to survive economically into the twenty-first century, it's essential that we look forward, not back, that we recognise we are a modern country at the end of the final decade of the twentieth century." He gestured at the Vicente. "This . . . for me to take this from you would be a retrograde step. I'm sure you understand."

"Not really." All Tess could think of was Vicente, the little frightened man, his back against a convent wall, the accusing guns pointing, the triggers tightening, and above him, the blue sky of freedom about to turn eternally black. It seemed imperative to stand up for the unheroic figure who had, in the end, proved himself a hero. "Not at all, as a matter of fact. What can be retrograde in such a painting? Quite apart from the intellectual confusion you seem to be making between the man who painted the picture and the times in which he lived, I can't see why owning a Vicente is suddenly going to put Spain back into the nineteenth century."

His face froze. For a moment she saw his ancestors massed behind him, all the haughty armoured nobles he was so proud of, the grandees with their fine thin faces. Despite his talk of the Common Market and twentieth-century democracy, his expression was a direct legacy of eight hundred years of autocratic power.

"In one way you are right," he said. He picked up the painting and thrust it at her. "But please take it away."

She set the painting down again. "It cost a lot of money," she said quietly. "I can't afford to buy it from you for the moment."

"Then perhaps we can come to some kind of an arrangement." He put an arm around her shoulders. "I'm sorry, my dear, if I sounded harsh. There are delicate matters at stake here about which you know nothing. But as we both feel so strongly about it, I have another suggestion to make. As you have pointed out, the painting is legally mine: why don't you borrow it from me for a while?"

"How can I do – "

"View it as a loan. Take it back home with you, and later, when you can pay for it, you will do so."

The arrangement seemed unbusinesslike. However, Tess did not feel inclined to argue. She *wanted* the Vicente, really lusted after it, quite apart from any personal connection with the subject. Besides, it would probably be only a matter of weeks, if not days, before Jonas's Will was probated, and she would be able to write a cheque to Don Pedro for the full amount. Mouth set, she began to repack the Vicente canvas.

"I'm sorry, Teresa."

"I'm the one who should be sorry," she said. "I should never have acted so impulsively. I jumped to entirely the wrong conclusions. I – "

"Why don't you let me buy you a hair-shirt?" he said. "I understand Harrods has them on special offer this week."

In spite of herself, she smiled. The old Don Pedro had reappeared; it was as though a light had been switched on.

"Incidentally," she said. "I'd like to take a couple of weeks off. I hope it won't be inconvenient."

She should be back before the next series of protracted negotiations taking place between the Banco Morena and one of the Japanese electrical giants. It was one of Don Pedro's pet projects; if matters proceeded smoothly, he hoped to persuade the Japanese to site their new manufacturing plant in southern Spain, instead of in Wales as a number of the company's directors wished.

"Take all the time you need, my dear." Don Pedro's kind eyes searched her face. "You seem tired."

"I am. And sad."

"Naturally. You miss Mr Fedor, I'm sure."

"He was more a parent to me than my own parents ever were."

The pen turned in his fingers; the gold casing glinted. "What will you do with yourself: take a holiday?"

"I'm going to Spain." He nodded. "To the place where Jonas died. I want to ask a few questions."

"Of whom?"

"I don't know yet. But there's something bothering me about the whole thing. I just want to get it cleared up."

"Then good luck, Teresa."

The telephone dragged her out of sleep the next morning. Groping for the receiver, she saw that the time was 7:08. "Yes?"

"Teresa?" She recognised Don Pedro's voice.

"Yes."

"We've just received a fax from Tokyo."

"And?" Tess leaned against her pillows.

"The Hayashima people want to move the meeting we had planned for next month forward to the beginning of next week."

There was a silence into which she was expected to jump. After a moment, realising she was not going to,

Don Pedro said apologetically: "You said yesterday that you wanted some time off. I'd appreciate it if you could postpone your trip. We need you at these meetings."

"I'm afraid I can't," Tess said. "I've already booked a ticket and – "

"Naturally the bank would cover any costs you might incur by – "

" – and made arrangements. Friends are expecting me."

"It's important that you attend the new round of negotiations."

"Martin García has sat in on most of the meetings we had with Hayashima. So has Peter Martin-Smith. Both of them are perfectly – "

"But you're the only person who really understood all the ramifications of this particular deal."

"I'm sorry," Tess said.

She realised that this was Don Pedro's way of reassuring her that his annoyance the day before had not affected their relationship, and was grateful. Swiftly, she ran through the details in her head: Martin García would be there, and Sir Peter, a former British Council man who had spent many years in Tokyo. Both of them were highly competent and astute; the negotiations would not be prejudiced if she were not there this time. Besides, the real work was done afterwards, in the palatial suites of the Dorchester or the Savoy where the Japanese liked to stay when in London, where she and Don Pedro had sat for many a long hour, talking of Van Gogh or El Greco, cathedrals in Spain and temples in Japan, cultural differences, anything but the subject at hand, until suddenly, delicately, the mood would change and they would be back on track, making the hard decisions before the next day's talks. Hayashima was a cultured man and chose his aides from western-educated graduates: Japan, despite its global economic success, was still a backward-looking insular country, he would say, and Don Pedro would nod, stretch out his feet to admire his handmade shoes with their rolled laces and thick expensive leather, and say Spain was exactly the same.

"But you know the importance attached to this deal," Don Pedro said sharply. "If we can swing it, I – the Banco, I mean – will rank as a hero in Spain."

It was impossible not to smile. She knew he saw himself in morning dress, besashed, sunbursts of decorations glinting on his breast as he chatted with the top ranks of Spanish nobility: dukes, duchesses, perhaps even the King himself.

"I can't, Don Pedro," she said. "Please understand." He deserved her loyalty, she recognised that. But so did Jonas. And for the moment, Jonas had to come first.

"Have I told you how beautiful you look tonight?" Dominic said.

"Three times."

"I won't bore you by saying it a fourth, then."

Tess smiled at him. "You look beautiful too. But then you usually do."

"In anyone else, I'd take that as a compliment. Maybe even an attempt to flatter."

"But not from me."

"Not from you," he agreed. "You only give praise where it's due. And in my case, not even then."

She laughed.

"Tess – " His face was suddenly serious.

"Is there any more wine?" she said quickly, stopping him from whatever he had been about to say.

He filled her glass. "What I don't understand," he said, "is why you haven't been back to the Casa de las Lunas before."

"I told you: because of my mother's stepmother."

"The old girl can't be as much of an ogre as you think."

"I think she can. My mother loathed her – feared her, too. I've seen her tremble when she talked about Mercedes. I remember her telling me that the woman once beat her so hard that she had to be hospitalised."

"Did you see Jonas on that TV arts programme, after he got the CBE?" asked Dominic.

"Yes."

"He was talking about evil people. Do you think Mercedes Ramirez was one?

"Yes."

"What about Jonas?"

"*What*?"

"Do you think he was evil? Or contained the seeds of evil?"

"Of course I don't. What an extraordinary question."

He leaned towards her and stared into her face with an intensity she had not seen in him before. "Has it ever occurred to you that Jonas was not what you thought him?"

"Never," Tess said, her face reddening with anger.

"Or simply *different* from what you thought him?"

"No. And I wish you'd stop saying such things." She tightened her mouth. "Let's talk about something else."

Deliberately he kept his eyes on her for a long slow second. Then he nodded. "All right. Will you go to your grandfather's house when you're in Montalbán?"

Later, she would wonder at his easy familiarity with the names of her past. Now she said: "I have to. I've never been there, I know nothing about the places or the people, because my mother had broken all the connections. I don't really know what happened all those years ago, but the Casa de las Lunas . . . I dream about the place, even though I've never been there – at least, not since the day I was born. It's become a kind of – of dragon's den for me. I have to go there. I have no choice."

"Even though you're obviously terrified of what you'll find?"

"Yes."

He put his hand over hers, gently stroked her fingers. "Are you the virgin waiting to be devoured?" he asked. "Or the knight in shining armour?"

"Maybe both," she said.

"I could come with you," Dominic said. "I've got to put in some time at Montalbán, in connection with the proposal for the book. And the Vicente Museum is finally opening this summer, after years of delay. So why shouldn't I go now? We could travel together."

"No."

He thought: I wish my imagination were less painterly, less vivid. I wish I didn't always see her spread before me like a picture, a white sheet under that amazing body, the linen creases meticulously in place as they are in paintings by the Flemish masters. I wish I didn't dream of the way breast and hip would curve under my hands, the colour of her nipples, the precise shade of her petalled skin. A blush heated the skin of his chest. *If she knew what I was thinking* . . .

The restaurant – The Orangery – was a place of potted palms and white wicker furniture set inside a glass conservatory. Mozart drifted unobtrusively; knives and forks clinked among quiet conversations; the food was superb. Even though she was leaving, he felt absurdly happy.

When he kissed her goodnight, guilt at turning down his offer to accompany her had lowered her defences. She leaned into his kiss, imagined his hands holding her breasts, his mouth slowly moving down her body . . . Breathless, she felt a fatal longing; she closed her eyes under his urgent mouth.

"Oh, God, Tess," he whispered and she pulled back, afraid.

There had to be something more civilised between lovers than mere physical attraction, didn't there? Sex alone was not enough: there had to be compatibility as well. And she ignored the tiny voice deep inside her brain which wondered why, in that case, making love with Henry had left earths unmoved and rivers unstopped in their courses.

15

MERCEDES

They named the new child Concepción. Paying a duty visit, Mercedes looked down at a second Ramirez baby in its crib and thought how insensitive a choice of name it was. The image of her own friend, white-thighed, shamed in death, flung down outside her own front door like so much garbage, flickered in front of her eyes. Concepción's elder brother had been Aunt Luisa's *novio*, her parents were friends of the Vicentes, of the Ramirez family, too. How could Ramirez have used such a name after what had happened to her? She remembered Concepción crying once, on the way to school, a little shadowed girl who seldom smiled, who was afraid of things and kept close to Mercedes because, she said, Mercedes was so strong. How she must have suffered at the hands of the monsters who killed her.

Standing in a Brooklyn nursery, remembering something which had happened more than ten years before, a familiar terror seized her. Why had she been allowed to see that white corpse? Why had it been left there for her to find? Concepción . . . it was not a name to give a child, it was not right to –

"Mercedes? Are you ill?" Behind her, Ramirez put an arm across her shoulders and she turned, needing comfort, to burrow against his chest.

"I feel a little faint," she said.

"Mercedes," he murmured, and as he did so, she realised he believed she was thinking of what might have been, of the children she might have had if she had married him – as she had already hinted she had hoped to do. Instantly she was strong again. Her instinct was to push away from him but she stayed where she was.

"Too much work at the gallery," she said, infusing weariness into her voice.

"Of course. Your new exhibition . . ."

"I know I've been spending too much time on it, but it's so important to me."

"Everybody's talking about it. I hadn't appreciated just how much of a reputation you had, Mercedes. I've been busy with my own career and my family . . ." He put his hand under her chin and tilted her head so she was staring up at him. "And what about you, my little friend? Isn't it time you had a family?" He smiled down at her. "Isn't there a man who interests you?"

It was the perfect cue. "Only one," she said. A sad smile touched her lips. She put one small hand flat on his chest, over his heart. "Only one, Carlos. And he is not interested in me."

His mouth tightened. He started to say something. He lowered his head until their two faces were only fractionally apart; when she closed her eyes, her lashes brushed his cheek. For a moment, she felt his mouth against hers as he said softly: "That isn't true."

274

"Oh, Carlos . . ." she breathed. She allowed herself to lean against him then stepped briskly away.

"Mercedes, I – "

"It's time I went." She pushed a wrapped present into his hand. "For the baby, for – for Concepción." *White thighs, red blood, somewhere a little girl crying . . .*

The man came in again at lunch-time, giving her a sideways look, his pale eyes sliding up and down her body. In the past month or two, he had come in half a dozen times; he had never spoken to her, never bought anything, just examined the paintings on the wall, stared at her, left.

He made her shudder; her heart thumped behind her demure striped blouse. She had never seen him before, yet she was seized with the feeling that he knew all about her. Although she tried to repel the image, she could imagine the slimy trail of his bloodless fingers crawling over her body like the slugs which used to appear after winter rain in Montalbán. His slightly hunched shoulders made him at first glance seem older than he was; she guessed him to be somewhere around thirty. She watched from under her eyelashes as he bent to study a painting more closely, his silky too-long hair falling from under his hat to swing against his cheek. His presence unnerved her; she wished Rabat would come back, that she was not alone in the gallery with the man. Yet people passed on the street outside; the telephone was in front of her; she could not possibly be endangered by him.

Why did he keep returning? Who was he? More importantly, what did he want? Strongly, she felt that he was there for a purpose, that his visits were deliberate, orientated in some way towards her rather than the paintings he examined so closely. When he left, it was as though a cloud had passed.

She saw him again at the party thrown by Erich Kostner, the flamboyant Hungarian Jew. A chaotic mix of artistic refugees, monied Yankees, Bohemian pairings of every possible sex milled about beneath the elaborate crystal chandeliers which were supposedly the only possessions Erich had brought with him into exile, and from which sudden drips of scalding wax fell every now and then onto the crowds beneath. They talked art, money, theatre, the new state of Israel. Even three years after the end of the war, service uniforms were plentiful. Europe had not yet succeeded in trying to pull the broken bits of itself together, to restore shattered lives, shattered countries, come to terms with the dead; the various postwar agencies of the United States were still deeply embroiled in the process.

Mercedes, seeing the man at the far end of the room, his back to her but his hunched posture and silky over-long hair unmistakable, asked who he was; nobody seemed to know.

"Rich," someone said. "A German."

"How does he dare?" someone else said, hostility bristling.

"He's an aristocrat, got out after the attempt on Hitler."

"I heard he was some kind of Scandinavian," chimed in another voice.

"Funny looking, wherever he's from."

The group stared at the man; as though aware of their scrutiny, he turned round and stared back. Mercedes quickly bent her head, hoping he had not seen her.

"Makes your flesh creep," a woman said. "Stick a needle into the guy and he'd bleed milk."

Not milk, Mercedes thought. Clearly in her mind she could see the needle intruding into that milk-white flesh, the tiny mark on his arm, the welling drop not of blood or milk but of poison, translucent and deadly. Looking up, she saw him listening as Richard Klein, her own creation, now well-established on the art scene, expounded his philosophy of painting while next to them, Schleeman listened attentively, head bent.

"I've never met anyone like you," Schleeman said. "You've bewitched me, I do believe. Enslaved me."

"Don't say that," Mercedes said sharply. The phantom of a goat with silver tipped horns rushed across her mind; she saw a dark cave, a wooden throne, musk-scented shadows . . . "Don't say it."

She watched Schleeman's mounting sexual hunger for her and tried not to remember Jonas but the images of those sweet and sweaty afternoons in the searing heat of a Madrid summer would not leave her. She thought: I want him so badly I could die from it; she was sadly aware that even if she never saw Jonas again she would not die, she would survive.

"But it's true."

Over the months their relationship had become an almost-friendship. Based originally on need – his erotic, hers ambitious – it had changed as they grew to know each other well. But friendship – even of the sort they shared – could not be allowed to stand in her way. True to his word, in the past months he had taken her about, introduced her to collectors, promoted her name and that of her protégés. But she wanted more than that.

When he had finished and lay stretched out beside her, she said: "We must talk, David."

"What about?" He was flushed with exertion, one hand on his chest as though to still the beating of his heart.

"The future."

"Marriage, do you mean? I don't know if I'm prepared to – "

"Not marriage," she said, instantly furious at the implication that while he had no objection to sleeping with her, *abusing* her, she was not good enough to be his wife.

"What, then?"

"I want," she said coldly, "to go into full partnership with you. Rabat has no vision, no true concept of art. Besides, he grumbles all the time. In spite of the fact that Klein's pictures are now getting huge sums from collectors, he still objects to putting artists under contract."

When Schleeman did not answer, she went on: "I can pay my way. I have money saved up. And you know yourself that I have a good eye, a sense of what will sell. Look at Jackson Pollock: Rabat could have had him, I recognised his talent from the very first canvas he showed us, but Rabat wouldn't agree, wouldn't even buy anything and now, with Mrs Guggenheim putting on an exhibition, he's the hottest news around." She took a deep breath, prepared to argue her case further, but Schleeman put a hand over her mouth.

"Hush," he said. "It's all right. I agree."

"You do?"

"I was going to suggest it myself." His fingers brushed the curve of her hip, then, rearing up on one elbow, he said: "As far as I'm concerned, you have only one flaw –

your complete lack of humour. It's the reason I haven't offered to marry you."

She thought: Why do the men in my life understand me better than I understand myself? "You think we would make a good partnership?"

"As soon as your new exhibition is completed, we'll start drawing up the papers, yes?"

"Fine." Mercedes could not prevent a smile spreading across her face.

"I don't know what sort of a contract of employment you have with Rabat but I don't suppose he'll make much fuss about you leaving."

"I think he'll be glad to see the back of me. It'll be more difficult to sort out the gallery itself though."

"How do you mean?"

"Didn't you know? I own a third of it."

"What?" Schleeman gave her an admiring look. "How long have you been in New York?"

"About three years." Mercedes hated to be precise.

"And already you own one third of the New Age gallery?"

"Yes."

"Did you sleep with Rabat too?"

She wondered if she should feel anger. "Certainly not. It was a strictly business relationship."

"Do you have any more surprises for me, Mercedes? Any more galleries you have a stake in? Any other artists you're bankrolling?"

She lied. "Nothing. Just some pictures I brought with me."

He laughed once more. "Still pushing your Vicentes, are you? I think you'd be wiser to stick with Klein."

She thought coldly: *You may regret that remark*. She gazed at him, her eyes growing dark and huge.

"I think we're going to get on very well indeed," he continued, unaware of her anger. "I suppose you already have a name picked out for us, do you?"

"Schleeman & Aragon sounds good, don't you think?"

"Are you sure you don't want it to be Aragon & Schleeman?"

"I thought about it," she said, wondering why he laughed yet again. "But I think the first is better – more rhythmic."

"Right. And tomorrow we go to the Guggenheim exhibition, right?"

"Right." She touched his shoulder. "Schleeman . . ."

"Yes?"

"That man you were talking to, at Kostner's party, the one with the silver hair: who is he?"

"Silver hair?"

"White, then. Or very pale blond."

"Oh, him. He's an Englishman."

"What is he doing in New York?"

"Working for one of the big oil firms, I believe. Why? What's your interest?"

"I have none," she said disdainfully. "It's just that he came into the gallery last week. Do you know his name?"

"He's called Lovel," Schleeman said.

Somewhere inside her, the blood stopped for a moment. In Montalbán it was whispered that her mother was a witch, possessed of the power to cast spells, to read minds, to forecast the future: was it part of her mother's legacy that although she had never heard the name before, she knew instantly that it was destined to be linked with her own?

He came again, two weeks later. At the sight of him, her stomach lurched; she came forward to meet him.

"Can I show you something, Mr Lovel?" she said.

He turned his head. "How do you know my name?" His voice was as thin and colourless as his hair, the skin of his face stretched palely across the skull beneath. His lips were bluely white; the black coat he wore emphasised his pallor.

With another customer she might have turned flirtatious; with this one, she merely said: "Someone told me."

The reddish-brown eyes fastened on her; she tried not to flinch. "I'm interested in Japanese prints," he said. "No-one in New York has anything to sell."

"Hardly surprising," she said. "After the raids on Pearl Harbor, you'd be lynched if you tried to sell anything from Japan."

"Memories are short," he said. "Wait until the Japanese economy recovers. Anyone with oriental works to sell will make a fortune."

What he said was true but it was not what he had come to say. He was not in the gallery for Japanese works of art; he had been in often enough to know that they had none. He bent his head towards her and she smelled him, a dry powdery scent which reminded her of the *cortijo* where Fernando's pictures had lain among the heaped-up almonds. She opened her mouth to speak.

The street door opened and a couple came in, loud-voiced, demanding information about prices and trends, wanting to look at everything, to be led round the walls. When she had dealt with them, Lovel was gone.

He was waiting outside for her at the end of the day. He took her elbow; even through the cloth of her sleeve she could feel the coldness of his flesh. "Miss Aragon," he said.

"Yes?" She hated the way he never seemed to blink.

"Or would it be more correct to call you Miss Vicente?"

At his words, the street around her receded; though she was aware of the passing street-cars, the shape of a woman's hat, the sharp gleam of lemons in the fruiterer's window opposite, it was as though the two of them had been cut off from the rest of the world, encysted in a transparent shell.

"What do you want?" she asked.

"It's ten years since they shot him," he said. His voice rustled in his throat like old leaves.

"As if I will ever forget."

"And those responsible still not brought to book."

"Not yet." She turned, pulling her arm from his grip, and began to walk towards the subway. "But they will be."

"By you?" He walked beside her, his coat swinging open. He reminded her of the big raptors which floated above the sierras, drifting with the thermals, wings flapping as they finally bore down upon their prey.

"Yes."

"You're not the only one hungry for revenge," he said softly.

"Is that so?"

"I could be helpful to you in settling old scores, just as you could to me." His pale hand brushed at his neck.

"I need no help," she said, walking faster, wishing he

would go, aware of some bond between them which she did not understand.

"You may do, some day."

They had reached the entrance to the subway. "I don't think so," she said firmly. She descended the steps; at the bottom she looked up and saw him still standing there, black against the darkening sky.

She came out of the New Age Gallery and turned to lock the door, Rabat having gone home early because his wife was sick. She was vaguely aware of a figure standing at the edge of the pavement which followed as she set off down the street. Lovel again? She ignored him, pretending not to have seen him – until a voice said: "Mercedes?" and she stopped, suddenly full of an old, a haunting passion and the voice said again: "Mercedes."

She turned – "Jonas? Oh, Jonas." – and ran towards it, knees melting, heart singing, – "Jonas, you came back to me." – as he gathered her into his arms. "Jonas."

"I have a room near by," he said. "Not much of a place but that doesn't matter."

"No."

"Will you come with me?"

She nodded, too full of emotion to speak. She knew herself to be strong and fearless; part of that strength derived from the way she was able to accept and ignore the parts of her life which would otherwise cripple her. Although she had never expected to see Jonas again, she had never once stopped hoping; although she longed daily for him, dreamed about him, she did not let that longing weaken her intentions. She had no time to waste on idle fantasising, although the thought of having lost him could still bring tears to her eyes.

He took her hand in his. The emotion which swept over her was so strong she thought she might faint; it seemed to her at that moment that their two linked hands generated enough force to fuel an atomic energy plant.

"How long are you here for?"

"Only two days. Then I have to travel to San Francisco, and to Texas."

"Why?"

"In San Francisco I have business. In Texas, an old friend I haven't seen since before the war."

"Business?"

He chuckled. "You aren't the only one who has been makink a career. You have obviously been too busy plottink and strivink to know that I have quite a name in the world of ceramic artists."

"Perhaps we could exhibit you some time."

"I'm not famous enough for Mr Schleeman. Which reminds me . . ."

He got up and rummaged around in the leather suitcase which sat on the floor. He was naked; she looked at his chunky body with a love she knew he would not wish her to express. He came back to her, carrying something roughly wrapped in brown paper. "I made this for you," he said.

She opened it. Inside was a pot; a sea-green glaze, a wide brim on a single elegant foot: she recognised it immediately. "It's like the one we saw in Granada," she said.

"I wondered if you would remember."

"I remember everything," she said.

He rarely smiled at her. He did so now. "So do I."

"Say you love me, Jonas."

"But I don't, Mercedes."

"You do. You know you do. You came across oceans to find me." The squalid little room juddered as the elevated railroad rattled past the window.

"True. But not from love."

"Don't you feel anything for me?" she asked, hating herself for wanting the answer, knowing that the one he offered would not be the one she craved.

"I feel many things for you," he said quietly. "Desire, of course. An unconquerable desire. But pity, too. And compassion."

She was astonished. "You're *sorry* for me? Why?"

"Because however hard you try to hide it, I know that behind your hard exterior lies someone deeply wounded, deeply vulnerable . . ."

She did not want to hear such talk. "Even if you do not, say you love me," she urged.

"Would you have me lie, Mercedes?"

"If necessary, yes."

He brushed her mouth with his, his fingers fluttered across her thigh and immediately the fires flared between them once again, hot and hungry, devouring.

Later, leaning back against the pillows, Jonas said: "And have you succeeded in buildink up your brother's reputation outside Spain? Have you forced the world to recognise Vicente's genius as a painter?"

"These thing always take time," she said, ignoring the sardonic tone of his voice. "But with the war over, it's easier. There have been several articles about him recently in the art journals." She did not add that she had written most of them herself. "His name is well-known to the dealers."

"Good. I have an investment in Vicente myself. I'd like to see it pay dividends before I die."

She stretched herself along his body, flesh against flesh, her breasts throbbing where they touched his chest, her hands loving. "Talking of that," she said, lying, "I've been thinking that one day I shall start a museum of my brother's work, perhaps in Montalbán where we grew up."

"Is that so?" He did not seem particularly interested.

"That's why I'm keen to buy back any Vicentes you have."

"How many is it?" he said idly.

"Three." She spoke too quickly, too much as if it mattered, and was annoyed with herself.

"Remind me," he said lazily.

She only wanted one, the important one. "Didn't you buy *A Monstrous Love*?" she said, feigning forgetfulness. "There was a still life, too: fruit and a skull. And – uh – *The Tears She Shed*, if I remember rightly."

He laughed, and she thought as so often before: Behind the mask he presents to me, there is a face I cannot see, and behind that face, another mask. She saw Jonas receding from her, saw the alternation of face and mask, mask and face, each stripped away only to reveal yet another while the true Jonas remained ever enigmatic, ever unknowable.

"Provided I recoup my investment plus a reasonable return, you can buy them back," he said.

She drew in a quick breath of relief, her fingers grabbing at the black hair on his chest.

"At least," he went on, and his eyes met hers in the

overshadowed light. "A couple of them. But not *The Tears She Shed*."

Anguish filled her. "Why not?"

"Why not?" He shrugged. "Because I like it best? Because one day, I want to give it to my daughter? Who knows."

"You have no daughter."

"Not yet," he said. Hard, ready, he stirred against her.

"Oh, Jonas," she said. "Touch me. Take me." She grabbed at him, forced him inside her. This at least was hers, this at least was knowable. For the moment, it had to be enough.

16

TESS

Some deaths are just a fading out,
   time shuffling past;
some fast, a shout
cut short, an ended song.

My death's life long.
            from Amador Ramirez' *Elegías españolas*
                translated by Teresa Lovel

On the other side of the plane's double-skinned windows, the sun beat down on eiderdown cloud. The air seemed intensely pure; if she were suddenly to find herself precipitated into it, Tess could imagine the gush of oxygen to the head, to the lungs, like chilled champagne. How long would she have to enjoy that intoxicating brightness – a minute? A second? – before she was frozen alive and, trapped in ice, diamonded with frost crystals, plummeted Lucifer-like through the atmosphere, through the cloud layer, into the warmer air above Castile and Catalonia, to disintegrate finally, melted now, above the dry hills, the burning plains.

*   *   *

At the airport, Spain rushed to meet her. Faint familiar smells of tobacco and coffee and flowering shrub fought with the gasolene fumes and the hot tarmac. Cold air rolled down from the black line of hills which lay against a sky pinkly pearled; a single rosy cloud moved lazily above them.

Before leaving England she had made arrangements to hire a car; as she turned out of the airport parking-lot, she took a deep breath, a new breath, as though to fill herself with a fresh resolve. She was here: she had finally taken the decision and come. "*You must go back to the Casa de las Lunas . . .*" her mother had said, all those years ago, "*I want so much for you to see how it all was once . . .*" Whether she would have come if it had not been for Jonas's death it was difficult to say; she hoped so.

Having found a parking place behind the church, she explored the little town on foot; in half an hour she had seen most of it. This was the place where Vicente had grown up: she even recognised some of it. His view of the valley from the terrace in front of the church hung in the Museum of Modern Art in Paris and the Tate Gallery owned a canvas depicting the dusty almond-spread hills which rose behind the town towards the snow-topped peaks of the Sierra Nevada. As she walked the sharp-shadowed streets, she was aware of being observed from dark doorways, from small balconies, from half-shuttered windows. In a town of this size, isolated from the cities on the plains, everyone knew everyone else, every stranger was noted.

There were only two hotels. She knew without asking that Jonas would have stayed at the Hotel La Viña, a precarious building of peeling cream stucco and faded green shutters. It faced onto the terrace in front of the church and was hung with small balconies trailing geraniums and the vines from which it took its name.

Despite the earliness of the season, an elongated diamond of blue neon hanging from the hotel's façade advertised someone's beer. Tables and chairs were set out beneath it, affording a vista of the *campiña* fields under a cobalt sky, dry earth enclosed by stone walls, the skeletons of vines, an orchard of black-branched almond trees. Inside, the man behind the counter was almost hidden by signs indicating that Mastercard and Visa could be used to pay the bill, by displays of brochures advertising coach trips to Seville and Granada and by a revolving wire rack which held postcards of local views. He flashed a gold-toothed smile as she approached.

"Welcome to Montalbán, señorita."

"I'd like a room," she said. "Looking onto the square, if possible."

He nodded, his smile wider than before. "There are plenty of vacancies at this time of the year. I can offer a splendid room with bathroom and an incomparable view."

"I'll take it."

"You have chosen wisely, señorita, to come now before the tourists spoil the peace and seclusion of our little town."

"Do you get a lot of visitors?"

The man shrugged, spreading his hands. "This is not a big town and there has been little to attract people. But from now on, they will come in their hundreds, maybe even thousands, to visit the town where one of Spain's great artists once lived."

"Fernando Vicente?"

He cocked his head at her. "You know his work?"

"Very well indeed."

"Good, good." He bobbed off his stool and ducked under the counter. "Come, señorita, I will show you something." Taking Tess's arm he pulled her towards the front door and pointed. "Over there, you can just see the house where Vicente grew up."

Half-way along the strongly shadowed street she could see a tall white house, with the curlicues of a balcony jutting out over the front door which gave directly onto the pavement. From the biography, she knew that it was from there Vicente had been bundled into the street, still in his shirt-sleeves; from there been driven away to imprisonment while the neighbours stared and whispered from behind their window-blinds and the plump aunts shivered. Had he stumbled? Had he hung his head? Or had he not believed that this could be the end of it all, that there would be no more bright mornings, no more lingering sunsets?

"A month from now, it will be officially opened as a museum," the hotel owner said. "A monument to a great artist. It will house the most important collection of Vicente's work anywhere in the world."

"I shall miss that. What a pity."

"It is already occasionally open to visitors. I can arrange it for you, if you wish."

"Does anyone live there now?"

"Not for ten years. The last of Vicente's aunts sold it then. It is only recently that it has been purchased by the Museum Trust."

"Which aunt was that?"

"The youngest, Luisa. Señora Ruiz-Barrantes."

The name was somehow familiar to her, though she could not remember why. She had a vague impression of a photograph seen somewhere, a plump woman with a huge knot of groomed hair doing something official . . . She tried to seize the memory but it slipped away from her. "Is she still alive?"

"Very much so, señorita. She was ten years younger than her nephew, although she was his aunt. His grandfather remarried in his seventies and Luisa Vicente was the result. Her elder sisters, of course, died many years ago. I remember the three of them very well. Always dressed in black. They often used to walk down here and sit on the terrace, looking out over the valley." He spun the revolving rack of postcards. "We have postcards of Vicente's more famous works, if you should wish to send them back to your friends in England. Also of the house where he lived. And, of course, of this very bar, where he used to come in the evenings to drink and laugh with his friends."

"What about the convent where he was kept prisoner before he was shot?" Tess said. If the town could celebrate the life, it must surely at least mention the death. "Is there a picture of that?"

His smile drooped. "It's on the edge of the town, a ruin now." He shrugged, grew brisk. "Your passport, señorita."

Tess handed over her passport for him to examine. "I was told about this hotel by a friend," she said. "He was here very recently . . ."

"A friend, señorita? We do not have many English people here. What was his name?"

"Jonas Fedor."

"Señor Fedor was a friend of yours?"

"A very good friend."

For a moment he stared at her, the smile still hanging from his lips. Then his face changed, as though a sponge had been wiped across it. Clearly deciding it would be pointless to pretend the name meant nothing to him, he said: "A most tragic occurrence. He was a charming man – we were devastated by what happened. It is a pity he could not leave things as they were."

"What do you mean?"

"He found himself involved in something which he should have left for others to deal with," said the man. He handed her a key. "Here, señorita. Your room is at the top of the stairs." He indicated a flight of steps made of polished composition stone which led up into dimness. "Over there, beside the lifts."

Tess stayed at the desk. "You said Señor Fedor was involved in something which other people could have dealt with? What did you mean?"

He stood very still. Then he said: "Perhaps I am confusing your friend with someone else."

"You seemed to know who I was talking about when I mentioned him first."

"I thought you referred to one of our American visitors," the man lied smoothly. "I remember now, his name was not Fedor but Faber. Yes, indeed, when we heard that Mr Faber had been shot in the subway in New York, we were truly sorry." He did not seem to care whether she believed him or not. "Señor Fedor, too, we were so very sorry to lose. I told him only that morning that he was overdoing it, no longer a young man and yet walking so strenuously all day in the hills. I was afraid that he would find the sun too much for him." He shook his head gravely. "Mad dogs and Englishmen . . ." He rattled a key at her. "You will find your room without difficulty, I think. It is next door to the one occupied by poor Señor Fedor."

He smiled at her.

She did not smile back.

The room was solid, old-fashioned, furnished with heavy pieces in a dark wood. She pushed open the shutters and stepped out onto the balcony. Six weeks ago in a similar room, Jonas had probably done the same. What had he hoped to accomplish by coming here? What had he expected to find? He had spoken of 'unfinished business': was it something to do with Julian Maitland, his former friend and partner? But if so, why had he chosen to stay at the La Viña when Maitland lived some miles away? Why not stay in his old friend's home?

Perhaps the reason behind his visit involved a more local matter, to do with the people he had known long ago, during the Civil War. She realised that she did not know exactly where he had been during those years, though it had been in the southern part of Spain. As though breaking through the concealing curve of a wave into the open air, she realised that the chances were high he had been in Montalbán, that the resistance group he had led was based in the mountains she could see from her window. And the 'unfinished business' he had mentioned must have concerned the identity of the man he had called El Malo.

Yet, remembering the unsigned sketches in his desk and the drawing of him hanging in Cramir's underground gallery, was it not possible that it might also concern Fernando Vicente himself?

There was also the cryptic note sent from New York, signed by the mysterious AR: there had been a reference in that to 'the Montalbán scheme'. She would have to try and find out what that scheme was. For a moment she envisaged hydroelectric installations, huge dams being built up behind the town, the siting of a nuclear waste plant. Like the Hayashima proposal, it would bring employment and prosperity to the town, but there might well be opposition. If so, whatever the suddenly impelling reasons behind Jonas's journey out here, they were ones in which Tess herself must necessarily become involved.

Below her, the hotel proprietor came into view; at the same time, a car drew up and a police officer got out. Something about the way the two men began to converse together made Tess draw back, instinctively certain that they were talking about her. From between the slats of the shutters she watched as the owner of the hotel jerked his shoulder towards her window; the policeman stared upwards and then nodded a couple of times. The two of them disappeared back into the hotel.

A few seconds later there was a tap at the door. When she opened it, an elderly woman in a checked wrap-around overall stood outside. "You must descend," she said, pointing at the staircase. "The police have come for you."

Although she had half expected such a summons, momentarily Tess found herself almost too frightened to move. Suppose they carted her off somewhere: who would know where she was? She foresaw a dank cell, a tin bowl of gruel, a sunless exercise yard and the pitiless faces of her jailers. Then common sense asserted itself. She had read too many books, watched too many movies. No-one was going to drag her away; she had only to scream, and if she disappeared, enquiries would eventually be made. After all, Martín García and Don Pedro knew she had come here. So did Dominic. The latter thought was less reassuring than she expected.

As she walked quickly down the stairs into the lobby, she wondered whether the police had come calling for Jonas too. The town was small and there could be few secrets: if the business he had come to finish adversely concerned someone local, officialdom might well want to be involved. It was obvious the hotelier had wasted no time in informing the police that a friend of Jonas Fedor's was in town. The speed with which they had responded merely confirmed what she already suspected: that there was something not quite right about the official explanation which had been given for Jonas's death.

In the dim-lit lobby, the man leaning against the counter straightened when he saw her. He was thin, narrow-moustached, wearing a uniform cut on military lines. "Ah, Miss Lovel," he said. "My name is Alvarez. Welcome to Montalbán." He took her hand and bowed over it.

"I understand you wish to talk to me," she said.

"That's right." He waved at one corner of the reception area, where a couple of hard chairs were set on either side of a tiny café table, its top made of tinted mirror glass. "Why don't you sit d – "

"I'd prefer to sit outside, if you don't mind." Despite her own attempts to convince herself that she was not in danger, she none the less felt it would be safer if they sat where they could be seen.

He hesitated. "It would be more convenient if – "

"You know how the English are," she said, smiling at him as she purposefully walked towards the doorway. "We have so little sunshine at home that we don't like to miss a moment of it when we go abroad."

She saw him conjure up a fog-wreathed island, slanting rain. "Very well." He called into the silent regions behind the desk: "Two coffees, please, José," before following her outside.

Seated at one of the terrace tables, he said: "Now, Señorita Lovel. You have come, I believe, to enquire about the death of Mr Jonas Fedor."

How did he know that when she had given no reason for her visit to the hotel-keeper? Since what he said was true, she nodded.

"And why did you feel it was necessary to do so? Such information as we had was given immediately to the Embassy and passed on to his family."

"Perhaps. But we felt we hadn't been told as much about it as we should have been."

The lines of his face lifted in enquiry. The leather straps across his shoulders gleamed like harness as he shrugged. "Forgive me, señorita: are you related to Señor Fedor?"

"Not exactly."

"A cousin, perhaps? A stepdaughter?"

"Neither."

"Then what right do you have to . . .?" He did not bother to finish the sentence.

"Jonas Fedor was my guardian. Apart from a nephew, he had no other family. It is this nephew who has asked me to come here." The half-lie sounded plausible.

298

"And what makes either of you think that the truth about this sad affair has been kept from you?"

"I've said nothing at all about the concealment of truth," Tess said. "Merely about the scarcity of information. I'm not accusing anyone of anything – yet."

"Not ever, I hope. The facts are these, Miss Lovel. Señor Fedor arrived here at the Hotel La Viña five days before he died. The hotel owner has testified that Señor Fedor stated he was here for a walking holiday and at the same time, wished to visit old friends. This we know he did: Señor Julian Maitland – do you know of whom I speak?"

She nodded.

"Señor Maitland has stated that Señor Fedor came to visit him two or three times. Our enquiries have made it clear that most days, he would walk into the hills, returning late in the afternoon. We have statements from witnesses who saw him – you are welcome to examine these if you so wish. Some evenings he would go out again. Where he went on these occasions I have not found out. He received two or three telephone calls, which we have not been able to trace, though one is believed to have come from Granada. A couple of times he was visited at the hotel but we do not know by whom."

"Someone must have seen."

"Oddly enough, they did not. But Señor Fedor was heard talking to someone . . ." With his head, he indicated the balconies above them.

"Who was this person? And how did they get to his room without anyone noticing? Surely the hotel owner or someone would have been manning the desk."

"Of course. But perhaps this person did not wish to

be seen and came in while the owner was temporarily elsewhere."

Or perhaps, Tess thought, someone had been paid to forget. "Did Señor Fedor have a hire car?" she asked, casually, already knowing what the answer would be.

"Of course. A Volkswagen Golf. And naturally we have examined the car very carefully." He lifted his shoulders, spread his hands, looking grave. "Nothing. Nothing, that is, beyond what you would expect: leaves, a feather, samples of soil from the hills where he had been walking."

"But I was told you had closed the case – you must have more information than this."

Deliberately he felt in the breast pocket of his uniform and pulled out a pack of cigarettes. He showed it to Tess and raised his eyebrows. "You permit, señorita?" When she nodded, he lit one with a Bic lighter and drew in deeply before blowing the smoke away from her.

"How did you know we had closed the file on Señor Fedor?" he asked finally.

"A colleague in England made some enquiries for me."

"You have friends in high places," he said, his expression hostile. He drew again on his cigarette. "We have closed the case because we know more or less what must have happened."

"And what was that?"

"We believe that in the course of his walks, Señor Fedor – perhaps resting during the hot time of the day, perhaps already feeling unwell – finding himself near an abandoned farmstead, sat for a while on the wall in order to recover himself. It is unfortunate that this particular *cortijo* . . ."

300

he checked to see whether she was familiar with the word, "backs onto a ravine so that when he was overcome, he had no chance of surviving such a steep fall."

"Do you have any proof to back up your suspicions?"

He nodded. "During our investigation we found the remains of several cigarettes scattered on the ground beside this wall. And there was also his rucksack, lying half-way down on a ledge almost immediately below the point from which he must have fallen."

"How come his body didn't land there?"

"Please, señorita, merely consider . . ." His hands sketched a bouncing movement. He spread his hands. "I am very sorry indeed that such a tragic event took place here, but the evidence seems fairly conclusive." He dragged again on his cigarette and drooped heavy eyelids over a calculating glance. He waited for her response.

Was it worth pointing out the gaps in his story, the implausibilities? Probably not. "I should like to see for myself the place where he died," she said. "Would that be possible? Is it far from here?"

"You have a car, I believe," he said. He dribbled smoke out through his nose, at the same time stubbing the cigarette into the red-painted tin ashtray which sat in front of him.

"Yes."

"Then I shall give you the directions: you will see for yourself how easily such a tragic accident could have occurred. It will be easier for you to drive there – it is quite a long walk from here."

"In that case, I'm surprised that Mr Fedor managed it," Tess said. "He was, after all, an elderly man."

The policeman shrugged. "I assume he must have driven

some of the way before beginning his walks. We took
it upon ourselves to return the car to the company
involved – the Agencia Andalucía, in Granada – once
our investigations were complete."

"Ah." Tess knew that if she was going to find out
anything more, she would do better to pretend that she
accepted his account. "If you are certain . . ."

"We are, señorita."

"Thank you for being so frank with me," she said and
was able to judge just how frank he had been by the relief
he was unable to hide.

After he had gone, the sound of his engine bouncing back
and forth across the narrow cobbled streets which led to
the town's centre, she sat for a moment, reassessing what
he had said. Jonas was supposed to have told the hotel
proprietor that he was going to visit 'old friends'. Yet
only Julian Maitland had been mentioned. Who were the
others? Who else had he gone to see? Who had come to
see him?

She clenched her fists tightly, wanting to drum them
on the table, wanting to dash the thick white coffee cups
to the ground. The account Alvarez had given her was
implausible from start to finish, the conclusion false.
Suffering from emphysema and arthritis, there was no
possibility that Jonas would announce that he had come
to Spain on a walking holiday: either he had lied to the
hotel-keeper in order to conceal his true object, or the
hotel-keeper himself was lying.

The turmoil of her thoughts made it impossible to sit
still. She walked briskly through the streets to where the
lower levels of the town gave onto a newly metalled

road which wound steeply away down the mountain-side towards the valley. Was it imagination that filled the shuttered windows with watching eyes? Was it her own uncertainty which interpreted the glances of the villagers as hostile?

She turned and walked back. At the upper end, the main street petered out beyond the last house into cart-tracks which passed a crumbling white wall topped with cracked orange tiles before winding round the side of a hill onto the slopes above. There were cypress trees inside; just visible, the remains of a rounded chapel. This must be the wall of the old convent. Going closer, she could see holes, hundreds of them and knew Vicente was not the only one who had died here.

As she climbed higher, small terraced orchards of almond and olive gave way to wilder ground: oleander and sage clinging to the dry soil, clumps of grey agave, the flat cracked discs of cactus casting strange shadows among the rocks. The houses of the town settled below her, their orange roofs drawn together, huddled above the lip of the ravine. From here, she could see how deep the chasm was, and how brutal, a straight drop of perhaps a thousand feet, falling between high walls of rock to what must once have been a river bed but was now a tumble of black boulders. At this time of year, the spaces of the ravine seemed insubstantial, the sparse undergrowth which clung to its sides blue-misted, indefinite; with the shrivelling heat of summer it would harshen, as the green parched into brown and ochre.

Somewhere down there, Jonas had been found.

She tried not to think of that fall, nor to wonder whether he had been conscious of the hurtling air as he crashed

towards oblivion. She remembered Hansl saying that
Jonas had long ago learned not to be afraid of death.

The light was starting to fade. A breeze blew dust into
her face and somewhere, olives whispered and stirred. In
the stillness, she could hear television voices from open
doors and a frenzied radio commentary on some big
football game in Madrid or Barcelona. The street itself
was empty.

Behind the houses, the road became track again, rutted
by the wheels of loaded carts. In the gloom a donkey
clicked its heels and stirred with the softness of feathers
on the end of its rope. On the shadowed side of the
hill, there was some kind of movement. She realised
how abruptly night had dropped over the landscape,
how little visibility there was left. Below her, in the
town, lights were beginning to glow dully behind shuttered windows; up here, there were shadows only, though
light still gilded the higher hills. Looking round, she
could see no sign at all of civilisation, though here
and there the *cortijos* gleamed like pearls in the gathering dusk.

She must have taken the wrong way: the Casa de las
Lunas had belonged to one of the principal families of
the region and would certainly have a more suitable
approach than this track. Leaning against a boulder,
Tess considered the terrain. The road she was on had
curved round on itself so that she now stood high above
a point midway between the hamlet and Montalbán itself.
It might be quicker to continue on a little further and then
drop straight downhill to the town, rather than retrace her
steps by the road.

Somewhere she could hear the knocking of a wooden

goat bell; at the same time, there was further movement and something came tumbling and skittering towards her. Instinctively she crouched in against the hillside, under a small overhang, as a rock the size of a tennis-ball bounced outwards and past her, dislodged by a cloven hoof.

Or had it been? Her heart thumped madly. All the choking horror of that unseen hand pushing her underwater returned: she was suddenly nauseous. Was it a goat up there, above her, or was it the same man? Had he followed her all the way from Cambridge in the hope of finding her in just such a desolate spot? Was he crouched up above her, waiting for her to show herself again? She held her breath, listening, but could hear nothing. If he killed her here, how long would it be before someone began to look for her? And if she ventured out again onto the hillside, would he use a more certain method to dispatch her next time?

Shuddering, she peered carefully out from her shelter and looked up. Against the dark blue sky a shape hovered, black and winged, some kind of large bird. The light played tricks; she could not see it clearly although it seemed to be only inches above her head, blocking out the sky. She fancied she could hear the rustle of wind through its feathers, the slow pulse of its wings matching the rhythm of her own heartbeat. The sound was infinitely malign. After a long moment, it flapped away into the shadows.

How long should she stay here? She could not even be sure that the falling stone had been deliberate, but did she dare take the risk that it was not?

She heard above her a voice calling; the plaintive

response of unseen goats filled the air above her hiding-place. The voice called again and again the goats answered, growing fainter, moving away.

And then, somewhere very near, a horse whinnied. She crouched even closer to the rock face and rested her forehead on her knees. She had no way of knowing whether the horse was riderless, or whether someone waited up there in the gathering gloom, hoping she would show herself. Time passed inconceivably slowly. Straining her ears, she heard no further sound, no thud of hooves on turf, no jingle of bridle, no fall of stone.

Hours, it seemed, passed before the pounding of her blood diminished, before she felt strong enough to stand up and carefully reconnoitre the terrain. She could see nothing, hear nothing, except the wind in the higher peaks, and the occasional call of some bird. Was it safe? How could she tell?

But she knew she could not linger among these inhospitable rocks. It was growing chilly, she was thirsty and hungry. She decided that to return by the road, which had only the ravine on one side and little hiding place on the other, would make her more vulnerable to any attack which might occur; her best hope would be to cut across the finger of mountain, especially since she would be climbing up into what was left of the daylight.

Fearing danger with every step, she finally reached the top of the bluff. Turning her head, she could look down and see, two or three miles away, alone on the hill above Montalbán, a rambling creamy house surrounded by clustered outbuildings. The jewel-blue of a swimming-pool shone briefly; she could just make out a tennis court, too, and a walled garden. Beyond, terraced vineyards gave way gradually to a silver sea of olive leaves.

The Casa de las Lunas, she thought, the House of Moons. *I was born in that house.* She stared at it, trying to imagine her sad mother walking through the rooms of her dreams.

A light blinked on in the distant house and was immediately subdued, as though a shutter had been pulled across a window. Behind her, feet scrabbled on rock and she turned, heart thumping, blood racing. But it was only a herd of goats, jostling for room on the path, who stared at her topaz-eyed, before they slipped like shadows between the boulders, leaving behind their particular pungent odour.

Dropping down at last to the little town, she considered what Alvarez had told her. She had no way of knowing whether Jonas's death had occurred the way he described. But someone was concealing the truth: if the police had nothing concrete to back up their theory, she herself had definite irrefutable proof that things could not have happened the way they said.

They might themselves be misinformed; that was perfectly possible. For the first time, she began to wonder whether the death was something quite different from what it had seemed. With a growing sense of both confusion and fear, the notion of murder began to take shape in her mind. For, however Jonas had reached the wall from which he had plunged, it had not been on foot. So he must have been taken there.

If so, by whom? And why? Was it possible – she shuddered – that Jonas had been deliberately thrown from that wall? It would explain why he had been found at the bottom of the gulley.

Instinctively, she increased her pace. Whatever the police said, one thing was certain. Jonas could not possibly have driven himself to the *cortijo*.

He had never learned to drive.

17

TESS

The kid sat on the edge of the bed, waiting for me;
it was obvious that she was terrified and I couldn't
help wondering what sort of men they were, the guys
responsible for her terror.

Blood is Thicker by I. C. Sanyoshi,
translated by Teresa Lovel

The Casa de las Lunas.

For the first time, she stood between the gateposts, for
the first time touched the copper crescents of the moons,
the one waning and the other waxing. The metal surface
was pitted, roughened by time and weather. In the picture
of the house which she had bought at the auction, the artist
had caught exactly the creamy grey colour of the posts,
the sullen green of the verdigrised copper. The house sat
above her, up a short steep drive, shaded by trees which
cast their shadows across the roof.

As in the painting, the ground floor was surrounded by
a pillared terrace and the windows were grilled with iron
bars, but little else was the same. There were gaping holes
in the roof now, the shutters on the upper windows were

309

peeling and the grilles were rusted. Rain pouring from
leaf-choked gutters had stained the cream stucco and
the pots on the verandah held only shrivelled stems. In
the garden the flowering shrubs had rebelled and tangles
of creeper suffocated the trees. Vicente's painting had
conveyed a house crammed with urgency, a sense of life,
however desperate it might be, teeming just beyond the
confines of the frame. In reality, the Casa de las Lunas
was fast tumbling into ruin and decay.

At the foot of the drive, Tess hesitated. This was
something she had waited all her life for, yet now that she
was here she wished she was not. The past crowded her: a
sick fear churned in her stomach. Only the memory of her
mother's face powered her slow walk up the drive onto a
tiled patio crunchy with dead leaves; only the thought of
Jonas gave her the impetus to tug at the rusty bell-pull set
to one side of the heavy arched door, though given the
state of the house, it seemed unlikely that anyone would
answer.

Yet the previous evening, she had seen a light come on
behind a shutter, she was sure of it. And her mother's
words pounded again in her head. "*You must go there,
Teresa . . .*" Once more she pulled at the bell.

The jangle bruised the quiet deep in the heart of the
house then shivered into silence; around her, the world
stilled itself, as though holding a deep-drawn breath. For
a long second, the only sound she could hear was the
drumming of blood in her ears, then gradually normal-
ity reasserted itself and she became aware of a tractor
thrumming somewhere in the fields, a dog barking, and
far away down the valley, a car engine turning over and
over, reluctant to start.

No-one came; after a while she turned away. To one side of the house a wing wall curved into impenetrable shrubbery but the doorway set into it, under a brick archway, must presumably lead into the area at the back of the house. She pushed at the gate and felt it give; pushing harder, she dislodged accumulated leaves and was able to squeeze through. A paved path, quilted with moss, led through jungled bushes and brought her out on the edge of the swimming-pool she had seen from above the day before. Close to, the blue tiled rectangle was empty; the mosaic pattern of mermaids and tritons half obscured by an accumulation of the curled corpses of leaves and twigs blown down in winter storms. Beyond the pool lay what had once been a tennis court; weeds had pushed through and the hard surface was pitted with holes.

Tess was about to make her way back to the side gate, when she became aware that the door which opened onto the patio at the back of the house was very slightly ajar. Within the dark gap, shapes shifted. Someone was watching her. Slowly she moved towards the house, heart pumping, apprehension and excitement making her breathless.

The door widened, its outer edge held by a gnarled hand, until she could make out an old woman, voluminously skirted, who peered at the sunlight, squinting at its brightness like an ancient tortoise.

Tess smiled at her. In Spanish, she said: "Good morning. I wonder whether I could talk to Señora Mercedes Ramirez."

The old woman shook her head. A sound which could have been a laugh emerged from her throat. "She's not here."

"Oh." Having psyched herself up to this visit, Tess was reluctant to let her preparations go for nothing. "When will she be back?"

The old woman shrugged massively. "Who knows? She stays in Granada when she is in the south. It's a long while since she came here." She pulled the door wider, giving Tess a view of the dark hall. "You can see for yourself, señorita, that it is not a place for the likes of her."

Behind her, parquet flooring stretched away into gloomy shadows. The surface was uneven, the blocks of wood long ago forced out of alignment by damp and neglect. A few dry leaves skittered in the draught from the doorway; the dull gleam of old polish still showed here and there. Massive in the dimness, a wooden settle stood isolated against dirty plaster. Tess could see daylight through the ceiling of the gallery which stretched across one wall.

As though anticipating criticism, the old woman said defensively: "I can't be expected to keep up a place this size, not on my own, without any help, not at my age. If she left money I could bring someone in, get it cleaned up. My nephew's always saying it wouldn't need a lot of work to get it back the way it used to be."

"Why does Señora Ramirez let it go like this?" Tess asked. She considered the symbolism of the copper moons: under the Ramirez the house had been strong, had grown, while in Mercedes' care, it faded, growing ever weaker. She stepped inside the house.

"What could you expect from such a marriage?" The old woman gave a shrug. She seemed to assume that Tess was acquainted with both the house and its former occupants.

As her eyes adjusted to the dim light, Tess wondered

if she would ever dream again of the Casa de las Lunas, and if she did, whether the dream would simply modify itself to embrace the reality. As her mother had so often described it, the walls were lined with wood, but instead of the reddish tones of her dream they were dark, funereal, bleached here and there with streaks of rain and emblazoned with the droppings of birds who had flown in through the holes in the roof. The life-size photograph of Fernando Vicente which dominated the dream-hallway was here reduced to nothing more than a paler rectangle on the wall, and cobwebs hung like ghostly curtains from the balusters of the gallery and the beams which crossed the high ceiling. Yet, in spite of the neglect evident everywhere, it seemed to her that the scent of the house was still familiar: tobacco and cedar wood and a fragile tang of citrus.

The old woman grumbled on. "We knew she would try to ruin him – well, you must know yourself, señorita. We knew she would spoil what she could. My own sister's husband tried to tell him – "

Tess cut across the bumbling monotone. "Do you mean this is deliberate? That Señora Mercedes . . ." As she said the name, she saw the old woman surreptitiously make the sign against the Evil Eye, forefinger and little finger of her left hand stiffly extended. ". . . that Señora Mercedes leaves the house like this intentionally?"

"She would have walked on her knees to hell, in order to cause him pain," said the old woman. "How she hated him, not just him but the entire Ramirez family. But what could you expect from either of them? They were tainted, their mother was a witch."

"I don't believe in – "

"I told the other one, the one who came knocking before, enquiring, I told him she wouldn't rest until the last of the Ramirez lies in his grave."

The semi-darkness of the hall, the croaking voice issuing from the puffy wrinkled old face, the draping cobwebs, lent a sense of unreality to the words. It was as though a fabulous reptile – a manticore or a salamander – had crawled from beneath a stone to spit out a curse.

I'm the last of the Ramirez, Tess thought, and could not repress a thrill of nervous horror. Was what the old woman said true? And had Jonas known?

"Who was this other person you keep talking about?" she asked.

"The one who came here before, a few weeks back. He thought I wouldn't recognise him, but I did, even after all these years." She brushed at her rusty black skirts.

"Who are you talking about?" Tess said.

"The one who's supposed to have fallen into the ravine and got himself killed. He was looking for Mercedes, same as you. And even though they said she was in London, I know better, I saw her, flapping about up there, I saw her."

"I was told his death was an accident, caused by dizziness or a heart attack."

"You must believe what you wish, señorita."

"But you. What do you believe?" persisted Tess.

"Only what I hear."

"And Señor Fedor came here?" Tess said. If Jonas had visited the Casa de las Lunas he must have had a reason. And if so, was it just to look up an old friend who no longer lived here, or had there been some other purpose behind his visit. "What did he want?"

"Said he would like to look round. 'Julia', he said, 'for old times' sake I want to look round.' I said: 'If you think I'm going up those stairs with you at my time of life, you can think again.' My legs wouldn't stand it," she added, in confidential tones.

"He went upstairs?" Tess was already crossing the ruined parquet towards the staircase which led up to the gallery.

"That's right. Poked around for a while and came down again."

"Do you mind if I go up?"

Behind the old woman, soot tumbled softly in the deserted hearth, as though a trapped bird was trying to escape. "There's nothing up there now," she said. "Except for memories."

At the top of the stairs, the coir matting, mouldering now, worn through in places to the bare boards underneath, stretched away from her along the passage, the doors stood open where in her dream they were shut. She passed her grandfather's room, the room of her vanished uncle, a linen-closet lined with empty slatted shelves. A tumble of discarded dust-covers, an overturned basket, a worn-out slipper kicked into a corner, were all that remained of the people who had once lived here. Yet though the house had been left to rot, it still seethed with secrets: she had a vision of them like so many insects, crawling, writhing, under the floorboards, behind the panelling.

She passed the bathroom where a tap dripped into a rust-stained bath, and the little room where the maids used to iron and repair the household linen. What had Jonas hoped to find here? Was he merely looking for his past, for lost innocence, a love once known? Or was his visit more purposeful, was there something particular he wanted to retrieve, something hidden long ago, perhaps, which might still be undiscovered? If so, it seemed unlikely he could have found it for there was nothing here.

Outside the room which had been her mother's, where she herself had lain for two brief nights before Conchita had fled, she paused, drawing breath deep into her lungs, warning herself that time passed, that dust settled and old wounds eventually healed. None the less, pushing open the half-closed door, she could not help feeling that the moment was significant. She had promised her mother she would come one day: now she was here, standing on dusty boards in an empty room – except that this room, unlike the others, was not completely empty. Set against the wood-panelled wall stood a magnificent four-poster bed. It was the bed of her dreams, the bed in which she had been born. The uprights were carved like the trunks of palm-trees; they soared towards the ceiling to spread into branches which supported the elaborate canopy garnished with fruit and flowers moulded in high relief. She guessed that it had been left behind, like the settle in the hall downstairs, because it was too big to move.

Had Jonas stood here too, only a few short weeks ago? Had he known this was her mother's room? If he was looking for something specific, had he found it? She should have checked with Hansl before she left England; if Jonas's possessions had been returned to him, there might have been something among them which could have provided her with a clue. But there was nothing here which could possibly have interested Jonas: just the four bare walls and the big bed, its mattress long since thrown away. As

Jonas might have done, she peered underneath, looked up at the canopy. There was a mark in the dust as though the bed had recently been shifted; she shoved at it to see if anything was lodged behind but found only a crumble of dust and the dried shell of a moth.

Walking back along the passage, she paused in the doorway of her uncle's room. After all this time, the dusty pink paint on the walls had faded to the colour of dried blood. He had slept here, Amador Ramirez, her never-known uncle, Conchita's brother. Lying on a windowsill was a paintbrush, stiff with caked paint. Tess tried to remember what she had been told about him. Her mother had loved him, had tried to protect him from their stepmother's cold loathing. At the age of sixteen he had run away from home and no-one had ever heard from him again.

She remembered her own questions as a child, hearing this story for the first time.

"Why wouldn't they let him be a painter?"

"Not they, darling, her." No need to ask who 'her' was. *"She used to laugh at him. She asked why he bothered to try when he had so little talent."*

"Was it true?"

"Of course not. Amador had all sorts of talents. He played the guitar like an angel. He wrote poetry, marvellous poetry. And his painting – that's what she couldn't stand, because he was a better painter than Vicente, her own brother."

"Where is he now?"

"I'd like to think that he was able to start a new life somewhere, away from her. I'd like to think he was able to do what he had always wanted. But . . . I know my brother is dead."

"How do you? Why?"
    Her mother was silent for a moment. Then she had
    said: "I feel it."
    She went downstairs again, leaving behind a weight
of shadowy griefs and lost loves, unseen patterns in
the dust.

It was the siesta hour. Montalbán slept. Sitting on the
hotel terrace, shadowed by the honey-coloured façade of
the church, with a glass of light Spanish beer on the table
in front of her, Tess looked out over the valley. All these
years, she had waited for the moment when she would
enter the Casa de las Lunas. Now she had done so, and
she felt nothing.
    What had she expected? Some kind of epiphany, some
fundamental revelation after which she would be utterly
changed, reborn? There had been nothing like that, no
sense of anything out of the ordinary. She had entered the
dragon's den and emerged unscathed. Was that because
she had focused her fears on the wrong object? Or because
the dragons occupied another, darker cave?

At some point, she would have to go down to the police
station and speak to Alvarez again, take a look at the
depositions he had gathered from witnesses. There was
also Julian Maitland to call on; the Vicente Museum could
wait until the following day when, the owner of her hotel
had told her, it would be open between ten and noon.
    The *comisaría* first, then. It stood at the top of a cobbled
street, tucked in beside the arched and whitewashed town
hall; from the paved square to one side she could look
across intricate patterns of ploughed fields to the jagged

peaks of the mountains. Bells clonked: leaning over the crumbling stone balustrade she watched as a jostle of goats went past beneath her, stirring up the dust of the narrow track. They were followed by a baggy-trousered boy plugged into a personal stereo attached to his belt. Further away, she could see the black surface of the road swinging away down the side of the hill towards the lower plains.

Alvarez did not seem pleased to see her, although he led her into his office courteously enough and asked if she wanted anything to drink.

"No thanks." She took the hard metal chair he offered. "I just wanted to go over the details of Señor Fedor's death again."

"Of course, if you wish." His puzzled frown managed to suggest infinite patience with the paranoia of foreigners. "What exactly do you wish to clarify?" Without waiting for a reply, he went over to a filing cabinet set against a wall. A drawer screeched open; he pulled out a file and brought it back to his desk, extracting two sheets of paper. "Here is a copy of the pathologist's report. And the list of contents found with the body."

Tess read swiftly through them. The laboratory report meant little to her, the vocabulary so unfamiliar that for all she knew, it could have been telling her Jonas had died of drowning or alcoholic poisoning, rather than from multiple injuries. Nor did the list of the possessions found with him hold any significance: watch, camera, guide book, stainless steel Parker pen, car key, wallet with major credit cards and sixteen thousand pesetas, spectacles in a leather case.

"These have all been returned to his nephew in England,

along with the bag he left at the Hotel La Viña," Alvarez said when she handed the list back to him.

"There are still one or two things which puzzle me," Tess said. "For instance, you said he went walking every day. But I know he found it difficult to walk for very long: he was a heavy smoker and his profession exposed him to dust. Recently he was having breathing difficulties."

Alvarez shrugged. "He told the owner of the Hotel La Viña that he was here to walk. And our enquiries show that – "

"You said that already. What exactly were these enquiries?"

"You can see for yourself," he said offhandedly. "Various witnesses who stated that at different times on the day of his death they saw him up in the hills." He gestured towards the window.

Tess picked up the sheets of paper he handed her.

". . . sitting under a tree, reading a book. He waved at me as I passed . . . red car, dark red like wine . . . when I came back again at around 4:30 p.m. he had gone . . . a backpack . . . green and blue, I think."

". . . said '*Buenos dias*' as we passed each other . . . track near las Platas . . . walking slowly . . . a maroon car further down the track . . . carried a walking stick of some kind . . . a bag on his back like hikers use . . . green or blue, I can't remember . . ."

"He was standing in the doorway of the empty *cortijo* up near las Platas . . . wearing a hat – the sun was fierce that day . . . I'd seen him up there before . . . he was usually on his own . . . he spoke sometimes, once he

said my goats smelled bad . . . I didn't see any car near
by though earlier I saw one parked further down the
hill . . ."

"Funny how they all mention the same things," she said.
"It's almost as if the words had been put into their
mouths."

The way Alvarez tightened the corner of his mouth was
the only sign of his annoyance. "For most of the year these
men live quiet uneventful lives," he said. "Peasant lives,
tending their olives or their fields. When a stranger comes
into their midst, naturally they take note of him, especially
when it is not the tourist season."

"This last witness," Tess tapped the paper. "He says that
usually Jonas was on his own. That implies that sometimes
– or this time – he wasn't."

"So?"

"Did you ask him about it?"

Alvarez frowned. "It didn't seem important." Like
Tess, he touched the paper with his forefinger, pointed
to a paragraph. "You see he particularly mentions the
fierceness of the sun. As I said to you, Mr Fedor was
almost certainly overcome by the heat."

Tess could not rid herself of the image of a man – not
Jonas – in the dark doorway, stooping perhaps, the wide
brim of his hat casting a shadow across his face, concealing
his identity.

"But if Jonas – if Mr Fedor was with someone that last
day, then the person should be found. He may know
something more."

"I can't see that there is anything more to know."

She said boldly: "So there's absolutely no substance

to the rumour I heard that Jonas Fedor was deliberately thrown over that wall?"

Lines of anger creased the policeman's face. "None whatsoever," he said.

"Then how come he was found at the bottom of the gulley? I've been up to look at the place myself and it's obvious that if he had simply fainted and gone over the wall, he would have landed on one of the ledges just below the edge of the cliff. Though if he *had* simply fainted, it seems far more likely that he would have fallen forward."

"Who has been telling you that he was thrown over? There is no truth at all in such a story. It is virtually certain that everything happened as I have told you."

He was uneasy, Tess could tell. He moved things around on his desk, straightened the two plastic baskets of correspondence, aligned the files, not sure how much she really knew and how much she was guessing.

"It was suggested to me before I came here that there might have been some kind of a cover-up," she said.

Alvarez spread his hands, placed them on the desk, leaned towards her. "Señorita Lovel: why should the police wish to cover anything up? Such a death is not good for our economy – we are a poor community, we rely on visitors in the summer to help us through the winter. It is in our best interests to be absolutely open."

"You might equally say that since such a death could damage your tourist trade, you have every reason in the world to sweep the whole thing under the carpet."

"Having investigated to the best of our ability, we naturally do not wish to see the matter stirred up again just before the opening of the Vicente Museum. You have doubtless heard of this?"

She nodded.

He went on: "It is expected to attract many tourists, many art-lovers. Naturally, if false rumours were spread, it could have an adverse effect on the livelihood of our citizens."

"I see."

"Do you? Señorita Lovel, this town suffered greatly during the Civil War. Despite the years which have passed, there are many people still living here who have not forgotten the atrocities, the bloodshed. Nor forgiven. In my own family . . ." He looked earnestly at her from under his heavy lids. "It is time that the divisions, the ruptures, were put behind us: the museum is more than just a memorial to a great painter. It is a chance for the town to pull together at last."

"I understand what you're saying," Tess said.

Yes: she understood perfectly. He was attempting to appeal to her better nature, to plead the most insidious of rationales – the greatest good of the greatest number – as a reason for her not to seek explanations other than the official one.

None the less, however persuasive he tried to be, however many copies he gave her of depositions by witnesses, or pathologists' reports, Alvarez' version of events simply did not ring true.

18

MERCEDES

Now.

The time had come.

Strength surged through the bones of her shoulders, lifting her arms; she felt her fingertips flutter, feather-light with the electric force of her power.

Across the crib containing the newest Ramirez baby, Mercedes smiled at Carlos and his wife.

"He takes after you," she said to Marguerite, and hoped her disgust was properly veiled. The child lay against a lace-edged pillow, eyes creased shut, cheeks blotched with rash, its over-large scalp crusted with some sort of skin condition.

Marguerite smiled palely. "Do you think so?" Her face was gaunt; despite having given birth only two weeks previously, her body had already lost all the accumulated roundness of pregnancy.

"We want you to be godmother to him," Carlos said.

Mercedes could see from the way Marguerite's mouth puckered that this was not a mutual decision. "What a compliment," she said. "I hope I can be worthy of such a trust. What is his name to be?"

"We thought – if you agreed – Fernando," said Carlos.

"Yes," Marguerite said. "We would both like that." Under her dark blouse her chest was flat and unnourishing. She spoke as though the effort of producing words was almost too much for her. "Fernando is a good name."

Too good, Mercedes screamed silently. Much too good for the brats of Ramirez. She would gladly have struck them both down then. Rage hurtled through her body like a pin-ball, rampaging along her limbs with the force of a bullet to collide with brain, sinew, muscle, to ricochet off and go racing through the bloodstream to smash against her heart.

She looked at the child and then at the uncertain mother; she saw how easy it could be.

"Six months old and still not thriving," she said.

"I know." Marguerite gazed down at the big-headed baby lolling in her arms. "I'm sure something's wrong with him." She seemed etiolated, emptied, as though the lifeblood was slowly draining out of her. Each movement cost her a visible effort.

"What do the doctors say?"

"They give him tests all the time but no-one seems to be able to say exactly why he's so sickly."

"Does Carlos have any suggestions?"

"Carlos?" For a moment some unreadable emotion blanked out the concern on Marguerite's face. "No. He leaves such domestic matters to me."

And to not much avail, Mercedes thought. There was dust on the grand piano at the far end of the room; the flowers needed changing; although it was already noon, a dirty glass and an ashtray full of cigar stubs still stood on the table beside the armchair where Carlos must have been sitting the evening before.

She walked over to the open window, the long swinging skirt and cinched-in waist of her New Look suit a sharp contrast to Marguerite's outmoded clothes. The cropped militarism which had been suitable during the war years had given way some time ago to the exuberance of calf-length hemlines and full gathers. She stepped out onto the small balcony and looked down at the oblong of green a long way below which constituted a tiny communal garden for the apartment dwellers. Distantly came the sound of hooves on cobblestones, invisible traffic. Yet though the Ramirez apartment was quiet and outwardly serene, Mercedes was sharply aware of tension, of an unhappiness almost palpable; it lodged in the folds of the drapes, seeped out from beneath the sofas, hid behind pictures.

Fertile ground, she thought.

Still on the balcony, she pulled aside the long lace curtains which lined the window so that she could see Marguerite leaning over her ailing baby. "Do you ever get a compulsion to fling yourself over?" she asked suddenly.

Marguerite looked up. "Is my state of depression so obvious?" she said, in her low voice.

"I didn't mean – surely you don't *really* . . . Most people have similar feelings in high places, don't they?"

"Perhaps," Marguerite said. "And some even give in to them."

Mercedes came hastily back into the room and sat down on the sofa beside Marguerite. Timidly, she took her hand. "You don't *seriously* consider throwing yourself over the balcony, do you?" she asked.

"I've certainly thought about it." The other woman's face was hopeless, her deep-socketed eyes sad behind the wire frames of her eyeglasses.

"But why? And think of Carlos."

"He'd probably hire a ninety-two piece band to broadcast the news," Marguerite said bitterly.

"Marguerite! How can you say such a thing? Carlos loves you."

"Carlos loves sex," Marguerite said harshly.

"But he is your husband."

"He doesn't seem to realise that unless you take precautions, making love means making babies. And when I ask him to be careful, when I say that the doctor recommends waiting before we have any more, when I say my health is suffering, that I don't want to, that I'm tired and it hurts me, he takes no notice, just carries on."

"Men are like that."

"Sometimes it's as though he's doing it to someone else, not me at all. As a matter of fact," Marguerite said, twisting her wedding band round and round, turning her eyes away from Mercedes, "I almost wish he *had* another woman." She began to weep, her thin chest convulsing.

"You don't suppose he does, do you? You don't think he is unfaithful to you?"

"I don't know." Tears squeezed from Marguerite's reddened eyes.

"How terrible for you," Mercedes said. "I had no idea." She paused, and added thoughtfully: "I don't know if I could go on living if I suspected my husband was in love with another woman."

"I didn't say he was." An ugly flush coloured the pale skin of Marguerite's neck.

"But it's obviously what you think."

"It's what I'm forced to think." Marguerite groaned. "Oh, Mercedes: you're too young to be burdened with the troubles of your friends. I shouldn't be talking to you about it. But you've known Carlos all your life – you probably know him better than I do."

"It is perhaps a terrible thing to say, but I know enough of him to be aware that one woman will never be enough. When he lived in Madrid, before he came here to New York, there were so many . . ." Mercedes let her eyes grow dark and huge; she saw Marguerite quiver under her gaze, raise a hand to her heart, as though in the black depths she had caught a glimpse of unspeakable perversion. "Pilar . . . Juanita, I remember them so well. And others, whose names I didn't even know."

"I don't know if it's true," Marguerite exclaimed wildly, her normally deep voice rising, out of control, "but if he's seeing another woman, I *would* kill myself. I can't stand the pain of knowing he no longer loves me, I simply can't bear it."

"Hush," said Mercedes. "What about your children?"

"They've been brought up by their nanny as much as by me. I don't suppose they'd even notice if I was gone."

"All marriages go through crises," Mercedes soothed. Gingerly, she put her hand on Marguerite's shoulder – had the baby thrown up on it? There was certainly a suspicious and nauseating whiff coming from the woman. And why couldn't she get a decent haircut? Those rolls and bobs went out with the end of the war. It was not surprising that Carlos was looking elsewhere. "You will weather this one, I'm sure."

"No! How could I allow him to make love to me if he's

slept with someone else?" sobbed Marguerite. "How could
I demean myself?"

"You're his wife. It's your duty."

"Never," Marguerite cried passionately. "My mother
keeps talking about duty, but what about Carlos's duty
to me? He made promises when we got married which he
hasn't kept; why should I keep the ones I made?"

"But you don't even know if he *has* been unfaithful to
you," Mercedes said, a little catch in her voice. "Though if
he has, no wonder you feel you can't stand to go on living.
The humiliation, the rejection, the horror of knowing he'd
come from one bed to the other . . ." She looked down at
her hands and murmured: "Too dreadful . . ."

A cold fury seized her when Marguerite, instead of
agreeing, wiped her eyes and sniffing, said: "Perhaps I'm
exaggerating. Things aren't nearly as bad as I've made out
– I tend to weep over the silliest things at the moment. It's
the baby, the aftermath of pregnancy. My doctor says my
hormones are bound to go a little crazy, three children in
three years."

"Of course they are," said Mercedes. She was thinking:
I must give her some proof.

Reluctantly she left the luxury of Doña Carlota's establish-
ment for the privacy of her own apartment. The old lady
wept. "You've been like a daughter to me, Mercedes,"
she said. "Please don't go."

"It's time I was independent," Mercedes said.

"I could make it worth your while to stay," said Doña
Carlota. She stared up at the girl; Mercedes wondered
if she knew about the pieces of jewellery, the occasional
small painting or *objet de vertu* which had ended up in

Mercedes' own room. For a moment she was tempted. The old lady was rich and careless; childless too. The long-term benefit could be very satisfactory.

But the years were passing; she had things to do. It was time to put her plans into action.

"I'm sorry," she said, kneeling in front of Doña Carlota, taking the plump old hands in her own. "I really am. But I need to have somewhere of my own, somewhere I can entertain my friends, my business acquaintances. I know you would never mind me bringing people back here, but it's not the same." What she meant was that it would be impossible to implement her plans for Carlos Ramirez under Doña Carlota's roof.

The years in New York, of visiting the houses of the wealthy and privileged, had refined her own tastes. She filled her new home – a four-roomed apartment only a few minutes' walk from the new Schleeman & Aragon gallery – with light, with flowers, with mirrors and paintings. Taking a tip from Schleeman, she had all her walls painted an uncompromising white, the better to display the rugs, the pictures, the sculptures, the few pieces of fine furniture she had accumulated. Surveying the rooms when they were completed, she told herself: this is the home of someone who cannot be stopped.

She bided her time.

Eventually, she knew, Carlos would come to the gallery, looking for her. When he did, she would invite him shyly round to see the apartment. After that, it was up to her own skill to see that events turned out as she wished them to. Meanwhile, there was Lovel to wonder about, Jonas to dream of, Schleeman to work with.

Without actually saying so, she had brought her physical

relationship with Schleeman to an abrupt halt as soon
as the papers of ownership were signed; he had been
philosophical about it. She was careful to hint at further
prospects; he was content to wait. She knew he had begun
to patronise the brothels once more and hoped there would
be no need for her to submit to him again. She found
him comforting; with the sexual element gone, she was
able to think of him as a friend. Like Jonas, he had no
illusions about her, he still professed to see in her the same
characteristics which had brought his own success.

Carlos came into the gallery one lunch-time. "You didn't
tell me you had moved," he said, taking off his hat and
staring at her with what appeared to be hostility. There
was grey in his hair, the first she had seen. It only made
him seem more handsome, as did the thickening of the
jowls beneath his jaw.

"I called in on my cousin," he went on. "She told me you
had left her house. You can imagine my embarrassment at
not knowing myself."

"But you are no kin of mine, Carlos. It did not seem
necessary to inform you."

"No kin," he said roughly. "I have to agree with
you there." More, much more than kin, his blue eyes
told her.

"Besides, you have problems at home," Mercedes said
delicately.

"What problems? Marguerite, do you mean? Even
though she is – "

"I meant my godson. Fernando. He is not well."

His face softened. "You are always so thoughtful of
others," he said. "You are – you have always been a
source of – of . . ." He broke off. "May I come and visit

you in your new home, Mercedes? Will you give me the address, allow me the privilege of calling on you?"

"Of course. But I am here during the day. And in the evening, you have your own home to go back to."

"I doubt Marguerite will grudge me a couple of hours with one who is, after all, as close to me as my own family," he said. His voice was tired; she wondered if he drank more than was good for him. Despite the easy charm, the gift for leadership he had shown as a young man, he had always been weak, she had known that. It was that very weakness which had made him so easy to manipulate.

"Then come when you will," she said.

"Tonight? Tomorrow night?"

"Whenever you wish."

He brought wine with him, Spanish wine, rioja. "I found a little shop which imports it directly," he said, unwrapping the bottle, removing the cork. "I drink it sometimes when I am alone. For a little while, with the taste of the wine on my tongue, I can imagine myself at home again."

"Carlos," she said. She reached out a small hand to him. "You too, then, suffer as I do, from a longing to be back in Spain?"

"God, yes."

"But I thought you were so happy over here."

"Happiness is always relative."

He looked round him, taking in the bright surroundings, the colour, the pretty things spread about the room, the drawn curtains shutting out the darkness, everything gleaming, not seeing the snare she had set, the honey-smeared trap. "You have made yourself a beautiful place to live," he said wistfully and she knew he was comparing it with his own dingy, neglected home.

"Thank you." She poured the wine into heavy goblets. "Sit down, Carlos."

When he had taken one end of the long pale-covered sofa, she nestled into the other corner and pulled her legs up under her. The lighting was behind her; she knew she looked young and fragile. "What do you miss most about home?" she said softly. "For me it is the way the light falls on the streets of Montalbán in the heat of the day. Everything is so clear then, so black-and-white, so stark. Here, there is always smoke or fumes, everything is grimy, no-one has time to stop or to spend time just looking." She wrinkled her nose. "But then here in the city there is nothing to look at."

"I long for my home," he said. "For the Casa de las Lunas. I don't think I have ever been entirely happy since I left it." He reached an arm towards her along the back of the sofa until his fingers were not quite touching the sleeve of her blouse. "That's not true, of course. But sometimes I think I shall never be content until I am there again." He drank deeply of the wine. "Though Montalbán was not all idyllic by any means. The ignorance, the poverty, the superstition – perhaps you're too young to remember that poor girl who was made pregnant by one of the landowners: instead of blaming him, they stoned her, actually stoned her. In the end, she left the village. God knows what happened to her. And the war, of course. The things that happened then left an indelible stain of bitterness and hatred."

Does he think I don't know that? she wondered angrily.

I, of all people? "But it is the house which means most to you?" she asked. "The Casa de las Lunas?"

"It means everything," he said simply. "My father was born in that house, and my grandfather, his father, too. It symbolises the family, the continuing line of the Ramirez. I want my sons to grow up there."

"What's to stop you going back? You're surely rich enough."

"I can't take Marguerite away from her family. Not that I want to. But, poor girl, she is already not very strong, perhaps even – " he looked at her with resignation, " – unstable. I feel she would pine away in an alien country."

"Don't you pine – at least a little – in this one?"

"Oh God, Mercedes . . ." To her surprise, his eyes filled suddenly with tears.

She got up, poured more wine into their glasses, sat down again, this time much closer to him. "Carlos, is it that bad?"

"You don't know how bad."

She felt a surge of elation. Things were turning out even better than she could have wished; other agencies were conspiring with herself to produce the unhappiness she was so determined should be his.

She produced an expression of sympathy and he reached for her hand. "I didn't come to burden you with my troubles," he said. "Tell me about yourself. I understand you're working for someone new now: another thing you didn't tell me. It was Mr Rabat who told me where to find you. Why didn't you do so yourself?"

She looked down at her hands.

"Why not, Mercedes?"

When she did not answer, he put a hand under her chin and lifted her face towards his. "Why not, Mercedes?" he asked again.

"Because," she whispered.

"Because what?"

"You know."

"Indeed I do not." His dark eyes smiled at her, then suddenly changed; in them she read comprehension, the possibility of delight.

"I felt it was time to get away from you, Carlos," she said, speaking as though it embarrassed her to utter the words.

"Why?" His voice was persistent; he moved closer to her until he was staring down into her upturned face. Rage and triumph filled her: she knew she was very close to the objective which had obsessed her for so many years.

"Don't make me say it," she whispered. His hand was on her back, pulling her towards him.

"Say it."

"I can't."

"Say it."

She looked at him, eyes huge. She bit her lower lip to stop its quiver. "It's not – "

"I'll say it for you." He pulled her up tight against him, and kissed her hard. His tongue forced her lips apart; against her open mouth, he said fiercely: "I love you. I love you, Mercedes. Oh God: I've loved you from the first moment I saw you, sitting like a Madonna under that olive-tree with the rocks behind you and the blue sky beyond."

"Carlos," she said, fluttering a little in his arms. As though by accident, her hand dropped to his lap; hastily she pulled it away, pliant against him. Her heart was as cold as an arctic wind.

"Do you remember how I carried you to my horse? How we rode down into the town? How I held you in front of me, in my arms?"

"I shall never forget," she murmured. "But you are married now. You belong to someone else."

He fumbled with her blouse. She waited until his hand was caressing her breast, letting him feel the hardening of her nipple. She thrust herself against him, uttering little cries, kissed him passionately as though she could not help herself. Then abruptly she pushed him away, gasping.

"No," she cried wildly. "This is wrong, sinful. We mustn't . . ."

"Mercedes." His groan was bitter, bone deep. "How could I have let you go? Why didn't I see what you meant to me before it was too late? Oh God: what have I done?"

In answer, she would like to have screamed at him that he had finally delivered himself to her. The words piled up inside her mouth, ready to spew forth, but she gritted her teeth and instead, pulled away from him, keeping her eyes cast downward, and began to tuck her blouse back into her skirt.

"I think you'd better go," she said. "Forgive me if I have behaved in any way which might have caused you to think – " She broke off, looked up at him, bit her lip. "No. I must be honest with you, Carlos. I wanted to kiss you. I wanted you to – to feel me. But it must stop. There is your wife to think of."

He looked distraught, leaning his head in his hands. "I've tried to hide my feelings from you," he said thickly. "But I can't go on."

"Carlos." Gently she touched his hair. "Please . . ."

"May I come again?"

"No. Yes. I can't think," she said distractedly, raising both hands to her head.

"Please." He took her hand. "*Please*, Mercedes."

"Not yet. Give me time to consider," she said. She stood very close to the sharp white of his shirt-front. "You know how much I want to see you, Carlos. It's just that – "

"I know." He laid a finger across her lips. "I understand."

When he had gone, she went into her bedroom. She took off her clothes and stood in front of the glass. Her body floated, milky-white, heavy-breasted, against the shadows of the room behind her. She smoothed her hips with her hands, felt the mushroom softness of her own skin, touched the triangle of hair which lay between her thighs. Jonas, she thought. There was an intolerable pain in her heart.

She put fresh lipstick on her mouth, watching herself, thinking how easy it was to deceive, how skilfully she had played the part of something she had been only once: a virgin trembling on the brink of revelation. In the darkened room, her white skin gleamed, innocent, illusory, like a toadstool among fallen leaves, which imitates an edible mushroom but is in reality deadly poison.

She leaned forward and slowly kissed her own image in the mirror, the glass cold against nipple and belly. Her eyes, open, were huge and dark; for a moment she stared into the depths of herself. Then, shivering, she took from a drawer a laundered linen handkerchief. She shook it out, wiped the mark of her mouth from the smooth glass, wrapped it in a chiffon scarf and hid it away again.

Although she had not attended Mass for years, she slipped into St Patrick's Cathedral on her way to work the next day. The stone floor was cold under her knees, and uncomfortable. She gazed up at the window above the altar and offered thanks, not knowing to what or to whom. She refused to believe in a conventional God but felt none the less that there had to be some supreme power which had helped her to reach her desired ends.

The night before, Carlos Ramirez had picked the toadstool, thinking it other than it was; he had lifted the fatal mouthful to his lips and one day, he would die of it.

19

MERCEDES

The world shrank. Once it had seemed wide with opportunity; now all other concerns appeared irrelevant, subsumed in the drive towards fulfilment of her goal. She sat like a spider at the centre of a bright jewelled web.

Carlos came frequently to the Schleeman & Aragon gallery; she looked away from him, spoke stiffly, refused his suggestions that they meet, yet clutched sometimes at his coat sleeve as though her emotions were stronger than she was. With satisfaction she saw him grow increasingly desperate. She lurked at the centre of her web, waiting.

Finally he came. Opening door of her apartment, she fell back in confusion, one hand drawing together at her throat the two edges of her satin robe.

"Carlos!" she exclaimed, "What are you doing here?"

"May I come in?"

"I'm not dressed," she said. "No. You must go away."

She started to close the door but he pushed at it. "Mercedes, let me in. I have to see you."

She pulled the belt of her robe tighter, as though armouring herself against him. "I'm getting ready to go out . . ."

"Please. I need to speak to you." Rain sparkled in his hair. He leaned harder on the half-closed door, his eyes reddening as though he was about to weep. "I'm going out of town at the end of the week. I can't leave until I've talked to you."

"This is wrong, Carlos," she said. "I thought we had agreed that – "

"Please."

"You can come in for ten minutes, no longer."

Concealing the triumph she felt, she led him into the living room, took his briefcase from him and set it down. Removing his raincoat, he watched as her breasts swung free inside the opening of her robe. Straightening up, she said: "Now, Carlos, what can I – "

He seized her, pulling her against him. His hands tore open her robe, held her breasts; his eyes were full of despair. She thought how tawdry the scene was as lightning calculations ricocheted through her mind. She had intended to inflame, merely. Would it further her ends if she allowed him to think he was raping her? Would it enslave him even more? There was the immense advantage that his rush to possession would be too precipitous for him to notice she was not a virgin. On the other hand, that could, if necessary, come later, without losing its advantage.

She struggled to get away from him as he crushed her face against his shirt-front; the buttons were painful against her cheek. "Carlos!" she cried, exultant. "You're ruining my make-up. Let me go."

He released her and they faced each other, breathing heavily. Mercedes pulled her robe together again and raised a hand to push at her dishevelled hair. "I told

you I was going out. Look what you've done to me,"
she said. "And your shirt – what a mess you've made."

He stared down at his smeared shirt-front. The sight
sobered him. "I can't go home like this," he said.

"That's your business." She stepped away from him.

"Perhaps I could sponge it – "

"You'd better take it off," she said coldly. "As it
happens, I have a couple of new shirts here which
Mr Schleeman asked me to pick up for him. They should
be about your size."

Ramirez took her hands. "You're angry with me."

"Of course I am. I told you that whatever our feelings
for each other we must not meet again, not when you have
a wife and children. And now you force your way into my
home, behave indecently."

"I'm sorry. I should never – "

"What did you wish to say to me? Why did you
come?"

He hesitated. "Mercedes, do you think we could
ever . . .?"

"Ever what?"

"If I divorced Marguerite, would you consider . . ."

She stared at him with horror. "But that would be
against everything we've been brought up to believe,"
she said. "How could you possibly imagine that I would
go along with such a – a terrible idea?"

"Of course not." His face was abject. "Forgive me."

"Oh, Carlos," she whispered, "don't look at me like
that." She touched his face. "So sorrowful."

And so weak, she thought, with contempt. She despised
him for being so easily manipulated, so out of control,
even though it was exactly those qualities which were now

working for her. She remembered her brother's cell, the lounging jailers, oil paint acrid on his fingers; that last winging bullet.

"Mercedes . . ."

"I'll get a shirt for you," she said, and turned away to hide her hatred.

As she had known it would when she bought it, the shirt fitted perfectly. "I'll wash this one," she said. "Come into the gallery next week and pick it up."

"Mercedes," he said urgently. "Can't we – "

"Not while things are as they are." She opened the front door. "Now, you must go." She smiled tentatively at him. "One of us must be strong, Carlos."

As soon as he had gone, she picked up the dirty shirt and examined it closely. She had feared it might be custom made, from one of the uptown shirt-makers; luckily it was ready-to-wear, bought from a Fifth Avenue department store. She went over it inch by inch, looking for distinguishing features: on the lower edge of the tail she found the laundry mark, an R, stitched to the seam in black cotton.

Marguerite lay back on the sofa, her face grey and hopeless. "There's no question," she said drearily. "None at all." More tears tumbled from her eyes and slid down her cheeks. "I'd been hoping that I was wrong, but there just can't be any doubt now."

"It does seem pretty conclusive," murmured Mercedes. Fastidiously she picked up the cosmetic-stained man's shirt which lay on the sofa between them. "You're sure this belongs to Carlos?"

"Absolutely sure."

"But how can you be? Bloomingdales must sell hundreds of these every week."

"Look." Marguerite turned up the hem of the shirt and showed Mercedes the initial sewn by the seam. Mercedes pretended a shocked interest; she already knew the mark was there since she had deliberately sewn it in herself. "My laundress marks all his shirts this way. There can't be any mistake."

"It's a pity Carlos is out of town this week, so you can't ask him. There's probably some simple explanation."

"The simple explanation is that he is having an affair with another woman," Marguerite said faintly. There were purplish shadows under her eyes; her cheekbones stood out in her bony face and her long nose seemed beakier than ever.

"The handkerchief is his too, I suppose."

"Yes."

"How do you know for certain? Couldn't anyone buy a handkerchief like this?"

"Look: it's got his monogram embroidered in the corner. I ordered them for him myself. Half a dozen, best linen. I know it's his. I packed three of them in his bag when he left yesterday and there are two others in the wash. He must have left this one at his – his *lover*'s house by mistake."

"I'm sure you're wrong," Mercedes said. She spoke with truth, having abstracted the handkerchief from Carlos's drawer herself, on one of her previous visits.

Somewhere in the house, the baby grizzled. Marguerite began to sob, as she had done off and on since Mercedes' arrival. "Why does Fernando cry all the time? Why can't he give me a little peace?" she demanded. She grasped her temples. "It makes my head ache so. Sometimes I'm afraid I'm going to hurt him, poor little thing. But he never stops. I can hardly think straight."

"What I don't understand is what this man hopes to gain by sending you such a letter," Mercedes said, frowning over the unsigned note which had accompanied the bombshell package delivered that morning to the Ramirez apartment. "He doesn't ask for money to keep silent, or threaten Carlos. He just goes on about Carlos seducing his wife. He doesn't seem to want anything."

"Perhaps he just wants to share his outrage and his – his grief with the only other person who could possibly understand – the other wronged partner," Marguerite said. "I've no idea who he is, or where Carlos might have met his wife, or how long this affair's been going on. I don't how he found out our address." She lifted her shoulders in a gesture of resignation and let them fall again. "Not that it matters. None of it matters."

"Have you told your parents?"

"No. It would kill my father if he knew. You know how poor his health's been recently." Again Marguerite sobbed, harder this time, her face contorted, her head hanging over her lap. "Oh *God.*" Uselessly she wiped her hand across a face smeared with tears. "What am I to do, Mercedes? How am I going to carry on?"

"You have to, however hard it seems, however lonely and unhappy you feel, however much you fear that the children will get on perfectly well without you," Mercedes said sternly.

The distant baby began a thin screaming which caused both women to glance at the open door. "Oh God." Marguerite's mouth twisted. Her voice rose to a shriek.

"I don't know why he cries so much. I wish he'd stop, I wish he'd give me some peace."

"You must try and be strong for his sake."

"Strong?" cried Marguerite. "How can I be strong? I'm an inadequate wife, a useless mother, no good to anyone."

Mercedes glanced at her wristwatch. "Look, I hate to leave you like this but I really must get off to work. We have an important dealer coming in from San Francisco. I wish I'd known about this earlier: I could have made arrangements to stay with you." She stood up, brushing at her skirt. "You will be all right, Marguerite, won't you?"

"All right? How can I be, with something like this hanging over me?" Marguerite raised a trembling hand and brushed ineffectually at her hair. "I'm no good to anyone, not to my husband, not to my children."

"You're not to say such things. You're not even to think them. Besides," Mercedes grinned crookedly at the older girl. "If no-one else needs you, I do."

"Not really. You're a working girl with a successful career of your own. I'm sure you wouldn't give up your job if you married, the way I did." Marguerite dissolved into choking sobs again. "I don't know what happened to me. I used to be capable and efficient too, like you. I used to have a job. All I've got now is my family, and I'm no good at it. When I think of the years ahead, the other children I shall have to bear . . ."

"If it's getting pregnant again which bothers you," Mercedes said briskly, "there are ways you can prevent that."

"I know. But somehow I never seem to have the energy to organise it. I just wish I was more like you." Marguerite clutched at Mercedes with a tear-wet hand. "As a matter of fact, I often think that you and Carlos might . . ."

"Might what?"

"If I wasn't here, I mean. He thinks he regards you as a little sister, but I've seen the way he looks at you."

Mercedes blushed. "I haven't. And if I thought there was any truth in what you're implying, I'd never speak to him again."

"It would be so suitable," Marguerite said. "A perfect solution, even if Carlos doesn't realise it."

Perfect for whom? Anger prowled the pathways of Mercedes' mind. Perfect? How could the woman be so obtuse? "I'm sure Carlos loves you still," she said, hearing the carefully calculated falsity of her tone.

"And I'm sure he doesn't," said Marguerite. "I must face the fact that to all intents and purposes, my marriage is over." She glanced at the balcony and then back at Mercedes.

"Look. I'll drop in again this evening," Mercedes said. "And meantime, try to be brave. Don't do anything silly?" She too glanced uneasily at the window leading onto the balcony, then leaned towards Marguerite and kissed her cheek. As though it was an afterthought, she added: "I'm going to take these away with me," indicating the contents of the anonymous parcel. "I'm not leaving them here for you to brood over. If you want to confront Carlos with them when he returns, I'll bring them back."

It all went more smoothly than Mercedes could have expected. The small tragedy in Brooklyn passed almost unnoticed by the press. The woman who had jumped from her ninth-storey balcony with her eight-month-old baby in her arms had been the daughter of one and the wife of the other partner in a small firm of lawyers specialising in cases of disputed immigrant citizenship. There seemed to be no particular reason why she should have jumped, though witnesses spoke of profound depression following the birth of her third child. As far as anyone was aware, there had been no strife between the woman and her husband, nor any money problems. Her distraught parents were at a loss to understand what could possibly have induced their daughter to take her own life; one of the witnesses, a Miss Vicente who worked in an up-town art gallery, stated that she had dropped in on Mrs Ramirez the evening before her death and found her, though somewhat low in spirits, none the less looking forward to her husband's return from a business trip the following day.

That was it: a verdict of suicide while the balance of the mind was disturbed was brought in. At the age of thirty-four, the short life of Marguerite Blevitsky Ramirez was over, done with.

Leaving the field clear.

20

TESS

Behind his smooth expressionless face, his blank eyes,
lurked a nightmare of secrets I didn't want to know about.
Too bad. Some of them might be interesting.
Here Be Dragons, by I. C. Sanyoshi
translated by Teresa Lovel

Julian Maitland's house lay up a rutted track, surrounded
by thick growths of oleander and fig. Palm-trees threw
black shadows onto its white walls; hens scratched in the
dry earth beneath them. To one side, in a patch of stiff
grass, a donkey stood tethered.

Maitland came out onto the verandah which ran round
the house as Tess parked her hire car. It was a relief to
have reached her destination safely; although she still did
not know whether the falling stone of the night before had
been deliberate or not, she was none the less constantly
on the look-out for danger, exhaustingly on the alert.

In the sharp light, Maitland seemed older than when
they had last met, and more weary. She felt a sudden
compassion for him, for anyone who had lived through
as many years as he had, known sadness and loss. What

was he: seventy, seventy-five? How many more years did he have before he too was gone? Since Jonas's death, she had become acutely conscious of the frailty of human life, of its fleeting nature, the narrowness of the gap between living and dying.

Julian led her into a round hallway which, despite the outside temperature, was amazingly cold. A small window let in what light there was. A couple of carved chairs stood at either end of a heavy table of dark wood which had been pushed against the rough-cast plaster of the walls; on it stood various pieces of pottery which she recognised as being Maitland's own work. A dark woodwormed painting of a suffering Christ hung above an empty fireplace set slantingly across one corner.

Trying not to shiver, she followed him through to the other side of the house; it was still too early in the year for the sun's heat to have penetrated the tiled roof, or for the thick walls to have had time to retain its warmth. On the plain white walls were a number of paintings.

"I suppose you've been collecting art most of your life," she said.

"Not in any organised sense. People give me things; I buy from friends."

Tess looked around the room more carefully. Two paintings in particular caught her eye, both still lifes, carefully unsophisticated, in vivid primary colours. "Where did you find those?" she asked.

"In New York. I was there a few years ago and saw these in a gallery window. Went straight in and bought them on the spot." Tess bent lower. At first she could see no signature, then, with a rising sense of excitement, she saw that both were signed with the initials AR, the same flowing letters as on the painting she had bought at the auction.

She tried to keep her voice even as she asked: "Who is he? Do you know his name?"

"I'm afraid I can't remember. Something rather prosaic, if I remember correctly, more like a civil servant's name than an artist's. Andrew Rogers – Arthur Rathbone, something like that."

"If you remember, or know how I could get hold of him, I'd be very grateful indeed."

"He's not very famous, nor likely to be. Andrew Rathbone – *that* was his name."

"I – I really like these. I'd love to buy one myself."

Was this the answer to why the Vicente signature had been so carefully painted over: in order that the mysterious AR could gain some renown for himself? But that couldn't be right: the two styles were completely different. No-one would believe they were by the same person. Still puzzling over the problem, she followed Maitland out onto the wide verandah.

It was not so cold outside; the sun was high and warm air was trapped under the verandah-roof. Above their heads, doves cooed. A bottle of wine and some glasses stood on a table. Julian Maitland pointed to one of the several basket chairs and sat down himself. His gaze swept the landscape in front of them.

"I never tire of this view," he said. "I've been visiting this area for nearly sixty years – I first came here when I was a schoolboy – and it still seems as lovely to me now as it did then."

He poured wine for them both. "Now, tell me how you are."

She hesitated, wondering whether to confide in him, then decided it would be wiser not to. Once the idea that there was something sinister about Jonas's final fall had lodged in her brain, the world about her seemed to have taken on a malignant hue. The incident of the previous evening added to what she still hoped was a groundless paranoia. It was perfectly possible that Maitland knew more about events than he had implied; equally, it was possible that he was in league with the police for some reason, eager to cover up. Carry the thought to its logical conclusion and it was not inconceivable that Maitland himself might have been responsible for Jonas's final fall.

"I'm coming to terms with Jonas's death," she said eventually. "Though I seem to have annoyed the local police force by asking questions about what happened."

"Alvarez cut up rough, did he?"

"A little bit. I had a terrible time getting him to give me the name of one of the witnesses. He implied that I would devastate the town's economy if I didn't shut up."

"Yes. The movers and shakers of Montalbán are expecting great things of this Vicente Museum now that they've overcome the local opposition. Some piece of minor Spanish royalty is even coming down from Madrid to cut ribbons and declare it officially open."

"Have you heard about a plan to develop the area round Montalbán?" asked Tess.

"In what way develop it?" Julian looked alarmed.

"I don't know. A dam? Industry?"

"Christ. I hope not. Anyway, the place is far too mountainous for that sort of thing."

354

"When you saw him, did Jonas say anything about why he'd come?"

"Nothing directly. We discussed old times, drank some wine. I showed him some of my recent work; we talked about an exhibition in Stockholm in which we were both participating. That's all. Nothing about any industrial development."

"I had a vague feeling that perhaps he wanted to prevent whatever it was – though for someone as law-abiding as Jonas, industrial sabotage is hardly the – "

Maitland laughed, his expression quizzical. "What makes you think Jonas was law-abiding?"

Taken aback, Tess said: "Wasn't he?"

"When I first knew him, during the Second World War, that was the last thing he was. Although I never knew exactly what he was up to, he was certainly involved in something outside the law."

Tess frowned. "What sort of thing?"

"Espionage, I'd have guessed."

"A *spy*? Who on earth for?"

"The Brits, I should imagine. Both before and during the War, there were a lot of Germans operating from Spain. He was an ideal candidate for recruitment by MI6 – a German-speaking refugee, fluent in Spanish, with a grudge against the Nazis. As you know, although Spain was officially neutral during the War, it leaned towards the Axis powers. Madrid was full of Nazis. Not that I could be sure about Jonas: you didn't ask too many questions in those days, for fear of the answers."

"Jonas a spy?" Tess did not know why she should feel so surprised. She knew, after all, that he had fought against the Falangists in the Civil War; what was so different about

355

spying in the World War? "But how could what Jonas was doing back then have any bearing on his death?"

Maitland moved his glass back and forth, holding it flat against the table with two fingers on either side of the stem. He looked up at her from under unkempt white eyebrows. "He was pretty familiar with this part of the world, you know. He worked for a while with one of the anti-Franco groups down here."

"I did wonder." Tess looked up at the craggy hills. "Alvarez mentioned atrocities in Montalbán. Was Jonas involved?"

Maitland did not answer straight away. Instead, he gazed towards the quiet hills. Then he said: "I sometimes wonder whether the Nazi-hunters have got it wrong. Perhaps people should forget what happens in wartime. Maybe it's best to paper over the cracks, try to carry on. But some of the things that were done . . . and all in the name of freedom." He ran both hands over his face. "There were so many atrocities, on both sides – but Montalbán's was a particularly bloody one." He looked at her. "How much do you know about the Civil War?"

"I've read about it, naturally."

"Then you'll know how confusing it all was, how many factions there were, all fighting against each other, only loosely united against one side or the other. The bigger groups formed themselves into armies but at a local level, many people were being denounced and killed by their own neighbours, being hauled before tribunals of their former colleagues and imprisoned by people they'd known all their lives, who'd set themselves up in judgement over their fellow citizens. They called themselves patriots or republicans or Falangists but often they were motivated by nothing more noble than personal revenge."

Again his gaze strayed to the red line of the hills and the high sierras beyond.

"And this was going on even in a place as small as Montalbán?"

"There was an army garrison at Granada. They sent down a particularly brutal officer to try and impose some kind of military order. He was the kind of sadist that wars so often throw up. Santiago, his name was. Capitán Santiago, though the people round here called him El Malo." He smiled sadly. "Everyone had a nickname then: it was best not to know real names if you could possibly avoid it."

"El Malo? But that's precisely what Jonas came here for – to try and identify the man." Vividly she remembered Jonas leaning forward under the bright studio lights, gazing at the camera in that determined way. Had he been passing on a message, hoping that among the viewers there was one who would tremble at his words? "Tell me what happened."

"A resistance movement grew up, centred on Montalbán. The numbers varied, but there was a hard core of about twelve – they called them the Apostles. This Santiago character was determined to hunt them down, so they took to the hills, living in some of the abandoned *cortijos*, moving about, never in the same place more than a night or two. They carried out some quite spectacular raids, considering how few there were of them. Once, they got so close to the barracks that they were able to ambush one of the senior officers outside the gates . . ."

"And?"

Maitland glanced at her and cleared his throat. "Uh – Jonas slit his throat, left him dying in his own blood outside the barracks."

Silence stretched out between them like a bloodstained ribbon. *Jonas slit his throat*: how strange the words sounded, how brutal, how unJonaslike. She remembered Dominic's question, the night before she left for Spain and felt her love for Jonas shift on its axis, not changed, but viewed from a different angle.

"He was a tough one, was Jonas, and utterly ruthless." Maitland sighed. "In the end, someone betrayed him and his group, poor devils. No-one knows who it was – except, apparently, Jonas. He told me that only a handful of people had ever known and they were all dead except himself. When he was here, he said that he planned to reveal everything in his autobiography, including the identity of El Malo – "

"How on earth did he – "

"– which could be bad news for Santiago, wherever he is," said Julian. He shook his head. "That evil bastard dealt with them in the most obscenely vicious manner. Most of them were so young, hardly more than boys. Though Santiago himself can't have been more than twenty or so. That didn't stop him from doing what he did." He stared sombrely at Tess. "He was something of an artist with the knife – I couldn't even begin to . . . wouldn't want to . . . people I knew, turned into so much . . . *meat*." Overcome, Maitland raised a hand to cover his eyes.

"Man's inhumanity to man," Tess said softly.

"Except that, in Montalbán's case, it wasn't just man. After Captain Santiago had . . . *barbarously* disposed of the men, they rounded up their womenfolk and children. Mothers, sisters, wives." He swallowed visibly. "What they did to them, to little children, for God's sake, to little girls, was so unspeakably vile . . ." He looked across at her and she saw his eyes were full of tears. "In front of their mothers, too. And when they'd finished, they would deliberately drop the bodies outside their homes, with a note saying: *Sorry, it was an accident.* Can you imagine what it did to the families round here?" His voice shook.

She wished there was comfort she could offer and knew there was not. What Don Pedro had said was clearly true: even after all this time, it still mattered, still hurt.

"Is that when Fernando Vicente was shot?" she asked quietly.

"He was the last one of the band to die: I don't know whether that was a blessing or a curse." Maitland said. He refilled his glass with a hand that was not quite steady, and drank its contents down. "I wasn't here at the time, you understand," he continued. "But . . . I've seen photographs of what those two butchers did. Unfortunately."

"Two?"

"He had a sidekick, a henchman with some refinements of his own when it came to torture. El Fantasma, they called him."

Tess sat in a silence, and after a while, he said: "Every time I go into Montalbán, I marvel at how normal it all seems, on the surface."

"But not underneath?"

His answer was oblique. "As you know, Jonas was here then, he was one of them, one of the partisans, resistance fighters, whatever you want to call them. Once, Santiago actually had him, but he got away on the journey to the barracks in Granada." Again Maitland drained his glass. "I only saw the photographs; Jonas saw the bodies. Did I say that they used to dump them in the street? With a note . . ." He stared at the sky behind the mountains.

"I can understand how terrible those days must have been for everyone, but what did it have to do with *now*? With Jonas? Do you think this Santiago lives here?"

"He'd be a brave man if he was still around here. The Spanish have long, long memories, and Montalbán is full of those whose close relatives suffered at his hands." Julian reached over and poured more wine into Tess's glass. Above them, on the roof of the verandah, the doves cooed; the palm clattered gently together, like clapping hands. The sombre air was thick with bitterness and the metallic smell of long-shed blood.

"On the other hand, no-one would recognise him, if he was, because the only ones who saw him face to face were the ones he tortured to death," Maitland continued thoughtfully. "He will undoubtedly have changed his name. I suppose in theory he could be the doctor, or the priest, or the chap who runs the grocery store in the Calle Vasquez Molina for all we know. Jonas was the only one who ever came back, and even he never actually saw the man."

"I can't believe he'd have stayed in the area. And wouldn't his – his bloodthirsty nature have come out over the years?"

"Not necessarily. A man can atone in later life for wrongs committed in youth."

"The sort of horror you talked about presupposes some basic ineradicable flaw," said Tess.

"Perhaps the flaw can be held in check. Perhaps that's the penance for someone like Santiago: for the rest of his life he has to deny a fundamental part of himself. That must be hard." Leaning forward, he tapped Tess's knee. "If you want my opinion, I think Jonas came back to jog a few memories and ended up jogging one memory too many. I think that's why he died."

He shook his shoulders, ran one of his long fine hands over his hair. "Let's talk about something more pleasant. Have you been to the Museum yet?"

"Not yet."

"When I came here as a boy, Carlos Ramirez – the friend I used to stay with – and I often used to come across Fernando Vicente when we were out riding in the hills."

She wanted to say: "You knew my grandfather. Tell me about him." But as she thought about them, the words grew more difficult to formulate. He would wonder why she had not mentioned it at the beginning; he would suspect her of picking his brains – and his memories – for reasons which had nothing to do with Jonas. Instead, she said: "Was he painting when you saw him?"

"Sometimes. Sometimes just sitting on a rock or under a tree, staring into space. He was a funny little man, very shy and frightened. We felt sorry for him." Maitland swallowed wine, his eyes fixed on the horizon. "Funny how things go. Carlos went to the States, married some American woman, who committed suicide, and ended up marrying Vicente's younger sister, Mercedes."

"Yes, I – "

"Not the happiest of marriages, that one." Maitland grimaced. "She was very beautiful. Very charismatic. Jonas and I met her years and years ago in Madrid, long before she was married. She had huge dark eyes set in an extraordinarily pale face. And that wonderful thick Spanish hair." He nodded at Tess. "Rather like yours. She always seemed to be dressed in floaty white things, like a phantom: it made us all feel terribly protective because she looked as if a puff of air would blow her away."

"I went to her house yesterday," Tess said, not enlarging on the reasons.

"Did you, indeed? I understand the place is virtually a ruin now."

"Pretty much."

"These days Mercedes seems to spend most of her time in New York, though since she's begun this project of hers – the Vicente Museum – she's been around a lot more. She must be a lonely woman: apart from Luisa, her surviving aunt, there's no other family left. Ramirez' boy is dead and the girl – Concepción – hasn't been back here for thirty years. She may well have died too."

Tess wondered how much to confide, whether to say that she herself was Concepción's daughter. Again, caution advised her against it. Until she established exactly what had happened to Jonas, it was better to say nothing unnecessary.

Maitland was shaking his head. "I haven't spoken to Mercedes for years."

"Why not?"

"She was responsible for making a lot of people very unhappy. In some ways, I think that's worse than killing them, don't you? I can never forgive what she did to

Carlos Ramirez, who was my friend. Nor to his children.
You'd have thought they had suffered enough, losing
their own mother like that, but she just made their
lives hell."

"What does she do in New York?"

"She owns an art gallery there," Maitland said. "The
Aragon Gallery, I believe. Very successful, very – "

"The Aragon?" Tess could not keep the surprise from
her voice.

"Yes: do you know it?"

"Not in a personal way . . ." A kind of bile was rising
at the back of Tess's throat, compounded of fury and
outrage. So Mercedes Ramirez was the person who had
sold fake paintings to Phil Cramir. Mercedes was the
person who had demanded that she, Tess, give her *The
Tears She Shed*, and when that did not work, had offered
to pay far more than it was worth in order to have it.

"Actually," Maitland said, frowning. "Although we
haven't spoken for years, I did see her recently. You
must have done, too."

"I don't know what she looks like. I've never seen – "

"But she was at Jonas's funeral," Maitland said.

Like a jigsaw puzzle half-done, Tess was beginning
to put pieces together without any idea what the whole
picture would look like. What Maitland had just told her
was merely another piece to be fitted in. So *that* was
Mercedes . . . Although she had no need to ask, she did
so none the less: "She has a – a mark beside her nose,
right?"

"Yes. The local people think she's a witch, of course,
as her mother was."

"So did Jonas." Tess said it quietly, trying to digest the

new information she had been handed, trying to decide its relevance to Jonas's death, unsure where any of it was leading.

For the moment it was impossible. It was time to change the subject. "Talking of recent work, did Jonas ever . . ."

Adroitly she led Julian back into the past, to the time after the war, to the days when the two of them had worked together to change the face of English ceramics.

Driving back to Montalbán, she tried to analyse her feelings. Twice now she had come across the woman whom she had grown to fear and loathe and not felt the emotions she might have expected. She tried to review the auction, that short moment of grief at Jonas's funeral, in the light of what she now knew, but they did not assume any new significance.

She was aware, however, of the possibility that the events leading up to Jonas's death were far more complex than she had previously imagined. Past and present were intertwined in a way she could not have foreseen. The long ribbons of time which bound her first to her mother and beyond that, to a younger Jonas, a vanished era, trailed behind her like the tails of a kite. It was beginning to look as though she might have to make sense of the past before it would be possible to make sense of the present.

Later that night, she stepped out onto the balcony of her room. Before her, in the darkness, lay Andalusia, the *campiña* spreading away from her down towards the coast. Out there, golden eagles soared. Out there, somewhere, lay the bones of Vicente and the spirit, indomitable, of Jonas.

The words the old housekeeper – Julia – had spoken that morning came back to her: *She will not rest until the last of the Ramirez lies in his grave.* Now that she knew to whom the words were attributed, she could well believe them true. What had begun as a simple desire to know more about the circumstances in which Jonas had died seemed to have turned into a kind of unacknowledged duel between Mercedes and herself.

She told herself she was being overly dramatic. This was Spain, now, not some vendetta-obsessed society in the eighteenth century. None the less, the fact remained: she herself was the last of the Ramirez, and whatever the reasons, Mercedes Ramirez wanted her dead. The night-time attack in her own home made a different sort of sense now; she was more than ever convinced that if the goatherd had not appeared on the scene the previous evening, another attempt on her life would have been made. Strangely, the realisation that the danger was real, rather than imagined, gave her strength.

Resolutely, she turned her thoughts elsewhere, remembering another balcony in another Spanish town. Then she had wept, mourning the urgings of her own body: now, instead of sorrow she felt fear. She should have told Dominic why she held back from him. She should have explained. But to do so would inevitably be to allow him closer to her heart, and that she was not prepared to permit, to him or to any man. Except Jonas. And even he . . .

In the town there were lights, voices, the sound of revving motorbikes and canned music. On the terrace below her window, people still sat at the tables. Most were couples or groups but at one, on the edge of the square, someone sat alone. Man or woman? It was impossible to tell. The night breeze carried herbs on it and leaves rustled. A bird squawked harshly. She pulled the windows to and closed the shutters.

The thin silk of her nightdress seemed inadequate cover against the cold. Yet it was the cold which lurks at the heart of a mystery rather than any physical chill. She was being drawn into something she did not understand, something far-flung and many-layered.

But the immediate mystery which occupied her thoughts was much more mundane.

Coming back across the pale polished floor of the hotel, she had seen the rack of postcards. Turning it round on its central axis, she thought about sending a card to Don Pedro, and to Dominic. She pulled out a poor reproduction of a Vicente landscape, the colours improbably bright, the outlines blurred, and another of the Vicente café scene which hung in the Prado. It was then she saw it: the thin shoulders and wide-eyed unfathomable gaze of the girl on the bed. She turned it over: *The Tears She Shed*, she read. *From a private collection. Printed in 1991*.

It was impossible. How could the picture have been reproduced in 1991, when for the past eight years it had been in her own possession? Was it connected in some way with the copy she had seen in the Cramir collection?

She picked the postcard up from the table where she had left it. There was something wrong with it, something she could not quite identify. Shivering in the night chill, she climbed into bed.

She thought back to Phil Cramir's paintings in Houston. It was increasingly obvious that all the events of the past few weeks were bound together into a pattern, linked by what might prove to be an ultimately fatal chain.

21

TESS

Time always decides to take an extended lunch break when you're waiting for something to happen.
Then There Was Nun by I. C. Sanyoshi
translated by Teresa Lovel

Ten o'clock. In the Calle San Miguel, the Vicente Museum would be opening its doors to such of the public as were interested. Not many, Tess imagined, since those that were had long ago had a chance to see over the house, and the tourists would not be flooding in for at least a couple of weeks, after the official opening ceremony.

The town was still half asleep, preoccupied with its small concerns. Shutters were being pulled inward as protection against the climbing sun, old ladies with shopping bags moved slowly between greengrocer and dairy, dogs barked. The elderly priest, a cigarette in his mouth, sauntered up the steps to his church then stood for a while, gazing over the valley, before stubbing out his cigarette and passing through the arched doorway. Someone switched on a radio which sent a blast of hard rock music rolling down into the square, while at the same

369

time a woman began to screech to her neighbour about her eldest daughter's shortcomings.

The former home of the Vicentes had been sold some years ago and recently been bought back by Señora Ramirez, the museum attendant told Tess, pushing a ticket and a thin catalogue under the plexiglass grill between them, while behind him, a bank of small screens patrolled the various rooms. It would eventually hold the most comprehensive collection of his works in the world. If the señorita would like to pass through into the room on the right and follow the arrows . . .

Tess was glad to do so. There were a few people ahead of her, admiring as they went. The conversion from home to shrine had been cleverly done: there were no glass-fronted cabinets, no labels, and the security system was sophisticated and discreet. Although the artist's three unmarried aunts had continued to live in the house until the late Seventies, someone with a long memory and a loving eye for detail had apparently recreated the house much as it must have been forty years before that, leaving plenty of room for the illusion that the *fascistas* had only that morning come knocking at the door in search of Vicente.

Tess wandered through the rooms, discovering from the catalogue which chair had belonged to the artist, which had been the everyday china, what newspapers the family had read, which of the many Vicente paintings and drawings lining the walls had been executed here in Montalbán and which had been purchased elsewhere by the Museum Trust and brought back to hang in the artist's birthplace.

In the dining room hung a portrait of the aunts: Isabella

and Rosita, Francisca and Luisa. The three older sisters sat rigid, gazing out of the canvas, reminding Tess of the famous portrait of the Brontë sisters. Standing by Francisca's knee stood a child, Luisa, the afterthought, the product of her father's late second marriage, dressed in a short white pinafore over a green dress, her dark hair caught up at one side in a green ribbon.

Tess was delighted to see a rough sketch of the Casa de las Lunas which justified her certainty that the painting she had bought at the Brantwell Manor auction was indeed a true Vicente. Which reminded her of the mystery she had not yet had time to resolve: who had painted over Vicente's signature and inserted other initials? Was it really Andrew Rathbone? Why would anyone want to conceal Vicente's signature and thus drastically reduce the value of the painting?

In the drawing-room – hard brocaded sofas, stiff arm-chairs, handsome pieces of furniture in satinwood – she saw, with astonishment, a familiar Vicente canvas. Surely it was impossible . . . She walked slowly towards it; as she came closer she realised that though it was an extremely skilful piece of work, it was only a copy of *The Tears She Shed*. The thick brush-strokes lacked real conviction; behind the dark eyes of the girl on the bed there lay no anguish, no resignation, and though the lemons in the Delft bowl were brightly yellow, they did not urge the viewer to reach in and pick up the sharp fruit.

In addition to which, there were six of them, instead of seven. The same deliberate error as in Cramir's version.

The catalogue confirmed that this was a copy, without saying who was responsible for producing it. It added that though the Museum Director – who had grown up in this very house – knew the whereabouts of the original, she had not yet succeeded in bringing it it back to its rightful place, though she hoped eventually to do so. Which explained the postcard in the Hotel La Viña: obviously it had been reproduced from this copy and the phrase 'Private Collection' had been used in order to disguise the fact that it was not the original. That meant there were at least two copies of the painting in existence, she reflected, in addition to the original: the one in Houston, and this one.

She followed the arrows which pointed up a curving flight of polished stairs. The bedrooms of the aunts still held the essence of their different personalities. As was fitting, Francisca's was the largest, containing not only a bed but a chaise-longue, numerous small tables covered in objects, a dressing-table loaded with silver-topped jars, a rocking chair, a cheval-glass and not one, but two wardrobes. Isabella's bustled with multiple chintzes. Rosita's was spare, decorated with faded water-colours, the covers and curtains pale, sprigged with tiny flowers. There were books beside her bed: Tess saw that the one on the bottom of the pile was the only available biography of Vicente. In such a careful reconstruction of a particular era in the house's history, perhaps even of a particular day, its bright cover struck an anachronistic note. Mercedes Ramirez had published it in the late Sixties, thirty years or more after the artist's death.

Passing the small cluttered room which had once been Luisa's, she came eventually to Fernando Vicente's own bedroom, kept as it must have been on his last day of freedom. In the wardrobe his clothes still hung; a striped collarless shirt lay carelessly across the bed, his shaving things stood on the top of the chest-of-drawers as though just set down.

Time frozen, time suspended, Tess thought. As though someone had hoped to defeat Eternity, not understanding that time can't be held back, that it continues, unstoppable, inexorable. Or was it something more tragic: an attempt to imprison time, pretend that this day was the only one which had ever mattered?

The catalogue informed her that the little room at the end had belonged to Mercedes, Vicente's sister, currently the Director of the Museum and President of the Museum Trust. Standing there alone on the braided carpet, Tess tried to capture something of the girl who had once slept there. The neat all-white room gave away no clue to the complex personality who had once gazed from that window and slept in that narrow bed – unless it indicated that the occupier was determined to let none of her feelings escape, to hide her real persona beneath unrevealing tidiness. So what had happened to turn the innocent child who had been Mercedes into the monster who terrorised her stepchildren, and betrayed her husband?

Was not the Museum itself an answer to the question? The obsessive love which lay behind this careful reconstruction, the captured moment inherent in Vicente's thrown shirt, the shaving kit, the detail of a forty-year-old moment: were they precisely what had changed Mercedes for ever?

Do I, too, hide the clamour of my inner self behind neatness? Tess thought. Is this what Dominic means when he says I'm too self-controlled? She thought of her own house, the unlived-in look she cultivated; it was not a notion which pleased.

As she climbed the narrow druggeted stairs from the bedrooms to the top floor of the house, the air grew distinctly colder. The servants had once slept up here and here also, the catalogue informed her, was Vicente's studio, kept exactly as he had left it that fatal day. The small room on the right was one where he occasionally used to sleep when caught up in the excitement of completing a canvas or beginning a new one. At such times, he would work fitfully through the night and on into the following day, his devoted aunts occasionally tiptoeing to the top of the stairs from the landing below to leave trays of food, most of which he did not stop to eat.

Tess stood at the door of the studio. Although at the time of his death Vicente had been based in Barcelona for some time, he always came back south to Andalusia for the summers to paint, to help with the hay harvest, to find spiritual regeneration in the hot hills. That was what he had been doing when they came for him; he was known for speaking out against the *señoritos*, the big landowners of the region, and their shameful exploitation of the peasant workers. He had been outspoken for years, and more or less tolerated; in a time of social ferment, it had been deemed necessary to silence him.

Poor Vicente. He had always referred to himself as a coward, inclined to take the easy way out; there was something deeply poignant about the fact that in the end he had stood up for his beliefs and been martyred for them.

Even all these years later, Tess fancied she could smell the tang of turpentine and the pungency of oils. His paint-spattered easel stood as it had the day the soldiers came for him; on a table near by lay his palette, an oily rag, a knife. It looked pretty much as all artists' studios look: a mixture of chaos and efficiency. The tools of his trade stood to hand, the rest of the studio was crammed with haphazard objects: a rosary of elaborately carved olive-wood beads, a moth-eaten antlered head wearing a dusty wreath of wax flowers, a crucifix of brass and oak, oddly shaped stones, an empty chocolate box, plaster busts, bones picked up on his walks, a top hat with a silk rose attached to the brim, a small bronze statue of a boy on a dolphin, a pair of white kid gloves with pearl buttons. Papers and books were piled randomly over a shabby chaise-longue draped with Indian shawls. On the walls were reproductions of Surrealist painters such as Dalí and Gris, Impressionists like Monet, a life-size copy of Picasso's *Demoiselles d'Avignon*.

If she had hoped, by some form of emotional osmosis, to feel the ghost of him painting there, head cocked to scrutinise the brush-stroke just made or the overall effect of a patch of colour, she was disappointed; she felt nothing. She moved on to the little room next door.

In the doorway, she stopped. The whitewashed wall of uneven brick, the high window, the bed, the cloth-covered table, were all familiar. In imagination, she had been in this room before a thousand times, she had touched that table, that embroidered cloth, had smelled the lemons which stood in a Delft bowl. All that was missing was the child on the edge of the bed. Although the furniture had been shifted around, this was surely the setting for *The Tears She Shed*.

She stepped forward – into a hideous noiseless clamour which ripped and hammered at her brain cells. Clasping her head in her hands, she squeezed her eyes shut. God!

What was it? Hastily she moved back, and the assault ceased. It was as though she had crossed into some invisible force-field surging with long-ago emotions so powerful that they had not yet subsided. Tentatively, she moved forward again – and again was assailed by a mixture of repulsion and fear so strong that she could almost see it hanging in the air, livid as a bruise.

Sick and shaken, she stood on the threshold of the room. What had just happened to her? It was terrifying – and degradingly familiar.

Footsteps. Someone was coming up the stairs. She felt an urgent need for solitude. Along the uncarpeted passage were doors on either side giving on to more attic rooms. The one furthest from the stairwell had a PRIVATE – NO ENTRY sign affixed to it: trying the handle and finding it open, she quickly slipped in and stood just inside the door, leaning against it, trying to catch her breath.

She had never had any psychic experience before, never been aware of other-wordly phenomena, never had a dream or foreboding of the future. Yet, carefully rerunning the past few minutes through her mind, she was certain that she had just endured some kind of subconscious re-enactment of events which had taken place there.

Had Vicente, too, tuned into them? Hitherto, she had assumed that the girl in the painting was taken from life, but perhaps not. Perhaps Vicente, with his artist's sensibilities, had also felt some of the same subliminal chaos, had reached into the past to transfer it onto the canvas and so created one of his finest masterpieces.

She wondered what had happened in that bare little room. Some long ago son of the house, perhaps, raping a young servant girl who was too afraid to cry out or to complain for fear of losing her job, her terror so strong that it took invisible shape in the room. What had happened to her? Was there some small tragedy to be unearthed here if she cared to dig for it?

Outside in the passage, she heard footsteps. As they came towards the room where she was hiding, she held her breath. Slowly, the handle began to turn and she pressed her full weight against the door. The stealthy twist of the brass door knob seemed infinitely sinister; her heart thudded with apprehension. Was she being followed? Or was the person outside, now exerting a steady pressure on the door, merely the caretaker? She knew she did not believe it was the latter; she remained as she was until, apparently satisfied that the door was locked, the footsteps retreated.

It was only when she heard voices that she dared emerge from the dusty little room and hurry downstairs and out into the street.

Sitting with a cold beer on the terrace in front of the Hotel La Viña, she looked through the Museum catalogue again. At the front, a paragraph explained that although Vicente's output had not been large, there were still many of his paintings unaccounted for, vanished during the war, hidden perhaps or stolen. The Museum's directors were actively engaged in searching for these pictures, and would welcome any assistance the public might be able to give them. On the last page was a list of Friends of the Vicente Museum; several of them were familiar to her. Julian Maitland. The British Consul who had owned Brantwell Manor. Other prestigious names: Spanish nobility, ambassadors, American millionaires,

well-known collectors, patrons of the arts of all nationalities. Even the Hayashima Corporation.

To her surprise, the name she would have expected to
head the list was missing. Surely Luisa Ruiz-Barrantes,
aunt to both the dead artist and also to the Museum
Director, should have been there.

Perhaps the señora, Spanish president of the global
charity, Save the Earth, had other calls on her time and
her purse. Perhaps she felt she already did enough to promote her nephew's reputation. Even so, it seemed odd.

Tess became aware that an old man wearing blue
overalls and a hat of tattered straw was watching her
from beyond the edge of the terrace tables. Catching her
eye, he said: "Señorita Lovel?" His voice was so gravelled
that the words seemed little more than a clearing of the
throat.

"Yes?"

"I am Juan Martinez. Don Alvarez says you wish to
speak to me."

The third witness. "Yes. Please sit down."

He did so, accepted a beer, waited while she scrabbled
in her bag for the papers the policeman had given
her.

"I wanted to ask you – you say here that Señor Fedor
was usually alone."

"Yes." He must be in his late sixties, she judged, yet,
clearly, despite the bent spine and arthritic hands, still
vigorous and alert.

"But not always?"

"Not always," he agreed. She watched the beer slide
down his throat and the tiny lift at the edges of his mouth
as the coolness hit his belly.

"The times when he was not alone, who was he with? A man? A woman? Always the same person?"

"I saw him maybe half a dozen times at the old *cortijo* where he fell. Twice he was on his own, four times he was with someone else. Once he was with two men, the other times with only one man, always the same person . . . a man, not tall, not young. They were far from me, you understand? I could not see all the details clearly."

Tess could not think of any questions to ask. Juan Martinez had just answered them all. "Was there anything about these other men that you might recognise if you saw them again?"

"Nothing, señorita. They wore hats and coats."

"Isn't that a bit bizarre?"

"How so, señorita?"

"Señor Fedor was supposed to have been overcome by heat. The others must have felt very warm, dressed like that."

Martinez lifted his shoulders. "Perhaps they were trying to disguise themselves a little." The glance he gave her was shrewd. She could not decide whether he was telling the whole truth or just a part of it.

"You're sure they were men?" she asked.

His smile was slow and wide, revealing tobacco-stained teeth. "I have a wife and four daughters, señorita; I think I would know the difference."

Not necessarily, Tess thought. Not if you were too far away to get a good view. "Was either of them from around here, do you think?"

"I couldn't see them clearly enough – and one I saw only once – but I should say not. On the other hand . . ." he paused, thinking about it.

"Yes?"

"The other one, he was not entirely a stranger. I mean, I have seen him before, somewhere."

"So you did recognise him?"

"Not him. But a man like him. Perhaps it was the way he walked. Or the way he held his head." Again the lift of the shoulders. "Difficult to say. I can only tell you of the general impression I got, not of any details."

"Did he and Señor Fedor seem friendly together?"

"That is a more difficult question, señorita." He tilted his glass and poured the last drops of beer down his throat, not objecting when she signalled to the hotel owner for another. "It is not a question I have considered until now, but thinking back, I should say they were not. They were not fighting, you understand. They did not seem to be exchanging angry words. But Señor Fedor held himself . . . like this." He clamped his elbows to his sides and stiffened his jaw. "You know. As if he did not wish to touch the other."

Tess waited while he took a long swallow of his second beer. "And that last day, when you say you saw Señor Fedor in the doorway of the *cortijo*, are you sure it was him, and not this other man?"

"No. I am not at all sure. In fact, I think perhaps it *was* the other. Since Don Alvarez said you wished to ask me questions I have considered the matter very carefully, and this is what I believe."

"So possibly Señor Fedor was inside the *cortijo*?"

"Perhaps. Or perhaps, señorita, by then he was already dead."

Tess started at him sombrely. "You think maybe this man killed him?"

Once more he showed her his discoloured smile. "It is not for me to think such a thing. I saw a man, that last day. The man in the hat. I mean. If it was not Señor Fedor but this other, then I did not see Señor Fedor. I do not know whether Señor Fedor was murdered, or merely fell, an old man overcome by the heat."

"But surely –

"I *do* know that it would be better for you not to be here, señorita, if you are a friend of Señor Fedor's." He spoke swiftly, urgently. "Of course we knew who he was and why he had come back. He hoped to find justice for us all at last. We had much reason to be grateful so, for his sake, it was best that we did not speak, did not let anyone know we recognised him. If he needed us, we knew he would ask. Alvarez? What does he know? He was not here in the time of the troubles."

He stood up and looked carefully around him, then leaned both his brown arms on the table and bent towards Tess so that she could smell the beer he had drunk, the cigarettes he had smoked, and something fouler, the stench of long-term poverty and neglect.

He said quietly: "I think you would do best to leave things as they are, for your own sake, to ask no further questions. Once, on the road to Granada, Jonas cheated death. This time, he was not so lucky."

Then he was gone, pulling his straw hat down over his ears, striding across the terrace with the step of a much younger man.

22

TESS

If there's one thing I've learned over the past twenty-five years, it's that if some eight foot bozo's coming at you with his fists swinging and a mean look in his eye, he's not going to be a Sunday School teacher.

Bodily Harm by I. C. Sanyoshi
translated by Teresa Lovel

She woke the next morning to find her brain in overdrive. It seemed clear that Señora Ruiz-Barrantes might be the very person to supply answers to some of the questions which clouded Jonas's death. The lines of interconnection were undoubtedly there: Phil Cramir had donated the proceeds from the sale of his Impressionists to Save the Earth; Luisa had strong links with Montalbán; Jonas had been in Montalbán during the most turbulent period of the little town's history, and had known Vicente, Luisa's nephew.

She sat up in bed. Although it was early, the day was already bright; through the half-open shutters she could see the fronds of a palm-tree limply sagging in the expectation of later heat. It seemed obvious that before she flew back to England, she must go to Madrid and talk to Señora Ruiz-Barrantes.

It did not take her long to pack. The hotel-keeper seemed relieved to hear she was going and she imagined him telephoning Alvarez as soon as she left to impart the good news. Despite the warning she had been given by Juan Martinez, she had had another fruitless interview with the policeman, who refused to listen to talk of another man seen in the vicinity of the *cortijo* around the time of Jonas's death.

Perhaps Martinez was right and she should leave things as they were.

Driving down the winding mountain road from Montalbán to the valley, she was conscious of relief, a lifting of burdens. She thought: I came here; I need never come again.

The road clung precipitously to the side of the mountain. On which part of it had Jonas escaped from the sadistic garrison commander who had captured him? Here, where the cliff loomed on one side and the mountainside fell vertiginously away on the other? Or further down on the plains?

Facts, information, half-formed theories crammed her brain; over the past two or three days she had learned of a very different Jonas from the one she had loved. She pictured him slipping between shadows, dodging down alleyways, perpetually looking over his shoulder for the fatal knife thrust or the unexpected bullet. She saw him with blood on his hands, bodies at his feet. Once, the images would have seemed grotesque; now they were entirely natural.

In her mirror a car appeared, fast closing up behind

her. He hooted, a long rude blast on his horn, and she instinctively put her foot on the brake. Something must be wrong. Was smoke coming from the boot? Was a wheel about to fall off? He was going much too fast to overtake; on a road like this, one misjudgement could be fatal. The barriers between her and the steep drop on her right seemed suddenly flimsy.

The car hooted again, the sound bouncing back from the sheer rock face towering upwards on the other side of the road. Staring into her mirror, she could see only a dim face mostly obscured by the sun visor. What did he want? What was he trying to say? She shifted uneasily in her seat; if her car was in trouble, this was not a good place to be caught without transport. Perhaps he simply wished to overtake, idiotic though it might be. If there was a widening in the road soon, she could pull over and let him pass. He was much too close to her; were she to brake suddenly for some reason, he would find it impossible to stop without ramming her.

Carefully she nosed round the curves, refusing to let the car behind pressure her into recklessness. It would only take the slightest of mistakes for her to hit the barrier and go plunging down to the valley far below. Her throat was dry; she prayed for a bend wide enough for her to stop. Finally, rounding an overhang of stone down which flood water slowly trickled, she saw one. She pulled over and stared straight ahead, breathing deeply, not wanting to see the person who was causing her pulses to drum and terror to rise in her throat. She had expected to hear an engine race past, perhaps even a last derisive hoot of the horn; instead she heard only the sound of her own car engine. Glancing up at the mirror she saw to her horror that the car following her had also stopped, its bonnet practically touching her offside rear door.

Should she get out and confront the driver? Ask him what the hell he was playing at? Or should she stay where she was, ignore him, pretend she was admiring the view? She surreptitiously pressed down the locking knob on the driver's side and heard the other three door-locks click into place. At least he could not, if he was so minded, break in. She told herself not to be paranoid but was none the less terrifyingly conscious that whoever sat in the car behind for some reason wished her ill. Why? Who was he? Her mind ran over the possibilities: Alvarez? The hotel owner? Julian Maitland? Was this yet another of the Mercedes-inspired attacks on her? She was, after all, the last of the Ramirez . . .

Or . . .

. . . the possibility struck with a thrill of terror so pure and sharp that it was like the sudden appearance of a sharpened razor . . .

. . . was it feasible, could it possibly be that the man behind her was – El Malo? Had her arrival, her subsequent questions, roused him from whatever tainted dormancy he had maintained over the past decades? Had Jonas, too, broken that long anonymity – and paid the price?

Feeling the tremble of her knees, the weakness in her wrists, she kept her engine running. If another car appeared from the direction of Montalbán she would swing in behind and follow it down to safety. Whatever the man behind intended, he would hardly dare to do anything when there were witnesses.

She heard his engine rev and squinted into the mirror. He was backing slowly up, swinging his car out. The sense of relief was enormous; he was suddenly innocuous, just another driver enjoying the view. And as she thought this, there was a massive crunch and her own car juddered, groaning against its brake pads, shifting on the gravelled surface in the curve. She grabbed the steering wheel, straining to turn the wheels towards the road, away from the edge. Whoever was in the car behind had driven slowly past her and at the last minute, swung his rear around to catch the side of her car. Helpless, she stared at the back of his head, at the broad brim of the hat he wore. She was trapped between his car and the edge of the ravine. Her body shivered as though she was running a high fever.

His hat: how many times had Martinez referred to the man in the hat? In that instant, she felt certain that her tormentor was El Malo himself, the man who had murdered Jonas.

"I'm going to die," she said aloud and felt nothing, nothing but a huge regret that she would never know how it would be to lie naked next to Dominic, never feel his hands on her breasts, his body entering hers. In this moment of terror, she remembered him asking if it had ever occurred to her that Jonas was not what she thought him, and her own angry reply. He had been right; he had known Jonas better than she did, he had dug deeper, whereas she had looked at the surface, and seen only what she chose to see.

She would like at least to have apologised . . .

The man behind cleared her car, stopped, put his own into reverse, began to back up towards her again. Her wrists felt weak with fear and anger. She was not tamely going to let herself be pushed off the side of a mountain. She too reversed, very slowly, then moved back into first gear, still looking over her shoulder as though continuing to reverse. He came after her. They were manoeuvering in a space of no more than twenty feet. She turned to look helplessly through the windscreen, showing a face as full of fear as she could: eyes stretched wide, mouth open in a scream. In his own mirror he was watching her, she knew. As he eased his car sideways in order to ram her again, she put her foot down on the accelerator as hard as she dared – harder, given the limited amount of space available – and then shot forward into the space between the front of his car and the edge of the road, not caring if another car was making its way up towards them.

She heard the crunch of metal against metal as her offside rear door scraped along the front of his car, then she was gone, conscious that she was driving dangerously fast, praying that she would reach the comparative safety of the main road to Granada before he could get close enough again to harm her.

Taking one of the corners too sharply, she skidded on the gravel at the side of road and twisted the wheel viciously to the left, hearing the car scrape along the barrier. At the same time, she heard something hit the glass in front of her as a stone flew up from the roadway. The windscreen shattered into opacity, so that she was suddenly driving blind, unable to see where she was going. Frantically she banged at the safety glass with her fist and it dropped away, leaving a hole through which she could see the road. Cold air rushed in, straining her hair back from her head: a loose bit of glass flew at her cheek. There was blood on the heel of her palm; she raised it to her mouth and felt the roughness of glass embedded in the flesh.

Behind her, the other driver hooted. She did not even look into her mirror, but kept her foot down, swinging round the tight curves almost out of control. Her eyes kept tearing up in the chilly air coming through the shattered windscreen but she dared not wipe them with her right hand because of the glass embedded in it; her left she needed on the gear lever.

Ahead of her there was a stretch of road which ran straight for about fifty yards; she stamped simultaneously on her brakes and the clutch, and felt the other car hit the back of hers with a bone-shaking jolt which propelled her forward. Letting her foot ease up on the clutch, she pressed down on the accelerator again and as she pulled away, saw in the mirror that the man behind had stalled, the hood of his car bent out of shape, half obscuring his windscreen.

Suddenly, he leaned out of the window. She saw, with disbelief, a gun in his hand. As though in slow motion, she watched him lift it, aim at her, pull back the trigger. Then she was screeching away from him at top speed, tyres skidding, the engine roaring as she fishtailed round the next bend and out of sight.

The sense of relief was euphoric. She punched her arm into the air, laughed aloud, screamed: "Serves you right, you fucking bastard." If he had appeared on the road in front of her, she would have mown him down without a second thought. Slowing as she skidded round the next bend, she listened but could hear nothing beyond the sound of her own engine and the clamour of adrenaline in her blood.

*   *   *

The Agencia Andalucía lay in a street behind the cathedral. She pushed open the heavy glass door and spoke to the girl seated at one of the several desks behind the counter.

"I want to check on a car which was hired here some weeks ago," she said. "Would that be possible?" She reached for the seat which stood beside the next counter and sat down, hoping that the uncontrollable shaking which seemed to have taken over the lower half of her body was not too noticeable.

"Um – " The girl looked behind her but the other desks were empty, her seniors absent. "I can't see why not," she said cautiously, pulling a thick engagement diary towards her. "What name?"

"I'm not sure. Jonas Fedor, possibly. The car was a maroon Volkswagen Golf."

The girl looked at her oddly. "Are you all right, señorita?"

"Yes, thank you." It was easier than the truth.

The girl flipped through pages, then got up and went to a filing cabinet against the wall from which she extracted a folder. "Ah yes." She looked more closely at the papers. "Mr Fedor didn't actually hire the vehicle himself," she said, pausing to look at Tess, holding the file half-way out of the drawer.

"I know that. I want to know who did hire it."

"But it was hired in Mr Fedor's name," the girl said.

"By whom?"

The girl spread the file on the counter and pointed to a line at the bottom of a form. "Here," she said. "I handled it myself. I think he was an American. He had a United States passport and an international driver's licence: there didn't seem to be anything wrong with his papers." She looked doubtfully at Tess. "Do you want to make a complaint of some kind?"

"I'd simply like to know the name of the person who did the actual rental," Tess said. Inspiration came to her. "It's for our files."

The girl understood about files. She nodded. "He was called Marlowe. Mr Lawrence Marlowe."

Tess did not allow herself to think until she was in Madrid. Originally she had intended to drive, taking her time. After what had happened, she decided she was less vulnerable in an aeroplane than on the road. It was late by the time she had dealt with the paperwork for her hire car, signed papers, extricated herself from an office manager worried about the smashed windscreen, and disinclined to believe her story of a madman on the road from Montalbán.

It was only when she had reached the city and was settled into a small hotel in a street off the Puerta del Sol that she gave herself up to thinking again about the events of the morning. On the flight from Granada, her knees had begun to tremble again: now she felt only an icy calm. The truth was that someone had tried to murder her: to her astonishment she was able to accept that fact without difficulty.

At first, it had seemed obvious that whoever had been behind her on that precipitous road had almost certainly been responsible for Jonas's death too. The reason for murdering Jonas were clear, especially if Julian Maitland was right and he had stirred up too much mud along with the memories. But the theory came up against a stumbling block when she considered the attack on herself. Why should anyone in Montalbán want to get rid of her? What did anyone stand to gain?

Was it possible that Mercedes Ramirez was behind both the attacks on Tess *and* the death of Jonas? If so, what was the common link: the Vicente paintings? Or were there *two* murderers on the prowl: one, who had killed Jonas, and the other – Mercedes – who desired to kill Tess?

A short while ago she might have dismissed all this as melodramatic nonsense. But no-one who had experienced the imminence of death could be so cavalier. What struck her as most strange was that she could feel herself almost physically changing as the threats to her multiplied. Asked, she would have assumed she would crumple, would dart in terror from one safe harbour to the next; in actual fact, the main emotion the events of the past week had called up in her was one of defiance. So far, she had survived two, possibly three threats to her life. She felt the stirrings of invincibility.

And who was this Lawrence Marlowe? At first she had assumed it was merely a false name, but the girl at the Agencia Andalucía must have checked his papers and not found any discrepancy. On the other hand, it was easy enough to get false papers if you had the money and knew where to look. But whoever he was, why should Jonas have gone off with him? Was he the man Martinez had seen in the doorway of the *cortijo*?

"I'm a friend of Don Pedro Morena," she said into the telephone. "Please ask Señora Ruiz-Barrantes if I might speak to her."

The maid at the other end of the line said she would see if the señora was at home. Waiting, Tess hoped she had chosen the right introductory link. The fact that Luisa was not involved even peripherally with the Vicente Museum suggested that her friendship with Don Pedro might be more useful than the family connection. She could explain later, if Luisa agreed to see her.

"Hello?" The voice was soft but firm.

"Yes. Hello. My name is Teresa Lovel. I'd very much like to – "

"Did you say Lovel?"

"That's right."

There was a pause. Tess wondered if she was correct in interpreting it as a cold one. After a moment, she added: "I'm here for a – "

"What exactly do you want, Miss Lovel?"

"It's far too complicated to explain over the telephone. If you could possibly spare me a few minutes or so, I'd – "

"Do you know my address?"

Tess had already worked out on the city map where the Ruiz-Barrantes house was. "Yes, I – "

"I am at home this afternoon after five."

"Thank you. I'll – "

The receiver was replaced.

Tess looked at her watch, it was just before two o'clock. Which gave her a couple of hours to work out a line of approach which would not alienate a woman she could already tell did not have time to waste.

The house was in a tree-lined street at the top of a hill. Waiting on the terrace to which the maid had shown her,

Tess could see the vast square of the Royal Palace and the spires of churches rising out of the smog-wreathed city below. Up here, the air was soft, the city noise muted, except for an occasional metallic snap which Tess finally identified as the sound of garden shears somewhere in the next street.

"Señorita Lovel?"

Standing in the doorway was a woman whose face she already knew. She wore a dress of white linen banded at the hem in navy blue; her still-magnificent hair was pulled back onto her neck in an elaborate chignon.

"You are a friend of Pedro's?" the woman said. She smiled; Tess saw that she had once been lovely, that in spite of her age she was still beautiful. Behind her was a drawing-room furnished with heavy mahogany, velvet drapes, gold-framed mirrors; Tess caught the glint of a crystal chandelier, paintings, many photographs. "A friend and a colleague," she said. "We work together at the Banco Morena."

"And how is poor Pedro? I understand he has not been well."

"He has been unwell but is now better." Tess explained the situation as her hostess motioned her to a wicker chair and chose another for herself.

"I see. We are all getting older; these health problems are only to be expected. But that, of course, is not why you have come to see me." She called softly; the maid appeared and tea was ordered to be brought.

"No. I – "

"As soon as I heard your name, I knew you must be poor Conchita's daughter, yes?"

"Yes."

"I suspected that one day you would come. I thought it would have been sooner than this."

"I've come because of Jonas Fedor," Tess said.

Luisa was taken aback. "Jonas? What trouble has he got himself into now?"

"He's . . ." Tess took a deep breath. ". . . dead." Even though weeks had passed, she still had trouble accepting it.

"Dead?" Luisa pressed a hand to her heart and closed her eyes for a moment. "But he was here – " She broke off, closing her eyes. "Naturally, at our age, one does not expect to live for ever. But Jonas was always so strong, so alive. It is hard to think of him dying. How did it happen?"

Tess recounted the story while Luisa uttered exclamations of horror.

"And this happened in Montalbán, you say?" she asked finally.

"Just outside, up in the hills. The police seem convinced that it was an accident, but I'm certain there's more to it than that."

"Why?"

"I think he was murdered," Tess said. "I think it may be something to do with the past."

There was a long pause. Luisa fanned herself slowly; Tess said nothing. Finally, she said: "I came to you in the hope that you might know something which could help find out who was responsible."

"Oh dear." The fan swished.

"What?"

"Don't you feel it is better that we get on with our lives, instead of mulling over matters which are best forgotten?"

"Not if they continue to haunt us."

"Perhaps you are right." Swish, swish.

"Not if they mean murder."

Luisa clicked her fan shut. "Of course you are right. Ask me what you want to know, and if I can, I shall answer."

"You were still living in Montalbán when the – the atrocities occurred," Tess said.

"Yes." Again Luisa closed her eyes, the frail lids falling with the heaviness of stone as though she hoped to shut out memories.

"Can you think of anyone who might have reason to want Jonas out of the way if he came back to stir things up?"

"My dear, there must be dozens of people. Although I was little more than a child, I was aware that the Civil War divided families, split relationships, set father against son and brother against brother. Jonas was in the thick of it all: it was he who organised the resistance against the Falangists."

"Yes."

"Those were bad times. I would prefer to forget them." Luisa sighed. "Though it is impossible to forget the day they took my nephew away between the guards."

"You must all have been very frightened."

"Of course. And with the child there – Mercedes – already hysterical, none of us dared say what we all felt: that we would never see him again."

She made a gesture with her hands, as though even now the memory of that traumatic moment could still make her heart beat faster.

"How many of those who survived the atrocity still live there?"

"As I said, there are still dozens of people who remember what went on."

"The group was betrayed. Do you know who by?"

"Jonas told me that only the smallest handful of people knew that. Whoever it was must have left Montalbán: it would not be safe for him – or her – to stay." The fan flicked open again and see-sawed across the aristocratic face as though to hide the melancholy outline of her mouth. "They were terrible days, my dear, full of death and blood. It is no wonder that some of us were left permanently scarred." The fan drifted across her features. She said: "When I go back to Montalbán now, I see the change in the people. Once we were a single unit; now, still, there is always suspicion, envy, hatred. If someone has done well, they whisper that it is because he betrayed people for favours during the war. If someone does badly, they say it serves him right for what he did then."

"It's not easy to plead a case for war," Tess said, "and yet there are unexpected benefits, threads of unsuspected gold. Like your nephew."

"How do you mean?"

"Cowards can prove heroic; the weak are made suddenly strong."

"And the strong are shown to be weak," Luisa said. "Talking of the strong, was Mercedes, my niece, in Montalbán?"

"I was told that she is in New York at the moment, that she doesn't often come to Montalbán."

"She is obsessed," Luisa spoke softly, not looking at Tess, gazing back into the past. "It is as though her life stopped that day, when she went down to the prison and discovered what had happened to Fernando. I realised years ago that she must be a little – or even greatly – mad." She shook her head. "Perhaps she had reason . . ."

"What reason could she – "

". . . and I cannot help blaming myself for some of it." She sighed and said briskly: "But you think I may have information about Jonas's death."

"Not exactly. I just wondered whether you had any explanations. It may just be a string of coincidences, but there was a Vicente sketch of Jonas in the collection of Phil Cramir, the American collector who donated so much money to your organisation . . ." Her reasons for coming seemed flimsy now, gossamer-thin against the solidity of the elegant house and the busy purposes of its owner.

"The donation from this Texan came as a great surprise to us," Luisa said. "It enabled us to complete and initiate a large number of worthwhile projects. We were most grateful."

"Did you ever meet this man?"

"No."

"Did he say why he was giving so much money to Save the Earth?"

"Not a word. The whole transaction was arranged through various banks – including the Banco Morena – and the only information we had was that it was donated 'for personal reasons'."

Tess was already thinking along an alternative route. If the Banco Morena was involved, was it possible that Don Pedro might know something about the transaction? He had never met Jonas, but it was possible he could put his finger on the connection between Jonas and Cramir,

Luisa and Jonas. Though even if he could, would it help in finding out who was responsible for Jonas's death?

Her head throbbed; she felt suddenly weary. Why did she not simply accept the police version of what had happened in the hills above Montalbán? She had no real reason – beyond her own instincts – for supposing that things had not been as Alvarez said. Besides, all that really mattered was that Jonas was dead. Compared with that stark fact, nothing else was of any importance. Words like 'revenge' and 'justice' slid about in her head but they seemed suddenly meaningless.

Luisa put down her teacup. "You look confused, my dear."

"I am."

"About Jonas?"

"And everything else."

"Do you mean poor Conchita? It must have been dreadful for you to lose her so young." She closed her eyes for a moment. "So many motherless daughters . . . My own mother died when I was four or five but my sisters – my half-sisters, I suppose they were – took her place so effortlessly that I was never aware of missing her." She touched Tess's hand. "Conchita, too, was left motherless. I remember so well poor Carlos – your grandfather – returning from New York with his two orphaned children. I was happily married by then, and his grief was almost too much for us to bear. My husband and I had no children: although we were not related to Carlos in any way, we were old friends, we offered to bring up the two little ones but he wished to take them back to the family home, to the Casa de las Lunas."

"When did he marry Mercedes?"

"They were already married when he came home."
Luisa shielded her face with her fan, head bent. Then
she said: "Although she was my niece, my own family, I
never understood what possessed him to take such a step.
None of us did. And in spite of her behaviour, he never
said one word against her, not one."

"Perhaps he loved her."

"How could he? She was so beautiful but so cold, so
cruel to those two small ones. She was . . . flawed." She
lifted her shoulders. "I suppose it is not surprising."

"You said that before. What did you mean?"

Luisa's eyes slid away. "The terrible shock of her
brother's brutal death, the loss of someone she adored
when she was at her most impressionable age, . . . losing
her own mother . . ."

Tess realised that this had nothing to do with Jonas.
Even if Luisa had known him once, the years would
have turned them into strangers. None the less, she
had to know. "Did Jonas come and visit you here, on
his last visit?"

Luisa breathed deeply. "Yes."

"What did you talk about?"

"The past, of course. Old people always do, hoping
that in some way they might change the things which
have happened and yet knowing they cannot."

"Did Jonas say why he was going to Montalbán?"

"Not really."

"What else did you speak of?"

"We mentioned my *novio* . . ." She bit her lip.

Tess remembered Jonas saying that the hurts of the
past grow stronger, not weaker, as time passes. Her

mother had told her about poor Aunt Luisa who had
been abandoned by the man she loved.

"Yes," she said encouragingly.

"He was part of Jonas's group, you know." Luisa said.
"We were to have been married, and then suddenly he
left, without a word."

"Did you hear from him again?"

"Never. I don't know where he went, whether he
did well or not. I don't even know if he is alive or
dead. Perhaps he was killed by one of the factions in
the war; perhaps he went abroad. Who knows?" She
shrugged. "Poor Felipe. As I get older, I think increasingly
of him."

"Felipe?"

"That was his name. Felipe Cabrera. At least, that's
what he was called in the village." Luisa stared past Tess,
her eyes fixed on the past. "His full name was Felipe
Cabrera Ramirez, but they called him Cabrera to distinguish him from the 'real' Ramirez. Your grandfather's
family."

Tess's blood seemed to grow warmer. The note she
had found in Jonas's desk, signed AR, had referred to
someone called Felipe. She was right: there *was* some
kind of link between Jonas and Luisa Ruiz-Barrantes.
She said nothing.

"It's a long long time ago." The old lady fanned herself.
"That was the worst day of my life: first hearing that
Fernando had been executed and then the news that
Felipe had vanished . . . I have told myself many times
that he could not have been captured. The Falangists were
very careful to let us know who had been taken, who had
been tortured, killed, so that we would suffer more."

"Did you ever meet this garrison commander, Captain Santiago?"

"Of course not. No-one did. At least no-one who survived. Except for Jonas, of course, who was caught by him but, thank God, escaped . . ."

"How did he manage that?"

"He was rescued by those of his men who were still at liberty. I always hoped that was the reason Felipe left: because it had become too dangerous, because he had helped to free Jonas and his identity was now known."

Delicately, the old lady lifted the fan to hide a yawn. Tess knew she ought to leave. But there was one thing more . . .

"What was my mother like when she was young?" she asked.

Luisa brightened. "Ah yes. Concepción . . ."

Their voices rose and fell on the quiet terrace, memories they could never share fell from their mouths quiet as bubbles, while each of them tried for a time to convey in words lives which had not until then touched. At some point they moved into the dining room to eat a meal of fish and fruit served by the maid. Listening, Tess felt herself melting like a candle, changing shape, fluid in the warmth of new-found affection as Luisa added colour to names and events which until now had been only words spoken by her mother.

She said: "Is your husband still . . .?"

"He died last year. I'm sorry that you never met him: he was a kind man, we had many happy years together." She smiled.

Tess looked around the room. "What a lot of Vicente paintings."

"Yes. I inherited those belonging to my sisters."

"You have a self-portrait." Tess looked at it. The artist had shown himself hunched on a high wooden stool, palette in hand, his eyes huge, his expression full of misgiving. "Is that what he was really like?"

"It's a good likeness. It says more about him than perhaps he wished us to know. I suppose I should leave them to this museum which Mercedes has so foolishly set up in Montalbán. But I don't wish to. Partly because she obtained possession of the house by deceit, against my express wishes. Partly because of the kind of man he was. And partly because he was never the great painter she has tried to make him out to be. I keep them for sentimental, not aesthetic reasons."

"Exactly what kind of a man *was* he?" Tess asked.

Instead of answering, Luisa suddenly spoke to the Vicente portrait. "Such trouble you have caused us all," she said fiercely. "Such endless trouble. It's time it ended."

But when Tess asked what she meant, she merely shook her head.

23

MERCEDES

The marriage between Carlos Ramirez and Mercedes
Vicente Aragon took place quietly on May 12th, 1949.
The groom had lost his first wife tragically the previous
year: the bride was involved in the setting up of a major
art exhibition in the gallery which she jointly owned
with David Schleeman, one of the most eminent and
respectable of New York's art dealers.

The revelation that this young foreign woman was
part-owner of Schleeman's gallery had caused something
of a sensation earlier in the year. Most people assumed
Schleeman must have signed away his rights in a moment
of besotted lust; only the wiser observers noticed that the
gallery had leaped ahead of its rivals in terms of both
income and prestige since the new partnership began.
While Schleeman provided solidity and funding, Aragon
injected flair and originality. To be taken on by Schleeman
& Aragon now meant guaranteed success for any artist
fortunate to find favour with either of them.

In the same way, to be invited to the wedding reception
was considered something of a social coup among the arty
élite of the city. Doña Carlota had flung open her doors

and hired a team of workers to beautify her house for the occasion. Ramirez looked like a man who had hit the jackpot; the bride, sultrily beautiful in a white lace dress which had been her mother's bridal gown, and surrounded by a gaggle of aunts from Spain, was suitably demure. Her modest glances at her new husband caused some sly amusement among those who had – to their cost – encountered the hard-eyed stare which accompanied most of her business dealings.

Richard Klein showed up drunk with a celebrated torch-dancer from a Harlem nightclub on his arm, and blubbered loudly throughout the proceedings; Simon Rabat told anyone who would listen that Mercedes drove a hard bargain. "Hard, but fair," he said, nodding wisely, remembering how much money Mercedes had made for him during their association.

Peggy Guggenheim gave the happy couple a Lalique vase; the Blevitskys sent a silver-plated tray but did not attend; Doña Carlota presented them with a doubtfully-attributed Goya etching and a dusty diamond brooch; Jonas Fedor made them a pot: shallow, tapering, beautiful.

Kissing the bride, he spoke into her hair. "You are a fool," he said.

She laid her cheek against his chest. "I love you," she said.

"You chase the wrong dreams, Mercedes, and they will turn into nightmares. You should not have married Carlos."

"Why not?"

"He is a good man. A man of honour."

"And you think I will make him unhappy?"

"I *know* you will."

"Good."

He stared at her with contempt until, flushing, she said: "If you're so concerned about him, you should have married me yourself."

"Oh, Mercedes," he said. "Perhaps I should."

She looked up at him, the emotion between them almost palpable. His mouth was regretful; staring deep into his eyes she saw something which made her afraid. "What have you done, Jonas?" she said.

"It is more a question of what I have not done, I think."

"You love me, Jonas."

He caught his lip between his teeth and briefly closed his eyes. Then he said: "I shall not wish you happy, Mercedes, because you are not happy."

"Except when I am with you."

"I shall merely hope that Carlos and his children survive."

He kissed her again, and she knew that if he asked, she would die for him.

It was nearly five o'clock by the time they found themselves heading northwards out of New York to the resort lodge in Maine where they were to spend their honeymoon. Carlos, his hand resting on Mercedes' knee, said:

"It's a long drive. Why don't we find a hotel in an hour or two and stop there for the night?"

"If you want," Mercedes said indifferently.

"I expect you're exhausted, aren't you?"

Mercedes shrugged. "Not really."

He looked across at her. "What's the matter, my darling?"

How could she explain? The first half of her plan was now completed, and yet her triumph was far less exhilarating than she had supposed it would be. Carlos might have – indeed seemed to have – completely forgotten Marguerite; she could not, nor that moment of revelation when she realised that despite her education and background, Marguerite was as suggestible as any superstitious peasant.

Yet Marguerite was an irrelevance. The battle for justice and revenge was between Ramirez and herself, and had little to do with the Blevitskys. Unaccountably, she felt herself close to tears in a way she had not been since those distant nights of mingled pain and pleasure, tortured love and hate. Sometimes, in the heat of a New York summer they came back to her as she lay alone between white sheets, and though she would cup her hands over her breasts, seek out the warm moist places between her legs, she felt nothing, and knew her body had long since been taken from her.

It was then she would perceive, with a terrible clarity, the barren waste her life had become, a flat empty space scoured by winds and pitted with encumbrances, each of which had to be overcome: bogs, boulders, dragons.

And Jonas's words lay across her heart. They were the nearest he had ever come to acknowledging that their strange intense relationship meant something to him as well as to her, that it was far more than a mere conjunction of bodies. If she had not had a goal to pursue, if she had been free . . .

"Poor darling," Carlos said, squeezing her thigh. "It's

over now. We shall be together for the rest of our lives."

The prospect set her shuddering. At the same time, she wondered how he could be so callous. Once he had loved Marguerite enough to make her his wife; she had borne his children, submitted to his careless desires. And now, it seemed, he had flung her memory into some emotional garbage can, just as he had forgotten that long-ago murder by the cemetery wall.

It became something further for which to hate him. When he patted her knee, she pulled it sharply away from him and was glad to see the hurt astonishment on his face.

Lights loomed in the dusk. A motel advertised vacancies; despite its sleazy exterior, some of the rooms were already occupied. Ramirez pulled onto the forecourt and booked them in. At the door of their room, he lifted her into his arms and carried her across the threshold.

"Our first night together," he whispered into her hair. "It drove me mad, waiting for you, but you were right to insist." He smiled down at her. "I promise you I'll make up for lost time." She saw, as though through fog, the pale ghost of Marguerite; she turned aside her face as his mouth sought her lips. He set her down, took her chin in his hand, holding her still as he kissed her, but she did not respond, allowing her lips to lie limply under his.

He was frowning as he opened the bottle of champagne he had brought with him, his eyes concerned as they rested on her. He poured two glasses for them and lifted his towards her in a toast: "To the two of us!" he said. Lamplight made the rising bubbles seem like solid gold.

She lifted her own glass. "To *all* of us," she said and

he laughed aloud, thinking she included the children, not recognising the ghosts which hovered. She began to shiver. Her heart lay in her breast as though carved from ice, chilling vein and muscle, blood and skin. If he touched her, he would find her stiff and frozen, as though she had been dug out of a snowdrift. After the years of waiting and planning, her path lay clear before her and suddenly she did not want to set foot on it. She felt herself cursed.

Carlos seemed to think that her silence in some way reflected her anxiety about their marriage bed. "Don't worry," he kept saying. "If you're unwilling, or too tired, I'll wait." He laughed again, his eyes kind. "I don't know how I'll manage but I'll do it somehow. I don't want to spoil our first time together. *Your* first time ever."

God. How she hated him. She could see the bulge at the front of his trousers, she could even see a darker patch, as though he was running over with desire. He seemed to view marriage as nothing more than untrammelled sex. Up to this point, she had been so certain: now she reviewed her strategy and did not know which course of action to follow. There were so many choices, so many ways to wound. She could submit to him without participating, let him see that he meant nothing to her. She could refuse him outright. She could keep him at arm's length until he could bear it no longer.

Yet her cold heart was not here. It was wherever Jonas lay that night, wherever his big hands could hold and caress her into warmth again. How had she embarked on this foolish notion of revenge? And would she be able to sustain it? Having once made the wedding vows, there was no way out. Even if she was no longer a practising Catholic, she was too much a child of the faith to contemplate divorce. Suppose Jonas finally admitted his love for her and asked her to become his wife? What would she do? What *could* she do?

She had never felt so unbefriended.

Tears came to her eyes. Seeing them, Ramirez sat down beside her on the bed. He began to undo the buttons of her jacket, and of the blouse beneath. Tenderly, as though she were his daughter, not his wife, he slipped the clothes from her thin shoulders. She heard his gasp of delight as he uncovered her breasts; his hand lingered then tightened on the soft flesh. He bent his head to kiss them, gently he took her nipples in turn into his mouth. She thought how odd it was that the same action performed by one man could send her into transports of trembling delight, while with another she felt nothing but revulsion.

His hands were quicker now. He pulled at the fastening of her skirt, dragging it down from her waist.

"Not tonight, Carlos," she said pitifully. She fell backwards against the pillows, briefly closing her eyes.

He pulled back. "If you don't want to, then we won't," he said. His hand hovered over her thigh then he moved away from her. "Come on, darling. You're exhausted. Tonight we shall sleep together in each other's arms, and perhaps in the morning . . ." His voice lingered over possibilities. He smiled at her lovingly, then got up and poured more champagne into both their glasses. Although he had removed his shoes and tie, his jacket and waistcoat, he was still wearing his shirt and trousers.

Handing her a glass, he said: "I've never seen anything

as beautiful as you." His voice was clotted with desire. "Never."

She came to a decision. "Please kiss me, Carlos," she said shyly. Rolling over onto her side, she covered herself with her arms. Artlessly she shifted, as though seeking a more comfortable position; he could not fail to see and be excited by the dark triangle of hair under the thin silk of her underwear.

He sat down beside her. He bent towards her and kissed her gently; she pressed her lips against his and felt the tremor of his passion.

He drew back. "There's time enough," he said, as though to himself.

"Carlos," she murmured, shivering her shoulders. "Put your arms round me: it's cold in here."

When he held her against his broad chest, she snuggled against him and began slowly to undo the buttons of his shirt.

"Mercedes . . ." His voice was not quite steady. She could feel his erection, she knew he was holding back for her sake, that he longed to make love to her. Over his naked heart she laid one of her hands and he covered it with his own.

"You do *know*," he said quietly, " – your aunts have explained to you what it's like between a man and a woman, haven't they?"

She shook her head. It was, after all, true, though Carlos took it to mean that she was ignorant of matters sexual. How could he have asked such a question? In the past, he had kissed her and felt her response; repeatedly she had urged him to wait, which must surely indicate a knowledge of what they were waiting for. She knew she

must not overplay her hand, that she had to encourage
him into taking her roughly if she was to keep up the
pretence of being virginal.

She slipped off the bed. Her heavy breasts hung invit-
ingly as she stood in front of him. He raised his arms and
cradled them in his hands. She pushed against him, his
face close to her flat stomach. "You'd better get ready for
bed," he said, not looking at her. "You're very tired."

Instead of stepping away, she moved closer until she
was standing between his knees. His mouth quivered as
he put his hands on her hips.

"Carlos." She pressed his lips to her uncovered breasts.
"Oh, Carlos." In the mirrored dressing-table, she could
see her face, cold, unmoved, and remembered with an
intolerable pain how she had looked, how she had felt,
when Jonas kissed her. Deliberately she forced herself
to think of Fernando and the passion which had guided
her through the years since his death, then reaching for
the belt around Carlos's waist, she fumbled with the
buckle, while he looked up at her with an expression
which mingled anticipation and concern.

"Darling," he said. "I don't want to rush you if you're
not ready. The first time between us should be as good
as it can be."

"I'm your wife now," Mercedes said bravely.

"I don't want to hurt you."

"For you, Carlos . . ." she murmured.

Carlos stood up, pushing down his trousers, stepping
out of them so that he stood naked before her. She stared
with apparent horror at the erect phallus which emerged.
There was a pungent odour of sexual musk. "If you're
sure . . ."

"What are you going to do?" she whispered.

"Nothing you don't want me to." His voice was reassuring. In the light from the bedside lamp, his eyes rested on her with love. He took her into his arms. "Don't be afraid."

She lay close against his chest. "I'm not," she said. "Not with you."

She thought of her brother again, using his memory as a stimulus to her hatred, remembering him as he must have been, defenceless against the convent wall with the rising sun in his eyes, remembering how they had heard that his body had been jolted away on a cart, along with the other prisoners who had been shot that morning, to be buried somewhere up in the hills.

Innocently she moved against his naked body, weighed down with hate, "Carlos," she whispered.

He was breathing heavily, his lower lip moist, his mouth open. She kept her legs closed; he pushed his knee between her thighs, gently parting them. She could feel his penis hard against the inside of her leg, could feel it moving, readying itself for entry.

"Carlos!" she cried, beating feebly at his chest with her hands. "What are you doing?"

"Nothing you don't want me to, my love."

"But I – " She lay stretched out under him, victim, sacrifice. His body was beautiful; she felt sudden desire but suppressed it. "Be gentle with me, Carlos," she begged. "I don't know what I'm supposed to do."

He looked down at her, his eyes travelling over her body. She felt him tremble, heard him draw a deep breath. "My lovely innocent," he said, and the possessive note of his voice infuriated her beyond bearing.

She tried to twist away from him but his weight pinned her down. "Stop," she said, meaning it this time. "Stop."

"I can't," he said, his eyes closed above her, teeth biting his lower lip as he entered her. She was dry; she began to scream, with not entirely simulated pain, bucking under him as he moved back and forth between her thighs. "I'm sorry, Mercedes. I love you so much."

She forced tears out between her closed eyelids, and moaned. His rhythm quickened; he opened his eyes to stare down at her for a moment, said quietly, "I'm coming," then did so, with a bursting gasp.

She lay passively under him. When she felt him begin to shrink inside her she pulled away from underneath him and turned onto her side with her back to him. She drew several sobbing breaths; she gave a series of tiny hurt moans, as though she were too frightened to make any louder sound.

Eventually he slept. Only then did she.

In the morning he awoke again and stretched luxuriously beside her. "God, you're marvellous," he said. He reached out a hand and began to stroke her breasts.

She slipped out of the bed before he could do more.

"Come back," he said lazily. "I want to make love to you again."

She walked round to his side of the bed and stood looking down at him. She made her eyes grow huge; she saw his flinch away and return unwillingly to gaze into those dark passionless depths. "Love: is that what you call it?" she demanded fiercely.

"What else would – "

"I will not come back to bed with you," she said,

through gritted teeth. "I ache. I'm sore. You've abused and hurt me."

"The first time is always hard on a woman," he protested. He held his arms wide. "Come to me, Mercedes. I won't touch you again until you want me to."

"That will be never," she said. She thought of Jonas, of her long-dead long-loved brother.

"But you seemed – I thought you were – "

"Don't ever again presume to know what I think or feel," she spat at him. His face grew pale at the change in her demeanour. She felt huge and dark, about to take off into the air. She spread her arms as though to attack and saw with both satisfaction and scorn how he shrank away from her. For a moment she was elsewhere, watching him cringe against an ochre wall, under the pearly sky of his last dawn. How would he have behaved as the guns clicked into readiness: like a hero or a coward? In the light from the window her shadow loomed over him like a giant bird.

"Mercedes . . ." he pleaded. He reached for her and she viciously knocked him away.

"This is how it will be," she said. "I will come back to Spain with you – but only because it suits me to do so, not because I am now your wife. I will not stay there long. I have a career, business interests, projects to which I am committed."

"But – "

"No," she said forcefully. "I have no intention of sacrificing my life for yours. No desire to give up my plans to become like Marguerite."

"There will be children . . ." he said.

"In that case there will also be abortions."

He stared at her as though she were a stranger. His expression was bewildered. "But I thought you – "

"You thought I lusted as you did. You thought you could use me for your gratification whenever you wished. You thought I would raise your children for you, be content to become housekeeper as well as whore." She spat at him and saw with satisfaction how he shrank away from the glob of spittle, how he snatched at the sheet and wiped it frantically from his body as though it might otherwise burn like acid. "You thought wrong, Ramirez."

He raised himself on one elbow. She saw realisation strike him. "You hate me, don't you?"

She nodded.

"But why?"

"Think," she said.

He pretended not to know what she was talking about. "My God," he said. "What have I done?"

She watched him look into the future and see that it was bleak. "So we won't make *love* again – if that's what you call it," she said. "Not now. Not today. Nor tomorrow or next week. Not ever."

It was probably not true: over the years, goaded beyond endurance, tied to her by his faith, he would sometimes overcome her, take her without consent. Each time he did so, she would think of Fernando and Ramirez would suffer the more.

24

MERCEDES

The years settled into a routine. Most of her time was spent in New York, the rest in Montalbán, not out of duty but in the belief that Carlos was more hurt by her presence than by her absence. She refused to share his bed; occasionally, however, she would wake to find his heavy body on top of her, his hands clutching at her breasts, or closed over her hips. If she resisted, he would force her; early on, she learned that she denied him pleasure if she lay passive while he grunted his way to what she hoped was an unsatisfactory conclusion. She was afraid at first that she would become pregnant but this never happened and after a while she came to the conclusion that she was barren.

The children, Amador and Concepción, were afraid of her. That fact exacerbated her hatred for them. Often, later, she was to think that if they had looked less like Ramirez, or if either of them had protested against her injustices to them, had fought back, she might have been less unkind. She was also to learn then one of the ironies of life: that although cruelty is a weapon used to put down resistance, it gives no pleasure when used against the resistless.

From time to time, Carlos came with the children to
New York to visit their grandparents, the Blevitskys.
On those occasions he would come to her apartment.
He never berated her; after that first night it was as
though he understood that this was a just punishment
for the wrongs he had done. Sometimes, as she saw him
with his daughter on his knee, or holding his son's hand
as they crossed a street, she was wistfully aware that she
had perhaps lost something valuable; she even wondered
whether her plan to destroy his life had not backfired, for
despite all her efforts, he was certainly happier than she
knew herself to be.

As the Forties gave way to the Fifties which in turn
rolled towards the Sixties, as money began to flow back
into an economic system impoverished by nearly six years
of war, and the market for fine art began to expand again,
she found herself moving at an accelerated rate towards
the goals she had set herself. The time would come when
the dealer and the collector would have as much impact on
world art as the artist himself; Schleeman had not needed
much persuasion to accept her pragmatic views. Both of
them were growing increasingly prosperous through a
programme which combined judicious buying, a nose for
the market and the careful building up of reputations. The
protégé system had worked well: her young unknowns
were beginning to pay for themselves as well as for her.

Klein, over whose work she had a virtual monopoly,
was selling for amounts which, when she first took him
on, would have seemed inconceivably high. She still could
not prevent him from dashing off drawings for friends, or
even giving his smaller canvases away as gifts. However
many times she pointed out that she had exclusive rights

to *all* his work, he ignored her. He was married now, to an ugly girl called Lorna Arup, a ceramicist; they lived in a farm in up-state New York where Richard, Mercedes realised, was carefully drinking himself to death.

He was not the only casualty among her protégés. Two or three years ago the arty circles of New York had given a delicious collective gasp of horror when Hal Howard had thrown himself off the Brooklyn Bridge. Wearing full evening dress under a purple-lined cloak, he had clambered onto the railings and turned to address the crowd of friends who had accompanied him to the middle of the bridge.

"I would rather die on my feet than live on my knees!" he had declared magnificently. Then, raising a bottle of Veuve Clicquot to his lips, he had jumped before any of them had fully realised what he intended.

A lot of people laid the blame for his death squarely at Mercedes' door, disregarding the fact that for the past four years he had lived entirely at her expense, in return for no more than a dozen paintings. There was talk of her protégés being forced to paint to order, and criticism that the system of patronage stifled true creative endeavour. Mercedes ignored such remarks. The Renaissance era, she liked to point out, was the high point in the patronage system, and look how art in all its manifestations had flowered under the Medici. Besides, the dozen Howard canvases were already changing hands at enormous prices.

Several times a year she returned to Spain, flying into Granada and then hiring a car for the drive to Montalbán. She did not inform Carlos beforehand of these visits, preferring them to come as an unwelcome surprise.

Once, arriving from Madrid after doing the rounds of the galleries and artists' studios, she had found the Casa de las Lunas empty except for servants; one of them explained that the children were spending the day with the aunts in the village. Going to the house, she was told that they were upstairs; when she finally tracked them down they were not in the big salon but on the floor above. They had not heard her stealthy climb up the attic stairs and she was able to stand at the door of Fernando's studio and watch them. Evidently the aunts were allowing the place to be used as a nursery; the sight filled her with fury. Aunt Isabella lay reading on the old chaise-longue, a box of chocolates at her side. Concepción, draped in an Indian shawl with a bridal wreath of wax flowers on her dark hair and a pair of long kid gloves drawn up almost to her shoulders, was playing some game of make-believe, bowing and curtseying to herself in the long mirror.

Mercedes' first instinct was to leap into the room, to snatch the things away from the child, to hit her. Those belonged to my brother, she wanted to scream. Don't touch them. Don't defile them.

Then she caught sight of the boy. He stood behind Vicente's easel, a paintbrush in one hand, a palette in the other. Mercedes stared at him in disbelief. At first she had thought he simply play-acted, as his sister was doing. But the colours squeezed onto the wooden board were fresh, shiny, squirming over the palette like brilliant slugs, and the brush he wielded was loaded with oil paint which he was busily transferring onto a stretched canvas on the easel.

For a moment, she was filled with such murderous rage

that she could not move for the weight of it. Then, as her body reacted to the rush, she erupted.

"What are you doing?" she screamed. She snatched the brush from the boy, tore the palette from his thumb, hearing a faint crack as though a bone had snapped. "Don't you dare touch those things, they aren't yours, they're my brother's, you have no right."

She knew she sounded incoherent, insane even; she felt as though she had come apart, that she could no longer control herself, as if pieces of her were flying away from the pure rage at her centre. She was aware of spittle on her chin, of Isabella's startled fright, the boy roaring with pain, the little girl backing away with the gaudy shawl clutched round her as though for protection.

Isabella finally got to her feet, swallowing the remains of the chocolate she had just bitten into. "Are you mad, Mercedes?" she said. "Have you finally gone completely mad?"

Words bubbled from her mouth: "They should not be here . . . no right . . . Fernando's studio . . . not theirs to . . ."

Like a hen, Isabella gathered the two frightened children to her sides. "To scream like that in front of the little ones," she said with distaste. "To behave in such a manner. I cannot believe it."

"They should not be here," Mercedes said, breathing heavily through her nose. "You should not allow them into this room." She was shaking, knowing that something had been damaged which could never now be restored.

"Perhaps I should remind you that this is not your house," Isabella said coldly. "You have no rights here."

"This is the room where my brother worked," Mercedes

said, and as she did so, saw with clarity that the lie she had told Jonas could be made fact. A monument to Vicente, a museum dedicated to his work, a place where his things would have their place, where children would not be allowed to touch and deface. Pilgrims would come from all over the world to worship at the shrine. It would be something solid to replace the fragile human life which had so carelessly been snuffed out.

Calmer now, she said: "These children should not be allowed in here."

"You cannot dictate what we do in our own home," Isabella said.

"It's my home too," Mercedes said loudly. And, as Isabella shook her head, added: "And Fernando's."

"Only because we allowed you to think of it as such," Isabella said calmly. "Besides, Fernando has been dead for years, and you are a married woman, you have your own home." Then, as though to placate the furious woman in front of her, she nodded at the easel. "Amador has talent. Look."

Mercedes did so. Through the angry pulsing of blood behind her eyes, she saw with amazement that what she had assumed was a child's daub was in fact a genuine composition, that there was a surety of technique, a visible awareness of line and shape which in one so young was astonishing.

She forced herself to remember Fernando standing there in front of the easel, his gentle voice, the way he smiled at her as he stroked paint onto the stiff canvas, the long afternoons, the smell of oils and turpentine, the way his eyes caressed her. He had called her his miniature muse once, and although she had not wept

for him in years, now she felt the sad tears prick at her
eyelids.

She substituted rage. Deliberately she wrenched Amador's
canvas from the easel. If she had possessed the strength,
she would have ripped it across. "A childish scrawl," she
said scornfully, tossing it to the floor. "I hope you know,
Aunt, how expensive paint and canvas is these days. Better
not to waste it on scribbles like this."

She turned to the two children, hating the cowed
expressions on their faces. "Get your coats," she said
harshly. "We're going back to the Casa de las Lunas,"
and saw with contempt how they both shrank against
Isabella's ample sides.

Over the years, her stock of canvases by the young
painters she had known in Madrid before the war had been
depleted. Sanchez, whose work she disliked but whose
commercial value was undeniable, was now commanding
high prices, Ramón O'Donnell, too, while both de León
and Pedro Castán were moving into voguish prominence,
helped along by her judicious feeding of information and
releasing of work. From time to time, as the art markets
swung skittishly this way and that, she had been forced
to sell off her Vicentes until the time came when the
last one had gone. It was time to collect the rest of her
inheritance.

She went back to Spain, calling on the aunts almost as
soon as she arrived. She took Amador and Concepción
with her. Although it irritated her to see the way the three
women attended to the children, she knew that they were
useful ammunition. However, as Rosita fluttered round
the girl, Concepción, exclaiming over the child's looks,

patting her hands, offering her cakes, Mercedes could not prevent herself from saying sharply: "For heaven's sake, Aunt. It's not good for children to have too high an opinion of themselves."

Rosita looked at her oddly. "But better than having no opinion of themselves at all," she said in her soft voice.

"What's that supposed to mean?"

"You are not kind, Mercedes," Rosita said, and on the overstuffed sofa plump Aunt Isabella, one arm round Amador, sighed and fanned herself.

"Are you criticising the way I handle my stepchildren?" demanded Mercedes. She opened her eyes, dilating the pupils, making them huge and black as her mother had once done, and was disconcerted when Rosita, instead of turning away, as she used to, stared back, unafraid.

"Yes."

"In that case, perhaps it is better if I take them home again." Mercedes began to rise then realised that she could not afford to antagonise the aunts, not until she had what she came for.

"Even if you do, Carlos will bring them back to us when you have gone," Rosita said, and there was a boldness in her which Mercedes found inexplicable.

"Not if I forbid him to do so," she said, but knew that she stood on shaky ground. Fleetingly she was aware that there was more than one kind of power; whatever her status in New York, here she was not approved of. The knowledge caused a sudden ache in her breast. The suspicion that perhaps she had deliberately turned her back on something infinitely more precious than anything New York could offer her was, these days, not an entirely unfamiliar feeling. She reminded herself that Montalbán was nothing more than a speck on the map, while New York was the hub of the universe.

She called again the following afternoon, this time without the children.

"I would like to talk business with you," she said, forcing herself to smile. She sat on the sofa and pulled off her gloves. The three aunts sat opposite her, upright in their corsets, their movements synchronised as they drank coffee from thin gold cups. They had lived together for so many years now, that they even shared each other's thoughts.

Francisca said coldly, "Why have you asked to see us, Mercedes? What exactly do you want from us?" Once her eyes had rested on her niece with love; now there was only hostility.

Aware of it, Mercedes crossed her legs and tried not to show her discomfiture. It was the children, she thought savagely. Ramirez' children. Without them, she would still be the adored child that the three women had shared and brought up together, instead of being dispossessed. Looking at their implacable postures, she was reminded of long-ago Sundays, the three straight backs at the altar rail. Everything had been so safe then, so certain; she remembered the smell of incense, the swinging censer, the singsong chanting of the priest. So safe. She had worn long black stockings under her Sunday dress, and a straw hat with a ribbon; her shoes were shiny, like black mirrors.

What does it profit a man if he gain the whole world and lose his own soul? she thought.

"We needn't take long over this," she said briskly. "I

would like to take some more of Fernando's paintings back with me to New York when I leave at the end of the week. The market for fine art is wide open now, and there is a great deal of money around. I can get good prices for – " She broke off as the aunts exchanged glances. "What's wrong?"

"I think you've already had your fair share of the canvases Fernando left behind," Isabella said.

"Fair share? How do you mean?"

"Presumably even you do not feel you are entitled to them all," said Rosita. Once she had fluttered; now she spoke boldly, no longer vague, uncertain.

"Fernando was my brother – " began Mercedes.

"I believe we are all aware of that fact," said Francisca.

" – and therefore, as his next of kin, I surely have some right to them."

"We brought him up." A vast coldness emanated from Rosita.

"I see." She forced a laugh. "And now you want payment for what it cost you, is that it?"

Francisca closed her eyes as though weary. "We do not see things in terms of money, as you seem to. Your aunt means that we too have certain rights in the canvases."

"And we've exercised them," put in Isabella nervously, raising her cup to her mouth as though to wash any further words back down her throat.

"What exactly does that mean?" Mercedes hoped she successfully hid the sudden chill these words brought her, along with the realisation that perhaps in New York she could successfully manipulate people but that these three middle-aged provincial ladies would not so easily be moved.

"It means that we have disposed of the remaining canvases," said Francisca.

Mercedes rose, advanced towards them. "In what way disposed?" At that moment she could easily have ripped out their faintly quivering throats. She stood over them, widening her eyes, and saw that they did not flinch.

Rosita started to speak but Francisca overrode her. "They are perfectly safe," she said pleasantly. "It's simply that we have not yet decided what to do with them."

"What to d – " Mercedes clenched her fists. How easy it would be to smash in those smug faces. She swallowed. "Did we not always talk of what we would do with them when the dealers came?"

"Not we – *you*." This was from Rosita.

"Well, now the dealers are coming – not here, perhaps, but certainly to my gallery in New York."

"You are wrong," Isabella said with triumph in her voice.

"In what way wrong?"

"They have come here too, these dealers."

"And did you sell to them?"

Francisca took over again, with hauteur. "Occasionally."

With an effort Mercedes controlled herself. From her bag she took out a leather-bound notebook and a solid gold pencil. "Perhaps you would let me know which paintings have been sold." She smiled at them but received no answering smiles.

They named a couple of paintings. "That's all?" said Mercedes, relieved. Two paintings was not so many to have lost control over.

"There were others," Francisca said vaguely.

Looking at her, Mercedes could see that the vagueness was illusory. "Which were they?"

They moved their heads about, their piled hair as solid as wood in the half-dusk of the shuttered room, hands lifting cups from golden saucers, shrugging a little. They did not remember which others, could not recall the subjects, they were sorry.

"And the rest," Mercedes said finally, returning the notebook to her bag. "May I see them?" She hated having to ask but recognised that she had miscalculated, that unless she was placatory she might end up without anything at all.

Francisca looked at her sisters then shook her head. "I don't think so," she said calmly.

Nothing Mercedes could say would change their attitude. The three of them sat there, smiling faintly, sometimes glancing at each other, shaking their heads, sipping their coffee. She demanded to know where the remaining canvases were stored but it was as though she were no more to them now than a mosquito, buzzing about their heads, at whom they must occasionally swat but could otherwise ignore.

She drove back to the Casa de las Lunas shaking with anger and frustration. On the gateposts, the copper moons hung like mocking symbols of a life that had risen and now was fading, without point or flavour. She strode into the house, flinging the door shut behind her and stood in the wide entry-hall, searching for a focus for her rage. Through the arch which led to the salon she could see Concepción: singing to herself, the little girl was looking at the objects on a shelf: an African carving, a candlestick of cut glass, a gilt clock. As Mercedes watched, she reached towards the pottery bowl which had been Jonas's wedding gift.

The sight brought all her rage to the surface. "Don't touch that!" she screamed. "Don't you dare."

The child turned, startled, and her thick braid of hair swung across her shoulder, knocking against the pot on its narrow delicate foot. For a long moment it hovered unbalanced while Concepción stared in terror towards the fierce voice of her stepmother. Then it tumbled and smashed onto the tiled floor.

Afterwards, Mercedes could never remember how she had crossed the space between her and the child. It was as though she flew towards her. Then she was holding the child between her hands, beating, kicking, tearing at her hair, scratching her face. "That – was – mine!" she panted, each word matched by a blow. She was beside herself, no longer aware of what she was doing. "You broke it – you horrible careless little monster, you . . ." she sought for a word of sufficient calumny and spat out ". . . Ramirez."

The child went limp. There was blood on her face. Behind Mercedes, Carlos shouted: "Leave her be!" He dragged Mercedes away, knocking her roughly to one side so that she stumbled against a table and nearly fell. He picked Concepción up in his arms, calling to Julia, the housekeeper, who stood horrified at the door, ordering her to telephone at once to the doctor in Montalbán.

Then he turned to Mercedes. "If you ever touch my daughter again, I shall kill you," he said quietly, and she realised in that moment that her power over him had gone. At the back of her mind, a truth struggled and took shape: *Those who fight on behalf of others are stronger than those who fight for themselves.*

But I am fighting for Fernando, she told herself; perceiving the loathing in her husband's face, the thought dropped into a hollow space somewhere in the region of her heart.

At a party given by Peggy Guggenheim, she had once heard Max Ernst complain to his fellow-Surrealists, Duchamp and Tanguy, that he was *dépaysé*. He had spread his hands, his beautiful face sombre, his quiff of white hair rising dramatically from his skull. "I am a man without a country," he had said in his heavy accent. "Without a home."

Not Mercedes. New York, for her, was home. It became increasingly important to her that she should succeed there, as a counter-balance to her failure within her own family. For the most part the exiled European painters who had fled to New York at the beginning of the war were now repatriated. She was one of only a handful of women dealers; the times were ripe for enterprise, receptive to new ideas. Having liquidated her precious stock of seed-corn canvases, she was constantly on the look-out for fresh talent to add to her own collection. Above all, she was determined to establish the reputation of Fernando Vicente.

Once, on a buying trip in Madrid, she had called on Luisa in an effort to discover where the missing Vicente canvases were.

"Missing?" Luisa said, and her expression was not kind. "I believe my sisters have them safe."

"But where?" Mercedes was enraged to see three or four examples of her brother's work blatantly hanging on Luisa's own walls.

"You must ask them."

"I have done so. They refuse to tell me. The point is," said Mercedes, tempering her tone, "they know very little about these things. If they would just let me see that the pictures were safely stored, I need not worry about them."

"There is no need for you to worry," Luisa said. "Besides, we have had expert opinions on the canvases and how to keep them in the best possible conditions."

"We?"

"Naturally my sisters consulted with me first."

"But not with me."

"You have not shown a great deal of interest in family matters in recent years." Luisa looked at her watch. In the absence of children, she had begun to devote her time to charitable concerns.

"But – "

"The pictures are well looked after, Mercedes. After all, did they not survive several years in the *cortijo* above Montalbán, hidden among the almond shells?"

"That was from necessity. Things deteriorate, canvases are susceptible to all kinds of damage."

"I can't see why you are so concerned. After all, you've already taken your share of them – without consultation with us."

"I should have thought that if anyone was entitled, I was."

Luisa rose. "I'm afraid I shall have to ask you to excuse me. I have meetings to attend to, a number of people to see."

Back in New York, Mercedes had time to wonder exactly

why and when her aunts had changed in their feelings towards her. The answer seemed obvious: Ramirez. He must have seized every opportunity to ingratiate himself with them, to blacken her name. Her lip curled as she thought about it: perhaps he hoped that they would leave the valuable legacy of remaining Vicente paintings to him, instead of to the rightful heir, Mercedes herself.

She circulated the information that she was willing to handle such Vicentes as might be available, hoping in this way to accumulate more. For the idea which had sprung into her head as she saw the boy using Fernando's easel, Fernando's brushes, seemed more and more feasible as time went by. Eventually the three older aunts would die; the house would either fall into Luisa's hands or her own. If the former, Luisa must surely be susceptible to pressure since she already had a substantial home of her own in Madrid. There was the Madrid flat, too; Mercedes was perfectly willing to renounce any rights in that for the sake of the house in Montalbán. Meanwhile, in order to pave the way, she would begin a biography of Fernando; it was more than twenty years since his murder at the hands of the *fascistas* and their instrument, Ramirez.

Minding the gallery one afternoon, she looked up from her desk to find the man Lovel in front of her. It was years since she had last seen him but he had not changed; the red-brown eyes were as unblinking as ever, the skin as pale. Looking up at him, she noticed something she had not seen before: a thin white line of scar tissue running across his throat, as though he had once tried to take his own life.

His mouth moved, opened in what she recognised as a smile. She stood. "Do you need any help, Mr Lovel?"

"No," he said. "But you do."

She frowned.

"I heard you were looking for paintings by Fernando Vicente," he said.

"Do you have one for sale?"

"Wait." He walked away from her across the gallery towards the door. He wore a black suit, a white silk tie, black shoes. He looked, she thought, like someone closely concerned with the intimacies of death: an undertaker, perhaps, or an embalmer. She wished she were not alone in the gallery; there was so palpable an air of evil about him that she feared it might somehow be transmitted to her, like some sinister virus.

In a moment he had returned, carrying a large flat package wrapped in brown paper. "This is for you," he said.

She tore the paper off and found herself looking at the painting which, years before, she had first sold to David Schleeman, the painting which had set her on the path to her present eminence in the art world. Staring at the skull-shaped face, the receding doors leading into infinity, she wondered what personal vision they had represented for her brother.

"How much are you asking for it?" she said.

"I'll give it to you." Something ugly flickered at the back of his oxblood eyes, then vanished.

"That's not necessary."

"But I want to."

"Why?"

"Because you value it more than I do."

"And you want nothing in return?"

Again the bloodless lips parted in his approximation of a smile. He said: "Perhaps some day you will own something I value more highly than you do."

"You shall have it," she promised. She remembered that he was interested in Japanese prints: it would not be too difficult to find him a Hokusai, an Utamaro, something by Hiroshige.

Yet she knew, even then, that it would be wisest to reject this poisoned apple of a gift. Even as her fingers caressed the contours of the subject's face, so like and yet so unlike Fernando's own, some instinct warned her not to accept, that when he came around to collect the debt she owed him, it would be something more important than a print or a painting he would require in return.

25

TESS

As the farmer does, so must the lover:
  Till the soil,
  Pull the weeds,
  Reap the harvest.
    from *Elegías españolas* by Amador Ramirez
    translated from the Spanish by Teresa Lovel

Cambridge lay submerged in the dark end of a winter twilight; shadows littered the cold pavements and frost-blackened shrubbery huddled in the front gardens. It was very cold.

Scooping her mail up from the doormat as she came in, Tess went into her sitting room, flicking on the switch as she pushed open the door. She saw immediately that, while she had been in Spain, the place had been searched. It had been delicately done; there was no mess, no emptying of drawers onto the floor, or tearing of pictures from walls. Yet the room's very spareness made it possible to see that cupboards had been opened and not quite closed, that the *tansu* chests had been moved and replaced millimetres away from their original position, that one of the Hokusai prints had been rehung not quite true.

A short while ago, she would have been terrified at the discovery of an intruder. Now, she simply squared her shoulders and picked up one of a pair of heavy candlesticks which stood on the table in the hall. For a moment she paused by the telephone. Should she ring Dominic, ask him to come round, wait in the street until he arrived? But for all she knew, it might have been he who had done the searching. Like Jonas, the Jonas she had never chosen to see before, there were elements of ruthlessness in Dominic. He had his own secrets. She was well aware that although he seemed to love her, that would not stop him if she had something he wanted. She was surprised to find this idea stimulated rather than frightened her.

Eventually she started up the stairs. Both of the bedroom doors were firmly closed, but if an intruder had hoped to find something of value, he would certainly have searched there too. Although she longed to turn and run downstairs, out of the house, she forced herself to take a deep breath then flung the doors wide. The rooms were empty of anything but their accustomed furnishings; the marks of the searching were as well disguised in both as they had been in the sitting room. None the less she could see that the pictures had been shifted, the rugs taken up, the beds pulled away from the wall. Even the philodendron had been lifted from its big brass container; there were crumbs of earth scattered around it, and a leaf had been bent sharply enough to break its ribbed surface.

There was something infinitely frightening about the

careful replacement. A hurried tumble of drawers would have implied vandals, a mindless search for valuables, the theft impersonal; this purposeful attempt to hide the fact of intrusion made her shudder, remembering the faint pad of feet on a bare floor, the glint of light on brocade, dragons and chrysanthemums.

What could anyone suppose that she possessed worth the risk of breaking in for? The only thing of value – *The Tears She Shed* – was still in its place on her bedroom wall. Did that mean this was not a raid by Mercedes or her agents? If so, what had he been after, this neat burglar? Since he had clearly looked behind her pictures, it would imply he was hoping to find a safe. What did he imagine she might have secreted inside it, suppose such a thing were to exist? Jewellery? Silver? Money?

Frowning, she finished her search and went downstairs. The red light on her answering-machine blinked but she ignored it. Instead, she picked up the mail from the hall table and carried it into the kitchen.

A letter from Jonas's solicitors reminded her that in their last communication they had indicated that they wished her to call at their offices. Some time had passed since then and they wondered if she would now do so as a matter of urgency.

Urgency . . . unexpectedly, she remembered a walk she had taken with Jonas one cloudy spring day. She had still been at school; she had dismissed what he said as the usual dramatic gloss he liked to give to even the most mundane of events. Now, because his words seemed suddenly relevant, she heard his voice rumble again in her brain.

"The ruthless ones will always have an advantage, Teresa. They don't care, you see. That is why they appear strong. They take, they kill, and never do they see the tears they will cause, nor the broken hearts they leave behind. So they are powerful. But always remember that their strength is also their weakness. Because they care only about themselves, their vulnerability lies in the urgency of their need to survive."

"What on earth are you going on about?" she had scoffed, fifteen and scornful, still isolated from the familiar world by the rigid grip of grief at her mother's death. They had been walking along the Backs, daffodils poking through dead black leaves beside the black water; tears had pricked the inside of her eyelids. Across the river, the spires of King's College Chapel stood dark against the grey-white sky. She had wished she too were dead.

"If you ever find yourself in danger," Jonas said, ignoring her tone, "you must keep to public places. Do not stay at home. Keep your options open. Go to visit friends, stay in hotels. Discard your routines, trust no-one, move among crowds. Even the ruthless ones do not often dare to kill in public. And remember that sometimes it is better to turn and face your adversary than to run away from him. Do not forget this, Teresa."

He had shaken her arm as though he were angry; a man walking past with two mufflered children had stared and hesitated, clearly wondering whether he should intervene.

Head down, mystified and embarrassed, Tess had walked on, faces turning to look at them like white discs in the drab light, while Jonas continued to talk, his voice loud and oblivious.

She leaped into wakefulness out of a familiar nightmare. The long road stretching across an infinite plain, the tiny

440

figure trudging towards the unknown, a red moon above the horizon, the knowledge that she was entirely and forever alone . . .

Her heart thumped against the covering sheets; the walk with Jonas along the Backs came back once more. Why had he been so insistent? Had something taken place to prompt such warnings? They were days she did not wish to recall, none the less, sorting painfully through her memories, she realised it must have been about that time that Lovel had made one of his rare visits to England, had turned up at the cottage, and despite Kate's refusal to let him in, had insisted on talking to Tess.

Even all these years later, the memory of Lovel made her sweat. The familiar terror had filled her that morning of her adolescence as he came into the sitting room where she sat reading, swotting up for the end-of-term exams. Japan – bare branches outside the window of her bedroom, white curled petals – came flooding back to her as she jumped to her feet and faced him, terror knotting her throat.

"What do you want?" she had demanded. It was the first time he had invaded the haven Jonas had provided for her.

The almost lipless mouth gave its familiar smile, edged with mockery. Under his jaw, the thread of white scar tissue shone in the pale light from the window. Even at a distance, she could smell the dry scent of him, like long-dead flower petals.

"Teresa," he said. His thin voice made her shudder with repugnance.

"What do you want?" she had asked a second time, her feet secure on Jonas's carpets, in Jonas's house.

441

"Nothing," he said. He shook his head again. "Nothing at all."

Somehow that made him even more sinister. Her hands were damp. She opened her mouth to speak and he added: "Except to see you, Teresa."

Behind him, Kate protested, insisting that he leave at once, that Mr Fedor had given her the strictest instructions . . .

"Surely Mr Fedor would not wish to come between a father and his daughter," Lovel had said, and his red eyes had rested on Tess without expression, so that she began to shake, reaching behind her for the edge of the table, hating him with such impassioned loathing that she feared she would faint.

"If you want to see Tess, you'd better come back when Mr Fedor is at home," Kate said.

"Tess." The skin of Lovel's forehead wrinkled. "Is that what he calls you?"

She could only nod.

"Tess," he repeated softly, and his voice crawled over her name like a slug, defiling, despoiling it.

Recalling the way he was, the way he had always been, she began to shake again, helpless under that ruby gaze even in imagination. Was it Lovel whom Jonas had been warning her against? Was it her own father he referred to when he spoke of turning to face her enemy? And if so, how could this years-too-late knowledge possibly help her now?

She awoke to a grey East Anglian morning of damp-pewtered pavements reflecting a wolf-coloured sky and rain spattering the windows. Standing in the bay window of her room, she looked down at the familiar street. A single lamp stuttered on and off, its breaker mechanism uncertain whether the night was yet over. Further down, a grey car waited against the kerb, its windshield opaque with cloud reflections. A man on a bicycle rode slowly by, head down against the wind.

The grey car abruptly shook into life and moved smoothly down the street towards her house. She remembered then that the car Kate had seen waiting outside Jonas's cottage had also been grey. As she was about to step back from the window, suddenly wary, the car slowed and the driver leaned sideways to look up at her windows, head twisting to avoid the obstruction of the car door's upper rim. She glimpsed a Russian-style fur hat and a thick coat with the collar turned up to hide most of the lower face. Whoever he (or she) was, the sight of her there was unexpected, causing the car to speed away from her, the driver ducking hastily out of sight. Tess shivered, aware that she had stumbled into areas where she did not belong, where unless she was careful she had little chance of survival.

The telephone rang.

She stared at it. Then, suddenly decisive, snatched it up. Whoever was out there was not going to turn her into a gibbering wreck.

"Yes," she barked. "Who is it?"

It was Kate. Through a confused gabble of speech Tess gathered that once again thieves had broken into Jonas's house.

"Ever so creepy, it was," Kate said. "I could tell something was wrong, soon as I got in the house, but I couldn't tell what. It was that press of his gave it away."

"How do you mean?" The press had belonged to Jonas's parents, a big clumsy piece of furniture carved from some black wood, which was far too big for the room where it stood.

"I did some spring-cleaning a couple of days ago," Kate said. "And I managed to shift the dratted thing so that it wouldn't leave a crush mark on the carpet. Whoever was in here put it back exactly where it had been before, instead of in the new place. Otherwise I wouldn't have realised quite what was wrong."

"Was anything taken?"

"Not that I could see." Kate gave a shaky laugh.

"Have you called the police?"

"It's hardly worth it, not if they didn't take anything – not that there was much left to take. Jonas's nephew's already collected most of the furniture and as you know, Jonas had cleared most of his papers before he went off to Spain."

Almost as if he suspected that someone would come looking, Tess thought. And as if he knew what for. She did not tell Kate that she too had been burgled: she was not even sure that the two break-ins might be connected.

"Kate, go and stay with your friend in Brighton," she said. "I'll drop round a bit later and have a look. But it'd be better if you weren't there on your own."

Kate took some persuading but eventually agreed. Later, Tess stood at the kitchen window with a mug of coffee in her hand. The back garden was unkempt: rough grass, straggling ivy, a few maverick leaves still clinging to yellowed branches, all beaten down by the rain. Her brain hammered at a question: if nothing had been taken from Jonas's cottage, or from her own house, what had the thief been looking for?

So many questions; so few answers. She sat down at the kitchen table with a paper and pen and forced herself to concentrate.

Julian Maitland had suggested that during the war, Jonas might have been a spy, working against the Nazis. Could an event so long ago possibly be the reason behind the break-ins? Had Jonas held on to some potentially incriminating piece of evidence, some piece of paper which could embarrass the government or the military?

Could it be that the Government itself was responsible for the search of her house? Every now and then a case emerged in the newspapers which made it clear that a vast and complex governmental organisation existed dedicated to the maintenance of secrecy. Was it possible that Jonas was the subject of just such a scheme? Were there grey men in Whitehall who had taken fright at learning of Jonas's memoirs and wanted to eliminate the manuscript before it reached the publishers?

But the war had been over for nearly fifty years, and Britain had been fighting a just cause against an unjust enemy. Anything Jonas had to say would be greeted either as irrelevance or a further confirmation of the rightness of the Allies.

She poured more coffee, felt the caffeine jolt her brain into further speculation.

What about – yes: what about the mysterious Captain Santiago? It was just as plausible to theorise that perhaps Santiago, knowing somehow that Jonas was about to publish his autobiography and terrified in case Jonas at last revealed his identity, was trying to suppress the manuscript. After all, the relatives of those who had died at his hands would still want revenge. She was hazy about it, but it was even possible that the Spanish government might try him for war crimes if they knew who he was. At the very least he would be pilloried by the Spanish Press.

The more she thought about it, the more she decided she must have stumbled on the right answer. Especially when she recalled the emphatic way Jonas had stared from the screen during his TV interview. With a start, she recognised that he had been *daring* Santiago to come after him. But Santiago, if he was still alive, would be living somewhere in Spain, would he not? Or in Latin America, or the States. Or had Jonas somehow known that whatever his current persona, Santiago was in England? Whoever he was, Jonas could not have been aware of his identity or there would have been no need for him to go to Spain, he could have denounced the man right then and there. Was that why he had looked so intently out at the unseen audience? *I'm coming after you, Santiago, wherever you are, whoever you are: I almost have you.* Is that what he had really been saying?

And Santiago had taken up the challenge. Santiago had followed him to Montalbán, killed him and was now – it came to her with the clarity of a magnesium flare – was now searching for the incriminating evidence in Jonas's manuscript.

The more she considered it, the more obvious it grew: someone desperately wanted something kept secret. And her own home had been searched because she was so close to Jonas. If she telephoned Hansl, would she find that his house too had been broken into?

But what did that have to do with the attacks on herself? That hurtling drive down the mountain in Spain, the remorseless pressure of the hand pushing her under water – surely they were motivated by something quite different than a desire to find and destroy Jonas's book.

As she formulated the thought, a connection which had nagged at her since her visit to the Agencia Andalucía in Granada suddenly made itself clear. Say the name El Malo aloud, and it sounded exactly like Marlowe. And Lawrence Marlowe was the name given by the person who had originally hired the car, the person who had almost certainly pushed Jonas to his death.

For she had no doubts any longer: Jonas had been murdered to keep him quiet. And El Malo, alias Captain Santiago, was the man responsible.

Another connection slotted into place. Luisa Ruiz-Barrantes had once been engaged to someone called Felipe. Felipe and Philip were the same names. Felipe Cabrera had disappeared the same day that Fernando Vicente, Luisa's nephew, had been shot. Was it fanciful to suppose that Felipe was the betrayer of the little band of guerillas? But if so, he could not also be El Malo, could he?

She wrote down the names:

Lawrence Marlowe.

El Malo.

Felipe Cabrera.

Phil Cramir.

What connection, if any, was there between the four? She remembered that Felipe's name was in fact *Felipe Cabrera Ramirez*: she wrote that down too, at the end of the list.

Somewhere among the names, some kind of truth was staring her in the face.

She scribbled: *Felipe C. Ramirez*. She changed the Felipe to Philip, eliminated the last two letters of the first name, and then, on impulse, for no other reason than balance, the last two of the last name.

It glittered up at her from the paper: *Phil C. Ramir. Phil Cramir*.

Had she unravelled the mystery of the reclusive Texan art collector's origins? Was Phil Cramir the *novio* who had disappeared so long ago? And instead of choosing a new name to go with his new life, and keeping his own initials, had he merely anglicised his Spanish name?

If she were right, so much was explained. The donation to Luisa's charity as a way of assuaging his conscience. The Vicente sketches in his collection. The reason why he spoke such good Spanish. The connection with Jonas. The obscurity in which he had buried his origins.

Another thought shot into her head. Was it possible that Luisa was wrong: that her *novio* had disappeared not because of the danger from the Falangists, from Captain Santiago, but because of the danger from what was left of the guerilla band? From their leader, Águila?

The phone rang again; with an effort, she dragged herself back from the bitter past.

"You're home," Martin García said unnecessarily. "Did you discover anything more about your guardian's death?"

"Enough."

"Enough for what?"

"For me to realise how much more I need to find out. I'm not sure yet what all this is about, but it's pretty murky."

"Be careful, Tess."

"Don't worry. What happened at the meetings?"

"Zilch. They were cancelled at the last moment."

"Why?"

"The Japanese didn't show. Just as well really, since Don Pedro was taken ill and had to stay home. Frankly, I don't know why they brought them forward in the first place."

"Probably some subtle oriental ploy to let us know they weren't going to be pushed around."

"Probably. Anyway, everyone would have said the same things they've all said a dozen times before. It wouldn't have mattered a bean that you weren't there."

"Any idea why the Japanese cancelled?"

"Haven't you heard? One of these simmering Japanese financial scandals has finally blown up and Hayashima's been arrested on charges of bribery and corruption. Political pay-offs or something. By the way, did you speak to Don Pedro yet?"

"I only got back last night. And I'm still officially absent. What's up?"

"It's that Cramir collection thing. I gather some art museum up in Vancouver is being a bit sniffy about the painting they were left in his Will. They say they've had their expert examine it and since it's a fake, thanks a lot, Phil, but no thanks."

"I'll ring him," she said, impatiently. "Some time."

"There was one other thing, Tess . . ."

"Can't stop," she said.

She dialled the number at the top of the solicitor's thick white letterhead and gave her name. She was put through to the partner who dealt with Jonas's affairs.

"Miss Lovel," he said, brisk and relieved. "Tony Matthews here. I'm glad you got in touch. When would it be convenient for you to come in? I'm tied up tomorrow but – "

"I can't make an appointment right now," Tess said hastily. "I only wanted to ask you something."

"You do realise that you are delaying matters, don't you? Probate and so forth?"

"Am I? I'm frightfully sorry. But what I wanted to know was whether Jonas – Mr Fedor – had deposited anything with you for safekeeping?"

"What sort of thing?" he asked, his voice cautious and legal.

"His memoirs. His autobiography. It's terribly important that I get hold of it as soon as – "

"I presume you would be talking about a considerable amount of manuscript, would you not?"

"A pretty thick wodge, yes."

"Then I'm afraid we have nothing like that in the office. But we *do* have the file about which I wish to speak to you. It is really quite imperative that you come in and – "

"I will. I really will, very soon."

"And there's this gallery owner who keeps telephoning from New York, demanding that we give her some picture which belonged to Jonas Fedor. Do you know anything about it?"

"What's her name?"

"Aragon. Something like that."

Tess found herself smiling. So Mercedes was not letting up the pressure to try and recover *The Tears She Shed*.

"Look: this file which I – "

"I'll get in touch as soon as I can," Tess said hastily.

She put the phone down then picked it up again. She dialled the number of Jonas's publisher, was put through to his editor, asked if the manuscript of his memoirs had turned up.

"Turned up?" the woman said. "That implies that you think it might be here in the office somewhere."

"Exactly."

"My dear, I only wish it were. I've seen enough of it to be aware that it'll require a considerable amount of editing if it's to be ready in time for the publication date."

"I see."

The editor's voice sharpened in alarm. "You do know where it *is*, don't you?"

"I – uh – I haven't really been looking. His housekeeper says he took the manuscript with him when he went to London just before his trip to Spain. I assumed you must have it."

"But I wrote and *asked* about – "

"I'll have a good search," promised Tess. "And let you know."

"Please do. It's really vital that we have the book as soon as – "

"I'll be in touch," Tess said, as she had to the solicitor. "It can't be far."

But where would Jonas have left his manuscript? Obviously he had not taken it to his publishers. Nor was it likely to be in some safe deposit box somewhere: the solicitors would have told her. There was one thing to the good: if she was right in thinking that the intruder was still looking for it, then it could not yet have been found and, presumably, destroyed. So where the hell was it?

Whatever the answer to the question, she realised that she herself was no longer safe. The car in the street, the break-in, the terrifying ride down from Montalbán only underlined the precariousness of her position.

Discard your routines, Jonas had advised. Very well, she would do so. *Keep your options open. Trust no-one*.

She picked up the telephone and dialled Emma Lybrand's number at work.

"Em," she said, "could you put up with a visitor for a while?"

"Of course. What length of while?"

"I don't really know. Not too long – I don't want to spend a lot of time in any one place."

"Are you in some kind of trouble?"

"I could be."

"Gosh," sighed Emma. "You do lead an exciting life. All I ever do is work and sleep. And bonk a bit, of course." She giggled. "Is it something to do with that wonderfully dangerous guardian of yours?"

"Dangerous?"

"You know what I mean: there was a touch of brutality about him that was terrifically exciting."

"Brutality? Jonas? Are we talking about the same man?" Tess said. But of course Emma was right. She would have seen it herself if she had not always been too frightened to look at the truth.

Emma went on: "The thing is . . ."

"What?"

". . . I'm not exactly living at home at the moment."

Tess groaned. "Don't tell me it's all on again with Josh."

"Sort of. We're having like, this trial whatever the opposite of separation is . . ."

"*Again*?"

". . . and my brother's away, so the flat's entirely at your disposal. You can water the plants for me: great!"

"Ever heard the name Andrew Rathbone?" Tess said.

"Vaguely." Emma thought about it. "He's a painter, isn't he? By the way, you know you were asking me about the Aragon Gallery?"

"Yes."

"The woman who owns it has been around for centuries. She's pulled off some spectacular deals in her time – she's one of those dealers who can literally make or break an artist overnight. Everyone calls her the Dragon Lady."

"I know who she is," Tess said quietly.

Behind Emma, someone could clearly be heard asking if she was coming out to lunch with them or *what*? "I must dash," Emma said. "Just tell me when you're planning to arrive at the flat. You've still got a key, haven't you?"

"Yeah. Thanks, Em. I really appreciate this."

She stood with her hand on the receiver, working something out. Mercedes had sold Phil Cramir (or Felipe Cabrera Ramirez) a copy of *The Tears She Shed*. Mercedes had written to Tess, demanding the same picture. Therefore she must know that one of them was a fake. The fraud she had perpetrated had been quite deliberate.

All art is illusion, Tess told herself wearily. The creation of a painting is nothing more than an attempt to persuade the viewer that something is what it is not. Now, her own reality was threatened; everywhere she turned, she was surrounded by falsehood and trickery. The lonely road of her nightmare stretched endlessly across her mind; increasingly it seemed that her private and professional lives were overlapping, that the menace which had for so long lurked outside her line of vision was coming closer.

"*Sometimes it is better to turn and face your adversaries,*" Jonas had said: she knew with sudden certainty that unless she confronted them now she would always be alone, never sure of what was true and what false.

She went slowly up to her bedroom. On the wall opposite the door hung *The Tears She Shed*; she stood in front of it, no more than a foot away, examining the technique, imagining the brush laying paint on the canvas, thick worms of white and blue and acid yellow, gradually smoothing them into bowl and sheets and fruit. Bending even closer to the swirls of paint, Tess noticed for the first time that what she had previously taken to be merely a consequence of the layers of pigment was in fact deliberate: a careful dot of dark brown paint laid alongside the girl's nose.

Tess was no great believer in coincidences, though prepared to accept that they happened. To find such a mark in a painting, to have seen a woman possessed of the same blemish, not once but twice, a woman who had wept at Jonas's funeral, a woman who was the artist's sister: it was not too difficult to assume that Mercedes herself had posed for this picture.

Not that it made any difference to anything; it was merely further confirmation, if she needed it.

She took the minimum she would need, using a duffel bag so that if she were observed, it would not be obvious that she was going away. The last thing she packed was the gun she had taken from Jonas's secret drawer; she wrapped it in two pairs of underpants and crammed it down at the bottom of the bag. Before leaving the shelter of her own door, she checked the street. It was empty. She walked fast into the town, the bag over her shoulder.

Once in the busy town centre, she slowed down. Her first stop was a travel agency; she chose one which operated as a concession within one of the big department stores. Having bought an airline ticket, she came out into King's Parade, where she spotted a single cruising taxicab. With no others around, no-one could follow her. She directed it to the station. A couple of hours later she was letting herself into Emma's spacious flat in Battersea, shabby and untidy but with a glorious view over the Park.

She could not have been followed; she had doubled back on her tracks several times on the Underground. Finally emerging at Paddington, she had taken a taxi south of the river. Emma's door had three separate locks on it as well as bolts top and bottom; the place was six storeys up and inaccessible to anyone but a rock-climber; there were neighbours above, below and on either side. No-one could break in without warning, and besides, they would have to find her first. For the time being, she was safe.

Even so, as she opened a bottle of wine, prepared a steak, her pulses thundered. There was a sense of disorientating exhilaration about living on the edge of danger; her senses seemed sharpened: the wine a deeper red, the steak more tender. The carpet floated a foot or so below the soles of her feet: if an assassin were to burst in and spray the room with bullets, she knew that, as though she were some comic-book superhero, they would bounce from her invulnerable flesh and leave her unharmed.

She longed to hear Dominic's voice, to tell him where she was and why. But Jonas himself had warned her to trust nobody. And there were questions which needed answering. Where had Dominic been while she was in Spain: could he be behind the search of her house? And how had he grown so friendly with Jonas in such a short space of time? Why did his eyes sometimes grow so bleak, just as Jonas's did?

She had assumed that Captain Santiago was behind the death of Jonas. But suppose Santiago was dead and it was his son or even his grandson who was trying to suppress incriminating information? Dominic still remained very much of an enigma to her: apart from his sister Valentine he almost never spoke of his parents or his upbringing. He had mentioned living in Spain: was that because Spanish blood, tainted blood, surged in his veins?

Thinking this, she found herself suddenly wanting the answer to a question which should have been asked long before. Though first suppressed by medication, then by preoccupation, finally by fear, it had hovered on the edge of her subconscious for days. Now, it burst out into the open, ripe and bloated with blood.

As clearly as though it were in front of her, she remembered how she had searched his wallet the night someone had tried to drown her. Credit cards, money, crumpled bus tickets, old receipts. And among them, the shiny cover of an Iberian Airlines ticket, the pink flimsy inside, the ticket gone, presumably used.

How could she have let so much time go by? Was it her deep reluctance to admit that Dominic was not at all what he appeared to be, but something much more sinister?

Because sitting there over the remains of a meal, an almost empty wine bottle in front of her, she could see, without any shadow of a doubt, the faint figures on that flimsy, figures which reinforced all her welling doubts about him. They were the dates of a return flight to Granada, and though they did not entirely coincide with Jonas's own time there, they covered most of it.

Including the day he was known to have died.

Nausea lurked at the pit of her stomach. Horror filled her. She wanted to weep, to scream. She had loved Jonas unquestioningly; she had learned to love Dominic.

Pressing her lips together so that they would not tremble, she telephoned Dominic's flat. When she heard the beep of the answering machine, she said levelly: "I'm going to the States on business. I'll see you when I get back."

Before she got into bed, she unwrapped the gun and put it beside her bed. *The ruthless ones*, Jonas had called them. She understood now that the reason he knew so much about them was because he himself had been one. Like Dominic.

She had thought at first that Mercedes might have killed Jonas, then become convinced that El Malo must have been responsible for his death. Now, a new possibility struck her. However much she yearned towards Dominic, however much she saw in him the key which might unlock the door to her own traumas, she had to face one chilling and inescapable question, however painful the answer might be. Until now, she had avoided it but now there was no escape.

Of the two men she loved, had one killed the other?

26

MERCEDES

She was riding high. Being female in the traditionally male world of hard graft art-dealing had occasionally been a minus factor. But as the Sixties moved towards the Seventies, it was precisely because she *was* a woman that she saw earlier than her male colleagues the need to create her own markets. If she was to concentrate on the sale of contemporary art, she had to persuade her clients that what they were buying was going to last.

Promotion had always seemed to her as important in the selling process as having the works to sell, especially now, when there were more millionaires than ever before. Having made fortunes during and immediately after the war, many of them were anxious to acquire social cachet and ready to spend lavishly to obtain it. Art – the acquisition if not the appreciation of it – was one way to buy social acceptability.

Realising this, Mercedes began to play on both the natural élitism of those with old money and the anxious ambitions of the newly rich. Invitations to her exhibition openings were considered a definite social cachet, identifying the recipients not only as seriously monied, but also as *cognoscenti*. It was flattery at its most blatant. Having issued her invitations, it was necessary to invest the occasions with the maximum glamour and excitement, to make being in attendance at an Aragon Gallery exhibition party one of the fashionable occasions not to be missed. New York socialites began to plan their diaries around the four major exhibitions at the Aragon; dressmakers were forewarned; pre-exhibition cocktail parties and post-exhibition dinner parties organised. The fashionable flaunted their invitations; those not invited to one showing angled and hustled for an invitation to the next. And all of them, once they had secured it, felt it necessary to buy from her.

Her stable of protégés grew. Though choosing an unknown to sponsor was always a gamble – she had had occasional failures – she grew more confident as she grew older, and more ruthless. Once she had established their work patterns, and their dependency on her, she was tireless in promoting their interests, for in so doing she promoted her own. Each one of them painted a portrait of her; as the number mounted, the collection only added to her legend in New York. It was not that the subject was always the same so much as the names who had painted her; some – Klein for instance – had painted her more than once. A representative from MOMA suggested a special showing of the paintings, to coincide with their latest exhibition of contemporary art. Although she refused, she made sure that the whole of New York knew about it.

Richard Klein died, sending up the price of his work and at the same time adding lustre to her, his patron for so many years, the one who had picked him out as a young artist and supported him, nurtured him, made it possible for his creative talents to flower. There was some adverse publicity, of course; there always was. Lorna Arup, Klein's widow, gave interviews in which she accused Mercedes of keeping them in virtual poverty. "Everything he did, every bit of work he produced belonged to her, for the price of a bowl of cornflakes in the morning and a hot-dog at night. That's all we could afford," she told the *Times*, "Even though Richard's work was fetching thousands, he hardly saw a penny of it, and all because of some contract he signed with her when he was just a kid."

She came into the gallery one day and hurled the same accusations at Mercedes in person.

"He seemed to have enough to pay for bourbon," Mercedes said coldly. "Besides, I know you've got pieces of his work stashed away somewhere."

"You cold-hearted bitch!" screamed Lorna. "Don't you think of anything but money? Is that all Richard's work meant to you: cold cash?"

"Of course not." Mercedes opened her bag. "If you're in need, I'll be glad to write you a cheque."

Any publicity is good publicity. Her own renown as a maker of artistic reputations grew.

In Montalbán, she had no reputation at all. Her visits to the Casa de las Lunas grew shorter and less frequent; there was an unreal quality about the time she spent there, for her true life was lived in New York. She had never made any pretence to love the two motherless children of Ramirez, indeed made every effort to display her indifference to their welfare, her lack of interest in their concerns. The boy was sixteen now, undersized and self-effacing, unwilling to meet anyone's gaze head-on. The girl, too, was timid and immature.

On one of her visits, Mercedes discovered that during her absence, Carlos had converted one of the rooms in the house into a studio for his son. The boy had messed about with paints and charcoal since an early age though she had always done her best to discourage him. She was furious to learn that the aunts had given him the easel at which Fernando used to work, although he was a Ramirez and no kin of theirs.

One afternoon she walked into the boy's room. She stood in silence beside the easel, watching his bony nervous hands as they worked, knowing that she unnerved him.

After a while the boy said: "Will you tell me the truth?"

"What about?"

"My work." He waved his brush at canvases leaning against the walls, at the one on the easel.

"I always tell the truth about art," she said.

"Well, then. What do you think?"

What she thought was that here was genuine talent, that if this thin sixteen-year-old were to walk into her gallery and show her his work she would put him instantly under exclusive contract. What she said – and it was far more difficult than she anticipated – was: "You'll never make an artist."

"Not everyone agrees with you," he said quietly.

"Who?" She was scornful. "The aunts, do you mean? They would think it an indication of genius if you drew a straight line on a piece of paper."

"My father," he said. His mouth flinched on the word as though he anticipated her contempt. She wished he was bolder, that he had the guts to look her in the eye and tell her he did not give a damn what she thought.

"What else would your father say?" she asked. "You're his son; he wouldn't want to hurt your feelings. Besides, he would assume that since you are a Ramirez, you must be good." She saw the flush grow along his neck and thought: He is as suggestible as his mother.

"There are others." His voice was defensive.

"People in the village? Your grandparents?" She laughed contemptuously. "I've often thought you only took up painting to be like Fernando Vicente, to be as loved as he was, as famous."

"That's not what – "

"He was a *real* artist," she said, deliberately cruel. "Not just someone playing about with paints."

"So you don't think I'll ever be as good as he was?"

"Never. If you could paint like he did, then I should consider your work worth something – and I should say so."

"Thank you." The blood had drained from his face; he looked at her with the sombre gaze of his father. "Thank you for being so honest with me."

The next day, he was gone.

Carlos came storming out to the swimming-pool where she lay relaxing, rubbing oil into herself. She wore a two-piece bathing costume which emphasised the flatness of her stomach and the ripeness of her breasts. From behind dark glasses she regarded him with indifference as he stood over her.

"You said something to him, didn't you?" he said.

"To whom?"

"My son."

"What are you talking about, Carlos?"

"Amador."

"What *about* him?"

"He's gone. He's run away from home. He left a note. What the hell did you say to him, you bitch?"

"I? Please, Carlos, control yourself." She thought viciously: You took away my brother's life and now, in a sense, I have taken away your son's.

"I told him not to ask your opinion, that you would lie if he did."

"I do have some integrity, Carlos, whatever you choose to think."

"You told him he was no good as a painter, didn't you?" Carlos leaned down, his face twisted with rage and grief. "That's what you did, isn't it?"

"He asked my opinion of his work; I told him what I thought."

"Not what you *really* thought. You can see the boy has talent, but you'd die rather than say so, even though you know how sensitive he is, how insecure." Carlos was shaking, his hand rough on her arm. She tried to pull away but he held her tightly round the wrist, hurting her.

"Let go of me," she said. He ignored her.

"You know his stuff's good, you know he's got a future. Far more than that deviant little shit, your brother, ever had."

Coldness filled her. Her head felt as though it was filled with freezing air. She had heard what they said about Fernando but knew it was not true. "How dare you," she said. "How *dare* you." She wrenched her arm away

464

from his grasp and took off her glasses to stare at him, giving him the witch's look, making her eyes grow huge as the pupils dilated.

For once, it failed to affect him. "I'll never forgive you for this," he said, and the loathing in his expression shook her.

"And I," she said, the words falling like ice into the heated air, "shall never forgive you."

"For Christ's sake," he said impatiently, stepping back as though he could no longer bear the proximity of her presence. "I don't know what it is you think I've ever done to hurt you, and frankly I no longer care. Amador is the important thing right now."

She put her sunglasses on again and returned to her book. "He'll get in touch when he needs money," she said indifferently.

But he did not. Weeks passed, turning into months and eventually into years, but they heard nothing from Amador. Though Carlos hired detectives, they could find no information about where he was, what he was doing, whether, indeed, he was still alive.

Francisca died, followed shortly by Isabella. Hearing the news in New York, Mercedes, heavily involved in mounting one of her quarterly exhibitions, decided not to attend the funerals. Time enough when Rosita went and the house in Montalbán became available.

The following year, Carlos brought his daughter to New York. Over the years, he and Mercedes had reached a kind of compromise, a state of neutrality in which they maintained an outwardly cordial relationship. She knew that he had never got over the loss of his son; seeing him on this visit, she was shocked at just how much damage his grief had caused. Last time she had seen him, he was upright and robust, but now he seemed diminished, bent, years older. The girl was small, shy, fearful, as frail as a sparrow in Mercedes' cold embrace.

Looking at her clothes, Mercedes told her to throw them away.

"You're in New York now," she said, "not in some backwater Spanish village. I'll take you shopping when I've got a moment. Or, on second thoughts, send you with my secretary."

"What's wrong?" Conchita looked down at herself. "Aunt Isabella's dressmaker made it for me."

"Exactly." Mercedes pinched a bit of the material between finger and thumb. "Some old peasant woman with pins in her mouth and a length of tawdry stuff from Granada."

Conchita flushed. "It's the latest fashion. We looked in the fashion magazines."

"There's fashion and fashion," Mercedes said. "And while you're here, you should aim to be New York fashionable, not Montalbán fashionable."

"I'd much rather be in Montalbán than here," Conchita said bravely. It was the first time Mercedes had ever heard her say anything even remotely rebellious.

"Well, I wouldn't," she said. "And while you're in town, I'd like you to reflect well on me as well as on yourself. I certainly don't want people nudging themselves, asking how Mercedes Aragon can allow her stepdaughter to go round looking like a shop assistant."

Dark colour came into the girl's face. "I thought your name was Ramirez," she said, as rudely as she dared.

"I use Aragon as a professional name," snapped Mercedes.

At her opening night party, Concepción appeared in a very short dress of black velvet with a fine lace collar. With it she wore low-heeled shoes and black tights; the extreme simplicity of the outfit only emphasised her air of youth and fragility.

"You must be proud of her," Mercedes said to Carlos, well-pleased by both the girl's appearance and Carlos's good looks, despite the fact that he seemed to have shrunk in the past year until his dinner jacket appeared to be a couple of sizes too big.

"She's beautiful," Carlos said simply. He waved at an elegant woman in green silk and diamonds.

"Who's that?" demanded Mercedes. The woman was unknown to her, but obviously rich: she was pretty sure the dress was one of Yves St Laurent's and the diamonds were real.

"A friend." Carlos moved away, making his way across the room, leaving Mercedes feeling, somehow, bereft.

"Your husband, I believe," said someone behind her. She recognised the curiously thin voice at once, although its owner had not been into the gallery for a long time.

"Good evening, Mr Lovel," she said without turning round. "What do you think of the exhibition?"

"I've not yet had a chance to look at it," Lovel said. "My interest lies elsewhere."

"Japanese prints, wasn't it?"

"Tonight I'm more concerned with people. To be specific, in one particular person."

"Which one?"

"Who is that child over there – the dark one, in black velvet?"

A voice spoke loudly inside Mercedes' head, warning her, entreating her to show mercy. "You must mean my stepdaughter," she said smoothly. "A pretty dress, don't you think?"

"Her clothes are irrelevant," Lovel said. He moved to stand in front of her. "It's what's underneath that interests me."

Mercedes gave him a hard stare. He was speaking in code, informing her the time for her debt to fall due was near. What exactly did he want? In spite of herself, she shuddered inwardly at the thought of the man's pale fingers on Concepción's immature body. She laughed, throwing back her head. "From where I'm standing, she hardly looks the sort to interest a man," she said lightly. "No bumps anywhere."

"That's exactly what I like about her," Lovel said, and his words were frosted with menace. "I'd very much appreciate being introduced."

Following him across the crowded gallery floor to where Concepción stood, she told herself that she really had no choice in the matter.

Much later that evening, when the last of the red stickers had been pasted to the works on the walls, when the last broken glass had been swept up and the soggy party food thrown away, she walked tiredly round the corner from the gallery to her apartment. All in all, it had been a success, even more of one than she had hoped. Several important contacts had been made, the critics had expressed approval of the names she had chosen to exhibit, she had landed a lucrative commission from one of her best clients to purchase a painting on his behalf.

She took off her Chanel evening suit and hung it up, turned on a bath. She lay for a long time in the scented water, thinking about Lovel. Although nothing had been said, she knew that he wanted something from her and that something was Concepción. She was not sure she would be able to deliver. These were not Victorian times, when girls did as they were told; even in Spain, where there was still a strong tradition of daughters obeying their parents when it came to a choice of husband, it was unlikely that Carlos would see Lovel as a suitable partner for Concepción. As for the girl herself, Mercedes had seen the visible flicker of repulsion in her expression as Lovel took her hand, holding on to it for a fraction longer than necessary, and the way she had bent her head away from his dead gaze. Once introduced, he had scarcely left her side after that; the girl was too inexperienced – and too polite – to know how to get rid of him.

Wearily, Mercedes closed her eyes. She could try, she supposed. If she failed, Lovel had nothing to threaten her with; if the worst came to the worst she could always return the Vicente he had given her.

She heard a knock. Who could that be? For a moment she was tempted to ignore it. Then, her heart banging about in her chest, she was splashing out of the bath and grabbing a towel, wrapping it around herself as she ran to the door of her apartment. She did not bother to check the spy-hole: she knew who it was.

"Jonas!" she said as the door swung open. "Jonas."

He came in on a run, propelling her backwards, kicking the door shut behind him as he tore away the towel.

"All these years," he said as she fell to the ground beneath him, "and still you bewitch me."

"All these years," she gasped. She ripped away his shirt as he pulled at his trouser belt. When he entered her, she screamed aloud for love of him, knowing that nothing mattered but this coming together of two halves, this making whole.

He was in New York to discuss with his agent the setting up of an exhibition to be called 'The New Ceramics'. The agent was giving a party to which Mercedes was invited; when she mentioned Carlos, Jonas told her to bring him too.

Carlos refused the invitation. "I'm dining with my – with a friend," he said, and Mercedes immediately visualised the elegant socialite who had attended her own exhibition party.

"I'll take Conchita if you like," she offered. After years of being known only as a hard-headed business woman, it would do her image no harm to appear as a dutiful stepmother.

"I should think it highly unlikely she'd agree to go," Carlos said, and Mercedes did not ask why.

But surprisingly, Concepción decided she would like to come. She appeared at Mercedes' apartment in a short coat of pale mink worn over a demure shift of garnet silk with a tiny collar of seed pearls. Mercedes was impressed: the girl had learned fast.

Mercedes called a cab, feeling an unaccustomed pride. Wonderful skin, huge soft eyes that were almost black, long shining hair bundled on top of her head: the girl was undeniably decorative in her own understated way, and a refreshing change from the cynical world of New York society. A dinner party, Mercedes thought, at a fashionable restaurant, cocktails at the apartment first, some of the Ivy League sons of her clients . . . she pushed away the memory of Lovel and his cool remorseless face.

Jonas's eyes widened as she came in with Concepción. She smiled at him secretly, remembering his body on hers the previous night, her own voluptuous surrender to the warmth of his mouth, the fire of his fingers on her breasts, their mutual passion. He worked his way towards them, and she sighed, taking his hand, wanting him again and forever.

"Jonas, this is my stepdaughter, Concepción," she said as he bent to kiss her cheek.

He held out his hand and the girl put hers into it. "The daughter of Carlos Ramirez," he said.

"Yes." Concepción twisted her head shyly. There were rubies in her ears; her piled hair emphasised the fragility of her neck.

For the moment, Mercedes thought, she is unaware of her effect. But when she realises . . . She laughed, mellow, taking Jonas's arm. "Come. Let's go and talk to people."

"Julian Maitland is desperate to see you again," Jonas said. He turned to Concepción. "He has not seen Mercedes since the war."

"Where is he?" asked Mercedes.

"Over there, waitink for you in the corner. Do not keep him in suspense or he may die."

Concepción giggled, a soft little sound.

"You do not believe me, señorita?" Jonas said in Spanish. "But I assure you it is true."

471

"Let's go over to him," said Mercedes. She pulled at Jonas's arm but he did not move.

"Julian is hopink to have you to himself," he said. "Besides, there is this beautiful señorita to be taken care of." He cupped a hand under Concepción's elbow.

"Someone will talk to her," Mercedes said impatiently. "Look at all the young men eyeing her."

"Oh, my God!" cried Jonas. He pointed a finger across the room. "Julian is cryink, you have left him alone, Mercedes, he thinks you do not wish to talk to him. See how he clutches at his bosom. His heart is breakink."

"You are ridiculous," Mercedes said, laughing, while Concepción giggled again, looking up at Jonas with soft dark eyes. She turned to the girl: "That young man over there is Carter, the heir to the Greeley fortune – you should make friends with him."

"I shall escort her over to this wealthy sprig," Jonas said. "Their eyes will meet and she will fall instantly in love. Do you believe in love at first sight, señorita Concepción?"

"Yes," Concepción said.

"Oh dear," Jonas said, pulling a face. "I am an old old man now, and you are just a girl, naturally you will fall for him and I shall be so-oo-o sad."

"I am seventeen."

"And I, my dear, am long past forty. Is that not right, Mercedes?"

"Age means nothing," Concepción said. "It is people who are important. Who they are, *how* they are."

It was the longest speech Mercedes had heard her make, the first time she had ventured to express an opinion. "Exactly," she said. "And you are still a boy, Jonas."

"Only in my heart." Jonas touched his chest. "Only *here*. Now, I shall take Concepción to meet her destiny in Mr Carter Greeley and then I shall rejoin you, Mercedes." And he was pushing his way through the crowds, pulling Concepción after him, before Mercedes could object.

She knew many of the people in the room; it was half an hour before she was able to look around for Concepción, check that she was all right, only to find that the girl had vanished. Narrowing her eyes, Mercedes looked for Carter Greeley but could not see him: he must have swept Concepción off for dinner at some fashionable restaurant. If not him, then some other of the young men about town who frequented occasions like this, fresh from Harvard or Yale and working their way up Wall Street. There was no need to worry, since they were all well-connected and impeccably bred. Whoever she was with would see Concepción home.

None the less, unaccountably, she did worry. Through a gap in the crowd, she saw Lovel appear and stand staring about him, searching for someone. Quickly she turned, but it was too late; he had already seen her and was shortly at her side.

"Is your stepdaughter with you?" he asked without preamble.

"No."

"Where is she?"

She raised her eyebrows. "I really have no idea, Mr Lovel."

"I thought she was coming here."

"Who told you that?"

"I . . . found out." His voice was very quiet.

473

"She was here earlier and now she's gone."

"Who with?" She saw his hands clench.

"Some people of her own age," Mercedes said, trying to ignore the fear which stirred at the pit of her stomach. There was something here that was unhealthy, obscene. He repelled her: the translucent skin, the reddish eyes, the way he stood moving his bloodless hands against each other so that they made a faint insect noise. Thinking of Concepción in her garnet-coloured dress, Mercedes made a sudden decision.

"Incidentally, I think it would be better if I returned your picture to you," she said, hating the faint tremor she could feel in her throat.

Lovel seemed preoccupied; he stood chewing his pale lip and did not answer.

"Mr Lovel?"

He shook himself. "Yes?"

"Did you hear me?"

"No. What did you say?"

"I said I wished to return the painting by Vicente which you gave me. Or else pay you a fair price for it. I shouldn't have accepted it in the first place but I was overcome by – "

"A bargain is a bargain," he said abruptly. "I expect you to keep your side of ours." He turned on his heel and disappeared into the crowd, heading towards the door, leaving her troubled.

He came into the gallery the next day. Mercedes had little time for him; near the door was one of the most influential art critics in New York, back for a second viewing after attending her opening party the previous week.

"She's staying with her grandparents, isn't she?" Lovel said.

Mercedes had to bend her head to catch his words but they made no sense to her. "Who is?" she asked. A favourable write-up could make a big difference to both the sales and the prestige of the two artists she was featuring.

"Concepción."

"Oh. Yes, she is." The critic was stepping back now, taking out a notebook, patting himself for a pen to write with . . .

"The Blevitskys, isn't that right?"

She did not ask how he knew. "Yes." It was time for her to make her move, to engage the critic in discussion, to mention how penetrating she had found his last article on the work being exhibited by a rival dealer, to drop the names of one or two clients . . .

"And when does she return to Spain?"

"For heaven's sake," Mercedes said. "I've no idea." She wished Lovel would go away and give her a chance to concentrate.

He planted himself in front of her, blocking her view. "No idea?"

"Next week, I think."

"That's too soon."

"Too soon for what?" She tried to see round him, anxious to net her prey before it fluttered elsewhere.

"Me."

"*You*?" He had caught her attention now. His unblinking stare was fixed on her; his ears were white, with a pinkish tinge on the lobes.

"Keep her here," he said. "I need more time."

"Time for what, exactly?"

But he had gone again, pushing rudely past the critic and out into the street, while she tried to compose herself, stifling her feelings of revulsion as she advanced towards the critic with a smile on her face.

Jonas left for San Francisco the following day. Although she doubted if Carlos would take any notice of what she said, Mercedes none the less repeated Lovel's words to him, hoping he would take some action to shield the girl. It was difficult to describe the dread Lovel inspired in her, or to convey exactly what she feared if he were not stopped. If Carlos would heed her and remove the girl from New York, Mercedes would at least feel that she had done what she could.

The thought of Lovel's reaction if he discovered she was trying to impede his chances with the girl chilled her. He was a man, she realised, more than capable of murder, a man who relished the pain of others. She was uneasy, filled with a sense of doom; she put it down to the fact that it was winter and the days were short. Even after all these years, she missed the way the light shone from behind the mountains above Montalbán on even the coldest days.

Carlos was dismissive of her fears, assuming that she was intent on making further mischief. She could not blame him, given her past behaviour. None the less, she persevered, aware that she had hitherto shown too little interest in the Ramirez children for their father now to believe she had Concepción's best interests at heart.

"Thank you for your warning," he said. He sounded uninterested.

"The man has taken the trouble to research her background and he's obviously been spying on her. Please pass on to her what I said," urged Mercedes.

"I will," he said and she felt a sinking of the heart, knowing he would not, that it might already be too late.

"Carlos, this man is dangerous . . ." she said.

"As it happens, Conchita is leaving for California to spend a week or two with Blanche and her husband. She wants to visit Death Valley, Alcatraz, the redwood forests – places she's only read about until now."

". . . and sick," she insisted.

"Once she has left New York, he will find other things to do with his time."

"I hope you're right," Mercedes said sombrely.

She had been dreaming recently, dreams which came back to her during the daytime with startling clarity: skulls and coffins, flames, herself at the mercy of a vast shapeless presence, the Devil himself. She told herself that these were merely the images of a Catholic girlhood brought on by overwork, but could not shake off the feeling of disquiet, nor the knowledge that she was embroiled in something evil from which there was no escape. Sometimes she woke to find she was sobbing; she knew herself to be lost.

Concepción weighed on her mind. Never having made any attempt to ingratiate herself with the two Ramirez children, Mercedes assumed they felt only dislike for her. Although the girl possessed a natural timidity, Mercedes was aware that she herself was responsible for much of her fragility of temperament. Lovel's intentions were not clear; because of this, Mercedes' fears were multiple. Concerned about someone other than herself for the first time in years, she was conscious of a new vulnerability.

In the days which followed, she had little time to think of Concepción. Lovel did not appear again and meantime, one of her long-term plans had come to fruition. A client asked her to undertake an overhaul of his collection of contemporary art, weeding out pictures he now regretted buying and filling in the blanks. It was the kind of influential commission she had long hoped for since it established her firmly and finally in the very top ranks of dealers.

At the same time, another client, a wealthy recluse from Texas, had begun sending out feelers with regard to his collection of Impressionists. If she were involved in the sale, however peripherally, the commission would be enormous, enabling her at last to move towards the realisation of her plans to establish her brother Fernando as the great painter of his generation.

When the time came, when Rosita died and she was able to start work on her memorial to her brother, she had decided to create a single day, that last day when he was taken away, stumbling between his guards. There had been a streak of blue paint on his shirt. He had looked back at her over his shoulder; she had never forgotten his look of entreaty, as though he hoped for forgiveness.

Sometimes, in the interval between waking and sleep, she would walk in imagination round the house once again, recalling that day in all its detail, what she had worn, Francisca's shoes, the way Isabella's hands had trembled as they opened a jar of fresh olives, a basket of oranges in the hall, the sound of Rosita sobbing, the newspaper headlines chronicling the progress of the Civil War.

Somewhere at the back of her mind was the thought that by bringing back that day, by stopping time, none of the rest would have happened, and all the rage and hatred might somehow be nullified.

And behind that was yet another thought. Once she had done that, she would surely have done all she need do to avenge Fernando's death.

Jonas returned to New York. There were pictures of him in *Life*, smiling behind a shelf of his pots; once she saw him in a restaurant with two young men, but although she waited, he did not come to her and she was too proud to contact him or ask him why.

Concepción, too, returned to town.

Lovel came into the gallery. "You must help me," he said. He was paler, more phantasmal than ever; his eyes burned in their bone-white sockets.

"Why?"

"She refuses to see me."

She did not need to ask who he meant. She busied herself at her desk. "I don't know what I can – "

He slammed his hand down violently in front of her. "Invite her to your apartment."

"She would not come."

"Make her." He was standing much too close to her so that she had to lean back to avoid contact with him; his clothes gave off a dry scent, like old leaves.

"And then?"

"Leave me alone with her." His mouth was cruel.

"And if I refuse to do this?"

"I think you will not."

"Why?"

"Because I knew your brother, Fernando Vicente." He looked down at her, unblinking. "The great artist."

She kept her voice steady. "So did a great many people."

"Perhaps they did not know him as well as I did," Lovel said. He rubbed one palm across the back of the other hand; the sound was exquisitely painful to her. She dared not ask what he meant but saw a void opening up before her, a blackness of waste and despair. For years she had known herself to be precariously at its edge; if she ignored him now, she was afraid he would say something that would make it impossible to maintain her balance.

For a moment she hesitated. There were two choices open to her: Fernando or Concepción. By betraying the girl, she would save her brother; she might save Concepción if she were prepared to defy Lovel and his threats, if she dared him to do his worst. But if Fernando's reputation was lost, then she was lost with him.

She said: "When do you want this to happen?" closing her eyes against her own betrayal, seeing all the other deceptions down the years and the way they had shaped her into a monster she could no longer control.

"As soon as you can."

As he walked towards the door, she said uselessly: "Don't hurt her."

He did not reply.

Looking at her own reflection in the mirror of carved Spanish walnut in her upstairs office, she shuddered. For a moment her features blurred; she heard the rush of wind among the stars and the tap of a cloven hoof.

Turning, she looked at the photograph of Vicente she kept on the wall, at his melancholy smile. "I do this for you, Fernando," she said and knew that he asked more of her than she ought to give.

When Lovel came again, she said: "Not my apartment. I will invite you there, and her, but I cannot be seen to be part of it."

At night the images crowded her: a cloth-covered altar, an operating table, a butcher's slab. Knives glittered across her dreams, and blood. Again and again she saw bullets thud against flesh and the blood-spattered convent wall.

She needed Jonas but he did not come; if he had, he could not have helped her.

She gave a small party, inviting a careful selection of guests, a smattering of older couples, some of their sons and daughters, the editor of an arts magazine, a museum curator. She told Carlos it could be useful for Concepción to meet some of these people; the girl might wish to stay in New York rather than return to Montalbán and they were the sort who could help her to find a job. She invited Jonas, but he was not able to attend.

"Not able, Jonas, or not willing?" she said into the telephone receiver, laughing a little.

"What do you think, Mercedes?"

"You prefer to see me alone, do you not? And preferably naked, yes?"

"Something like that," he said and she laughed again, remembering the many times they had made love, and the ways they had made it, secure in the exclusivity of his desire for her if in nothing else.

"I leave town tonight," he said abruptly. "I don't know when I shall be back."

She had never shown her hurt at his sudden departures, nor would she do so now.

"So I shall not see you again this time."

"No."

"Before you go," she said lightly, "we have business to discuss."

"What business?"

"My picture. *The Tears She Shed.*"

"*My* picture," he said.

"Let me buy it back from you, Jonas." She told him of her plans for the Vicente Museum she would open, the shrine to her brother she planned.

He listened in silence, then said: "But I told you, I wished to give it to my daughter."

"You have no daughter."

"Then you may have it when I am dead," he said.

The thought of a world without Jonas was abruptly appalling. Tears clutched at her throat. "Tell me you love me, Jonas," she begged. "Just once. Say it."

"But I do not."

"Do you love anyone?" she asked.

"Yes."

"But not me."

"Not you."

"You are hard, Jonas."

"I have needed to be."

"Oh, Jonas." She closed her eyes. Her life was full of angles, sharp edges; only with Jonas was there anything soft. "So have I."

"I know that," he said quietly. "Which is why I cannot condemn you."

*   *   *

Concepción was in a dress of deep pink silk with a single strand of pearls around her neck. Her dark hair, worn loose, emphasised her extreme youth though she had none the less matured in some way since Mercedes had seen her last. She hesitated at the sight of Lovel, nodded briefly at him and moved away but her eyes constantly returned to him. Each time, she found him staring directly back at her; each time she found it more difficult to look away. After dinner, Lovel took a seat beside her. He did not speak. Mercedes realised that his personality blanketed the girl; he was devouring her like a cancer. If someone addressed her, Concepción turned blindly towards them as though recalled from sleep.

Towards the end of the evening, one of the young men offered to drop Concepción at the house of her grandparents, but Lovel intervened.

"I'm going that way myself," he said. "I will see Miss Ramirez home."

Refuse him, Mercedes thought. Fight him. She was frightened. The girl simply nodded and turned away, expressionless.

"She's pregnant," Carlos said through clenched teeth.

"By whom?" Mercedes stared at him in horror.

"She won't say."

"What will you do?"

"I don't know. She says she doesn't care what happens to her, she wants to go home, but I can't take her there."

"Why not?"

"For God's sake, Mercedes, you know what Montalbán is like as well as I do. An unmarried girl with a baby?

They would crucify her. Besides, she has dishonoured me. Dishonoured the name of Ramirez."

"Then find her a husband." Mercedes felt nothing but contempt for him. Dishonour, indeed. Who was he to talk of dishonour?

"Where would I start looking. I don't know if any of the boys she has been seeing fancies himself in love with her, let alone wishes to take on a wife who is pregnant by another man."

Her self-control broke. She ran at Carlos, beating him with her fists. "I warned you," she shouted. "I *told* you, Carlos, to keep her away from him."

"You know who is responsible?"

"Yes."

"He must be made to marry her."

"Was it – did he rape her?"

"Who knows."

"But didn't you ask her?"

Carlos groaned. "She refuses to discuss it."

She wished he cared less about the burden of shame which his daughter's loss of virginity had brought to him, and more about Concepción, whether she had suffered, perhaps suffered still.

"If he agrees to marry her," Mercedes said, "you must persuade her that it is the best thing."

He looked immeasurably relieved. "Do you think he will?"

"Possibly."

Faint and sick, she telephoned Lovel, her loathing for him so great that she could scarcely dial his number. "Come and see me immediately," she said, and put down the telephone before he could reply.

"Concepción is pregnant," she said when he arrived an hour later. She put one hand against the wall to steady herself. "What did you do to her, Lovel?"

"What do you think?"

"Did you . . . force her?"

"Only enough to make it interesting for both of us."

"Was it just the one time?"

"No."

"Surely she cannot – " Mercedes broke off.

"Enjoy it? Is that what you were going to say?" The bloodless lips widened. "No. She does not enjoy it. I would not like it if she did."

"Then how do you – "

"She comes to my apartment of her own accord," Lovel said.

"But why? Do you drug her?"

"Of course not. But some people are so filled with self-disgust that they relish their own degradation. And other people enjoy degrading." The blood-coloured eyes slid away from hers; his pale fingers smoothed the back of his silky hair. "There is very little she will not do," he said

Bile rose in her throat. "I don't believe you," she said, feeling nauseous. "The girl is of good family, carefully brought up."

"She was not a virgin," Lovel said.

"Nons – "

"Which does not make her any the less desirable."

"Do you still want her?" She could feel her mouth curling with disgust.

There was a long pause before he said: "Oh yes." His fists were clenched so hard that the tendons of his neck stood out. "But maybe she would not have me after – after what has passed between us."

Mercedes shut her mind to the sense of his words. If she was to remain strong, she must not imagine that first seduction, the girl weeping, beating her hands against his chest, the final forcing, must not imagine the subsequent occasions nor what Lovel asked the child to do. "She needs a husband," she said faintly.

"She would not have me."

Mercedes ignored that. "She is at the stage where she doesn't care what happens to her."

She longed to ask if that first moment of release inside innocent flesh was everything he had expected it to be. Lovel's claim that the girl was not a virgin she dismissed. In these days of regular exercise it was easy for a girl to appear impure; there was a tennis court at the Casa de las Lunas, as well as a swimming-pool and horses, all of which Concepción used regularly.

When he did not answer, she said: "Well? Will you marry her?"

"God." He paused for a moment. "Have you ever known what it is to feel passion for someone? Have you ever found your mind, your heart, your entire life taken over by thoughts of another person? From the first moment I saw Concepción, I have scarcely slept for thinking of her, I have done nothing but dream of possessing her. I don't mind that she hates me, is repelled by me, I simply need to have her there, ready for me to take whenever I want. And having her only fuels the need to have her again."

"That's not love," Mercedes said, thinking the man sounded insane.

"Love? Who said anything about love. I'm talking about obsession." His mouth was wet. He added: "Once we are married, you will have discharged your debt."

"In good measure, pressed down and running over," said Mercedes, and turned away.

The marriage of Concepción Ramirez and Richard Lovel took place in Montalbán. Throughout the ceremony the bride, though beautiful, appeared apathetic to the point of semi-consciousness. None of the bride's family looked at Mercedes Ramirez, or spoke to her. She seemed ill, her face sallow, her eyes hidden behind sunglasses; she left immediately after the bridegroom had taken his new wife away on their honeymoon. No-one knew about the incoherent telephone call she received from Jonas one night, nor his accusations that he would never forgive her. She could tell he was drunk; her demands to know what he was talking about were only met with further ravings.

Some months after this, Rosita died. Mercedes travelled from New York, arriving from Granada on the morning of the funeral. Standing beside the grave as the priest intoned the last sentences of a funeral Mass, she again shielded her face with dark glasses, watching the villagers stare at her, whisper.

Heavily pregnant, looking far older than her eighteen years, Concepción stood with her father, absorbed in some dream of her own. Her husband, it was understood, was in Japan; when the child was born, she would join him there. Next to them was Luisa, now a handsome woman in her fifties, some years older than Mercedes.

Afterwards, Carlos Ramirez escorted his daughter to a waiting car for the short drive back to the Casa de las Lunas, leaving his wife to make her own way to the cemetery gates. Mercedes paused there, looking back, waiting for Luisa, who was approaching with her husband.

"Luisa!" Mercedes offered her face for a kiss but the other woman drew back.

"How are you?" she said coldly.

Mercedes looked regretful. "Horribly busy," she said gravely. She looked at her watch. "In fact I must get back to New York as soon as possible. Even for a death, business does not stop. Which is why I would like to know what you intend to do about the house in Montalbán." Her lawyers had already checked out the terms of Rosita's will; as she had been afraid, the house was left to Luisa.

Luisa's plump pretty face narrowed into suspicion. "Why do you ask?"

"Because if you are thinking of selling it, I should like to have the first option on it."

"We certainly have no reason to hang on to it," the husband said. "We already have two other – "

"*I* may wish to hang on to it," Luisa said brusquely. "Besides, my sisters did not wish you to own it."

Francisca had already hinted as much, years earlier. Concealing her anger, Mercedes said: "I can't see why. I intend to turn it into a museum housing as many of poor Fernando's paintings as I can collect together. It would be of enormous benefit to the town."

"How?"

"I should have thought it was obvious. Tourists will come from all over the world."

"You delude yourself, Mercedes, as you always have done," Luisa said. "How many people have ever heard of Fernando? Besides, I doubt if the townsfolk would appreciate your plan."

"It seems quite a good one to me," began the husband, but Mercedes cut across him.

"You underestimate people's greed," she said. "I have spoken to the mayor, to the priest, to the doctor. They feel it would bring prosperity to the town. They would certainly back my plan."

"All of them are newcomers," Luisa said. "They were not here when – when everything happened."

"When Fernando was killed, you mean." Mercedes tightened her mouth. "Perhaps, too, the village owes me – *us* – something. Some of them were involved in his death. Some might even have been able to save him."

Luisa frowned, shaking her head a little. "Anyway," she said, "I've arranged for it to be let; I've signed on a tenant for a ten-year lease."

"What tenant is this?"

"A lawyer from Barcelona who wants to bring his family down here in the summer."

"Ah." Mercedes turned away to hide her hatred. Luisa had done this in order to thwart her, for no other reason. Had they been alone and unobserved, she might not have been able to restrain herself from leaping at Luisa's triumphant face and tearing her head from her shoulders. For a moment she pictured it, the wrenching flesh, the spurting blood and Luisa's screaming mouth. Then she turned back. "I see I shall have to wait a while. But one day, I swear it to you, Luisa, there will be a Vicente Museum here and Montalbán will be proud to have it."

Luisa walked away. After a shrugging second, her husband followed her.

From her bedroom at the Casa de las Lunas, Mercedes telephoned her financial advisers in New York. "I want to set up a company," she said. "I don't care what it's called or how you organise it, but it must not be traceable back to me. London-based, perhaps. Or in Madrid."

When the accountant wanted to know what kind of company she had in mind, she laughed. "It's a property company," she said. "But there is only one property in which it wants to invest, and it may not be able to do that for ten years. Organise it how you please – just hide the company's origins. I want to be able to move on the property the minute it comes on the market, either to lease or to buy. Do you understand?"

He said he did; she knew he did not, could not possibly.

As she replaced the receiver, she saw a flicker of movement. The door, which she was sure she had carefully closed, was now slightly open. Had someone been listening? Had she been overheard? If Luisa were to hear of the arrangements she had just set in train, then she would never achieve her goal. She ran to the door and looked along the coir-matted passage. Concepción was walking rapidly away, looking over her shoulder; had she heard, and if so, would she tell Luisa? Mercedes ran after the girl and seized her by the shoulder.

"You were eavesdropping," she said fiercely. "Did she tell you to? Has she set you to spy on me?"

Concepción was frightened; she clasped her swollen

belly in both hands as though for protection. "What are you talking about?"

"You were listening at the door, sneaking around trying to catch me out," Mercedes insisted. She shook the girl, digging her fingers into Concepción's shoulder.

"I was passing, that's all. I heard nothing."

Mercedes gave her a shove and she stumbled, clutching at the banister rails to stop herself from falling. "I shall have the house in the end," Mercedes said, and heard her own breath whistle through her teeth. Making her eyes grow big, she touched the witch's mark at the side of her nose and looked intently at Concepción's pregnant belly.

The girl screamed, backing away. "Don't!" She staggered along the rail towards the stairs which led up from the hall below. "Don't harm my baby."

"I swear to you," Mercedes said, "if Luisa hears one word from you I shall kill it."

"No!" Sobbing, Concepción made for the stairs, half falling, half slipping down them, trying to get away as Mercedes advanced towards her with raised arms. "I don't know what you're talking about. If Luisa hears anything it won't be from me, I swear it."

Her words merely confirmed Mercedes' suspicions. "Remember what I say," she said. As she started down after the girl, Concepción screamed again, grabbing at the rail behind her and, failing to find it, falling the last two or three stairs to land awkwardly on the polished wooden floor of the hall.

Looking down at her as Julia came rushing out to help her to her feet, Mercedes thought contemptuously: For a while I felt compassion for her, even warmth. But she is not worth bothering with. She is like a caterpillar, flimsy, crushable with a single pinch of the fingers.

Later that afternoon, Concepción began to go into labour. The child, a girl, was born early the following morning. When Mercedes entered the room where Concepción lay in the carved four-poster bed, the baby at her side, the girl grabbed the infant and clutched it to her breasts.

"Go away," she said. There was sweat along her upper lip. Although she sounded calm, there was hysteria under the words, so much so that Carlos and the midwife, both in attendance, stared at her in surprise.

Mercedes said nothing. Watching the girl in the bed, she touched the side of her nose and smiled a little.

Two days later, Concepción, like her brother before her, was gone. Carrying the basket with the newborn child in it, she had crept out during the night. Later, Carlos found a peasant farmer who remembered a shawled woman walking along the road with a basket; she had seemed ill, exhausted, he said, but inured to exhaustion both in himself and in others, he had not thought about it until the Señor came asking, nor, once the woman was out of sight, had he thought to wonder where she might be going.

Eventually, Mercedes received a card from Lovel in far-off Tokyo, saying that the girl had reached him. He added: *Though I doubt if you care, both mother and child are well*. She tossed the card into the wastepaper basket. He was right: she did not care.

Nor would she have cared had she known she would never see Concepción again. There was so much still to do.

27

MERCEDES

He came into the gallery in the late Seventies, a thin young man, carrying an artist's portfolio. She heard him from her office; even through the intercom she could hear the determination in his voice. He had an occasional stutter.

"I want to see S-Señora Ramirez."

Upstairs, unseen, she stiffened.

"Ramirez? I think you've come to the wrong place." Jane Vandening, her assistant sounded cool, off-putting.

"I haven't."

"There is no-one of that name working here," Jane said. Mercedes heard the sound of her chair scraping across the wooden floor as she stood up.

"The owner of the g-gallery, then."

"Ah. You must mean Señora Aragon."

"Perhaps."

"I'll have to see if she's in," Jane said. "She usually doesn't see anyone without an appointment."

"I'll wait, if I have t-to."

"And your name is?"

"Rathbone." He did not elaborate further.

493

"As you can appreciate," Jane said smoothly, preparing him for disappointment, "she has a great many calls on her time. Was there something specific you wished to speak to her about?"

"Yes."

When he added nothing further, Mercedes heard Jane open the door at the foot of the stairs leading to the upper gallery.

"Who is he?" she said, as soon as Jane came into her office.

"I don't know. He's carrying a portfolio: probably wants you to look at his work."

"Anything else?"

"No. You heard him yourself: he's not giving a lot away."

Mercedes stared out of the window, chewing the corner of her lower lip. Instinct told her that the man downstairs represented a danger she could not afford to ignore but without seeing him it was impossible to determine in which direction the threat might lie.

And he had called her Ramirez, the name she had never used.

"Send him up," she said. "I'll talk to him."

At first sight he was the least threatening thing she had ever encountered. Slightly built, his hair cut close to his scalp, he had the large soft eyes of a domestic cat used to being cosseted beside its own hearth and terrified of now finding itself alone in the urban jungle.

Long afterwards she was to admit that she should have remembered then that the cat is the direct descendant of the tiger, and the jungle is in its blood.

"Rathbone," he said. There was no expression in his

494

mild gaze; he did not stretch out a hand. Instead, he
laid his portfolio flat on top of the papers on her desk
and began to undo it.

"What do you – " she began, then stopped. He was
pulling something out of his bag; he held it up in front
of her and she blinked, not believing what she saw.

"I heard you wanted Vicentes," he said.

"Where did you get that one?" she asked.

"It d-doesn't matter, d-does it?"

He was right. "How much do you want?"

"F-five hundred thousand," he said.

"Five hu– You must be mad." The painting glowed in
front of her, reviving old memories: the smell of almond
husks, tumbled sheets, love, pain.

"P-perhaps. But that's the p-price."

Her longing to repossess the painting was so strong that
her desire almost overcame her natural business sense.
She reached towards the canvas – then pulled back. "Do
you have any documentation for this?" she demanded
sharply.

"No," Rathbone said. His hands were very small, the
nails bitten down; on one finger he wore a ring, made of
silver, in the shape of a skull.

"How do I know this isn't a – isn't a fake?"

"You don't." He stared at her. The pupils of his
cat-eyes were so dilated that she could no longer tell
what colour they were. She leaned towards the console
and switched off the intercom.

"You don't," he repeated. "But how c-could it be
a fake?"

She thought about it. Could Jonas have sold the painting to someone else, thus providing an opportunity for it

to be copied, either by this young man or by someone else? Or had he allowed someone to copy it? She did not believe that to be true. But in that case, how could it have progressed from Jonas to Rathbone?

"Did you steal it?" she asked.

He laughed without amusement. "Do I look like a thief?"

"If not you, then a friend of yours. Or are you a fence?"

"Neither of those."

"I could call the police." She nodded at the telephone.

"If you do, I'll destroy the picture." Before she had time to cry out, he had produced a knife from his pocket and was holding it at the painted surface, so close that she thought she saw a flake of paint lift from the canvas.

"No!" She felt the knife as though it had plunged into her own heart.

"Five hundred thousand d-dollars," he said in his gentle voice. He put the knife away. "It's not much. Not when you c-consider."

"Consider what?"

"That it was p-painted by one of the finest artists of his generation. Or would you not agree?"

"Of course I agree."

"If you are worried, you c-could c-call in the experts to examine it," he said.

"That would be pointless. I am the expert."

He said: "I know."

She bent over the canvas, seeing the sworls and lines of oil paint, the white sheets, the still-sharp yellows of the lemons in their bowl, remembering the very feel of the cloth which covered the table. And the glass beads.

Fernando had told her that each bead held a reflection of himself, painted so small she could not see it. At the time, she had been young enough to believe him.

Again she stretched a hand towards the picture; this time she allowed herself to caress the signature. Vicente. The sweeping V. The voluptuous curve of the 'c' and the 'e'. The slash of the 't', like a cross.

If she closed her eyes, it all came back to her; like poison poured into a flask, the old pain filled her. She had so often watched him finish a canvas, lean forward, the brush circling and dipping in his hand, head hunched between his shoulders, the little smile on his face as he looked round at her and let out his held breath with a sigh, reluctant to leave the imaginary world behind the scene he had created, yet eager to start the next.

When she looked up, Rathbone was watching her without expression. "Well?" he said.

"Why did you call me Señora Ramirez?" she asked.

"Because it is your name."

"But not one I ever use."

He shrugged.

"I'll give you one hundred thousand dollars," she said firmly. "Take it or leave it."

"Leave it," he said. The little hands picked up the painting and began to wrap it up again.

She opened her mouth to protest, to negotiate, then closed it again. Take it or leave it – but he knew she would have to take it.

"All right," she said quietly. "You win."

"Who's f-fighting?" he said.

He had it all worked out. On his instructions, she telephoned her bank and informed them that she wished to withdraw a large sum, in cash, which she would be collecting in one hour's time. While they waited, Rathbone sat in front of her, the portfolio on his knee, saying nothing. When the hour was almost up, he rose. Together they walked to her bank, where together they watched the money counted out. She handed him the big envelope; at the door, he turned to her and said: "This will help."

"I should damn well think it would," she burst out.

The mild eyes blinked once, as though offended by the violence of her tone, and then he was off, walking away from her down the street, the empty portfolio hanging from one of his hands.

She remembered Ramirez walking away from her like this. For a moment, it occurred to her that she had once been offered a golden ball and all she had done was to kick it into a dung heap.

Often, now, there were moments like this. Revenge had not proved sweet; with the rolling years she was aware of waste, of barrenness. The taste in her mouth was not triumph but ashes.

Two months later, Rathbone came back. She was out, visiting a client. When she returned, Jane said: "He was here again this afternoon."

"Who was?" But she knew; she had thought of nothing else since he was last here.

"Rathbone. There were two of them this time."

"What do you mean, Jane?" She was deliberately brusque, hoping to hide the rapid beating of her heart. With certainty she knew this was the danger she had anticipated. "Two Rathbones?"

"He came with a friend. I assume it was a friend. He was in a wheelchair – the friend, I mean."

"I don't suppose he said what he wanted."

"To see you." Jane shook her head. "More specifically, to see the Señora Ramirez."

Ramirez. "Don't call me that," she said murderously, and turned away from the surprise in Jane's face. "Did the young man say when he would return?"

"Tomorrow morning."

Upstairs, she sat at her desk, fists clenched, nails digging into her palms. Ramirez: why did he use that name? Carlos had died five months ago; five months ago she had seen Jonas again. She had not been present to ease Ramirez' passage out of life, but had attended the funeral. As the coffin was lowered into the grave in the Montalbán cemetery, she had felt some of the burden lift. *He* would lie alongside his ancestors; no-one knew where Fernando Vicente lay scattered. She had done what she could to make amends. It was no-one's fault that time had blunted what should have been the sharp edge of her triumph.

As the red soil pattered down onto his coffin, she caught a sudden movement beyond the crowd of mourners; looking up, she had found Jonas watching her.

She could be out when Rathbone returned tomorrow, but she knew he would simply come again and again until he found her. Why was she so certain he brought ruin with him? She looked out of the window at the buildings rising about her into the sky and wondered whether it was time to leave this city where she had spent the last thirty years. But you can only run so far; Jonas had said that, later, as people were leaving the graveyard and the commiserative phrases had been spoken, not for her loss but for their own. With Carlos dead, Montalbán had lost one of its leaders; Carlos's son had gone years ago and they knew he would not come back.

"How are you, Mercedes?" Jonas had asked gravely.

"All right, I suppose. Sometimes things seem to be . . ." She left the sentence.

"To be what?"

She shrugged. "Out of control. As if I am running down a steep hill and cannot stop."

"You can only run so far, Mercedes."

Looking up at him, she had touched his cheek. "It is not you I run from. Never you." Though both of them were old now, settled, if he asked her to, she would go with him wherever he wished. She wanted nothing but to be with him, to shelter in his strong shadow.

"Not from me," he agreed. His eyes were not kind. "You run from Nemesis."

As though they heard, a group of the 'townspeople turned at the cemetery gate and looked back at the two of them. Their expressions would have frightened her if she had planned to stay.

Though his tone was serious, she tried to laugh. "Nemesis? What does that mean? Do they think I don't remember what they did to Fernando?"

"They?"

"Someone betrayed him," she said forcefully. She stared fiercely at the open grave. "The one whose finger was on the trigger now rots in Hell, but someone betrayed him first. They are all guilty."

500

He pushed her away from him; she stumbled, surprised by his roughness. "You are a fool, Mercedes," he said.

"Jonas!"

"A sad, sad fool." He turned, then looked back at her again, taking her shoulders in his two hands. "Children must not be hurt," he said. "So always I tell myself you cannot help what you are, what you have become. But it seems to me you should be able to see the past for what it was, that there is no need for you to remain inside the cage you have built for yourself. The door is open, Mercedes; you could fly free if you wished."

"I don't know what you're talking about," she said.

"You are afraid to know."

He began to walk towards the gates, passing between the headstones. She followed.

Outside the gates, he turned to the left to where the wall of the old convent curved away along the dirt road. "That is where it happened," he said. "Right there."

She wanted to faint. "What are you talking about? How can you say such cruel things?"

He grabbed her upper arm, his fingers digging painfully into her flesh. "But Mercedes, you are a realist, are you not?" He began to march her along the road towards the convent wall, stopping when they reached a certain point. "You have spent nearly all your life in pursuit of vengeance, is it not so? Surely you have looked before at this wall and wondered how it happened."

Of course she had. Night after night, feeding her resolution, for years. The ball of pain in her chest swelled until she thought she might choke. "I know how it happened," she shouted. "They brought him out in the early morning, they stood him up here,

they let him see the sun rise over the valley and then
. . . then they . . . shot him, like an animal, like ver-
min."

He jabbed at one of the holes in the wall, its edges
smoothed by the passage of time. "If you look, you will
see the mark of the bullet," he said, his voice brutal. "The
first bullet."

She banged at her chest with one hand. "Oh God,"
she gasped. "I keep thinking it will get better, and it
never does."

"Cry," he said.

"I cannot."

"Cry, Mercedes. They will think it is for Carlos, and
judge you less harshly."

"Tears water the soul," she said. "Do you remember
saying that to me?"

"Of course." He touched her cheek. "I remember
everything."

In her New York office, she thought: So do I.

Rathbone came again the following day. Jane called her
down. "He can't come up because he won't leave his
friend," she said, over the internal telephone.

As soon as she opened the door into the lower gallery,
Mercedes knew. Rathbone was examining some of the
displayed paintings on the wall, his portfolio leaning
against Jane's desk but she did not look at him. The
man slumped in the wheelchair held all her attention. She
took in the hollow eyes, the clawlike hands, the purplish
blotches on the emaciated face.

"We thought you were dead," she said, in Spanish.

He laughed weakly, answering in the same language. "To all intents and purposes I am."

There was so much to ask that she could not begin. "You are ill?" she asked.

"It's an immune deficiency thing. Lots of us have it."

Us? What did he mean? Then, seeing the tenderness in Rathbone's eyes, the protective hunch over his friend, she understood. She thought of Carlos, of what he would have felt, and before she could prevent the treasonable thought, wondered: Was Fernando worth this?

She turned to Jane. "Why don't you take a break?" she said. "Have an early lunch-hour."

When Jane had gathered her coat and purse and gone, she said: "I presume this is not a social call."

He did not answer. Instead, he asked: "How did you recognise me? It's been years."

How *had* she known, as soon as she stepped into the ground-floor gallery, that the man in the wheelchair was Amador, the boy she had persecuted, the boy who had seen his own mother plunge to her self-inflicted death, who at the age of sixteen had run away from his father's home, his father's wife? She wanted to say: *It was not recognition.* There was, after all, little enough resemblance between that lost boy and the wasted figure before her. She waited to hear the reason behind the visit.

It was not long in coming. Rathbone picked up his portfolio and laid it on Jane's desk. "You might like th-this," he said.

The skull on his finger glinted as he drew out a canvas and spread it in front of her. In silence she took in the figure on the bed, the high window, the fruit in the bowl, the beads.

"Powerful, isn't it?" Rathbone said.

She nodded, feeling the earth sink under her feet so that she stood on the very edge of an abyss.

"Painted by one of the f-finest artists of his generation. Isn't that what you called him?"

"How much do you want?" she said dully.

"Nothing," said Amador. "This one is a gift from the artist."

Mercedes raised her eyes. "Which of you –?"

"I did," said Amador.

"Why?"

"To avenge myself, to avenge my father and my sister." He gave a savage grin. "These aren't the only ones I've done. There are false Vicentes all over the place. They're very good. You told me once I would never make as good a painter as Vicente. I've spent my whole life proving you wrong."

She looked again at the painting in front of her and then at Rathbone. "The one you brought before . . ."

"That's a fake, too."

"I gave you five hundred thousand dollars for a *copy*?"

"Yes."

To Amador she said: "Then you must have had access to the original."

"Of course."

"Who – " She had to clear her throat. "Who owns it now?"

"Jonas Fedor, the potter."

She kept her head high though her spirit wilted. Of all the betrayals this surely must be the most painful. "Did he know why you wanted to copy it? Who you were?"

Again the death's head grin. "Of course," said Amador.

"And why have you brought these to me now?"

"Because I don't know how much longer I'll be alive. And with my father dead . . ."

"How pleased he would have been to know that you were still alive," she said.

"He knew."

"What?"

"He has always known."

"He knew?" She could not hide the consternation in her face, though she could see the pleasure it gave him.

"You can't have imagined I would let him think me dead. Of course he knew. Once we had re-established contact, he used to send me money."

"Too late, of course," Rathbone said.

"He came to visit us many times," said Amador. "*Many* times. He was with us only a month before he died."

The acid rush of deceit caught her unawares. She staggered back against the solidity of Jane's desk, feeling a pain like a knife-blade in her chest. From time to time, she had felt that her determination was misguided, that Carlos did not deserve the unhappiness she had brought him. Having tried to prevent any communication between him and his son, to discover that he had been playing a double game left her breathless with fury.

"He came with us to stay with Jonas earlier in the year," Amador said.

"He was very proud of his son," said Rathbone. He looked fondly at his friend. "Immensely proud. As he sh-should have been."

When they had gone, she went upstairs, carrying the second copy of *The Tears She Shed*. She slid out the first from its recessed hanging rail and studied it closely, comparing it with the second one, and the two of them with what she remembered of the original. How many years was it now since she had sold it to Jonas, out of love, out of need to bind him to her? And this was how he repaid her? She reached towards the telephone. Should she ring him, ask him what he was doing, why he had behaved like this towards the woman he loved?

But they almost never spoke on the phone, and she was reluctant to start now. Besides, she was a tiny bit afraid of what his answer might be. Always she had waited for him to come to her, and she would do so still.

Meanwhile, she must decide what to do with the two brilliantly executed copies in front of her. If she was smart, she might be able to turn what those two queers had hoped was a disaster into a triumph. She thought for a moment. Then she picked up the telephone.

The voice on the other end was known to her; they had negotiated several times over the past few years. Speaking softly in Spanish, she explained what she had to offer, emphasising the fine condition and rarity.

The voice at the other end listened in silence then said abruptly: "How much?"

"Six hundred thousand dollars."

"That's a lot of money."

"Paintings like this don't often come onto the market. And Vicente's output was very small. The upside investment potential is enormous."

"I don't buy for investment."

"Forgive me, Señor Cramir," she said smoothly. "On the other hand, when such sums are involved, potential cannot – *should* not – be ignored."

"How did it come into your hands?" the voice asked.

506

This was the tricky question. Jonas had proved devious; she had no way of knowing just how devious. And the man to whom she was speaking had known him once, years ago, might still, for all she was aware.

"The person to whom I sold it myself many years ago has now decided to sell it back. In spite of the way the economy is booming, not everyone is doing well. And sometimes, as people reach retirement age, they wish to consolidate their assets . . ." She allowed the sentence to dangle like a necklace with, suspended from it, the image of some elderly international tycoon wishing to put the sordid world of commerce behind him and retire to his condominium in Florida, his schloss in the Black Forest, his country estate, his château.

The gruff voice said: "The usual arrangements, then?" and she felt a moment of exultation.

"Yes. And the usual precautions?"

"Naturally."

She smiled. She knew perfectly well that the man on the other end of the line had begun buying art because his tax advisers told him to. Over the years he had built up a certain expertise, even a certain taste, but basically he remained what he had always been: an ignorant peasant, with more money than sense. Naturally, when she was with him she was careful to hide her opinion of him; he had spent too much money with her – starting with the Goya which Doña Carlota had given her on the occasion of her marriage to Carlos Ramirez – for her to wish to jeopardise the business relationship which existed between them. Because of his insistence on absolute secrecy about any of the transactions he undertook, his would be the perfect collection in which to bury one of the copies produced by Carlos's son.

And already she had the glimmerings of an idea, or rather the fulfilment of a dream, where the other one could go, until Jonas relented and resold her *The Tears*.

In her apartment that night, she thought: Secrecy is one thing, but Rathbone must be allowed to know that the two of them did not outwit me.

Rathbone came to the Gallery again, this time to tell her that Amador was dead. He pressed the sides of his face with his little hands, as though to hold back the tears and Mercedes was moved, knowing how she would feel if Jonas died.

On impulse, she went to the funeral. The two of them stood side by side looking down at the grave and she wondered if this was all there would be, now, only dying and funerals.

To her surprise, he came again. And again. She bought some of his work, promoted it; he became a minor figure on the art scene. Sometimes she wondered if he came because she was still capable of exerting a fascination, or whether she was simply his only link with Amador.

From time to time they dined together; she told him of her plans for a Vicente Museum in Montalbán.

"But he wasn't much of an artist," Rathbone said. "Be honest, Mercedes. If he w-walked into your gallery tomorrow and showed you his w-work, would you buy it?"

"Of course I would."

"I wonder."

"You don't think I'd have bothered to spend most of my adult life in promoting a second-rate artist, do you?"

"Is it the artist you remember, or the m-man, Mercedes?" They were on their way home from the theatre, for he sometimes accompanied her to public events; she found him a useful escort, though never certain why he agreed to come.

"Aren't the two inseparable? The life and the work are simply two facets of the same persona."

"Perhaps. I must say I've always wondered what lay behind *The Tears She Shed*. What kind of life produced a painting like that?"

She looked sharply at him but his face was bland. "A sensitive loving life," she said.

"Come on, now, Mercedes. Most of the Vicente canvases I've seen are full of self-loathing, full of hideous suffering. Surely you must have realised that. It's just, I've often wondered who was doing the suffering in *The Tears*."

"Like all artists, Fernando was occasionally unhappy," she said, uncomfortable. "It's part of the artistic temperament."

"I wouldn't know about that." His tone was ironic.

Each year, on the anniversary of Amador's death, Rathbone took her out to dinner. "I don't want to stay home," he said. "It's too miserable, remembering it all."

One year, as they sat across from each other eating pasta, she realised with astonishment that it was ten years since Amador had died. Time was slipping past now, faster with each succeeding year. Her own death had become a fact she accepted, rather than a remote possibility to be ignored, as when she was younger. The Vicente Museum had become more important to her, now that she had at last been able to buy the house. Luisa

509

had not suspected who was behind the purchase and the sale had gone through smoothly; when she discovered she tried to renege on the sale but it was too late. The letter she wrote had been so virulent that Mercedes had thrown it away without reading beyond the first paragraph.

"Ten years," she said. "Unbelievable."

Carefully Rathbone turned his fork round inside a nest of tagliatelle. "I believe it," he said. "Every one of them has been a torture without him." His eyes filled with tears.

When he had arrived to pick her up, she had smelled bourbon on his breath. He had drunk most of the first bottle of wine and was half-way down the second. Not for the first time, she wondered if he had a drink problem, whether he was, in fact, drunk at the moment.

"Perhaps," she said slowly, "you are luckier than most. Not everyone has an abiding passion, as you did for Amador."

"And still do." He wiped his eyes. "An abiding passion. Yes. Are we blessed, you and I, Mercedes, to have recognised what it is we love, and not wavered? Or are we cursed?"

"Perhaps both," she said. She thought of Jonas, and of Fernando.

"Perhaps." Rathbone straightened his back, as though coming to some decision. "Your museum: how many Vicentes have you collected now?"

"A lot. There are still a number hidden away somewhere: my aunt Luisa refuses to tell me where they are." She shrugged. "I'll find them eventually, I suppose."

"I know where there's one," he said. He refilled his

glass, drank it in one swallow, poured more. "What's more, it's for sale."

"Where is it?"

"In England."

Immediately she thought of Jonas. "Which one is it?" she said.

"The *Casa de las Lunas*."

Memories flooded her: she saw again the hills, the gateposts past which she had ridden so many times after Fernando's killing, hoping to encounter Ramirez. She had not foreseen then that it would become her own home, that she would have the right to walk between the gateposts and the copper moons. It had seemed so solid in her childhood, so impregnable; now it mouldered, becoming more of a ruin each year, a symbol of her achieved goal, the destruction of the Ramirez.

"Who owns it?" she asked.

"Some diplomat who's just died. He was a consul in Spain. His house and its contents are up for sale by auction. I half thought of going over for it, since the painting used to belong to Amador."

"To *Amador*? How did that happen?"

"One of the aunts gave it to him when he was just a boy. He told me it was the only thing he took with him when he ran away from home."

"I never knew that."

"He took care that you should not," Rathbone said.

Mercedes stared down at her plate, working it out. "It was one of Vicente's best works: if you do go to England, perhaps I'll come with you."

"I hoped you might say that." Rathbone wagged his head; his mouth seemed to be sliding about in his face and she decided he must be very drunk indeed. "But there's something about it you should know."

As soon as she saw it, she remembered Fernando painting it, laughing, saying that perhaps the Ramirez would pay a fine price for the canvas and he would have some money at last. "Then I will buy you a present," he said, smiling at her as she stood in front of the long mirror in his studio with the wax wreath in her hair, wondering who she would marry, whether she would ever fall in love.

She leaned down to examine the initials Amador had painted over Fernando's signature, thinking she was probably the only person in the room who knew who had really painted it. But a girl arrived, a young woman, who stared at the canvas, who bent to look for the signature as though she knew what she was looking for and seemed surprised not to find it.

When the girl straightened up, Mercedes caught her breath. The face, though stronger and more character-ful was, by some trick of physiognomy, exactly like Concepción's. The same dark eyes, the same beautiful hair and wounded mouth . . . Amazed, Mercedes remembered the last time she had seen Concepción, at Aunt Rosita's funeral. The past came flooding back: Concepción in New York and meeting Jonas, Lovel's sinister face, standing in the doorway of Concepción's bedroom in the Casa de las Lunas, deliberately staring at the child in Concepción's arms and touching the mark beside her nose.

Remembering, she widened her eyes now, as she had then, and the girl stared unflinchingly back at her, not moving, as though somewhere at the back of her brain she saw images of stars and dragons, images of witchcraft.

Mercedes did not care how much she paid, but once the bidding had started, she sensed behind her in the panelled room a will to own the painting even stronger than her own. At first she ignored it, but as the bidding increased, she began to realise that however high she went, her antagonist would go higher, that she was fighting Mercedes for possession. She twisted round in her chair but could not see the person bidding against her; she did not need to see in order to know it was the girl, the one with the look of Concepción. In the end, it seemed easier to let it go and find some other way to get the canvas.

Afterwards, furious, she raged at Rathbone, cursing the unknown woman.

"How do you know it was a woman?" he asked.

"I feel it. I saw her earlier, she knew the picture was by Vicente. She was *fighting* me for it. I must find out who she is. I curse her."

She and Rathbone drove up to Scotland and slowly back down through the historic parts of England. In Cambridge, she left him to look round the colleges while she drove out to the village beyond which Jonas lived. There was a lane running along the back of his garden; she parked on the verge, looking at the thatched roof, the green hedges, a tumble of ruined outbuildings covered in climbing roses, bare now, waiting for summer. Where was he? *How* was he? Did he ever think of her?

A light came on in the house and she started the engine,

drove away, not wanting to intrude on a world he had never shared with her.

In a hotel near Stratford-on-Avon, she switched on the television set and found herself watching Jonas. The years flooded back to her, the lost loves, the betrayals, the life she might have had, the warmths she had rejected. For the first time since her brother's death, she wept, feeling the manacles drop, the chains loosen. "Oh God," she said aloud in the empty room. "Oh Jonas. What a terrible waste we have made for ourselves."

She heard the interviewer ask whether he had known any evil men and found her face growing hot, the tears withering as Jonas frowned. He said he had known two, that one of them had betrayed his family, his friends, his honour, his art.

She heard him say: "He died the death he deserved," and felt her heart grow cold again.

On the little grey screen his image stared at her, and she felt nothing. He knew. All these years, he had said nothing, and yet he knew.

They were still in England when the newspapers carried the news of Jonas's death. She went to the funeral – yet another funeral – and listened in a daze to the singing. Julian Maitland, an old man now, white haired, delivered the address. This was a Jonas she had never known; their lives had abutted but never adjoined and when they were together there was nothing else but the two of them. Now she saw that a whole life attached to him with which she had nothing to do: a life full of friends, fame, pictures, music, colour from which she had been excluded.

When Julian spoke of Jonas's art, his love, his zest for life, she began to weep. She had never wanted anything else; now she realised how little she had asked him for, how little she had been given.

The wind blew coldly in the churchyard. A priest intoned the final words from a prayerbook, there was a muffled sound of sobbing. How shall I proceed, she wondered. Without Jonas, it is as though the centre of my life has been sucked away, leaving only the dry crust of myself.

She thought: I am an old woman now. She had not seen him for nearly twenty years but she knew that if he were to walk between the yew-trees and ask her, she would still lie down for him.

There had been so many men but only two had ever meant anything to her. Oh Jonas, she thought, how I loved you. And you never ever said you loved me back. Not once, although it was all I ever asked of you.

Except *The Tears She Shed*.

She wrote to Jonas's solicitors, demanding the picture; she had a letter back from someone refusing the request, saying it was hers. At the sight of the signature – Teresa Lovel – she reached for the phone.

"Lovel," she said. "This is Mercedes Aragon."

"Who?"

"Mercedes Ramirez." The word came with difficulty from her tongue.

"It's been a long time," he said, his thin voice drier than a desert.

"There has been no reason."

"And now there is?"

"Yes. Your daughter . . ."

"Teresa, you mean?"

". . . appears to be in possession of a painting my brother did. I want it back."

"Have you asked her for it?"

"Of course. Years ago, Jonas forced me to sell it to him," *the hot room in Madrid, the tangled sheets, his strong body*, "but promised to let me have it back when he died – you did know that he was dead?"

"One could hardly miss the fact," he murmured. "The papers were full of it."

"I told your daughter that it was supposed to be mine, but she insists that he gave it to her some time ago and she has no intention of handing it over."

"What do you want me to do?"

"Get it from her."

"How?"

"She's your daughter," Mercedes said. "You must know how to persuade her."

He said slowly: "We aren't in communication. I haven't seen her for some years. Jonas took it upon himself to look after her during her school holidays after her mother was . . . after she died. I haven't really seen her since. It was her decision, not mine."

Mercedes was silent. Then she said: "But your fault, I should imagine."

She caught sight of herself in the mirror on the wall opposite her desk and thought, with shock, that he must be old too. When she was young she had considered people of the age she was now to be immeasurably ancient. She felt no older than all those years ago; her blood still ran as strong, she still fought for what she wanted.

516

"I owe you nothing," Lovel said. "I have no need to do what you ask, nor any desire."

"Nor do I have any *need*," she emphasised the word, "to tell the world about you – and your colleague."

He said: "I take it that by colleague, you don't mean the man I work for."

"Quite right. I meant the man you *worked* for, long ago."

She was glad to hear the slight vibration of fear in his voice. "And how do you know about that?" he asked.

"Perhaps you were too good at your job. Frightened men don't keep secrets."

He tried to bluff it out. "You're too late, Mercedes. I only work in a consultant capacity now: I'm too old for scandal to ruin my job prospects."

"But you still have a position to maintain, Lovel. A time of retirement to live through when you might have anticipated the admiration and respect of those around you."

"Even if you carried out your threat, it would be a small and not very long-lived scandal. And since I have few friends, there is nothing to keep me here in Tokyo if I decide to go. I could live anywhere I choose."

"Except that you are not a man who could hide in a crowd. Besides, I would make it my business to see that wherever you went, people would know. You would be ostracised. Is that how you want to spend your last years?"

"You'd do it, too, wouldn't you?" he said.

"Believe it, Lovel."

"Very well. I shall be in England soon; I'll see what I can do."

She sighed. "I am in England now. I'll stay on. Where can I contact you?"

He gave her his address, adding: "I promise nothing, Mercedes."

Putting down the receiver, she wondered if she had been wise to display her hand quite so openly. She knew him to be a dangerous man, a man who had killed for gratification. Was there anything to stop him killing again, this time for expediency? It might be wisest to take precautions, to find herself – did she really think him that dangerous? – a weapon.

28

TESS

Turning the corner of my life, I found
Myself facing myself – but stood my ground.
        from Amador Ramirez' *Elegías españolas*
        translated by Teresa Lovel

Houston was hunched beneath driving rain and dull grey
skies. Rain bounced off seal-slick blacktop; along the
freeway into town trees drooped disconsolately. From
her motel, Tess called the manager of the bank charged
with handling the local details of the Cramir Will.

Identifying herself, she said authoritatively: "I need to
check the Cramir collection again."

"I don't know if that will be poss – "

"It's extremely important," said Tess. "The Banco
Morena needs some of the information urgently."

"But I've received no formal – "

"There have been certain . . . developments," she said
with heavy significance. "I'm sure I don't have to spell
them out for you."

She could almost hear the tick and whirr as he tried to
recall his reading of the financial pages over the past few

days. "I still don't see what – " he began, but once more she cut him short.

"It's imperative that I look at some of the paintings again. As you must be aware, the authenticity of some of them has been questioned. I have the full authority of the Banco; you can call London if you wish to confirm." She, who liked certainties, was gambling now, counting on the fact that it was after office hours in London to prevent him from doing so. By the time he contacted Don Pedro the following day, she would, with any luck, have got what she came for and be gone.

"Well . . ."

"I'm assuming you will want to accompany me out to the Cramir place," she said. If he insisted on going with her, she would be in trouble. "Or perhaps I should contact Mrs Westlake direct . . ."

"That might be the best way," he said. "I'm fully occupied for the rest of the afternoon. If you had let me know earlier I might have been able to arrange to – "

"I'll call her now," Tess said quickly, before he could suggest doing so himself. "Perhaps she could meet me there."

"Good idea." She could hear his relief at having one less problem to deal with.

"The keys?" she said.

"They're here."

"I'll pick them up. Naturally I shall expect to sign a receipt. I'll return them to you tomorrow morning at the latest."

"Fine." He thought of something: "Several of the paintings will have gone since you were last in town."

"It's the unassigned pictures with which the Banco is concerned."

"Of course." He seemed reassured by her air of brisk efficiency. "And you'll call Mrs Westlake?"

"Right away," lied Tess. Until now it had not occurred to her what good cover a respectable profession like banking provided for someone hoping to pull a scam.

There were lights showing in the Cramir house but she guessed they were on automatic time switch, that the house was empty. She turned off the engine of her rental car and hurried through the rain to the steps. If Mrs Westlake should turn up, summoned after all by the banker, she had a story ready, but hoped she would not have to use it. During the drive out here, she had checked her mirror a hundred times to see if she was being followed. At the turn-off in the direction of the Cramir place, she had put her foot down on the accelerator and gone past, only to exit at the next junction and circle round to drive back onto the freeway. Heading back towards Houston, she checked the mirror again: as far as she could tell from the press of traffic, no-one behind her had performed the same manoeuvre. She hoped she was safe.

Using the keys she had picked up in Houston, she opened the complicated locking system on the front door and went in. Her nerves throbbed with apprehension. She was assuming that the sprawling house was empty but each unseen room now seemed full of menace and possible danger. Walking uneasily across the hall, she waited for sudden attack: the gun, the knife, the garrotting wire. The floor of polished slate spread before her like an oily pond; the house smelled musty, unused. Watery light filled the long living room; cobwebs outside the huge windows glistened with raindrops, each one reflecting the blank white sky.

Opening the door beside the hearth, she went down the iron stairs to the gallery. Once inside, she locked the door behind her, her stomach contracting as she did so. She had no idea where the emergency exit was: suppose the electricity failed or – despite the banker's protests – a fire started: how would she ever get out?

She hurried down the long vaulted chambers, past the painted eyes of Madonnas and martyrs, rich patrons and unknown peasants. The air-conditioning purred, recycling air which smelled as though the rodent control people had recently sprayed. When she came to the two rooms where the Vicentes hung, she stopped at the first of the charcoal portraits bequeathed to Jonas.

These were why she had come. It was the remembrance of the dozen sketches, coming to her in the limbo-consciousness before sleep which had prompted her impetuous flight to Houston.

Pulling her camera from her bag, she quickly snapped each one of the grim young faces, boys forced into maturity by troubled times, denied the irresponsibility of youth, and eventually betrayed.

For if she was right, these twelve sketches were the faces of the *Apóstoles*, the small band hunted down so ruthlessly by Captain Santiago. All of them had died hideously, except Jonas and the man who had betrayed them – Cramir himself. It seemed so obvious now. In later years, he had sought to redress the wrongs he had done by giving back to the town the portraits of its heroes, drawn by its most famous son. Just as he had given the proceeds from the sale of his Impressionists to the charity organised by his former *novia*, Luisa Vicente.

She looked again at the drawing of Jonas, the only one of the group's members to slip through Santiago's fingers, apart from Cramir himself – and realised that the face next to Jonas's *was* Cramir's, much younger than in the portrait which hung above the hearth in his living room upstairs but none the less recognisably the same. Though she searched the Judas face, she saw nothing of the implicit weakness, the cowardice, which might indicate that this was a man prepared to betray his fellows in order to save his own skin. That meant nothing: appearances, as by now she knew all too well, are all too often deceptive.

There was a noise behind her and she whirled round, her lips suddenly white. Empty of any but painted faces, the gallery stretched away from her towards the door; knowing she would have to, she was none the less unable to begin the long walk towards it. Painfully she swallowed. What an idiot she was to have come here without letting anyone know. Even the banker would by now assume her to be with Mrs Westlake and therefore no longer his responsibility.

The tons of earth above her head pressed down on her; she hunched her shoulders as though she experienced their actual weight. In Orwell's *1984*, rats were the ultimate horror for Winston Smith; for Tess, it was confinement in a small space. Merely the thought of not getting out of this underground room was enough to bring her out in a claustrophobic sweat. Terrified, she thought: suppose there really is someone on the other side of the door, suppose they switch off the lights. If I am left here in the dark, I shall lose my mind. She could imagine nothing worse.

Keeping her eye on the door-handle, she forced herself to move towards it, willing it not to turn. Close to, she leaned against the panels, listening, but could hear nothing, no breath, no movement, which would indicate someone on the other side. Jonas's gun had been left behind in Emma's flat; she longed to have its solidity in her hand.

In the end, she realised that if there was danger awaiting her, she would have to face it sooner or later. As quietly as possible she turned the key in the lock; to her horror, it would not move.

She stepped back and closed her eyes, telling herself not to panic. Taking a deep breath, she tried again. Whatever the reason, the key would not open the door, however much she twisted and shoved it against the levers. She was sweating heavily, despite the air-conditioning; she could feel the damp patches under her arms, and the slow crawl of perspiration down her spine. Vividly she saw the discovery, weeks from now, of her own mummified corpse, reduced to a husk, her dried-up claws scrabbling at the locked door in their death agony, skeletal fingers still showing signs of blood. Frantically she turned the key this way and that, fingers clumsy, slick with perspiration.

It was useless.

She stared down the long stretch of vaulted rooms. Where was the emergency exit? She had enough presence of mind to leave her own key half-turned in the lock, to prevent anyone from getting in from the other side, then began running. There'd been a small glass-fronted box on a wall in one of them, she was sure; the certainty that she had been prevented from opening the door by human agency rather than by accident had heightened her senses. She knew, without doubt, that any minute now, the lights would be turned out, and the air-conditioning off. She would be left there to suffocate in the pitchy dark, just as she had so feverishly imagined.

The box was unobtrusively positioned; inside was a black rubber flashlight, a couple of packs of batteries, and a key. She swung open the little door and as she did so, the lights went out, just as she had feared. The sudden darkness dropped over her, as heavy and solid as leather, absolutely impenetrable. Panic swept her, a tidal wave radiating out from her heart and rushing through her body to weaken her knees, her fingers, her self-control. Scrabbling, she located the torch then dropped it on the floor; she began to scream, the sound rolling away from her and then, by some curious acoustical quirk, coming back at her from all sides so that for a few mercifully brief seconds, she stood in a whirlpool of terrified self-generated sound.

Half sobbing, she dropped to her knees and felt around for the flashlight, sweeping the floor with the palms of her hands. It was too heavy to have rolled far; eventually she found it and pressed the switch.

Nothing happened.

Choking down the inclination to give up, simply to scream herself hoarse, she concentrated on the little ridged catch under her thumb. She pressed it again. Again there was nothing. Blackness weighed her down. She knew that there was no way she could fight against it long enough to find the secondary way out. Wherever it was, it had clearly been designed to be unobtrusive, the door flush with the wall or even hidden behind one of the larger canvases. She could be in here for a week and not find it in the darkness, even supposing the air lasted that long. Already she fancied she could feel the temperature rising; her linen dress felt as though she had worn it into the shower.

Forcing herself to keep calm, she located the catch and pushed it one way and then the other. This time, a faint glow rewarded her. It looked as though the batteries were almost finished. None the less, the faint beam gave her back some of her hope. Carefully she stood up and felt for the wall-mounted box, took down one of the packets of batteries and replaced those in the flashlight. Immediately the beam brightened, cutting through the fearsome darkness, catching the dull gold of picture frames, a sudden bright piece of painted landscape, the gaze of an indifferent eye. She put all the remaining batteries, including the old ones, into her pockets, then switched the flashlight off so as not to waste the batteries and sat with her back against the wall, considering the options.

Reason told her the second door out of the gallery would be at the opposite end to the main door. Which meant three rooms further on from here, where the Vicente sketches were. On the other hand, was it not more likely that rather than go to the expense of tunnelling out thousands of extra tons of earth, the designer would have placed the second door somewhere near the first?

Yet if there was a fire down at one end, it would certainly be much safer to locate the second door at the other. And Cramir was a millionaire: the extra cost would hardly have worried him.

So start this end.

She stood up. Switching on, she walked quickly through

the three remaining rooms, flashing the light up and down the walls as she passed. There was no visible line where a door might be hidden, nothing obvious to indicate a way out. *The Tears She Shed* loomed up in front of her. The dark eyes of the girl she now presumed to be Mercedes met hers; in a moment of intuition, Tess wondered if the two of them shared the same ugly secret. And as she extinguished the torch again while she considered what to do next, she had a sudden startling thought: was it that secret which lay behind all this terror and uncertainty?

It was not the time to pursue the notion; she knew she would return to it later, was aware that the epiphany she had hoped for on visiting the House of Moons, and failed to find, had perhaps come to her here, in the entombing darkness of an underground vault in Texas.

She considered her position once again. If the second exit was not here, or not obviously here, at the end of the gallery, then perhaps it was somewhere in the middle. If she remembered correctly, there were a dozen of the open vaulted rooms. She would look for the sixth then cast about on either side of it, in the seventh and then the fifth. Quickly she made her way back to the sixth room and shone her light about. Again there was no obvious indication of an exit. And in this room, the canvases were all too small to conceal a door.

She went on, into the fifth room: again there was no clue as to where the door might be. To avoid drilling through hard rock, Cramir's construction team could have put it anywhere; it might take her hours to find it. None the less, she searched the walls of the seventh room and then the eighth. Nothing. Only the blank white walls, curving over her head, the pictures, the passionless watching eyes.

It was in the ninth room, on the opposite wall from the glass-fronted box, that she found what she had been looking for. Set close to the archway leading into the tenth vaulted room, she saw a darker line set into the wall, some of it covered by one of O'Donnell's splashy canvases. She tried to keep self-recrimination to a minimum, while all the time her thoughts screamed at her for her own stupidity in not looking there first. It was the obvious place. Carefully setting the flashlight down on its end so that the light beamed up at the ceiling, she tried to lift the O'Donnell from the wall. Would it set off alarms? Would it alert whoever had locked her in here? Or had he already left, satisfied that she would be unable to escape, already relishing the thought of her gasping death as the air supply dwindled and vanished?

She reasoned that, with the lights and air-conditioning already off, the alarm system too had probably been de-activated. Besides, what did it matter if she set it off? Even if he was still out there somewhere, he was not to know that she had found another way out.

With some difficulty, she lifted the painting from the wall to reveal a Yale lock set flush into the plaster. She took the small key from her pocket and fitted it into the lock. It opened easily, to reveal a dark passageway lined with unplastered brick carelessly cemented together. She listened. Was there movement somewhere ahead of her? Was she safe or would she be walking into more danger? Quietly she closed the door again, extinguished the light, thought about it. If the person responsible for locking her in here had known of the existence of this second exit, would he have bothered with all this? Or was he such a sadistic psychopath that having enjoyed the thought of her panic and desolation when the lights went out, as she painfully searched for and found the way to freedom, he was none the less still waiting for her to emerge so that he could finally get rid of her?

If she thought that, she told herself, she might just as well give up now.

Somewhere she had read that keys held in the palm of the hand with the ends protruding between the fingers made a good protective weapon. Not much use against a gun, she told herself. None the less, she felt in her bag for her key-ring. Opening the door again, with the heavy rubber flashlight in her other hand, she moved noiselessly along the rough cement floor of the passage. The torchlight showed her a flight of wooden steps with a door at the top. She crept up them: there was no line of light around the edges of the door, nor any kind of keyhole. Despair gripped her. Had she come this far only to find herself blocked at the last hurdle? Leaning against the door, she listened but heard nothing. Carefully she felt for a switch, a lever, a button, anything which would release her. She pushed at the door.

To her surprise, it opened, moving soundlessly on some kind of balanced hinge, and stepping through, she found herself in the big entrance hall. There were traces of mud here and there on the slate floor and damp marks leading to the front door – or were they the remains of her own footprints, made on entering? Had she imagined the whole thing? Had she merely panicked over a stiff lock? She glanced through the open door of the living room. Nothing stirred. The stiff sofas, the plumped-up cushions, glass surfaces skinned with dust, everything was as it had been when she arrived.

She could not stay in the house another second. Racing towards the front door, she ran for her car. For a moment she stood in the drenching rain, fumbling with the keys. Then she was away, heading into the rain, leaving behind the wet road, the empty house and the bitterness of old betrayals, while from her soaked hair drops ran down her face like tears.

It was raining in New York, too, a wetter, dirtier rain than in Houston, splashing up from the sidewalks, rushing along litter-filled gutters. A cold wind blew up from the river, flinging the needled rain into the faces of those unwise enough to be out of doors instead of inside, watching television, eating take-away, quarrelling, making love: all the busynesses which mark the passages of everyday lives.

The water had soaked into Tess's shoes. She stood in the darkness, across from the featureless red-brick building, nerving herself to cross the road, find the name she wanted, press the buzzer. Although it was late in the evening, she could smell fried chicken and stewed tomatoes and a hot buttery smell like popcorn, as if a cinema was near by.

Though reluctant, she finally crossed the street. She pushed in the white plastic button and seconds later heard the intercom crackle. A tinny voice asked who she was.

"Teresa Lovel," she said, raising her own voice as she spoke her surname.

"Ah. And why do you w-want to see me?"

"It's a business matter," said Tess.

"This is a strange hour for discussing b-business, Teresa Lovel."

"I've just arrived from England." Tess leaned closer

530

to the little grille out of which the voice issued. "Via Houston."

"Houston?" There was a small silence. "And w-what were you doing in Houston?"

Caught him, she thought. She said firmly: "Taking a long hard look at the Cramir collection."

"I see." After a moment, the heavy door of the building suddenly clicked off the catch. "You'd better come up."

She pushed open the door and went inside.

From outside, the building had appeared to be a two-storey warehouse, ugly and run-down. Inside, it was apparent that substantial structural work was in the process of being carried out, involving the demolition of the second floor to create a single cavernous space surrounded by a first-floor gallery. Sheets of polythene hung from the first floor. Dust lay thickly everywhere. A yellow light burned dimly at the top of a flight of new open-tread stairs; in the gloom Tess could make out wooden planks, builder's rubble, a cement mixer, piles of concrete blocks. Above her head a door opened.

"Come upstairs, Teresa Lovel," a voice said.

The polythene sheets stirred gently, like ghosts waiting in the wings of some spectral theatre as she climbed the wooden steps, gritty with powdered brick. Dust sifted and resettled about her legs.

At the top of the stairs there was a gallery, its wooden floor covered in dust-sheets. At the end of it, someone waited for her, a black figure centred in a rectangle of light. She was aware of both apprehension and excitement, as though she had journeyed to the heart of a mystery. Was she about to reach the core at last, or were there unexpected corners still to turn?

One black arm gestured at the disorder below. "Take your shoes off, please." The figure turned and led the way into the light.

Following, she stepped into a vast room, perhaps sixty feet long. The roof was held away from the floor by a complicated system of black steel, almost sculptural in its beauty. White spotlights hung from the sculptured ribs and hanging constructions of crystal moved slowly back and forth in front of them. The long room was divided by waterfalls of chains hung with chrome and mirror glass which shimmered with the slightest movement of air so that the space was in a constant state of gentle fluidity.

Tess stared. On the white walls hung scores of canvases, all of them by Fernando Vicente.

The man behind her laughed and she turned to look at him properly for the first time. Recognising each other at once, both of them stepped back a little, both of them spoke: "You?"

The man wore velvet trousers and a cashmere sweater, both dramatically black; on his feet were loafers in Italian leather, worn without socks. He was small, hair cut close to his scalp. She recognised him at once as the man who had been at the Brantwell Manor auction.

"*You're* Andrew Rathbone?" Tess said.

"And *you're* T-Teresa Lovel – or, rather, Teresa Lovel is *you*?" He smiled. "If I'd realised w-who you were at that auction . . ."

Tess indicated the paintings. "I don't understand," she said. "Who did these?"

He came further into the room, with the curious dancing step she remembered from the first time she had seen him. "Would you like a d-drink?"

"Martini," she said. "Very dry."

She turned back to the pictures. So many Vicentes –
except they were not, could not be. There were at least
two copies of *A Monstrous Love*, three of the *Casa de las
Lunas*, three of the last self-portrait, two of the famous
composition in black, white and red called *Corrida*. Still
lifes, landscapes, the well-known *Madonna*. Once again
she said: "I don't understand."

"It's very simple." The little man gave her a glass.

"Is it?"

"You obviously recognise them as V-Vicentes."

"Except that they can't be."

"They're copies. Fakes. Forgeries. W-Whatever you
want to call them."

"And you did them?"

"Not me."

"Who then?"

"My friend. My lover." He tasted his drink, stirred it
with one finger. As though recollecting that she was a
visitor, he pointed to one of the chairs. "Please, Teresa
Lovel, sit down. And t-tell me why you have come. How
did you find me?"

"It wasn't very difficult," Tess said. "I called the telephone company."

"You said you were here on business: is that t-true?"

She sank into a vast chair covered in black linen piped
in scarlet. "Personal business," she said. "Have you ever
heard of Jonas Fedor?"

"Of course." He smiled, as though the question was
superfluous. "He's your guardian, isn't he?"

As so often since Jonas's death, she felt like someone
standing blindfold and ear-plugged outside a door, trying

to understand what was going on inside. "How do you know that?"

"I know who you are, T-Teresa Lovel, even though I was not aware of your identity when we m-met in England earlier this year."

Questions choked her; she forced herself to keep to a single point. "Then you may also know that Jonas died recently, in Spain. I'm trying to find out exactly what happened."

"Why do you come to m-me?"

"Partly because I think you sent him a note shortly before he died. I believe it may have been because of what you wrote that he went to Spain."

"Do you think I killed him?" Rathbone said, raising his eyebrows.

"I'll reserve judgement on that," Tess said coolly.

"In order to p-persuade me to open the door to you, you spoke of Houston and Phil C-Cramir. W-What do you think that has to do with Jonas?"

"Somehow – I haven't worked out how – they're all connected."

"And you thought I might have some answers?"

"Looking at the stuff you keep on your walls, I *know* you have."

"I keep these here to remind me." Rathbone's mobile face twisted. "To m-make myself remember."

"Remember what?"

"My hatred."

"Hatred?" It was a strong word. The crystal sculptures caught diamond points of light from the spotlights as they shifted. Tess raised a hand to shield her eyes from the glare. She wondered if she were suffering from jet-lag.

That would explain her sense of disorientation, the way the room, the paintings, the words he spoke, the liquid in her glass, seemed to ebb and flow, curling away from her like a wave only to crash back again at her feet.

"It's not an easy emotion to m-maintain," Rathbone said. "You have to keep fuelling it, s-stoking it up. You need an obsessive nature to be a good hater, s-something I don't have. That's why I keep these p-paintings on the walls, even though I loathe them. For my lover's s-sake."

"Where is he?" It did not occur to Tess even to wonder whether the lover was female.

"Dead." Rathbone danced across to the bottles which stood on a sheet of plate glass and poured himself another drink. "We m-met at art school. He was terribly young, only a kid. We had the s-same initials. We became friends and, much later, lovers. He died about t-ten years ago. I have to keep remembering him in the last d-days before he died, those p-poor th-thin hands s-still trying to t-turn out these d-damned Vicentes." Emotion exacerbated his slight stutter. "Each b-brush s-stroke was an effort, but he w-wouldn't give in. S-Sometimes, I felt as though he was p-painting with his own b-blood." He rubbed a hand across his face and she noted the bitten nails, the silver skull-shaped ring. He took a deep calming breath. "I loved him," he said.

There was nothing Tess could say; she stared at her hands.

Rathbone said harshly: "He was called Amador. Amador Ramirez."

She looked up at him, half-rising from her chair. "What?"

"Yes. Your uncle. You're v-very like him."

"You *knew* about me?" She felt the beginning of a terrible pain.

"When I saw you at that auction, I knew there was something f-familiar about you. I knew Amador had a niece called Teresa Lovel, but of course I didn't know what you l-looked like."

"But why didn't he come and see me? Especially after my mother died?"

"We tried. Once we had tracked your m-mother down – and it wasn't easy – we did go and visit her. But it only m-made things worse for her."

"Oh God." Before she could stop it, an image, long repressed, filled her mind, the way a bruise floats up under ivory skin, amorphous at first, faint, then gradually taking on shape and colour, darkening from rose to lilac, from lilac to purple. *If you touch the child I will* the words rose out of memory, *if you touch the child . . .*

She rocked back and forth, hanging on to thoughts which could not hurt her, neutral things: the rain-drenched pines in Houston, the olive in her glass, clouds over the gothic spires of Cambridge. Better to keep the pain bottled up, under control; better not to remember.

Rathbone put a hand towards her. It rested on her shoulder, fragile as the claw of a bird. "Are you OK?"

OK? She wanted to laugh. She had not been OK for years. "Why didn't he come?" she whispered. "After she died, I was so alone."

"What can I say?" Rathbone withdrew his hand. "By then Amador w-was terribly ill. I was busy nursing him, getting on with my own w-work, trying to earn a living for us both. I'm afraid there just w-wasn't time for you."

She heard the indifference in his voice but could not blame him. A child never seen, in a foreign country: what could it have meant to him when set against those other greater problems?

He moved with his balletic step towards a cabinet of dull red lacquer. He took out a leather-covered book. "Here's something you might like," he said. He held it out to her and she could see the reluctance in his fingers to let her have it.

"What is it?" she asked.

"His poems. He wrote some w-wonderful things. Apart from the canvases, they're about all he l-left behind."

Tess took the book. The letters AR were stamped into the leather, set between the symbols of the moon which adorned the gateposts of the Casa de las Lunas. On the first page she saw the words ELEGÍAS ESPAÑOLAS written in dark blue ink on thick, good quality paper. Many of the pages were still blank; others contained poems written in formal elegant Spanish, mostly about love or the loss of it. Her translator's brain took in the words, created new shapes with them, tossed them around like a kaleidoscope to assume fresh patterns, fresh meanings, just as beautiful but none the less different.

"Keep it," Rathbone said, and his voice trembled slightly. "You have more right to it than I do."

It was the only piece of her uncle she would ever know; she wanted it to be hers. "No," she said. "The poems are yours. You loved him, I never had the chance to. But perhaps one day you'll allow me to translate them into English."

He smiled. "Thank you, Teresa Lovel." He put the book back into the cabinet.

"What did my uncle die of?" she said.

"He had no money. Before we . . . got together, he s-sometimes s-sold himself, his body. Eventually it caught up with him. Do I need to s-spell it out?"

"Couldn't he have got money from his family?"

"His grandparents were dead. He had no idea where his m-mother's sister lived. He asked his father, of course he did. But his letters w-were never answered. It wasn't until years later, when it was much too late, that he realised they must somehow have been intercepted and was able to make direct contact with his father. At first, he w-was desperate: he did what he had to do in order to survive."

"Intercepted by Mercedes," Tess said.

"Who else?" He stared at her, and she could see the dilated pupils of his eyes, like a cat's, almost colour-less, deceptively mild. "M-Mercedes. The beautiful, the powerful, the m-mad." He waved his drink about and little rainbows danced across the room as the spotlights caught the patterns chiselled into the glass. Tess wondered if he were drunk. Or stoned. "Mercedes, who hated her own husband so much that she s-sacrificed his children in order to hurt him. Mercedes, the Dragon Lady."

"But she was away most of the time. How could she have intercepted letters?"

"Servants can be bribed," Rathbone said. "J-Julia, the housekeeper, might have had a hand in it. Or one of the girls in the kitchen – it's not difficult to make people do things when you have m-money."

Tess remembered something else. "That auction," she said. "I bought the *Casa de las Lunas*."

"I know. Mercedes was not pleased."

538

"Is it a Vicente?"

"Of course."

"Then why did you overpaint it with your initials?"

"Not me. Amador. He sold it years ago to the owner of the house in England – s-some kind of diplomat, was he?"

"But why? It would have been worth much more if he'd sold it as a Vicente."

Rathbone sighed, the skin stretching tight across the facial structure beneath. At the roots of his cropped hair, his scalp showed pink. "It would have been worth m-more, but it wouldn't have achieved his aim."

"Which was?"

"Always and c-continually to hurt and annoy the Dragon Lady." Tipping back his head, he threw what was left in his glass down his throat and moved back towards the bottles. "Like I said, he was obsessive. And she was the obsession. The easiest way to hurt M-Mercedes is through her brother. So he painted over Vicente's signature and substituted his own initials. He loved to think about that: the *Casa de las Lunas* hanging unappreciated in some English country house."

"How did Mercedes discover it was there?"

"I'm afraid I got drunk and told her." Behind the words she sensed hours of loneliness eased by alcohol, days made tolerable only by the slipping away from reality into boozy comfort. "She was not v-very happy about losing it to another bidder."

"Me."

"Exactly." He groaned suddenly, putting his hand over his mouth. "Amador could have m-made it as an artist, you know. That was his tragedy. He was brilliant; if only he could have resolved his hatred for his stepmother, he might have b-been one of the great names of the age." Rathbone nodded dreamily over his glass. "Instead, he spent his life trying to out-Vicente Vicente, trying to paint Vicentes b-better than Vicente himself could."

Tess shivered; behind her, the silver curtains tinkled faintly. Her mother's voice sounded in her head: *She used to laugh at him. She asked why he bothered to try when he had so little talent.*

"Rightly or wrongly, he also blamed Mercedes for his mother's s-suicide. He used to tell me about it endlessly: it was one of his clearest memories. He was sitting with his mother while she nursed the new baby. She got up with the child in her arms, went over to the window, he heard this t-terrible thudding sound. He was only f-five years old . . . He ran and looked over the balcony and there they both were, the mother and the baby, broken and bleeding." Rathbone swallowed. "He had t-terrible dreams."

Unexpectedly, Tess found herself less moved by this story than she ought to have been. Bad blood, she thought. *Weak* blood. What kind of a mother kills herself in front of her five-year-old son? She thought of her own sad, beautiful mother, who had never fought against the circumstances in which she was embroiled. It seemed that Amador, too, had not been able to look beyond Mercedes.

She sat up straighter in the linen-covered chair, spread both hands along the arms, feeling the nubby material under her fingertips. She realised, with surprise, that she was stronger than either of them had been. "Is she in New York at the moment?"

"No."

"Damn," Tess said. She had hoped to catch up at last with Mercedes, the dealer responsible for selling pictures she knew to be fakes to Phil Cramir, a client of the Banco Morena. Mercedes, her own stepgrandmother.

"Did you wish to see her for any specific reason?" enquired Rathbone.

"She's knowingly sold at least one fake to a client of my bank."

"Which one?"

"*The Tears She Shed.*"

"Ah." Rathbone stared up at the ceiling, ashimmer with reflections from the curtains and the crystals. "J-Jonas's picture."

"How on earth do you know Jonas had it?" asked Tess.

"Because we travelled to England together, years ago, in order to copy it. That was what Amador did, before he got s-sick. Spent his time tracking down Vicentes. The Louvre, the National Gallery, the Prado, private collections: wherever they were he c-copied them."

A faint memory of being in the Rijksmuseum in Amsterdam on a vacation from the Courtauld and seeing a gaunt-eyed man in front of the Vicente there came back to Tess. Was that – could it possibly have been her own uncle? It was like travelling in time, a paradox which could now never be resolved.

"Yes," Rathbone said. "He did two copies of *The Tears.*"

"Did you sell them both to Mercedes?"

"No," he said, smiling a little. "We only sold her one. She thought it was the original. That's how good Amador was. Vicente's own s-sister thought it was the original."

"And the second?"

"We *gave* her the second. Just so she'd know what we'd done. What Amador had done."

"And she sold it to Cramir, knowing it wasn't the original?"

"Absolutely correct."

"And this was part of my uncle's plan?"

"Yes. Like him, she spent her whole life obsessed with just one thing. In her case, it was the glorification of her b-brother. She was determined to have him recognised as one of the leading painters of his generation. So far, we've been able to stop her."

"How?"

"We had copies of nearly every extant painting by Fernando Vicente – some of them which M-Mercedes herself had not seen since her brother was shot. She authenticated some of them herself, in order to make a prestigious sale; we could have exposed her any time we wanted."

"Why didn't you?"

"Amador wanted her fall, when it came, to be spectacular. He d-died before it could take place. And now the time has come to make a move, with the opening of this Vicente Museum of hers in Montalbán. That's what my note to Jonas was about. The place is being officially opened by someone from the Spanish royalty. If it goes through, she'll have achieved her twin aims of ruining the Ramirez and having Vicente idolised by the public – who don't know twat about him."

"But why does it still matter so much?"

"Partly because of the damage she had done to Amador and his family. And partly because Fernando Vicente was a shit of the first water. Not even a very good painter, and a sexual pervert as well."

"Someone else said that to me recently."

"It's true."

"Do you mean because he was . . ." she paused, delicately aware of sensibilities not to be disregarded, ". . . homosexual?"

"That's one of the things he was *not*."

"But I thought – "

"Besides," he glanced at her quizzically. "I personally don't consider homosexuality a perversion."

"So wha – "

"What Vicente liked best was little girls."

Again Tess shivered, although the room was not cold. "How do you know that?" she demanded. Her voice was unsteady; it was an effort for her to keep hold of her glass.

"Why do you think Mercedes is so determined to own *The Tears She Shed*?"

"I've no idea." Understanding began to take shape as she remembered that screaming room in the Vicente Museum in Montalbán, emotion compressed into almost solid form.

Rathbone stood. Somewhat erratically, he refilled his glass. "God!" he said violently, swinging round to look again at Tess. "I b-bet that sick b-bastard loved looking at it. And who do you think the model was?"

"I'd already guessed it must have been Mercedes herself."

"And why do you think she's so determined to have her brother recognised as a genius?"

"Tell me."

"Because she knows that the world forgives its geniuses for their sins. And if the world forgave, then perhaps she could forgive too. Otherwise, if she has to acknowledge that it's not love she feels for him but hate, then her whole life has been nothing but a waste."

Keeping her voice steady with an effort, Tess said: "What does it have to do with Jonas?"

"You ask, even though you've seen the Cramir collection? Didn't Jonas ever talk to you about Phil?"

"Never. Until after he died, I didn't even realise Jonas knew him."

As Rathbone opened his mouth to answer, she suddenly knew what he was going to tell her. She thought of him, the little man in his white shirt being led off between his guards, the fine painter's hands trying to hide their tremble. Was it possible to feel sorry for him, to understand why he had done what he did? She thought of Mercedes; she thought of the small band of men, coming down from the hills by night to visit their families, to dandle children, to sleep with wives, to comfort mothers, and finding themselves caught in a trap from which only a cruel death would release them.

"It was him," she said, and wondered if the crack inside her signalled the breaking of her heart or merely the smashing of her illusions. "It was Vicente who betrayed them."

Rathbone nodded as she went on: "He drew them for Captain Santiago and his men, so they would recognise them. He told them when they would be coming down to visit their families, didn't he? He gave them all away, one by one."

"Jonas was the only one to escape. So you see, don't

you," Rathbone said, "why Jonas felt that the Montalbán Museum must be stopped?"

Tess nodded. "And why Mercedes, at all costs, had to stop Jonas."

29

TESS

Birds fly westward;
Clouds drift towards the sun. And I?
I watch the trees and weep.
    translated from the Japanese by Teresa Lovel

She took the Piccadilly Line in from Heathrow, changed
onto the Circle Line, at Victoria changed again. Stepping
out of the tube station at Pimlico, she walked a bit before
hailing a taxi on the other side of the street. Precautions,
necessary ones. It was unlikely that anyone had been
hanging about at the airport on the off-chance she might
appear. On the other hand, she had presumed herself
safe from being followed to Houston – and been proved
wrong.

Vividly aware of both fear and lethargy, as though she
inhabited some fatalistic limbo between the two, she
journeyed towards Cambridge. In the Tube, a hand
pressed the small of her back. Whirling round, she had
seen only the bored exhausted faces of other travellers,
eyes vacant as they stared past her. Quickly she moved
until she was standing with her back against the curving

walls of the station. The vaulted ceiling reminded her of
Cramir's underground gallery; nausea bit sharply at her
stomach, bile rose in her throat. She was shocked by the
realisation she had no-one to turn to. Jonas was dead,
Dominic not to be trusted.

She thought of Don Pedro. But that was primarily a
business relationship, and anyway, in view of their last
meeting, it was best not to think of him as a friend. There
was Emma Lybrand, of course. But she could not possibly
understand the uncertainties which now faced Tess.

Fear heightened her perceptions. Crossing the market
place in Cambridge, she noticed with sharper awareness
the immaculate pink-grey smoothness of a pigeon's chest
and the whiteness of the band round its throat; saw,
too, how solid were the reflections in shop windows,
how brilliant the stripes of an undergraduate scarf, how
clearly defined the puffy cloud above a Tudor gateway.
For the first time, she truly understood why hostages
were able to adapt to appalling conditions, how people
strive for normal routines in even the most dangerous
of war zones. Matter of factness, attention to minutiae,
is one way of coping with the constant razor edge
of fear.

There was an accumulation of letters and newspapers
on the doormat; after firmly bolting shut the front door
and putting it on the chain, she carried them into the
kitchen.

While the kettle boiled she sorted the letters, threw
away the days-old newspapers, glanced rapidly at the local
freesheet and, about to throw it away too, paused. Sweat
prickled under her arms; she stared at the smudgy front
page then suddenly she was running for the downstairs

cloakroom, bending over the pedestal, violently throwing up.

The doorbell rang several times. Registering it through a haze of cramping discomfort, she made no move to answer it. The bell sounded again, fiercely, demanding to be answered. Slowly she moved along the passage towards the front door. As she unlocked it, the person on the other side shoved at it hard until brought up sharply by the chain. She gasped, pushing ineffectually, trying to close it again.

"Tess?" It was Dominic's voice. "Are you there?"

Relief loosened the joints of her knees. "Oh, Dominic," she said, and for a moment felt like weeping – until she remembered her suspicions of him, and asked herself how he could have known she was back home. "What do you want?" she asked.

"Let me in, for God's sake."

"Why should I?" she asked.

"Why *should* y – " Indignation made him choke.

"How did you know I was back?"

"I didn't. Open the door, Tess."

"You must have or you wouldn't be here."

He gave an exasperated groan. "I've come round each day, just to check. Every time I telephone you I get nothing but your blasted machine. What's going on, Tess?"

"Don't you know?" she asked bitterly.

There was a pause. She looked at him through the gap between door and frame and saw he was frowning. "All I know is, it's to do with Jonas and the things which happened in the Civil War."

"Why do you think that?"

"He told me some of it. Some of it I guessed. Some –
the worst part – I can only imagine."

Tess bit her lip. She longed to believe him; she dared
not. "Dominic, I . . ."

He stared at her incredulously. "You bloody well think
I'm mixed up in all of this, don't you?"

"I – " The desire to believe him innocent was over-
whelming.

"You think it was me who tried to drown you, don't
you?" he demanded.

She stared at him. A small voice whispered inside her
head: *It might have been.* Misery welled inside her. After
a while, she said: "If you don't go away, I shall call the
police," and closed the door on his furious face.

As she walked slowly back to the kitchen, she heard the
rattle of the letter-box and his voice, shouting: "Tess, for
God's sake be careful."

She did not even turn her head.

The freesheet was still spread across the table. The
front page was dominated by a photograph: at first
glance, the grainy black-and-white face could have been
Tess's.

The text beneath the picture indicated that it belonged
to a local woman called Heather Armcoat who, two
evenings ago, had been murdered as she walked home
late at night from the station. Witnesses had noticed
her travelling in the rear coach of the train back from
London; the ticket-collector remembered seeing her walk
off towards the town. The police were busy eliminating
people from their enquiries and still wished to interview
the man who had not travelled on the train but was seen
following the woman across the station forecourt and into

the night. They added that whoever had perpetrated this 'grisly deed' would have been covered with blood and easily identifiable; someone must have noticed him.

Unable to prevent the trembling of her mouth, Tess read further. The dead woman had worked as a secretary in a London law firm. On the night of her death, she had been to the theatre and had taken the late train back to Cambridge. The attack had occurred as she took a short-cut between two roads; she had died within a hundred yards of her own home.

Once more, Tess examined the anonymous newspaper photograph. Was the likeness more than a mere coincidence? Was it remotely possible that Heather Armcoat had met her death precisely because of that likeness, because she had been mistaken for Tess herself? The short-cut was one Tess herself always used.

Only Emma knew she had temporarily moved into the Battersea flat. If someone had been watching for her to step off a train from London, it was more than possible that seeing Heather Armcoat instead, from a distance and in the dark, the murderer had struck under the impression that his victim was Tess. Once, she would have dismissed such theories as the purest nonsense; now they seemed all too likely.

Which made her – did it not? – indirectly responsible for someone's death? And made it clear that she was now being stalked, just as Jonas had been on those hot southern hills.

Events had suddenly taken too terrifying a turn; she could not handle them on her own. She *had* to talk to someone, if only to hear them say that she was being unecessarily alarmist, that Heather Armcoat had been a victim of random violence, that Jonas had simply been taken ill and fallen.

Don Pedro. He was the only one, older and wiser than she, more versed in the ways of the world. Despite the conclusion she had come to earlier, she remembered that until the unfortunate purchase of the *Casa de las Lunas* he had been a good friend. She would not willingly have trespassed over the line between a personal and a business relationship. Yet he himself had done so, by asking her to attend the Brantwell Manor auction.

Before she could persuade herself out of it, she lifted the telephone.

Don Pedro seemed delighted to hear from her. "My dear, I'm so glad you're back," he said. "Did your trip to Spain help to clear things up?"

"In some ways, it raised more questions than it answered," she said slowly, relieved by his warmth. She did not say she had also been back to Houston. "You were absolutely right about the Civil War still being a living issue over there."

"Of course."

Tess took a deep breath. "Don Pedro: I'd really like to come in and talk to you if I might. While I was in Spain, I learned a few things which – "

"When do you wish to come?"

"As soon as possible."

"Then come tomorrow morning," he said simply. "If you need me, I am here to help."

"Oh, thank you. Thank you so much."

She stayed that night in Battersea, the bolts drawn, the curtains closed against the night. She slept sitting up, propped against the pillows, Jonas's gun near her hand.

Her life had never seemed bleaker.

A pale sun shone through the window behind Don Pedro's head. The branches of the plane tree were beginning to break into tightly curled leaf bud, green shading into red. Don Pedro got up to greet Tess as she was shown into his office, raising her hand to his lips then holding it closely in both of his.

"My dear," he said.

Tess fled from his kindness into defensive flippancy. She opened her eyes wide in mock awe. "There's been an addition to the Celebrity Collection, I see." She picked up one of the silver-framed photographs and pretended to be overcome. "Heavens!" she cried. "Royalty, no less."

"The Princess was very gracious."

"This week the Princess; next week the Queen herself, I shouldn't wonder."

"There *was* mention of a visit to Sandringham," agreed Don Pedro complacently.

"One word of warning," said Tess. "Don't mention Sanchez or you'll be out on your ear. Her Majesty is known to be a woman with a highly developed artistic sensibility."

"I'll try to remember." Smiling, Don Pedro indicated a chair. "Now, Teresa. To business. First yours, then mine."

"Funnily enough," she said slowly. "The two seem fairly closely linked."

"How is that?"

"What did you know about Phil Cramir? Why did he insist that the Banco Morena handle so many of his affairs?"

"I've no idea. But if a rich client wants to pay for the Banco's services, I'm hardly likely to question him about his reasons for choosing us rather than one of the big international banks, am I?"

"Did you ever meet him?"

"No. I knew nothing about him at all. Sometimes over the years I have wondered whether he was a Spaniard, partly because he did, as you say, choose us when he could have chosen a bigger concern, partly because when he sold off his Impressionists, he chose a Spanish-based charity as the recipient of the proceeds."

"Why do you think he did that?"

Don Pedro shrugged. "Who knows. As people grow older they begin to try to put right the wrongs they did in their youth. If they have the means, that is. And a sufficiently guilty conscience."

"And assuming they've done wrong in the first place."

"Exactly. Most people have not." He wrinkled his forehead at her. "What is your interest in this man?"

She said slowly: "It has to do with Fernando Vicente."

His face changed. He frowned heavily. "And this is something you learned of while you were in Montalbán?"

"I realise it seems very tenuous . . ." Quickly, writing them down as she spoke, Tess explained about the matching of the names, the connection she had conjectured between Cramir and Montalbán, between Cramir and Luisa Ruiz-Barrantes, between Cramir and Jonas. "It's impossible that it's simply coincidence," she said. "And I know Jonas's death is mixed up with it all."

"In what way?"

"I think I know why he went," she said.

"Why was that?"

"To try and stop the opening of a museum of Vicente's works: Cramir was involved, too, I'm sure."

He looked astonished. "Vicente was not someone I can pretend to admire," he said, "either as a man or as an artist. But why should your guardian wish to prevent this museum from opening?"

"Because . . ." Even though she had had time to digest the information, Tess still found it painful to recall the passion with which she had once regarded Vicente. ". . . he was a traitor."

"I knew that."

"He betrayed the men of Montalbán to someone who tortured to death not only them but their families, in the most hideous way."

"Teresa." Gently he took hold of her hand again. "This is surely not something for you to concern yourself with. Let those who suffered be the ones to deal with it. If they are prepared to let the museum go ahead, that is their business, not yours."

"Except that someone killed Jonas when he went out there. And then tried to kill me."

"What?" His hands tightened over hers. "What do you mean?"

She recounted the hair-raising scramble down the mountain road, the dislodged stone, the imprisonment in Cramir's gallery. "The horror of it," she said, her voice almost failing. "Each time, I thought I was going to die. And now – " she had to swallow, " – a woman was killed in Cambridge while I was away – and I'm sure it was because of me."

He seemed to accept her story at once. "My poor Teresa . . ."

"I think I know why Jonas was killed," she said. "And by whom."

He frowned. "Then you yourself could be in further danger."

"I'm taking it all quite seriously," she said. "I'm taking precautions."

"What sort of precaution?"

"I've moved out of my house for the moment."

"Very wise. How many people know you're not still in Cambridge?"

"None. Except the friend who's lending me her flat in London."

He pulled a pad towards him, then pushed it away again. "I was going to suggest that you give me the telephone number, but perhaps you'd prefer not to."

She left the question open, not wishing to offend him. "Then there's the sketches that Cramir left to Jonas. Since he was still alive when Cramir died, they're technically part of his estate. He wanted them to be sent to Montalbán in order to – "

"You mention them in your report, I believe. There were twelve of them, yes?"

"That's right. Unmistakably the work of Vicente. And Jonas had two more: I don't know who they were – at least – " She hesitated. "I know who one of them is. Cramir's ones, I'm sure, are the twelve Apostles."

"I hadn't realised they were religious works."

"That's the name the people in Montalbán gave to a group of resistance fighters during the Civil War." She knew she sounded confused.

"Of course. Your guardian spoke of them in his television interview."

"Because of Vicente, they were all picked up and murdered by some sadistic fascist commander called El Malo. His real name was Santiago."

"Santiago?"

"Yes. And Jonas was going to expose him in his memoirs. This Santiago is obviously still alive somewhere in Spain and doesn't want his identity made known, so he killed him."

"And all this is connected with the Fernando Vicente Museum?" Don Pedro shook his head, the movement causing a blackbird to fly up from the plane tree, one wing brushing the window as it wheeled in sudden panic.

"I think so."

"Tess," Don Pedro said gently. "Although I do not wish to pour cold water on your theories, it was all a long time ago."

"But you yourself said that people in Spain still haven't forgotten. Nor forgiven."

"I meant it theoretically." He swivelled his chair to look out at the tree. "I was old enough to fight in the Civil War," he said. "It is one of my shames that I did not. But I was the only son of a doting mamma." He shrugged. "She nagged my father until he emigrated, taking us with him. We didn't return to Burgos until well after the war." He turned to look at the branches behind him, picking up his gold pen, turning it in his fingers. "I owe something to the men like Jonas: tell me how I can help you and I will do so."

"That's just it, I don't know. But Cramir's pictures have something to do with it, one way or another. And the ones I queried in my report were sold to him by a dealer called Mercedes Aragon, the sister of Fernando

Vicente. And, incidentally, the driving force behind this museum."

"This becomes more confusing by the second. Are you suggesting that this woman killed Jonas?"

"Maybe." Mercedes was a monster; even Luisa, her own aunt, had suggested she was not entirely sane. Tess remembered the woman cursing her, the way she had spat into the fire as though sealing a bargain. She remembered that uplifted agonised face at Jonas's funeral.

But in that case, where did Santiago fit in? Or was he irrelevant, a mere red herring?

"Or," Don Pedro's voice said, relentlessly. "Do you think this Santiago person is responsible?"

"I don't know. I just don't know."

"Wouldn't it at least be helpful if you read your guardian's memoirs yourself to see if your theory is correct? If this man is not mentioned, then that would at least serve to eliminate him from your enquiries, no?"

Was he laughing at her? Tess looked up quickly but he seemed as concerned as ever. "That's part of the trouble," she said. "Nobody knows where they are. I've checked with his solicitor and with his publisher. I haven't got them, and I've thoroughly searched Jonas's house. I can't imagine where they might be . . ."

And as she spoke, she thought of one place Jonas might have left them.

Don Pedro read her expression. "Ah," he said gently. "You have remembered something."

"A friend of mine may have it," she said slowly. That must be what Dominic had wanted to tell her the previous day.

"The art expert you told me of once before?" Don Pedro said, raising his eyebrows.

"Yes."

"Then check and see if you are correct. After that, if you think it will help, I shall be happy to talk to you again." He looked at his watch. "Meanwhile, if you will forgive me, I should like to discuss this other business. I think you are right when you say your affairs and mine are interconnected."

"What makes you say that?"

"I've now had time to go through your report on the Cramir collection in more detail, and it seems to me that the implications are fairly serious. If Cramir was fooled, how many others were too? Strictly between ourselves, Teresa, the Banco could be in trouble."

"Why?"

"Because at various times in the past, we have lent substantial sums to known and trusted clients, using their art works as collateral. Now I have discovered that several of these works were bought from the very dealer you mentioned in your report: the Aragon Gallery. You can see for yourself how disastrous it would be if some of those paintings turned out to be fakes. So they must be checked. And you're the obvious person to do the checking. You're loyal, knowledgeable and discreet – and discretion is vital. Some of the people involved are extremely well-known."

"How urgent is all this?"

"In one instance, very much so. There have been certain . . . um . . . developments. Perhaps you heard that Michio Hayashima is involved in the current corruption scandals in Japan."

"I did indeed."

"One of the paintings I'm worried about is kept in Mr Hayashima's flat at the Corporation's London offices. It must be looked at as soon as possible."

"All right. How do you suggest we organise it?"

"The simplest way would be for you to present yourself as a representative of the Banco Morena wishing to inspect the picture for insurance purposes, in case the premiums need updating. After all, the Corporation can hardly object, as it technically belongs to us."

"Very well."

"Not that it will be Mr Hayashima himself you will speak to, since the most recent information we have suggests that he's in prison. But someone from the company will be there – business seems to be carrying on as usual, for the moment." He slammed a fist down on his desk and he added vehemently: "*Dios*! This could turn into a nightmare – suppose all those paintings turn out to be forgeries."

"It's extremely unlikely," she said. "Where are these clients of yours?"

"Hayashima is the urgent one."

"I could go there this afternoon."

"Excellent." She saw him relax, shoulders dropping, smiling. The scar below his lip echoed the curve of his mouth. "I shall telephone the Corporation's offices in Kensington and tell them to expect you."

Before leaving the Banco, Tess went along to Martin García's office. He looked good, his blond curls haloing his tanned face above a suit she had not seen before and an expensive silk tie. He was playing with an executive toy, a pile of magnetised silver flakes, trying to turn them into a sculpture. "Tess," he said. "How's things?"

"Fine," she lied.

He looked contrite. "I'm sorry I didn't get back to you about that flight list," he said. "Things have been hectic round here recently."

"Flight list?" Vaguely she remembered calling him from the airport on her way to Houston. So much had happened since then . . .

He searched the immaculate piles of paper on his desk. A glass vase of early narcissi stood on his desk, tiny open trumpets pale against yolk yellow petals. "Yes. And you were absolutely right." He looked at her expectantly. "What'll you give me if I tell you all about it?"

She opened her mouth to answer impatiently, then caught an unexpected glimpse, behind his jokey exterior, of something she had never suspected. They had worked together for years: she realised with shame how little she knew about him. The grandfather who had fought alongside Franco – or was it against him? A former girlfriend called Sue. A smartish bachelor flat in the Fulham Road. For a while he had escorted Emma Lybrand about town, but when she went back to Josh, he had not taken up with anyone else. Was it possible that handsome successful Martin García was lonely, even unhappy, and she had never bothered to find out?

She did not like this tiny revelation of herself. Was she really so self-obsessed that she could not tell when a friend needed something from her? Was she incapable of judging other people as they really were?

"I'll give you anything you like," she said lightly. There

were two scratches down one side of his face and she leaned forward to touch them.

"Dinner," he said. "Just the two of us. Soon."

"OK."

"Here's the business: you were right – someone called L. Marlowe took the same flight to Spain as your guardian," he said.

A jolt of pain shook her heart. Dominic. She remembered the airline ticket stub she had found in his wallet. She nodded, hoping to hide her sudden desolation. L. Marlowe. El Malo. "Thanks."

"You won't forget our date, will you?" he said anxiously.

"As long as it's my treat."

He looked shocked. "My Spanish *machismo* would never allow a woman to pick up the tab."

"You're only half Spanish."

"That's the half with the *machismo*."

She put her hand lightly on his fair hair, feeling years older than he was. "Martin, I'm staying at Emma Lybrand's place for a few days. If anything comes up unexpectedly, you can get me there. I'll ring you very soon about dinner, promise."

Waiting for a lift to street level, she thought about him again, remembering the drunken revelations about his Spanish grandfather to which she had only half-listened in Houston. Could this same grandfather have been called Santiago? Could it possibly be *Martin*, by his own admission dominated by the dead man he had never known, who was determined to see to it that Jonas's memoirs were never published, in order to preserve his grandfather's memory?

But that made no sense at all.

Even as she thought this, she realised it made all the sense in the world. And she had told him where she was staying . . .

The Hayashima Corporation's London offices were impressively sited near the Victoria & Albert Museum in Kensington. From the outside, the building seemed no different from the cream-painted town houses on either side. It was only on pushing open the smoked-glass entrance doors that Tess found herself in a world at once familiar and alien. A flight of three steps led from the doors up to a wide reception hall. Whoever was responsible for the décor had gone for a general impression of oriental sumptuousness rather than true Japanese minimalism. The floor, of shining black marble, looked like a pool of still water, reflecting the clumps of bamboo in carved planters which were set here and there. Large upright glass cases stood against the walls, holding a series of elaborate robes: *atsuita* and *karaori* for Noh performance; silk *kosode* hand-painted with plum blossom or embroidered with dianthus sprays; costumes of hemp or satin, gorgeously tie-dyed or stencilled with butterflies, peonies, and bellflowers.

A girl dressed like a geisha appeared and bowed; her piled hair and powdered face with its delicate, almost non-existent features, made Tess feel over-large and coarse.

"Teresa Lovel," she said, bowing in her own turn. "From the Banco Morena."

"Yesss." The girl bowed again, motioning her to a set of lifts situated behind a pair of decorated screens. In front of them, two flat-topped cabinets displayed a group of *netsuke* in ivory and wood; Tess glimpsed miniature carp, stag-beetles on a shell, a group of turtles, each elaborately carved in exquisite detail. She longed to stop and take a closer look but to do so would imply discourtesy to the man she had come to see so she hurried past.

Explaining that the lift would take her directly into Mr Hayashima's penthouse apartment, the girl pressed the button and stood bowing as the doors closed on Tess.

When they opened again, she found herself stepping into a paper-screened apartment full of lacquered tables and chests. The floor was the same shiny black marble as the reception area, mirroring arrangements of black branches and orchids set among low sofas of embroidered silks. Immediately facing her was a suit of *nimaido gusoku* style armour, flanked by a pair of Chinese lion dogs in green glazed porcelain.

There was a view from the windows of the Kensington skyline: roofs, trees, the slate spire of a nearby church. She stood for a moment, remembering – remembering cherry blossom, fragility, a time before she learned to hold tight onto her life, to clutch it to her so that pieces did not break off and swirl away from her. The moon-coloured screens, the paper lamps, bamboo. It's gone, she told herself, it's gone, and I've survived.

There was movement behind her, the whispery slap of thongs on the floor and she turned, a smile ready.

The man facing her opened his bloodless lips but did not speak. He bowed, and there was mockery in every line of his body beneath the *kimono* of heavy brocade he wore. As though mesmerised, Tess stared at him, unable to move. The blood in her body seemed to have stopped moving, grown heavy as lead. She saw the writhing dragons on his robe and the way the embroidered chrysanthemum petals swayed as he moved towards her. She saw the pale pale face, the silvery too-long hair, eyes the colour of torn flesh. Once, years ago, she had wondered whether blood flowed in his veins or simply water; later, older, she had decided that his body was filled with a clear and lethal poison.

She was terrified. The last twenty years might never have been. Although the length of the room separated them, she was as helpless under his unblinking gaze as she had been when a child; around her, defences cracked, buttresses crumbled. She felt that the essence of herself was about to leak away, to drip softly to the shining floor and there evaporate, leaving only a husk of the woman who was Teresa Lovel, the child who had once tried to close herself to the sounds, the tastes, the smells of violence, and had not succeeded.

Blood. She could smell it again, thick, metallic, clogging her nostrils.

The pale lips parted again. "Teresa," he said in the thin attenuated voice she knew so well, had hoped never to hear again. "Or perhaps I should say Tess."

"Wh-what are you . . .?" Her mouth felt as though it was frozen, unable to complete the sentence.

"Didn't you know I work as a consultant for Michio Hayashima now?" he said, and his voice was as soft as the rustle of a viper in the grass. She knew him to be over seventy yet he was like a monstrous boy; there were no lines on his face and the hair was not white but of a gold so pale it was indistinguishable from silver.

She shook her head. She could not speak. Years of loathing, a childhood of terror were weighing her down, slowing her reactions. She felt as though she were slowly petrifying under his gaze, shrinking, turning to bone, to ivory, becoming nothing more than one of the carved *netsuke* in the cases downstairs.

"Quite a prestigious position, I assure you," he went on. "I have often wondered if our paths would cross again, having seen your name on some piece of translation for the company's negotiations with Morena."

"If I had known, I would never ever have come here," she managed.

"But you did." The cold mouth widened; it was almost a smile. "It's a pleasure to see you again after so many years, Tess."

She wanted to shout at him, tell him not to call her by that name, but found herself transfixed, as though she were a rabbit caught in the mesmerising gaze of a stoat. She felt a wave of longing for Jonas, the security he provided, the protection he had so generously offered to a child who was not even his own.

He moved towards her, the *kimono* widening with his movements; she tried to take a step back. "Don't come near me," she said urgently. "Don't touch me." His hands were hidden within the wide sleeves but she knew how they looked, those cold fingers, the chilly trail of them on her skin . . .

"What will you do to me if I do?" he asked, his thin voice jocular, his eyes as chill as snow. She heard the echoes of grotesque childhood games of punishment and reward.

"I'll . . ." Once again her mouth would not form the

words. Instead, she asked: "Why did you hate us so much?"

"Do you really not know?" Inside the brocade sleeves, something glinted.

"I wouldn't ask if I did." She felt the weight of her bag on her shoulder and touched it carefully, remembering what it held. "It just seems so . . . so unnatural."

As he took a quick step in her direction and another, the words screamed in her brain, pounding to be let out *If you touch the child I will* . . . She would have no hesitation in taking out the gun which had once belonged to Jonas, nor any compunction about using it, if she had to, on the man who was now moving almost at a run towards her, a syringe in the hand now freed from its enveloping sleeve.

The man called Richard Lovel.

Her father.

30

TESS

Belief in witches is still strong in this isolated mountainous region. To this day a girl with a mark or mole on her face is viewed with suspicion even by those anxious to prove that the Basque country is a modern and sophisticated culture with every right to self-government.

The Basques, by Pablo Laínez,
translated by Teresa Lovel

Bulge-eyed dragons snarled; petals writhed amid swirls of formal fire. Somewhere above her head, a voice roared and whispered. When she moved her limbs, her hands felt as though they were made of sponge. The dragons moved and she tensed, waiting for the familiar pain but it did not come. There was another pain, instead, somewhere at the edge of her body, though nothing was solid enough for her to be sure of its location.

She was lying on a hard mattress. When she turned her head, clouds moved at the corners of her eyes. She was vaguely aware that words had been spoken, information passed.

The roaring voice rushed towards her again and then subsided. "Are you awake, Teresa?"

Was she? Or was she still trapped in some sad nightmare she had thought escaped from long ago? Debating her answer, her tongue thick as a slipper in her mouth, she tried to sit up. Immediately she felt nauseous. At the same time, she realised that although her clothes had not been removed, she lay exposed, her blouse unbuttoned, her skirt above her hips. She tried to cover herself and heard, through ears full of mist, a laugh which filled the inside of her head.

"You're safe from me, Teresa. As you know, I dislike the bodies of women. I merely wished to see how you had changed."

Hatred burned *If you touch the child I will* as she struggled into a half-sitting position, ignoring the waves of sickness which rose and fell. She blinked hard and shook her head from side to side. Her vision cleared so that she was able to focus on the room about her. Apart from the futon sofa on which she lay, it was empty of anything but a gold-lacquered chest and a large porcelain jar. The only relief from the austerity of the furnishings was a group of decorative mountings for the ceremonial swords worn by the *daimyo*, feudal lords of the Edo period.

Leaning on one elbow, she swung her legs down so that she was sitting with her feet on the floor. When the mists had cleared she would stand, but for the moment it was easier to remain as she was; her arm throbbed. Years ago she had discovered that the best way to protect herself from her father was to keep still, not to struggle or scream. She said calmly: "You drugged me."

"Nothing very much," he said. "Sodium Pentothal."

570

He stood over her, tall and pale as a ghost; beneath the brocade kimono she glimpsed his body, white and hairless.

"The truth drug," she said. "What did you make me tell you?" And as she asked the question, knew the answer. "Oh God," she said.

He smiled his ugly lipless smile. "It's too late now."

She felt a shudder of apprehension. Her brain had been dislocated by the drug, the separate parts of it scattered. Now, they reassembled, locked into place, began to operate.

Beside the futon was her bag. She reached for it, pulling it towards her by the strap. Was it the same weight as when she arrived? She dared not open it to check in case Lovel saw the gun inside – unless he had already removed it.

There had been two of them questioning her, she remembered now, though the other one had remained out of her sight, speaking in a sharp unidentifiable whisper. She had told them something: under the influence of the drug she had said she suspected that Dominic had Jonas's memoirs, given them Dominic's address in Cambridge. Where was the other person – was it man or woman? – now? On the way to Cambridge to find the memoirs? A wave of fear washed over her: would they hurt him?

At the same time, she tried to work out what connection Lovel had with Jonas, and why he should want to know where the manuscript was.

He floated in front of her like a ghost, a phantom. Something teased at her, tugged her memory, moon-shaped, white as a bone, something seen recently, the key to it all. Pressing both hands down, she pushed herself

up onto her feet. The floor seemed a long way below her
and the walls melted when she stared straight at them. She
suspected that as well as the Sodium Pentothal, she had
been given something else, to keep her quiet. She was
more or less in control of her body now but it seemed
expedient to appear not to be. Deliberately she staggered
a little, blinked and shook her head. "I feel terrible," she
said weakly.

Time had passed; the light coming in behind the paper
screens was of a different quality from when she had first
arrived. It was now early evening, she would guess.

"There are no lasting effects," Lovel said. "I've used
it many times before."

"Yes," she said. She slung her bag over her shoulder
and carefully undid the flap. "That's how you killed my
mother, isn't it?" The question had lain like a thorn in her
heart for years, demanding to be asked, ever since that
winter afternoon when she had seen Jonas walk across
the kitchen floor to answer the phone, seen his agonised
face and his tears. "An overdose, was it?"

He looked at her warily. "What did you say?"

"I know you killed her." She had not been this close
to him since adolescence and was amazed to realise how
slight he was. In her imagination, he had loomed over her
like a tree, monstrous, repellent. Now, she was taller than
he, and bigger; their roles had changed; she was the strong
one. The realisation was like the loosening of a manacle;
chains dropped from her mind.

*Just like Jonas said, I should have turned and faced him
years ago, I should have exorcised him.* She had thought
him a monster and saw now that he was no more than a
mirage.

"It was an accident," he said, and the words echoed; she had heard them somewhere else, not long ago.

"You mean," she said coldly. "You didn't intend to kill her?"

"You are being ridic – "

"What I have never understood is why she married someone so . . . *ugly*," she said with deliberate cruelty and was glad to see him wince.

The silky hair lifted briefly, as though a breeze had passed over it. He said: "Do you think I like looking like this? Do you think I don't revolt myself, as well as others? I decided that if I couldn't make people love me, then I could at least make them fear me."

"We certainly feared you, my mother and I."

He turned his head to the ceiling. "I would have given anything in the world to have you both love me instead."

"You abused us."

"It was the only way I could get near either of you. Especially you. You were always so much stronger than Concepción." He sighed. "At first she represented all the things I would never have: colour, brilliance, richness. After that, I simply found myself excited by her terror and revulsion, and the way she did whatever I wanted."

"To save me," Tess said.

It all seemed so clear to her now. Squeezed from her subconscious came words heard once and carefully not remembered, a child waking in the hot Tokyo night, smelling petrol fumes through an open window, and the fierce whispers from the next room:

"Unless you leave her alone I shall tell."

"And ruin me?"

"Yes. Let her be and you can do what you will to me."

"You wish to spoil my fun?"

"If you touch the child I will kill you."

Beside her bed the clock had ticked, ticked, the luminous hands pointing out the time in the darkness, 4:18, and already the traffic starting up in the street below, the slap of slippers in the flat upstairs where the Dutch oil executive lived with his Japanese wife. The words did not make sense. At the same time they made all the sense in the world. She heard the familiar sound of his blows, a gasp, a faint moan and then the curious sucking noises; dimly she perceived that her mother offered herself as a willing sacrifice.

In the darkness – the seconds moving on: 4:19, 4:20 – she had added under her breath: *"And if you don't kill him, one day I shall."*

The past faded as, through the intercom, the distorted voice of the receptionist below announced the arrival of a visitor, now ascending in the lift.

Lovel turned. The lift doors opened and Mercedes Ramirez stepped into the room. She wore a white silk dress, the full waist gathered with a bold scarlet sash.

"Ah," she said, peering across at Tess. "You have Teresa Lovel."

"Teresa is here, yes."

"Has she agreed?"

"Agreed to what?"

"To give back my picture, of course."

Tess felt no surprise at the realisation that Mercedes and Lovel knew each other. One more knot in her tangled past was unravelling. Closer, the older woman stopped suddenly, seeing Tess clearly. "You?" she said, surprised. "The girl at the auction?"

"My daughter," Lovel said.

Tess thought: However strong I grow, I shall never be reconciled to the fact that his blood runs in my veins, his poisoned blood . . .

"Then she must have the *Casa de las Lunas* as well," said Mercedes. There was a wildness about her, an insanity of hair and eyes and mouth which made her appear as though she were about to fly apart. She turned directly to Tess. "I want both the paintings back. I will pay a fair price. I must have them both."

"Shut up," Lovel said savagely. "We aren't here to talk about pictures."

Mercedes seemed astonished. "No? What, then?"

"She has something far more important than that, far more dangerous. For all of us."

"All of us? How am I connected with this?" Mercedes said haughtily.

"The memoirs," Lovel said. "Your lover's memoirs." He stared at Mercedes and then blinked, once. The small movement had the effect of a drum beat.

Lover? Jonas and this woman had been lovers? Tess found it impossible to believe. "You and Jonas?" she said scornfully. "Never. Jonas would never have touched someone like you."

The mark beside the woman's nose flared, darker than before and bigger. The voice of the old housekeeper at the Casa de las Lunas came back to Tess. *Her mother was a witch, they were tainted, what could you expect from either of them*? She knew about the witch's mark. Looking at Mercedes now, she could almost believe it true.

"He loved me," Mercedes said, before turning back to Lovel to ask: "What about these memoirs?"

"They tell everything," snapped Lovel.

Mercedes drew in a sharp breath. "*Every*thing?"

"About me, about Santiago, about Vicente. Everything."

There was fear in Mercedes' expression. "How do you know?"

"He told us. We followed him to Spain."

Strength surged back into Tess's body, expelling the last of the drug from her bloodstream. "You?" she said. "You killed Jonas?" She took a step forward, hatred surging inside her like an angry sea.

Lovel fell back before her, shaking his head violently. "Not me. I wasn't the one who – "

Tess rounded on Mercedes. "I thought it was you," she said.

"Me? Kill Jonas?" There was a look of bewilderment about the older woman which made it clear she was telling the truth. "Don't be ridiculous. I would have died for him."

"He went to Montalbán to stop the Vicente Museum from opening, didn't he?" asked Tess. It was getting too complicated; what had seemed like certainties now were suddenly no more than fragile possibilities.

"He tried. Of course he did," said Mercedes. "I saw him on the television. I – I telephoned him." It had been the first time in their long acquaintance that she had ever done so but seeing him under those bright lights, she had realised how much she needed him. "He told me all sorts of lies about Vicente. He said he would expose him for what he was. I didn't pretend to understand him, poor

Jonas. I assumed that perhaps he had grown too old, that his mind was going."

Tess opened her mouth to protest, but Mercedes carried on. "Besides, even if what he said were true, nothing could stop the Museum. The plans were too far advanced for anything to bring them to a halt. Why should I want to kill the only man I ever . . ."

Tess thought: I was so sure. But if Mercedes was not the one, then – she turned back to Lovel. "You tortured him in that *cortijo* to make him tell you where the memoirs were hidden, didn't you?"

"I had nothing to do with – "

"And when he wouldn't, you threw him into the ravine to hide the marks of what you'd done to him." Tears blinded her. "I *knew* he hadn't just fainted." She felt as though she were choking. "You killed Jonas," she repeated. "He was the best person I ever knew and you *killed* him. Why? What had he ever done to you?" She was weeping now, sobbing, mouth open, not caring how ugly she looked. For the first time, she truly understood that Jonas would never come back. She raised her hands to tear at the white skin of Lovel's face.

He grabbed both her wrists. "It was an *accident*," he said, as he had said about Conchita, and again she had the sense of having heard the phrase before. "And as for the harm Jonas Fedor did to me, look at this." Still holding her tightly, he lifted his head so that she could see his throat and the familiar white line of scar tissue which ran from one side to the other.

Mercedes said, in an odd voice: "*You*, Lovel? *You* killed Jonas?"

"No! Not me!" Lovel's voice was almost a scream. He

ducked his head as though to avoid a blow. "Not me! Him." He pointed.

A man was standing in the archway leading from the next room. For a moment, adjusting her eyes to the increasing gloom, Tess could not make out who it was. Then she gave a cry of disbelief, wrenching her hands out of Lovel's grasp. "Dominic!"

He wore jeans, a blue-checked shirt open at the neck, a navy sweater. He came towards her, and she began to move away, light-headed with shock. Dominic? All this time her suspicions had been correct: it was Dominic who had been behind Jonas's death. She thought of how she had kissed him, desired him, and was suddenly shaken with self-disgust.

He stared at her for a moment, then he said quietly: "Thank God. I thought these two devils might have hurt you."

It was then she saw that he himself was hurt. One eye was swollen and almost closed; there was a bruise on his jaw and blood ran down from his ear into the gap between his shirt collar and his neck. And behind him, shadowed in the doorway, stood another figure.

Mercedes began laughing wildly. "Jonas," she said. "Oh, Jonas." She raised her arm; there was a gun in her hand. Before anyone could move, she had fired haphazardly at the second man as he stepped forward.

Sound-waves crashed against their ears as the room filled with the smell of explosive.

"You bitch," the man said, astonished, raising a hand to his neck. "You stupid fucking bitch." He stared at his fingers, already dripping blood. "Look at what you've done."

He faltered, took a step forward, crumpled slowly to the ground. Blood was pouring from his throat; there seemed no end to the red stream of it. Even as Tess watched, he grew paler, fading in front of her like a petal.

"This is so stupid," he said. His cold eyes met Tess's. "Help me."

She wanted to rush forward, to cradle him in her arms; she would have done so if Mercedes had not waved the gun at her and said angrily: "Stay where you are!"

Not daring to disobey, Tess stood quietly beside Dominic. When he put out his hand, she took it gratefully, glad of his warm strength, while the man on the floor visibly shrank, obscenities falling from his paling lips.

"We can't just let him lie there," she said.

"Can't we?" Dominic's mouth twisted. "Don't you realise who he is?"

"Of course I – "

"He's the one who threw Jonas over the cliff. He's the one who tried to drown you, who tried to push you off a mountain."

"I don't understand," Tess said. He lay in front of her, his face bleaching as the blood continued to spurt from his neck. That single wild shot had obviously severed an artery. She knew she was watching him die.

He caught her eye again. "Do something," he said dully, but no-one dared move as Mercedes again aimed the gun at them. His eyes were glazing. "My daughter . . ." he said, trying to press his hand against his neck. "Help me," though he must have understood, as they did, that it was too late, as blood streamed between his fingers and onto

the marble floor, black and red mingling, the colours of
the Spain Tess had never dared to look for.

The mad voice cut through her thoughts as Mercedes
pointed the gun towards Lovel. "You next," she said.

"No," he said, "I didn't kill him. I had nothing to do
with Jonas's death."

"What about Fernando Vicente," Dominic said suddenly. "Who killed him?"

"Not me, I swear it," Lovel said. In the gathering dusk
he seemed increasingly insubstantial, unreal, the shadow
of a ghost.

"Nor Carlos Ramirez," Dominic said. He spoke slowly
and clearly as though to a child. "Definitely not Carlos."

The words hung in the darkening room, silent now
except for the shallow breathing of the man on the floor.
The sky behind the roofs of Kensington was the colour
of a mussel shell, promising rain and, indeed, a few early
drops hissed against the windows as wind threshed the
tops of the trees.

Into the quiet, Tess said urgently: "You can't just leave
him there to . . . die."

"Why not?" Dominic's voice was steely. "How many
people did he leave? How many did he kill?"

The words seemed incomprehensible. "But even so
. . ." She realised that like Jonas, Dominic was not a
man who easily forgave those who trespassed.

"You can't do anything for him now."

The words spurred the dying man to feeble action.
"My daughter," he said. Tears gathered in his eyes
and fell slowly down the pallid cheeks. Heedless of the
gun, Tess ran forward and knelt beside him, reaching
for his hand. Whatever he had done, no-one deserved

to die alone, and briefly, in imagination, she glimpsed Jonas, falling into that unfathomable blue, past jagged rock and cactus and dry clumps of esparto, floating like the eagle he had always been towards oblivion.

"You're wasting your time," Dominic said. "He had no compunction at all about trying to get rid of you."

"I don't believe it," said Tess. "There's been a mistake."

Mercedes spoke again, half-screaming. "It was Carlos Ramirez who shot my brother."

"No," Dominic said decisively. "It was not."

"How can you possibly know? You weren't even born."

"Because I know who did it. Jonas told me. He knew who was responsible and it wasn't your husband."

Mercedes did not argue; it was as though in some secret place she had known for years. "My life," she said in a kind of wail. Again she seemed bewildered as though she was trying to grasp some important fact which continued to elude her. "My whole life wasted?"

"Yes," Dominic said. "Wasted in the interests of a sad little inadequate man, terrified of women, a coward who betrayed his friends one by one and then raped their daughters. Just the way he raped you."

"No," Mercedes screamed. "No. It's lies."

"You know it's not." Tess sensed that Dominic was playing for time, provoking a situation which would enable both of them to get out of the room intact. "Remember your friend Concepción?"

Mercedes gasped. "The Falangists," she said faintly. "The soldiers." As though it had been that very morning she saw again the innocent white thighs, the gathered blood, heard the child's weeping as they walked past the house to school . . .

"I'm afraid not." Dominic's voice was colder than a knife-blade.

"But he was in prison too. I saw him there, I went every day with food for him." Mercedes closed her teeth over her lower lip and moaned. "I loved him."

"The *fascistas* put him into prison so that it would look as though he too had been captured," Dominic said. "They always intended to let him go. It's all in Jonas's book. It was only when they released Vicente that it was decided justice must be done."

"Justice? What justice?" spat Mercedes. She saw Vicente going away from her, out of the dark hall, into the street, the blue splash of paint on his shirt. If what this Englishman said was true, why would he have looked back with that anguished expression on his face? "What kind of justice is it when innocent men are set up against a wall and shot?"

"At least it was a better death than he granted to those he betrayed," Dominic said.

Mercedes stared at him. "Who shot my brother?" she said. "Lovel?"

"Not Lovel. Nor him." Dominic nodded towards the bloody figure lying on the floor with its head in Tess's lap.

"They told me it was Ramirez," Mercedes said sadly. She smoothed the silk of her dress, remembering the hunt, the trap, the capture, remembering heat and wine and shadowed afternoons of love.

"Jonas had checked it twice already with those of the guards he could find." Dominic said. "Even though you were only a girl, they were frightened of you, they knew your mother was a witch, and that you yourself bore the witch's mark. They tried to tell you that Fernando had been set free but you assumed he had been shot. When you demanded a name, the young guard – Ramón, was it? – said: 'Ask Ramirez'."

Mercedes thought back. It was more than fifty years ago. She smelled again that prison odour of pain and cigarettes and blood; she remembered the weight of the basket on her arm and how they had spoken of orders; someone played a guitar as she made her eyes grow huge, forcing Ramón to tell. He had looked down at his scuffed shoes, unwilling to meet her eye, and muttered the name. Surely he had said one word only. Surely she could not have misheard what he said. "Ramirez," muttered under his breath, but even fifty years later, she realised that the Englishman was right, he had told her to ask Ramirez, meaning not Carlos Ramirez but the *alcalde*, Felipe Cabrera's father, Federico Cabrera Ramirez. Ramón was from the next village: he would not have known that they called the mayor Cabrera in order to distinguish him from the powerful Ramirez who lived in the Casa de las Lunas.

"If it was not Ramirez," she said, and felt the words lie in her mouth like unripe olives, dry and bitter, "who shot Fernando?"

"When they let your brother out of jail that morning," Dominic said, "he was met by the only Apostle left. It was explained to him that he did not deserve to live, that he must be executed to pay for the deaths he had caused. He begged for his life. He grovelled on the ground, pleading for mercy."

583

"No!"

"But since he had shown none himself, none was shown to him. He was dragged over to the wall and when he refused to stand up, he was shot where he lay." He paused, then added sardonically: "It was not a hero's death."

"The only Apostle left," Mercedes said. "But that was Luisa's *novio*."

"There was also their leader," said Dominic. "Águila."

"Jonas?" When Dominic nodded, Mercedes raised her hands to her face, covering her mouth. She thought of her black hatred for Carlos, the way it had glinted through her life like a seam of coal. She had vowed to avenge her brother's death and had ended up loving his killer. She thought: My aunts were right; I have been mad all these years.

"Fifty years ago, and I remember it as if it were yesterday," she said, in a little voice. "Only yesterday."

Tess saw that she meant it quite literally, that for her those cataclysmic events had indeed taken place only yesterday and all the intervening years were unreal, insubstantial, her present rooted firmly in those moments when the door of the jail had slammed behind her, shutting out the mid-afternoon heat, and a voice had tumbled out the news: "Fernando is dead."

Time had ceased for her then, Tess realised. The present had moved towards now in a series of todays, there had never been a tomorrow after that, and only one yesterday. In her lap, the dying man stirred feebly and she laid her fingers on his forehead.

Mercedes turned to her. "Jonas loved me. Why did he give you my picture, the picture my brother painted of me? There's obviously been a mistake. He was going to give it to his daughter, if he had one. Otherwise it was to come back to me."

Something stroked the base of Tess's spine like a feather. "He gave it to me," she repeated.

"But you aren't his daughter."

The two women stared at each other; both of them instantly recognised the truth. Mercedes grew suddenly pale.

"Why else would he give it to me?" Tess said. She breathed through her mouth, the beginnings of a vast elation making her breathless.

"Did he say so?"

"He didn't need to."

"It was *me* he loved," insisted Mercedes. In the fading light, the signs of age were blurred; dressed in white, she seemed to have reverted to the girl she had once been, beautiful and flawed.

For Tess, it was as though a sheet of ice had shattered, revealing and at the same time releasing the water beneath, clear as glass despite the mud at the bottom. She thought, surprised: This is me, this is what I am. Jonas's daughter. The experiences of childhood would always be there, but that did not mean she could not go on living, enjoying. Lovel had spoiled her mother's life; thanks to Jonas, he could not spoil hers.

The knowledge was a revelation. She felt suddenly lighter, superhuman. Jonas was her father – it was so obvious it scarcely needed thinking about. And over the years, his strength had become hers. She thought: Dominic and Jonas are two of a kind; that's why I love them both. Ahead of her shone warmth and wine, afternoons of love, happiness.

"It was me he loved. And my mother," she said positively.

"He loved Concepción? That's impossible. When would he have had . . ." But even as she spoke, Mercedes remembered the girl going to California, and Jonas, too. He had not come to her ever again, and later, the girl announced that she was pregnant and Lovel had married her.

"I am the proof," this Teresa Lovel was saying. And indeed, there was the strongest look of Jonas about her. Something withered inside Mercedes, some long-held hope, and at the same time, she remembered the gun she still held. Slowly she raised her arm. She would eliminate this impostor who insisted that Jonas loved her more than he had loved Mercedes. But before she could take aim, Lovel, moving in from the side, smashed her viciously across the face with one of the sword mountings he had carefully lifted from the wall.

With an audible crack of bone, the heavy wooden scabbard broke her jaw: she staggered backwards, cannoning into the wall then falling onto the futon. The gun fell from her hand.

Before either Dominic or Tess could move, Lovel had picked it up and pointed it at them both.

"Nobody move," he said.

"You won't get away with this," Dominic said. "You can't kill us all." As he spoke, he stepped forward slightly so that he was in front of Tess and the man on the floor.

Lovel raised the gun. "Perhaps not. But unless you

tell me where those memoirs are, I shall certainly cause considerable pain to Teresa." He motioned at Tess with the barrel of the gun. "Get up and move over here," he said.

"Why does it matter so much to you?" Tess said. The head in her lap was heavy, no longer animate. She would have thought the man lying against her was dead except that every now and then his eyelids fluttered and he sometimes struggled to speak.

"You'd better ask *him*," Lovel said. "He said we would never be traced, and as the years went by, I started to believe him."

"Then Jonas got the CBE and appeared on the TV, gave those interviews to the Press," Dominic said. "And you realised that it was all about to come out."

"What was?" asked Tess.

Lovel ignored her. "If you don't tell me immediately where the memoirs are, Mr Eliot, I shall take a great deal of pleasure in shooting Jonas Fedor's bastard in the stomach, then we shall all wait here and watch her die, in great pain."

Tess sensed the hesitation in Dominic. Carefully she stood up, her bloodstained skirt already stiff, pretending to fumble in her bag for something to wipe away some of the mess. Her hand closed over Jonas's gun. She thought: Because of me, my mother dared not face up to him.

"I could tell you anything," Dominic was saying. "How would you know whether it was the truth?"

"You forget I am a powerful man at the top of a powerful organisation," Lovel said. "I only have to pick up the telephone and ask for someone to follow your instructions and bring the memoirs back here. If, of course, you lie to me, then the consequences could be even more unpleasant for Teresa than I have already described." Behind him, Mercedes stirred, her hand to her face, moaning with pain.

"You're bluffing," Dominic said.

"Try me," said Lovel. He waved the gun. "Move aside, Mr Eliot. Or perhaps I should shoot you somewhere relatively harmless first, just to show you I mean business."

Tess said coldly: "You wouldn't dare." She remembered the quick pad of feet across the bedroom floor, the brocaded dragons, the dry smell of his fingers on her, touching her in places he was not supposed to touch. *Daddy loves you*, he would say, and his thin lips would nibble at her, *Daddy loves his little girl*, but she had seen his eyes on her, those dead eyes the colour of dried blood, and knew he did not.

Behind Lovel, Mercedes rose to her feet. Her face was grotesquely swollen and the side of her mouth hung open, as though she had suffered a stroke. For a moment she hovered, arms outstretched, like a giant bird. Then she pitched forward, falling against Lovel, pushing him off balance, knocking the gun out of his hand.

Instantly Dominic was there, his foot on the weapon as Lovel scrabbled for it. He bent down and picked it up. "Thank goodness for that," he said. "I was wondering whether we'd make it out of here."

"You didn't show it," Tess said. She looked at him. "Dominic . . ."

"Yes?"

"I – " Something fastened round her ankle and she screamed. The man who lay on the floor stared at her and she could see his approaching death as clearly as a cloud crossing the moon. "Help me," he whispered. Beside his mouth the crescent-shaped scar was white as bone. His lips twisted in a half-smile and he died.

Tess stared at him without flinching. "Captain Santiago," she said softly. "El Malo."

"And El Fantasma," said Dominic, indicating Lovel. "Didn't you realise?"

"Not until now. How could I have done?" Tess knelt in the pool of blood and touched the dead man's brow gently. "Goodbye," she whispered. Although she wished to, she could feel no hatred for Don Pedro. In spite of what she now knew, he had always been her friend, as well as her betrayer.

31

TESS

Fire leaps in my brain;
Your kiss is like music on my mouth,
Your touch eases my old pain.
Kiss me, touch me again.
　　　　from *Elegías españolas* by Amador Ramirez
　　　　　　　　translated by Teresa Lovel

"I still can't take it all in," Luisa said.

"I don't suppose we'll ever know all of it," said Tess. "But you can see how some of it must have been."

She leaned back against Dominic's arm. He smelled of garlic and wood-smoke; if she closed her eyes she could almost believe that . . . but Jonas was dead and it was time to begin the new life he had always hoped she would have.

"Pedro Morena," Luisa said, shaking her head slowly from side to side. "I've known him for years and never suspected a thing."

"He lied so often that he probably couldn't remember himself exactly what happened," said Dominic. "But Martin García – someone from the Banco Morena –

has been able to track down a few facts. For instance, in spite of what he pretended, he *was* in Spain during the Civil War, and went to the States immediately after, where he called himself Lawrence Marlowe. It's one of those grim puns that people like him go in for."

Luisa shook her head again. "Who would have believed it? Any of it."

"Then he came back to Spain and changed his name again – Morena was his grandmother's name – which was easy enough in the confusion after the war. With a little help from Franco's government – "

"Payment for services rendered," Tess put in.

" – he was able to prosper. Eventually he came to England, married a girl he'd met in America, became a respectable banker."

"And then," said Tess, "two things happen: firstly, his adored daughter becomes engaged to a diplomat. And at the same time, he sees Jonas Fedor on the television and realises to his horror exactly who he was, and what he could tell about Captain Santiago if he chose."

"Not just what he *could* tell, what he had every intention of telling," Dominic said. "Bang would go his daughter's marriage, for a start. Bang would go his own reputation, everything he's built up over the years, all his fancy friends. When he heard that Jonas was about to go to Spain, he seized the opportunity, sent Tess off to Houston with García, and flew to Spain himself, travelling as Lawrence Marlowe."

"And then what?" Luisa's hands were clasped to her chest; she looked frail, battered by the shock of what she was hearing.

Dominic and Tess glanced at each other. "You tell," he

said. His hand moved slowly down her sleeve to stroke her fingers, his thumb running back and forth across the curve of the ring she wore.

"He hired a car in Granada in Jonas's name – "

"Why?"

"Covering his tracks had become second nature by then. He drove to Montalbán where he had arranged to meet Lovel. The two of them found Jonas and tried to persuade him not to publish the memoirs. At first they just talked, in his hotel room, or in the hills where they couldn't be overheard. When Jonas wouldn't agree, Don Pedro – he – "

"He killed him," Dominic said quietly.

"Then all he had to do was find the memoirs and destroy them. The only one who knew who Captain Santiago had become was Jonas, and Jonas was dead."

"And how did Jonas know?"

"That's one of the things we're not quite sure of. Research, I should think. There's a strong possibility that Phil Cramir – or Felipe Cabrera – knew."

"Or perhaps," said Dominic, "Jonas put two and two together from looking at the two sketches he had obtained back during the Civil War, when he realised what Fernando Vicente was doing."

"Except that it wasn't as easy as he thought," said Tess. "First of all I came back from Houston with a tale of forged paintings and a list of twelve sketches which Don Pedro immediately recognised as the big giveaway."

"Is that why he attacked you on the Montalbán road, when you came here?"

"I think so. I was the one most likely to make a fuss about them; with me out of the way, he would at least have time to think, maybe even to destroy the sketches when they arrived. Don't forget they'd have gone to the Banco first, before being sent on to Jonas."

"So Mercedes and the forged paintings were nothing to do with it?" Luisa said.

"Not really. Or perhaps they were everything," said Tess. "It was Vicente who betrayed the others. But Martin has come across a paper which gives the impression that Vicente was about to be charged with assaulting his own sister; perhaps he was blackmailed into the betrayals."

"Is it all my fault?" Luisa leaned back in her chair. Her fragile eyelids dropped. "I heard him summon her once. I followed her, I was only a child myself, I didn't understand but I could see her face and I knew he shouldn't be doing what he did. It was in that little room next to his studio. She was always saying how much she loved him but it wasn't love, it was fear, repulsion. She hated what he did to her, I know she did. So I told my sisters. They must have informed the police – or the military: it was much the same in those days." There were tears in her eyes. "We loved him. But in the end we betrayed him."

"He betrayed himself," Dominic said forcefully.

The three of them sat in silence for a moment, thinking of the little man with whom they were all, in their various ways, so intimately connected. Then Tess said: "Jonas kept the drawings Vicente had made of Captain Santiago and El Fantasma – "

"Alias Richard Lovel," Dominic said. "Tess's – as we now know – unpleasant stepfather. Who started off in the International Brigade, but changed sides and ended up doing what he liked best: hurting other people."

"I should have realised much earlier who Captain Santiago was," Tess said.

"Why?" asked Dominic. "How could you?"

"I should have recognised that scar from Vicente's drawing. After all, I recognised Jonas immediately when I saw the drawing of him in Houston."

"Except that Jonas hasn't changed much over the years: if you look at early photographs, you can see that he was always round-faced and curly-haired, beefy, even as a boy. Whereas Morena had done everything he could, short of plastic surgery, to change himself."

"I still feel a bit – " Tess broke off, knowing the kind of brusque reply Dominic would make. But in spite of everything, she *did* feel sorry for Don Pedro. Not telling Dominic, she had gone to a memorial service for him and could not help thinking how Don Pedro would have loved it. The handsome fiancé, untouched by scandal, supported the stern wife on one side and the weeping daughter on the other. There was a fine sufficiency of lords. Representatives of the great and good were in plentiful supply. It was impossible not to like Don Pedro, Tess reflected. And perhaps he had been right: perhaps you could atone, in some measure, for wrongs done. She remembered Julian Maitland saying that the hardest part of repentance might be the repressing of a fundamental part of yourself.

They were back in Jonas's cottage. Dominic's presence brought it to life again, gave it back the vigour and eagerness it had always contained when Jonas was alive.

Tess, working on the translation of I. C. Sanyoshi's latest hardboiled detective novel, looked out at the summery garden. Tobacco plants bloomed, there were roses round the door. One of the outbuildings had tarpaulins stretched across its roof, since Dominic had decided to turn it into a study. She could hear him singing somewhere, horribly out of tune, as he hammered nails into new wood. It was not a Jacuzzi, but she knew Jonas would have been pleased.

She remembered her last birthday, the feeling of aloneness she had experienced then. Jonas had been her only friend.

Now, she had Dominic. It seemed more than enough. But there was also Aunt Luisa in Madrid, and Hansl's family in Muswell Hill, who had proved every bit as welcoming as she had pictured them. Andrew Rathbone seemed to have attached himself to them, and was full of plans to convert the rickety barn into a studio where he could give classes to art-lovers. And there was the Casa de las Lunas, the House of Moons, her house, now that Mercedes was dead, with the shutters flung wide and the copper moons shining on the gateposts. She felt as though she had emerged from a forest onto a sunny slope.

She stood up and walked over to Jonas's desk. It bulged with Dominic's correspondence: bills, promises of Ford Sierras from promoters anxious to sell time shares in Spain, letters from his sister Valentine, his nephews and nieces, his mother, his Scottish uncles. She pressed the little lever and the secret drawer sprang out.

Inside was a letter, the last Jonas had written, which she had finally collected from his solicitor, who had been instructed to put it personally into her hands.

She had read it a hundred times: she read it once again:

My darling Teresa,

In two days' time I leave for Spain and I am very conscious of the fact that I may not return. For some time now I have been followed; my house has been broken into, and my car. I think I know who is responsible, and by going to Spain, I may be able to bring them into the open. If not . . .

If you are reading this, then I am dead. And I can at last tell you how proud, how pleasing it is to me that you are my beloved daughter. I have wanted to tell you so many times, particularly when you were so little and bewildered, but Conchita would not let me, perhaps out of some misplaced loyalty to her husband or to her church, perhaps because while Lovel was still alive, she thought it would be easier for you not to know.

I have always considered her wrong on this point; I think you would have been infinitely happier if you had been aware that you were not tied by blood to him. But I felt I had no rights in you and did what she told me, as I have always done.

Your grandfather Carlos and uncle Amador came to visit me when you were just a little girl: do you remember them? I said nothing because I knew that both of them were ill and it might have been too cruel to give them to you, only to snatch them away again.

I hope I did not do wrong: we talked it over and decided it was best, for Conchita's sake.

I have tried to make up for it, my darling Teresa, to be grandfather and uncle to you, as well as father.

You will wonder why I did not marry your mother. I went away not knowing that she was pregnant with you, leaving no address because I was wandering. When I came back to her, it was too late. She was a girl unused to happiness; she had not expected me to be true to her. And you must remember that in those days, in a strait-laced country like Spain, a girl with an illegitimate child could be ostracised, mistreated, even assaulted. When Lovel appeared, he seemed to her like an answer to a prayer. Or a curse.

But I cannot be sure that Conchita would have married me even if I had been free. She loved me once, I am sure of it. But sometimes I wondered if I was merely a means to an end for her, that through me, she hoped to damage her stepmother, knowing that I was the lover of Mercedes.

As for Mercedes, God knows I loved her. Always she was sad rather than wicked; she had been abused; she could not help what she was.

By now you will have learned that Fernando Vicente was not the hero you always believed him. Him, too, I felt sorry for: his blood, like that of Mercedes, was somehow tainted. But he could not be allowed to live when so many brave men had died. I shot him without compunction, as I would have killed a sick animal.

By now, you will also know what he did to his sister. Poor child: how could she have grown up straight with such a beginning? Teresa, she was a beautiful thing, so pure, so innocent. I wanted to love her, but she could think only of Vicente because she dared not do otherwise. I loved her but I knew she was flawed; perhaps it was cruel of me not to give her the only thing she ever asked of me, which was to tell her that I loved her.

Sometimes I wonder if things would have turned out differently if I had followed the destiny I recognised as soon as I met her. I could perhaps have changed her, made her happy. Who can tell?

Beyond everything, my darling, I hope you will follow *your* destiny, and that you will find the kind of love I knew with Mercedes, that burning inescapable drawing of two people into flame.

It may not always be the marrying kind of love, my darling, but no-one should marry until they have known it.

If you go back to the Casa de las Lunas, there are more Vicente paintings there. Years ago I helped Carlos and the aunts to hide them. The panels behind the four-poster bed are in fact a cupboard under the roof: in there you will find several paintings. It's up to you to decide what to do with them.

If you meet Andrew Rathbone, be kind to him.

Your loving father,

He had added a PS.

I think you would be deliriously happy with Dominic – but who am I to try to make you do something you do not wish to do!

It was signed, as were all his letters to her, with the long-tailed J, curled into the suggestion of a heart.

* * *

The night before her wedding-day, Tess dreamed again of the Casa de las Lunas, the House of Moons, the house where she was born. In dream, she passed through the panelled rooms, past the shaded windows, the lemon-coloured shadows; in dream climbed the wide staircase, the baluster rail smooth against her palm.

The passage stretched away from her, white walled, hung with paintings. Slowly she walked towards her mother's bedroom; the carved four-poster bed was empty now, the white sheets crisp, a bowl of lemons on the table beside it. The house smelled as always: of wood-smoke, of tobacco, of fresh linen and fruit. There were flowers lying in the passage, red flowers leading to another room, a half-open door. The dream had no sound-track but she knew that somewhere there was music.

The door opened wider; a man came towards her. She could not see his face but she knew that when he reached her he would take her into his arms and hold her against him, she would hear his heart beat and would know that at last she could be happy.